Praise for the novels of
*New York Times* and *USA TODAY* bestselling author

# KAREN HARPER

"A strong plot, a pair of well-written characters and a genuinely
spooky atmosphere add up to yet another sterling effort from
Harper. Fast-paced and absorbing, this one will keep readers
turning pages far into the night."
—*RT Book Reviews* on *Deep Down*

"The story is rich...and the tension steadily escalates
to a pulse-pounding climax."
—*Publishers Weekly* on *The Hiding Place*

"Strongly plotted and well written, featuring a host of
interesting characters, Harper's latest is a winner."

"Ha                                                    ly evades
effo                                                   final act,
pro                                                   ement."

"                                                      nating
her                                                    strands.
M                                                      ust no

*Watch for the other books in the Home Valley Amish series*

RETURN TO GRACE March 2012
and
FINDING MERCY November 2012

*Romantic suspense novels also available from MIRA Books
and Karen Harper*

DOWN RIVER
DEEP DOWN
THE HIDING PLACE
BELOW THE SURFACE
INFERNO
HURRICANE
DARK ANGEL
DARK HARVEST
DARK ROAD HOME
THE FALLS
THE STONE FOREST
SHAKER RUN
DOWN TO THE BONE
THE BABY FARM
EMPTY CRADLE
BLACK ORCHID

# KAREN HARPER

# FALL
## FROM
# PRIDE

MIRA®

Recycling programs for this product may not exist in your area.

ISBN-13: 978-0-7783-1249-9

FALL FROM PRIDE

For questions and comments about the quality of this book please contact us at Customer_eCare@Harlequin.ca.

www.MIRABooks.com

Printed in U.S.A.

First Printing: August 2011
10 9 8 7 6 5 4 3 2 1

For my family and friends who love those relaxing, lovely trips to Ohio Amish country.

As ever, for Don.

# 1

Saturday, May 22, 2010
The Home Valley, Ohio

"SARAH, YOU WON'T BELIEVE WHO JUST DROVE in. Passing by, that's what he said. It's Jacob! In a fancy car, too. He's right outside the barn."

At her younger brother's words, Sarah Kauffman's insides lurched. She had once cared for Jacob, but since he'd been shunned, it was *verboten* for him to be here. No way she wanted to see her former come-calling friend, but someone had to get him away from Gabe and his buddy group. Her family had invited the young people for a barn dance tonight.

"If the kids won't tell him to leave, I will," Sarah said as she circled the long plank table laden with food. "He's a bad influence, and you *youngie liet* don't need that in your running-around days!"

She hurried outside and down the sloped approach to the barn, her eyes scanning the clusters of boys huddled by their courting buggies or the two cars someone had driven in, and beyond all that, with its headlights still glowing golden, Jacob's red car stood out like a beacon.

No, she thought, the glow was not where headlights should be, but higher, farther off, behind the car and buggies so that they stood out in stark silhouette.

She moved to the side and squinted across the dark distance. The glow was growing, wavering. It was coming not from something on her family's property but from across the newly planted fields that stretched to those of Bishop Esh.

Ignoring Jacob's calling her name, she pointed, stiff-armed, at the distant blaze of color, but Jacob must have thought she was gesturing for him to leave.

"Hey, just came to say hi to all my ol' friends, 'speci'ly you, an' I'm not leavin' till we talk," he slurred, but she hardly heeded him.

What was that strange light? The moon rising low on the horizon? Someone burning trash? No. No! The Esh barn, where she had begun enlarging the quilt square she'd painted there two months before...the Esh barn was on fire!

"Fire!" she screamed. "Fire, over there—the Esh barn! Does anyone have a phone? Call the fire department!"

Sarah lifted her skirts and ran through the scattered boys, past a smooching couple who jumped to their feet. She almost tripped over some beer cans on the grass. Smooching and drinking—now she knew why their guests hadn't spotted the fire.

She raced past their *grossdaadi haus* where her younger sister, Martha, was tending to their eighty-year-old *grossmamm* tonight, past the family garden and into the field.

Laboring through the rich, damp soil, she sank ankle-deep with each lunging step, once falling to her hands and knees, but this was the fastest way to get there, even compared to a buggy or Jacob's car. *Schnell! Schnell,* hurry, hurry, she urged herself. Human lives, the horses, the stored hay and straw, the old barn itself...and her bold painting of an Amish quilt square. She jumped up from her knees and clambered on, hearing voices behind her of others coming, too.

Out of breath, a stitch in her side, she ran on, to warn the Eshes—Bishop Joseph and his wife, Mattie, almost her second parents because she and their girl Hannah had been so close.... Were they home tonight? Already gone to bed? Their house looked dark, but the glow of kerosene lanterns didn't show sometimes. Didn't they know their livelihood, their future, was on fire? The flames seemed high in the barn, reaching downward as well as up. Maybe the firemen could use her painting ladders to spray water.

It seemed an eternity until she reached their yard, screaming, "Fire! Fire!" She prayed no one would be trapped in the barn, that they could get the work team and buggy horses out if they were in for the night. She knew that barn as well as her own. It was where she, Hannah and Ella had played as children, tended animals, the barn where the bishop had been brave enough after much discussion to let her paint her very first quilt square and then let her enlarge it when he saw how well the others were received.

Exhausted but energized, Sarah stumbled into the Esh backyard, her dress and hands smeared, clods of soil clinging to her shoes. The belching heat slapped her face. What had been a glow in the hayloft was now a red-and-orange monster inside the barn trying to get out, licking at the windows, curling its claws around the eaves. Shouting, she beat her fists on the back door of the dark house, but no one came.

Turning back toward the barn, she saw that Jacob, Gabe and several other boys had followed her across the fields.

Using someone's jacket to avoid burning their hands, they lifted the bar on the barn door and pulled it open. That only fed the flames, which made a big whooshing sound and drove everyone back. The beast's breath came hotter, orange fires from hell. She could see its fiery fingers reaching for the pattern of the six-foot-square Robbing Peter to Pay Paul quilt square she'd been enlarging from her wooden ladders and scaffolding earlier today. She'd left them leaning against the barn. Maybe they'd been burned up by now.

Her agony was not only to see the barn burn but her quilt square, too. How proud she had been of her work, the beauty of the striking design. Bishop Esh had chosen that repetitive, traditional pattern because he said it would remind folks that Paul and Peter were equal apostles—a Bible lesson, even on a barn.

Sarah watched in awestruck horror as the flaming beast devoured her neat white and gold circles within the bright blue squares. The paint crackled and blistered. Was it her imagination that the colors ran like blood? Was this a sign that she should not have asked to place it on the bishop's barn—shouldn't have been so worldly in her pride over it? She'd even felt a bit important when the local newspaper had put this painting and her picture—not of her face, of course—on the front page. But for so long she'd felt different from her Amish sisters and friends.... She stopped herself, knowing her line of thinking was a danger and a sin.

"Their plow team's in the south field!" someone yelled. At least that was a blessing. The six big, blond Percherons that pulled the farm equipment were safe.

"The Eshes must not be home!" Sarah shouted, ignoring Jacob, speaking to her brother and the other boys.

"I called the fire department on my cell," Jacob yelled, coming closer. "They'll be here ASAP."

She wasn't sure what "a sap" meant, but she asked him, "So there are no buggy horses inside, either?"

"Naw or we'd hear them, even over the roar, that's sure!" he shouted as he came closer. She hadn't seen him for months and she couldn't see him well now, only his bulky, black silhouette etched by leaping lights. The fire made a deafening roar. Inside, something heavy fell and little golden lines ran madly between the old, weathered boards. Barn swallows from under the eaves circled madly around the increasing clouds of ash-and-cinder-laden smoke.

It seemed an eternity before the fire engine pumper truck screeched in from the closest town of Homestead with six volunteer firemen, three of them Amish. When Sheriff Freeman's car pulled in with the siren sounding, several other firefighters spilled out to help. They pumped what water they had in the truck through two hoses, then, when that was quickly gone, rigged a hose to draw water from the pond. It was too late to save the barn, so they watered down the roof of the house and outbuildings to keep flying debris from burning them, too.

As word spread or they saw the seething sky, other Home Valley Amish arrived in buggies, some *Englische* neighbors in their cars. Even before the Eshes raced up the lane in their buggy, back from visiting Mattie Esh's sister on the other side of the valley, even before the local newspaper editor, Peter Clawson, started taking pictures, the big, old barn with Sarah's bright painting on it had burned into oblivion.

Nathan MacKenzie took the call on his cell phone. His digital clock read 3:24 a.m. Something terrible must have happened, and he hoped it wasn't bad news about his foster mother. His heartbeat kicked up. It was his boss, Mark Lincoln, the state fire marshal of Ohio.

"Nate, I need you to check out a big fire in Amish country, pronto. I want you there shortly after dawn."

"Amish country?" he said, raking his fingers through his short hair. "Northeast but south of Cleveland, right? That's Stan Comstock's district."

"Our northeast supervisor's in Hawaii for his daughter's wedding and won't be back for about ten days. It's a barn fire, Nate. Went to the ground—no one inside but for them a huge loss. Two volunteer firefighters were slightly injured when a beam fell. They should have been outside at that point, and I'm not sure how much correct protocol was followed. I just got calls from both the county sheriff and the local newspaper editor. I'll input what I know to you online including GPS specs for getting there. It's in a rural area called the Home Valley outside Homestead, Ohio, in Eden County. Real pretty rolling-hill country."

"And it was arson?"

"We won't know until you take VERA up there and get a good look. But the thing is, the newspaper guy says the Amish in Pennsylvania had a rash of hate-crime barn arsons a couple of years ago, and we can't take a chance with this. You'll have to handle things with kid gloves, not go in like gangbusters, even with VERA, you hear?"

"Of course," Nate said, fumbling in the dark for his jeans. VERA was one of the two expensive, state-of-the-art technology-laden vehicles that served the state Fire and Explosion Investigation Bureau, usually called the Arson Bureau. And VERA was Nate's idea of the perfect date to investigate arson on the road.

"You know much about the Amish?" Mark asked.

"Good food, handmade furniture, quilts, buggies, black clothing, no electricity, old traditions. How's that?"

"When you get a chance, research their belief system or find someone Amish you can trust there to translate their ways for you. Whatever you turn up, they're going to tell you this was God's will. They'll rebuild and forgive the arsonist—if that's what it was."

After Mark hung up, Nate muttered, "They may forgive, but I won't."

# 2

SARAH GLANCED OUT THE WINDOW OF THE Esh farmhouse again. The beast that had devoured the barn left only a pile of blackened bones. The emergency vehicle carrying the two injured firefighters—Levi Miller, Amish, and Mike Getz, *Englische*—to the regional hospital had pulled away. Both had been struck by debris when a flaming beam fell and temporarily trapped them before they were rescued. Word was that, despite broken bones, both were expected to recover just fine.

Jacob had been asked to go, but other than that, no one had left. It was as if the circle of Home Valley neighbors were mourning a mutual, fallen friend. Since the Amish held worship services in their homes or barns every other week, and it was an off Sunday, many had buggied in. Others had arrived, including Ray-Lynn Logan. The owner of the Dutch Farm Table Restaurant in Homestead had parked next to the sheriff's car and was handing out doughnuts and coffee. Ray-Lynn was Sarah's friend and an outspoken admirer of her painting skills.

Sarah was exhausted and filthy, but to please her devastated hosts, she sat at the Eshes' kitchen table to eat. Mattie Esh and her two oldest daughters, Ida and Ruth, both married and living nearby, were turning out scrambled eggs and bacon to be washed down by hot chocolate. Sarah had been thanked repeatedly for spotting the flames and for rushing here to warn the family. But she still felt as if someone had died, not only the old barn, but the painted square that had meant so much to her.

"Still can't figure a cause," Bishop Esh muttered to his wife. "No kerosene lantern out there, no green hay to smolder in the bays or loft, no lightning storm, and at night."

"God's will," Mattie told him, tears in her eyes. "We may not understand His ways but must learn to accept."

"So who's the preacher now?" her husband said, his voice tired but kind. "We'll rebuild, Lord willing."

Sarah offered to help clear the table, but they wouldn't hear of it, so she went outside again. She wanted to head home to wash up and relieve Martha from taking care of their grandmother, but she just couldn't leave yet. If—when—the Eshes rebuilt, would they want another painted square? It had gone a long way that the bishop had let her put one on his barn, even though it was fairly small at first. What was worrying her most was that some of Gabe's friends at the *danze* last night had been smoking around her family's barn. It was a fair distance across the field, so surely none of them had sneaked over here to get more privacy for their doings, then carelessly thrown a butt or match down. The Amish never locked their barns, even if, in these modern times, some had begun to lock their homes.

From the back of her van's tailgate, Ray-Lynn, still handing out coffee in paper cups, motioned Sarah over. The

Kauffman women, Sarah's *mamm* and married sister, Lizzie, made the half-moon pies for Ray-Lynn's restaurant, and Sarah delivered them fresh daily in her buggy. Like most everyone else around, she loved to talk to Ray-Lynn. Even in the grief of this morning, she was like a spark of sunlight.

The shapely redhead was about to turn fifty, a widow whose dream had always been to have her own good home-cookin' restaurant in Cleveland—that is, before she'd fallen in love with Amish country. Her husband had suffered a drop-dead heart attack six years ago, just before they were to buy the restaurant, once owned by an Amish family who couldn't keep up with the state's increasingly strict health inspection codes.

But newspaper owner and editor, Peter Clawson, had gone in as Ray-Lynn's partner, and she had made a real go of it, expanding to three rooms and a big menu. The Dutch Farm Table was the most popular place to eat and meet in town for both the local English and Amish, and, of course, tourists. They used to come by the busload, though they'd been in shorter supply lately in the far-reaching American recession.

"Good for you to spot that fire, Sarah," Ray-Lynn said, and gave her a one-armed hug. "Gonna get your name in the paper again."

"It didn't save the barn. Maybe you can tell Mr. Clawson not to overdo it, especially so soon after that article about my barn quilt squares."

"It may be a biweekly paper, but he's putting out a special edition over this. I'll bet we get folks here to gawk at the burned barn, let alone your other paintings. And if the Cleveland or Columbus papers pick this up, especially if it turns out to be foul play—"

"Foul play? Did you hear that someone set the fire?"

"The sheriff just wants all the bases covered, so he called the state fire marshal's office," she said with a roll of her snappy brown eyes. "But barn burning's not the way we'd like to get buyers and spenders 'round here, is it? Personally, this painting," she went on, pointing at the patch of empty sky where Sarah's quilt square used to be, "was my favorite so far. Hi, ya'll," she called to someone behind Sarah as she gestured them over. "Coffee here, doughnuts all gone."

Though Ray-Lynn had lived in Cleveland with her husband for years, it was no secret she'd been born and bred in the deep South, so she drew her words out a lot more than most moderns did. She even had a sign in the restaurant over the front door that Sarah had painted. It read Southern Hospitality and Amish Cooking—Ya'll Come Back, *Danki*. And she was always trying to talk Sarah into painting a huge mural of Amish life on the side wall.

Secretly, Sarah yearned to paint not static quilt patterns but the beauty of quilts flapping on a clothesline, huge horses pulling plows in spring fields, rows of black buggies at church, one-room schoolhouses with the *kinder* playing red rover or eckball out back, weddings and barn raisings.…

But all that was *verboten*. No matter what Ray-Lynn urged, Sarah knew an Amish painter could never be an Amish artist.

The moment he turned off the highway onto the narrow, two-lane road at the sign Homestead: 4 Miles, Nate MacKenzie felt as if he'd entered a beautiful but alien world. Another road sign bore the silhouette of an Amish buggy, so he cut his speed way down. Farmers plowing or planting in the fields used four-horse hitches and all wore black pants, blue shirts and broad-brimmed straw hats. Here and there, little boys dressed the same way as their elders, and girls in long dresses and white aprons fed goats or played some kind of beanbag game barefoot. Clothes flapped on lines and no electrical or phone wires existed around the neatly kept houses, which all boasted large vegetable gardens. Though the roads were nearly empty, he passed one black buggy and saw many others sitting beside barn doors or in backyards. The fields, even the woodlots in this broad valley, seemed well tended, almost as if he had driven his big vehicle into a painting of the past.

He noted a beautiful painted square, of what he wasn't quite sure, on one old barn. Despite his need to get to his destination—"Two miles on Orchard Road, then turn left onto Fish Creek Road," his sweet-voiced GPS recited—he slowed and craned his neck to look at the painting. The design was amazingly modern, yet he figured it was something old-fashioned. Not a hex sign, for sure. A quilt? Maybe they sold quilts at that old farmhouse.

He turned his eyes back to the road and tried to shake off his exhaustion. He'd felt burned out from too much work lately, but he'd managed about five hours' sleep before Mark called, enough to keep him going. He thrived on adrenaline, one reason he loved this job, though this case could be a bit of a challenge with the unusual culture and all.

At age thirty, Nate MacKenzie was the youngest of the state's twenty-one arson investigators. Though he'd told no one but his foster mother, his goal was to work his way up to become a district supervisor and then chief. He had both law enforcement and fire training. He saw himself as a detective who dealt with the remnants of a crime, the clues hidden in the rubble and ruins. After the tragedy that had happened to his family, his career was his calling, his only real passion.

He passed a one-room schoolhouse with a set of swings

and a dirt baseball diamond. Man, it reminded him of something from the old show *Little House on the Prairie*. But surely a group of old-fashioned Amish couldn't be too hard to handle, especially with his experience and the state-of-the-art technology at his fingertips. He would make a quick study of the Plain People by picking VERA's online brain so he'd know how to deal with them and in case he needed their help.

Sarah was about to head home when she saw something big and black coming down the road, then turning into the lane. It looked like a bulky, square, worldly emergency vehicle but it was bigger than that—why, it could almost swallow four buggies in one gulp. She hoped it wasn't some kind of hearse and one of the injured firefighters had suddenly died and was being brought back for burial.

She and the rest of the Plain People stood their ground and stared at it. Even Ray-Lynn quit talking. It had a truck cab and real fancy writing on the side, but, as it pulled in and stopped, the large lettering didn't really make sense except for the first word: OHIO. OHIO FEIB SFM VERA it read in big print with some smaller script under that.

Bishop Esh, her own father, Ben, and Eben Lantz—the three farmers whose lands adjoined—walked over to greet the man who emerged from the truck cab. Even without his big vehicle, he stood out as an *ausländer.* Bareheaded, he was a good foot taller than the bearded Amish men, even with their straw hats. He was clean-shaven like unwed Amish men. His short, almost ebony hair looked strange amid the blond and brown heads she was used to. His body seemed all angles and planes, maybe because he didn't look as well-fed as the Amish men. He wore belted jeans and a white shirt under a brown leather jacket, a kind hardly seen in these parts.

She wished she could hear what they were saying. The men shook hands and walked together toward the broken, still-smoking pile of beams and rubble. Sarah sidled a bit closer while some of the boys went over to peek at the vehicle.

She saw the visitor was not only speaking with the men but was talking into a little wire that hooked over one ear and curved around his face and stopped at the side of his mouth. It was either a small kind of recorder or a microphone like some workers wore at the McDonald's in Homestead when you gave an order and they passed it on to the kitchen. The stranger seemed to be repeating some things the men told him. Bishop Esh was pointing and gesturing, then he swung around and scanned the crowd and motioned—to her.

Feeling exposed, maybe because she was bonnetless, since it was still back in her own barn, wearing only her prayer *kapp* on her head and suddenly aware of her soil-and-ash-smeared appearance, Sarah went over to join the men.

"Sarah Kauffman is the one who spotted the flames from her own barn, over yonder," Bishop Esh was saying as he pointed across the fields, and the man turned his head away to look toward their barn. Her father nodded to her. He'd said earlier he was glad she had done the right thing to run across the fields because it took him twice as long to hitch up the buggy and come over to help.

Their visitor spoke something into his curved wire, then turned back to look at Sarah. Their gazes slammed into each other, right between the two men who held the most sway over her life, and yet it was like they weren't there at all.

"I'm Nate MacKenzie, Mrs.…Miss…" he floundered.

"Just plain Sarah is okay," she said, crossing her arms over her waist, as neither of them broke their steady gaze. She bit her lower lip. She hadn't meant to make that sound like a joke about the Amish being called the Plain People, but no one seemed to notice.

"I'm from the state fire marshal's office in Columbus, here to determine the cause of the blaze," their visitor told her.

*The cause of the blaze.* His words rotated through her head. Funny but she was starting to feel warm, as if the seething fire was still sending out flames. She was usually real easy with strangers, enjoyed talking to moderns with their outside experiences, so why should this man be different? Well, maybe it was just that big version of a worldly buggy he drove and his different looks.

Nate—that was probably really Nathan, a good Old Testament name—had strong features, a little cleft in the middle of his chin, which, along with his sharp-slanted cheeks, was peppered with beard stubble, like he'd been up all night and in a hurry, which he probably was. His lips were taut, his nose broad with a little bump, like maybe he broke it once. A thin white scar on his forehead slanted into his left eyebrow, but it was his eyes that entranced her. He had deep blue eyes when she thought dark-haired people mostly had brown ones. What a color that lake-blue would be for a painted quilt square—probably for the pattern of Ocean Waves, because that design, like her other favorites, seemed to shift, to move and beckon.…

"The state fire marshal's office received calls from the sheriff and the newspaper editor about this blaze," Nate said directly to her. "I understand you ran across the fields. I'd like to interview everyone who saw the early stages of the fire. Actually, if it's okay, I'd like to have you show me the exact spot at your place where you first saw the blaze so you can describe size, color and positioning to me. A time frame of its spread pattern will really help."

Ordinarily, Sarah would have waited for the bishop or her father to approve, but she said, "I'd be glad to help. I was just going to go back over, and I can meet you there, or you can come calling—I mean, visit us when it suits."

Her father cleared his throat and said, "Sarah had a big loss here, too, Mr. MacKenzie. She's been painting large quilt patterns on barns to help draw visitors to our area, and this was her first one. Enlarging it lately, just yesterday, too."

"Please, call me Nate. I saw one of those on the way in. Very striking. Did you lose paint or paint thinner in the barn last night?"

"Yes, but the cans were all closed up tight," she told him, her voice steady now. "I tap them back in their grooves when I'm done. Besides, I use exterior latex paint, water soluble, not oil base that needs turpentine or something like that. I left my scaffolding and two ladders just outside the barn, leaning against it. That's the bigger loss, moneywise."

Nate, still watching her, nodded. The sunshine shot more directly into his eyes. She saw he had sunglasses in his coat pocket, but he made no move to put them on, maybe trying to blend in with her people just a bit. He no doubt felt like the outsider he was. Though she was Amish born and bred, sometimes even she felt like that, unwed at the lofty age of twenty-four, a painter, not a sewer of quilts like other women.

"Like I said, Mr. MacKenzie," Bishop Esh put in, "no lanterns inside the barn and only seasoned hay, not the green stuff that can catch itself on fire."

"No open accelerants from paint supplies, no spontaneous combustion from methane-emitting hay," Nate said into his mouth wire. "Would it be okay if I take Sarah over to your farm in my vehicle?" he asked her father.

"Sure, and I'll ride along," *Daad* told him. "My son, Gabe, can bring our buggy back over."

Sarah knew better than to feel prideful or important, but her people parted for the three of them like Moses at the Red Sea as they walked toward the big, black truck. "We call her VERA for Vehicle for Emergency Response and Arson," Nate explained, patting the shiny hood as Sarah might her buggy horse, Sally.

"Arson," Sarah repeated. "Then you do think someone set the barn on fire?"

"Yet to be determined. Arson's the easiest crime to commit but often the hardest to prove. I know this barn—all your barns—are important to your way of life. If we can eliminate accident and act of nature, arson's what's left, and then I'll investigate that."

Nate wasn't sure if the Amish woman and her father were awed or frightened by VERA, but they climbed in the big front seat with him, Sarah between the two men. He was surprised they didn't fumble with their seat belts but clicked them quickly in place. She wore no wedding ring, but then he hadn't seen one piece of jewelry on any of these people.

Amazing that, with her honey-colored hair parted in the middle and pulled straight back under her messed-up small cap and with her old-fashioned dirty apron and dress—a peach-colored one, not black—with not a bit of makeup on her face, Sarah Kauffman was a real looker. She was a natural beauty with auburn, perfectly arched eyebrows over heavily

lashed amber eyes that seemed to have little flecks of gold
swimming in them. Surprisingly, mixed with the scent of
smoke, she smelled faintly of lavender. Her full mouth pouted
as she looked wide-eyed at the dashboard computer screen.

"Why, it has a map of our area on it," she said.

"It's called a global positioner, and it talks to me in a nice
female voice if I want it to," Nate said as he backed up, careful that none of the crowd, especially the gawking boys, were
behind him.

"Oh, now it's changed to a kind of TV screen that shows
what's in the rear when you back up," she said. Her voice
was mellow without a trace of the accent that the older men
seemed to have.

"Sarah, Mr. MacKenzie knows what's in his truck," her
father said.

"Oh, right."

"So could you tell me what you were doing when you
first saw the fire?" Nate asked as he drove them out of the
dirt lane to the road.

"My family was hosting a barn dance for my brother's
buddy group," she explained. "Gabe is seventeen and during
the mid to late teenage years, our young people are given a
time of freedom called *rumspringa,* kind of a running-around
time before they decide—or not—to join the church. I went
outside to ask someone to leave and looked up above his car
and—"

"His car?" Nate said.

"Right. Jacob Yoder's. He shouldn't have been there, and
he was drunk, I think, and making noise, and I was going
to ask him to leave."

Her father put in, "Jacob Yoder has been shunned for
breaking the *ordnung,* Mr. MacKenzie. Lied to the bishop

and aided an illegal theft ring of stolen cars, and was unrepentent."

"So he and Bishop Esh have a history—not a good one?" Nate wanted to ask more about shunning and breaking the *ordnung,* but he let it go for now. Mark was right about this being a foreign world, one he was going to have to navigate his way through. Find an interpreter of their ways, their culture, Mark had advised. He supposed he should rely on the bishop whose barn had burned, but sitting next to this interested, interesting young woman, he had a better idea. He needed a translator all right, because, despite all of VERA's space-age charms, he felt like a Star Trekker who was about to go where no man had ever gone before.

When her *daad* said he'd be out later and went into their house, Sarah was surprised. It was unusual for her father to leave her alone with an outsider, a man at least, so *Daad* must trust this man. Instead of taking time to change clothes, she decided to get his investigation going right away. She led him toward their barn since he had asked her to show him where she had been when she first noticed the blaze.

"By the way," she told him, "our barn is almost a replica of the Esh barn, if you want to see how it looked before the fire. Except it's usually neat as a pin, and we all ran out and left it like this last night." She gestured inside where a table with food sat and bales of straw surrounded a now-empty circle.

"Yeah, it would help immensely if I could study its structure," he said, lifting his eyebrows and looking intrigued by something. He had left his mouth wire in his truck. She wondered if he wanted to make her feel more at ease with him, which probably wasn't going to happen, because he just plain disturbed her somehow.

"Feel free to look around," she said, noting he at last pulled his gaze away from her to glance high and low inside their barn. "So," she went on, "I was helping *Mamm*—my mother—serve food behind that long table there, and I came across this threshing floor—"

"Still used for threshing at harvest time?"

"Sometimes, but we haul modern gasoline threshers now, pulled behind the horses, of course."

"But animal horsepower pulls them, so they're not actually fueled by gasoline? That means the hay baler Bishop Esh says he lost in the fire would not have had gasoline in it even off-season?"

"Right—modern equipment but real horsepower."

"In your field and the Eshes', I saw them—beautiful horses, big as the Budweiser team. But go ahead. You walked to what spot before you saw the fire. And what did it look like then?"

"I honestly don't know what time it was, if you need to know that—"

"I have the exact moment the call came in, so that will help."

"Anyway, I shouted for someone to call the fire department. Later, Jacob told me he'd called it in on his cell phone."

"Right. I have that info from the sheriff."

"When the buzzers alert the volunteers, it takes a while to get to the firehouse and then here," she said as she led him out of the barn.

"I've got all that and will be checking everyone out."

"Oh, sure, to get their descriptions of the fire, too. So I

would say I was right here when I saw the golden glow in the distance, which was growing fast and turning orange. And it seemed to start high, then burn downward."

"Really? That could be a key clue." He was taking notes with just a regular ballpoint pen on paper now, nodding, looking across the fields where she pointed.

"I thought at first the fire might be the headlights of Jacob's fancy car," she added.

"If he was exiled, why—"

"Shunned."

"Okay, shunned. Then why was he here?"

"It really doesn't have anything to do with the fire," she assured him, hesitant to get into all that about Jacob's past, especially how it meshed with hers.

"You need to let me decide that, Sarah," he said, turning to her. "Just in case the cause of the fire is incendiary and criminal, I have the right to investigate anyone who could have caused it, even make an arrest."

"You're a policeman, too?" she blurted. Although her people rendered to Caesar what was Caesar's and got on just fine with Sheriff Freeman, the Amish way was to steer clear of government authorities like the ones who had persecuted— burned to death by the hundreds—her people in Europe centuries ago. Her *grossmamm,* Miriam, was always reading to her from the Plain People's heirloom book, the *Martyrs Mirror*—talk about horrible burnings!

"I'm a law officer under certain conditions," he said. "So what's with this Jacob Yoder I've heard mentioned more than once? He was shunned by Bishop Esh?"

"By all of the church, really. I—it will take some explaining."

"Then we'll do it in a later interview. Go ahead and take

me across the field the way you ran last night and tell me how the fire appeared to change as you got closer, how the flames spread."

Happy to have a topic besides Jacob Yoder, she nodded, looking up into his intense gaze again before walking toward the fringe of the plowed field. In his work clothes, *Daad* came out of the house, and she told him where they were going. He nodded and headed for the barn past the *grossdaadi haus* where Sarah stayed at night with her grandmother and where poor Martha had been stuck during all the excitement.

"Wait a sec," Nate said so loudly she jumped. "Your barn doesn't have lightning rods. The Esh barn didn't, either?"

"Lightning rods show dependence on man, not God. If the Lord wants to protect a barn, He will."

"Then, ultimately, if the fire was arson, God's to blame?" Nate challenged, frowning.

"Not to blame," she insisted, but she'd never thought of it that way. She supposed there were other sides to some of the things she'd been taught since birth. "We live in an evil world," she went on, her voice more strident. "The Lord might allow it for a lesson, for our better good, to teach humility or bring our people closer—all positive things, gifts from above. We will work together to rebuild, to raise money for that if we must."

"So I heard. On the other hand, at least you don't have electrical wires coming in that could have caused a spark. I didn't mean to criticize your beliefs, Sarah. I'm just used to lightning rods on barns. Those or smoke alarms or fire extinguishers can save lives and buildings. And maybe God gave the inventors the ideas for those things through inspiration, like positive, useful gifts from above."

She had to admit that, in his own way, he was right. She

must remember, she told herself, that this man was here to help them but that he was not one of them. She had to keep her fences up, however much she wanted to work with him to help the Eshes.

So, with Nate MacKenzie at her side, she plunged into the field following the trail of her frenzied footsteps, back toward the burned barn.

# 3

SARAH HEARD THE PURR OF A BIG MOTOR EVEN before she peeked outside the barn where she was cleaning up the *danze* debris. As if her thoughts had summoned him, Nate MacKenzie had returned in the masculine-looking vehicle that had a woman's name. After Sarah had walked him across the field and back, he'd driven VERA over to the Eshes' again to do some preliminary work, but now, midafternoon, here he was.

"Hi, again," he called to her as he headed for their back porch but then did a U-turn toward her.

He came over, carrying something in a sealed plastic bag, wearing his sunglasses this time. They wrapped around his eyes like dark brown twin mirrors in which she could see herself getting larger as he came closer. At least she'd washed up and changed clothes but, not planning to go out in company, she still didn't wear a proper bonnet over her clean prayer *kapp*.

"I did an initial walk around the ruins," Nate said, stopping at the bottom of the banked entrance to the barn.

"Everything's still too hot to sift through and may be for a couple of days."

"Sift through? All the ruins?" she asked. That meant he'd be staying for a while.

"I may not have to, actually, to get proof of arson, though I'll need details for my report that point to how and who. The why may be harder to come by, but I found something key to my investigation. A rubber band around a bunch of about twenty matches," he said, lifting the plastic bag so she could see what was in it. "I found them on the ground about thirty feet from the back of the barn—not in this bag, of course. Bishop Esh says no one smokes in his family, nor does he keep matches around like this to light their kerosene lanterns."

"Oh, no!" she blurted. "But why would kids who might be smoking on the sly put a bunch of matches together with a rubber band?"

"So some of the kids in the neighborhood last night were smoking, kids who were here at your barn dance?"

"During *rumspringa,* it's fairly common. When the fire happened, I thought of it and worried a bit. But those matches are unburned, so you mean they might have dropped that bunch, but threw another pack like that into the barn?"

"Sarah, I'm not jumping to the conclusions you seem to be. It's just that this is part of an old arson trick amateurs use. They get some kind of long trailer—a wick—light the end of it, maybe far away from the object to be burned, and have it ignite some kind of combustibles."

"But you found no wick?"

"No. If one led into the barn, it would have been consumed in the inferno. Besides, you said the fire seemed fiercer high up, so that means someone had a very long wick if they were on the first floor. Of course, kids could have gone up into the loft."

"We can ask them."

"I will."

"Or a long wick means the person could even stay outside the barn to light the fire."

"That's another possibility," he told her with a nod. "A trailer, if it's long enough—sometimes soaked with an accelerant—can give the perpetrator up to fifteen minutes to vacate the property before the fire ignites. So it could have been kids, but before I look around your barn to get an idea of what I'll be searching for in the remnants, let's have that little chat about why Jacob Yoder was hanging around if he'd been shunned."


Deciding not to take notes or record Sarah as she talked, Nate listened carefully as they sat together just inside the barn door on bales of straw. His cell phone even rang once, but he glanced at it—a coworker in Columbus—then put it away without answering.

Sarah explained how she had broken her betrothal to Jacob even before he was shunned for helping hide stolen cars. She said that Sheriff Freeman could have brought aiding and abetting charges that would have sent Jacob to prison for a while, but he didn't because he thought the Amish could make him shape up better by shock treatment—that is, ostracizing him from the church, his family and friends.

"He could have blamed the bishop and wanted revenge against him," Nate said after she stopped talking. He hadn't interrupted. He found her fascinating, the way she managed to keep control while emotions obviously rampaged through her. Her full, lower lip had quivered, but her voice never wavered. Her naive beauty was riveting, and he tried not to let that distract him from what she said. "Or, he could have picked that barn because of your wall painting there," he added, "or because it would hurt the Eshes *and* you. Can you give me more details about shunning?" he asked.

"If he hadn't been a member of the church, he wouldn't have been shunned. But, once you're a member and you break the set of rules—the *ordnung*—that's that. But I don't see how he can be vindictive. Not only did he bring it on himself, but he was not sent to prison when he could have been. Besides, the church will take him back with open arms if he atones and returns to our ways."

"Since he was hanging around at your barn dance, does he think you'd take him back with open arms? Sorry, that's too intrusive."

"It's okay. To tell the truth, though I once cared for Jacob, it was a relief for me when we got unmatched—before he helped those car thieves. I knew he was keeping something from me and he was flying too high and too fast in worldly ways and questionable company. Now, if you want to look around our barn or ask more questions, go right ahead while I finish cleaning up."

He supposed he'd overstepped, pushing her about Jacob, but whatever cages he had to rattle, he would. As polite as she remained, her demeanor had shifted a bit from helpful to huffy. She started toward the long table, but he walked with her. "Can you tell me a little more about your quilt square paintings?" he asked.

"Painting is…dear to me," she began, her voice almost faltering. She stopped and turned to face him. "I've done decorations on birdhouses and gazebos in my father's wintertime carpentry shop for years, but I thought I could do more than scrollwork and leaves and birds—if it was allowed."

"Allowed by your father and by Bishop Esh, I take it—and the church *ordnung*. As I said, the painting I saw was beautiful."

"Best say it was purposeful. Just like the rest of the people in the country, shaky financial times have hit Amish businesses hard. Busloads of visitors used to come to eat in our restaurants and buy homemade goods like furniture and quilts, but not so many lately. So I thought, and convinced our church leaders, that it would be good to have something new to draw them in—a quilt trail, so to speak, where they could go from barn to barn, maybe buy things, even garden products or eggs if the more expensive items were too deep for their pockets. Besides farming, I guess we've learned to lean on the tourist trade a lot."

"Maybe someone attracted to the decorated barns has a hidden agenda. Has anyone ever said something to you about not liking your paintings?"

"Not visitors. In general, our people don't believe in doing things just for pretty, as we say. Things can't only be pleasing as a decoration. Quilts, scented lavender sachets or candles, furniture—all has to be useful, purposeful for the common good."

"And some of your people thought the quilt squares were just for pretty?"

She sighed. "Despite the bishop's and the church elders' permission, a few of the brothers and sisters, yes. Some think I'm being too different painting squares instead of quilting them. The local newspaper did an article and made me sound prideful when I try hard not to be!"

Emotion swelled her voice and flushed her cheeks with

color. He wanted to comfort her. Was he nuts? He had to stay objective here, but he decided his best bet was to change the subject because, before she turned away, she almost looked as if she'd cry.

"I hope you don't mind," he said, "but Bishop Esh said I can park VERA and live on the woodlot at the juncture of the three farms while I'm here. He told me the best approach to it is from the lane that runs off your driveway and cuts behind this barn."

"Sure, that's fine," she said, heading again toward the long plank tabletop set on sawhorses. "I can point it out to you." She started to wipe the oilcloth-covered table with a vengeance.

"I've got food in VERA and I've been invited to eat with the Eshes when I'm over there working, but I don't want to impose on them more than tonight. I'm told the Dutch Farm Table Restaurant is good."

"The best, if you don't want McDonald's or Wendy's—a big battle between those two with all kinds of specials. If you don't mind day-old half-moon pies, I've got some here you can take with you. My mother and sister make them for the Dutch Farm Table. Here, help yourself," she said, opening a cake-size box and extending it to him.

"One more thing," he said. He took a bite of one of the crimped-edge, glazed pastry half circles, this one filled with apple and cinnamon. Delicious. He talked with his mouth a bit full. "Mmm, this is fabulous," he said. "I just want you to know that I need to be suspicious of everyone, every possibility. Not just of kids smoking, not just of Jacob, who may have a double motive, but even of the firefighters themselves. If a closer survey of the evidence in the ruins points to arson by a burn pattern or residue of accelerants, I'll be looking at everyone, even them."

"At the firemen? That doesn't make sense, Amish or English."

"It's the so-called dirty little secret of firefighters. A few of them want to fight fires because fires mesmerize them, make them feel powerful, release pent-up feelings. They revel in being the first one into a fire, the hero, or, if they're injured, even the victim who gets the glory or sympathy."

"So that means you'll even talk to the two who were hurt and not just to see how they describe the blaze? They were the first ones in."

"Exactly." He held the half-eaten, small pie up to his mouth and stared at her again. He was surprised she didn't protest that, if an arsonist burned the barn, he—or she, though a female was unlikely—could be Amish, even one in good standing, especially if they thought both the bishop and the artist had overstepped with "just for pretty" painted quilt squares. He hadn't mentioned that directly, but he couldn't afford to ignore any possibilities.

"The Eshes can prove where they were before the fire, and our people don't believe in insurance, so no one would burn his own barn for that," she said, anticipating his next line of questioning.

"The Eshes have an alibi, but in the modern world, as you call it, sometimes people do burn their own property to get the money for it."

He almost choked on the bite of half-moon pie he took to cover up the catch in his voice. What he'd just said hit too close to home—his own lost home and family. All he needed was that old nightmare he had buried deep to resurrect itself. But what scared him even more was his gut feeling that it would be so easy for someone to burn another isolated, unprotected barn. He had to act fast to stop that from happening.

"Are they burning our people again?" Sarah's grandmother, Miriam Kauffman, asked her the night after the barn fire.

Her voice shaking, her expression distraught, the old woman stood in the doorway to the bathroom with her toothbrush in hand and her white hair in a long braid, ready for bed. Sarah told Martha, who had stayed last night in the small *grossdaadi haus,* that she'd take over. But Martha had wanted to hear every last detail about the fire and the fire marshal's arson investigator, so she was waiting in the living room. *Grossmamm* and Martha had watched the fire from the kitchen windows, until Martha had convinced her charge to go to bed, but talk of the fire was what had probably set *Grossmamm* off right now. That, and the fact she insisted on reading a few pages from the *Martyrs Mirror* every night before she slept.

"No, *Grossmamm,* it's all right," Sarah assured her. "No one is burning our people."

"*Ya,* the authorities are coming again for us!" she insisted. "They tried to burn the Eshes out, and they'll be here next! Soldiers like that man you were talking to outside today are going to slaughter us again."

"That man is here to help us," Sarah promised, putting her hands on the old woman's shoulders. "We are safe here on the farm, in America."

Sarah had considered taking the *Martyrs Mirror* away from her grandmother more than once. But that precious book had come down through her family, an heirloom. Poor *Grossmamm,* afflicted with Alzheimer's, sometimes thought the Amish were still under siege as they'd been in Europe, hundreds of years ago.

Sarah kept talking, slowly, calmly. "That man was sent by the state government in Columbus to find out about our neighbor's barn, why it burned. No Amish were burned or will be."

"I was afraid you would be lost in the fire."

"Me? No, I'm just fine. All I lost were some paint cans, my scaffolding and two ladders."

"They killed our people on tall scaffolds as a warning so all could see. They tied women to ladders, then tipped them into the fires just because they disagreed with the state religion."

"That's all in the past. No one is going to burn. Even the horses were safe from that fire. Now brush your teeth, and I'm going to read to you from the *Budget,* all kinds of news about our people visiting and how well things are going."

"Except for Amish martyrs being burned," Miriam Kauffman mumbled as she thrust her toothbrush in her mouth and bent over the bathroom basin where she'd left the water running.

Sarah sighed. She knew she resembled her grandmother in her height and coloring, so she sure hoped she wouldn't inherit the mental hauntings that plagued her. She'd been better lately, but seeing that barn fire across the fields had obviously set her off again.

The *Martyrs Mirror,* with its lifelike etchings, was in almost every Amish home, along with the Holy Bible, of course, and the *Ausbund,* which contained the words to the traditional Amish hymns sung in the regular church meetings every other Sunday. As for the *Budget,* that newspaper was the Amish community glue that held the Plain People together wherever they lived. Births, deaths, marriages, horse sales, new addresses or endeavors and chatty tidbits were listed on page after page. Yes, she was going to spirit away the *Martyrs Mirror* and substitute it with the *Budget* right now.

Later, Sarah was glad she did. Not only did the chatty items in the *Budget* calm the old woman, but Sarah noted one about the Eshes that explained why they might have been out last night. Mattie Esh's niece had just given birth to triplets, and they probably went to see them.

As usual, *Grossmamm* fell asleep quickly, and Sarah took the kerosene lantern with her down the hall and into the living area. Most Amish farms had a *grossdaadi haus* for the older generation. When the grandparents who had worked the farm and raised their children were ready to retire, they voluntarily turned over the big house to the eldest married son, or the one who wanted most to keep the farm going, and moved to the smaller place on the property. No rest home, retirement village or shuffling off the older genera-tion among the Amish. They cared for their aging parents or grandparents on-site and included them in as much of life as they cared to be a part of. After their *grossdaadi,* Gideon Kauffman, had died five years ago, his widow had started to slip into another world. Alzheimer's, sure, and she'd had a doctor's care, but they were still going to keep her here and look after her themselves.

Sarah found Martha sound asleep, sprawled on the sofa, breathing heavily. She covered her up with a quilt. That sofa made into a double bed, so where was she going to sleep? They both had their own rooms in the big house, but it was Sarah's turn to stay here tonight. Should she wake Martha and send her away so she could have the hideaway bed?

She sat down in her grandfather's big rocking chair very

carefully, because she knew it squeaked. Her eyes were so heavy. She hadn't slept last night…was dead on her feet today, except when Nate MacKenzie was around twice because he seemed to give her energy.

When her lids drooped, she saw fire, saw Nate's intense gaze. She wondered how he was doing living in VERA down by the pond on the woodlot…. And what if the woods, all those trees around the pond, caught fire and the blaze burned him, burned her, too, crackling…popping…

She jolted alert. Her heartbeat pounded. That sound! Gravel against glass, against the window? That was the signal she and her friend Hannah Esh had always used during their *rumspringa* years to get each other up at night when they wanted to sneak out. Not to meet boys like some did, but to go for a night swim in the pond in the summer or just stuff themselves with candy or listen to a transistor radio until dawn while Sarah sketched pictures and Hannah sang along with every Top Ten hit. They knew better than to get their friend Ella from the Lantz farm for such goings-on. No way Ella, as much fun as she could be, would take a risk sneaking out like that.

Again, she heard the sound of gravel against the window. As she stood and looked, the glass was like a big black mirror since they hadn't pulled the curtains closed. Sarah turned down the kerosene lamp and peered out, seeing at first only her own reflection. The *Martyrs Mirror,* she thought…now why had they put the word *mirror* in the title? She'd never thought about that. Were the Amish all martyrs to something or other? Did it mean to look deeply into your own life, to see yourself as you really were or to decide what you were willing to die for?

And then Hannah's face appeared, not the old Amish

Hannah but the new one her parents were so riled about. Hannah and her friends in Cleveland had gone goth. Whereas Hannah was a natural blonde with eyebrows and lashes so pale they hardly showed, she now had red, spiky hair and eyeliner dark as sin. Sarah was used to seeing her friend in the soft pastel dresses unwed women wore, not in black, partly ripped and fringed tight pants and wearing silver chains and pins and piercings. Even now, Hannah looked like some kind of worldly Halloween freak. And she was gesturing for Sarah to come outside.

Sarah held up one finger and, her hands shaking, scribbled a note for Martha. "I had to leave for a little bit. Stay with G., please—S."

She grabbed the windbreaker she wished she'd worn last night and tiptoed out. Hannah here! She wasn't shunned so she could come back anytime, but she didn't. After she'd had the argument with her father almost three years ago, she'd left for Cleveland. Their daughter's loss was the cross the bishop and his wife bore, and Sarah's and Ella's loss, too. When Hannah's plan to record and sell her own songs didn't work out, her friends and family prayed she would come home. Instead, her worldly boyfriend got her a job in a recording studio mixing something or other, answering the phone and greeting people at the front desk, looking just like this.

Sarah and Hannah hugged hard. Hannah smelled of an exotic scent Sarah could not name. Something smoky. She'd had incense burning in her little apartment the one time Sarah and Ella had visited her in Cleveland. Or had she been over to her family's burned barn?

"Jacob phoned me," Hannah told Sarah as they stepped awkwardly apart. "I couldn't believe the barn was gone. It's

supposed to be in the Cleveland paper tomorrow, but I had to
see it first, before all the gawkers in the world come flocking
in."

"You didn't have to come at night. Everyone would have
been glad to see you."

"Give me a break. About like they'd be glad to have Satan
himself drop by. But I knew I could come to you, that you'd
go with me. I just can't go see it alone, any more than I could
face my father. I parked back down the road by the graveyard
and walked here. He—Jacob—said you were the one who
spotted the fire and he called it in, but that you weren't back
together yet."

"Yet? Never. He crashed our party for Gabe's friends.
That's why he was here."

"Jacob also said there's a superhero here to save the day,
solve the crime—if it's a crime."

"Word travels fast, because Jacob was asked to leave before
the state arson investigator showed up."

"Will you go with me, Sarah? I can't go to Ella. I don't
need her telling me I've got to mend my ways and come
back. She never did quite get the 'judge not lest ye be judged'
bit, did she?"

"I guess accepting that comes with suffering, and she's
been all wrapped up in traveling the road of her perfect
Amish life."

Sarah instantly regretted she'd said that with such a sharp
tone. But sometimes she resented Ella's sticking to the
straight and narrow, when she herself would like to go her
own way at times. How she yearned to paint entire land-
scapes instead of the geometric quilt squares that called for
no more creative decision than what color of hardware store
paint to use.

"In other words," Hannah said with a bitter laugh, "she still hasn't found out 'it's not all cakes and pies.'"

"I've been thinking lately that it's not all *quilts* and pies."

"You never did like to stitch quilts. And you think I'm a freak? But your painting—that's you. Jacob told me about the quilt square you did on our—my family's—barn."

"A real font of information, isn't he?" Sarah said, surprised again her voice was so sharp. Maybe Hannah's rebellious nature was rubbing off on her. And was Nate right to be suspicious of Jacob? Nate had said that some firefighters loved the attention from a blaze, but did Jacob, too? Nate had also said that some arsonists returned to the scene of their crime, not only to watch the fire, but even later to relive the excitement. Maybe that's why Jacob stopped at the very next farm. Or did he think his phoning in the fire would build bridges back to his people—and her?

The two young women started down the Oakridge Road that linked their farms. Sarah was glad Hannah didn't insist on a run through the fields, like she'd done last night. They didn't worry that there would be buggies or cars on the rural road now, because traffic was rare even in the daytime, unless a buggy clip-clopped past or tourists pleasure-driving some back byways happened by.

As they sneaked around Hannah's childhood home, not going up the lane but skirting along the fence, Hannah cursed. "Damn! There's a hole in the sky where it should be! Nothing but blackness and stars! It's so—I can't believe it, all of that destroyed to almost nothing!"

Her family's team of horses plodded over to the fence as if to commiserate about the loss of their stalls, feed troughs and harnessing gear, the wagons and equipment they used to pull. Hannah put her hand out to one's muzzle, and he snuffled against her palm as if he were crying.

"At least you guys still know me," Hannah whispered.

"Why don't you write your family a note!" Sarah suggested. "They'd love to hear from you, know that you cared enough to come see it."

"It won't help them to know I was here and saw this," she insisted. Even in the darkness, with only the wan quarter moon rising, Sarah could see her friend's tears track down her cheeks. "The heart of the farm, so many good times here... I'm so sorry, so sorry about what I've done," Hannah cried, and began to sob so hard that some of her mascara ran down her face in dirty lines and smeared against Sarah's cheek as she hugged her again.

"Good evening, ladies." The deep male voice came from behind them. "Sarah, I thought you were going to stay all night with your grandmother, and what is this person confessing she's sorry she's done?"

# 4

"WHAT ARE YOU DOING HERE IN THE DARK?" Sarah demanded.

The other girl glared at Nate and tugged her arm free. He was so shocked by her appearance that he let her go. He read in her defiant stare that she wouldn't run, but he kept a light hold of Sarah's arm. It was the first time he'd touched her. She radiated warmth from what must have been a walk down the road from her farm.

"I'm going to ask the questions, Sarah," he said more harshly than he'd intended. "I'm Nate MacKenzie, state arson investigator," he told the other young woman, riveting his gaze on her. "I want to know who *you* are and what *you* are doing here in the dark."

Since he'd been in a sleeping bag near the back of the barn, Nate knew they hadn't come across the fields. He'd seen the Eshes turn off their house lamps over an hour ago, so he'd been startled to hear women's voices. Earlier, the bishop had sat outside with him for a while, over milk and cookies, no less. Nate had explained to him that he had obtained a search warrant to examine the ruins of the barn, but the bishop had said he had his permission and didn't need anything from the government to say so.

Bishop Joseph Esh had also reminisced about the barn, which his father had bequeathed him. Amish barns were almost a part of the family, he'd learned, the cornerstone of their way of life, necessary not only for running their fifty-or-so-acre farms but for keeping the generations working and worshipping together.

"This is Hannah Esh, from Cleveland," Sarah said when the stranger continued to glare at him in silence. "She's the Eshes' third-oldest daughter, but she hasn't lived here for three years because she's away building her career."

"It's okay, Sarah," Hannah said. "I can talk for myself. He just surprised me. I thought, at first, it might be my... Never mind. Mr. MacKenzie, a friend phoned to tell me my family's barn burned to the ground, and I wanted to see it without bothering them. I'm a big disappointment to them and am living in so-called worldly exile."

Hannah Esh, Nate noted, had a bitter tinge to her voice and a defiant expression on what could be—with that harsh makeup, he wasn't sure—a pretty face.

"She's not being shunned like Jacob. She left home before joining the church—perfectly permissible," Sarah said.

"Then she's able to be welcomed back with what you called open arms," Nate said.

"I'd appreciate it if you don't tell my parents I was here," Hannah said. "And I certainly don't want to see them to-night."

She stared straight at him when she talked. Like Sarah, a strong woman—or were all Amish women?

"I would think they would be happy to know you cared," he said.

"But only to visit to see a—a dead barn? I don't think so."

"Hannah, I need to know where you were last night, when the barn burned."

"Why?" she countered instantly, and this time her steady gaze did dart away from him, back toward where the barn had been. He heard Sarah suck in a breath, so she no doubt recalled what he'd said about arsonists possibly returning to the scene of the crime. And Sarah's quick mind would get it that Hannah, just as Jacob, had a motive to hurt the Eshes for rejecting her.

"All right," she said, cutting off Sarah, who seemed ready to leap to her friend's defense. Hannah folded her arms over her breasts. "I was in the recording studio, making a demo and mixing my own audio background."

"You're a singer?"

"I am, and trying to be a professional one."

"She has a great voice," Sarah added.

"So you're saying you were alone last night," Nate said, looking only at Hannah. "Who called you to let you know the barn burned?"

"No one you've met. Jacob Yoder."

"But someone I'm going to meet real soon. I need all your contact information, Hannah, including the name and address of the owner of the studio where you work—just in case there are more questions."

"And I'll just bet there will be," she said, her voice slightly shaky now. Ordinarily, he felt he could really read suspects, but with the barrier of her appearance, he couldn't. It was tough enough to try to read the Amish, but an Amish woman who had rebelled? Maybe he could get more out of

Sarah about Hannah later. She was becoming his touchstone here—his translator, as his boss had put it.

"I'd like to be able to drive you ladies back to Sarah's but I jogged over from where I left my vehicle in the woodlot behind the Kauffman farm. So I'm going to walk you back."

"Not necessary," Hannah said. "No one's out in Amish country in the dark."

"Someone was out last night," Nate said, handing her a small pad and a pen to write down her contact information. "Someone, I'll bet, who had a big beef against either your father or Sarah, or both."

Sarah loved her job taking *Mamm*'s and Lizzie's half-moon pies to Ray-Lynn at the Dutch Farm Table Restaurant six mornings a week. Honoring the Amish tradition of no Sunday sales, the place had been closed yesterday. Sarah had to get up before dawn, but she didn't mind. *Grossmamm* was always still asleep and either Martha, if she wasn't in school, or *Mamm* if she was, came over to stay.

Some amazing sunrises greeted Sarah as she went out to the barn to hitch Sally to her buggy, but, she had to admit, never one as stunning as the orange, fuchsia and apricot blaze in the sky today. Cirrus clouds and feathery floaters made the heavens look like a kaleidoscope quilt—one with Nate MacKenzie standing near the barn, silhouetted by it all. *Ya,* if he'd only been wearing an Amish jacket and straw hat, what a painting that would make. As good as his word, he'd walked her to the *grossdaadi haus* last night and Hannah to her car down the road at the Amish cemetery. He seemed to turn up everywhere.

Somehow she managed to find her voice. "So you're an early riser as well as a night owl," she said as she carried her big flat basket with four boxes of half-moon pies into the barn. *Daad* and Gabe were already out in the fields with some of the work team, and the barn door stood open.

"I do what I must to solve a crime."

"You're sure it is?"

"I'll start going through the debris today, and then—if it is—I'll be interviewing others. Hannah just more or less knocked on my door before I was ready for her."

"She's had a hard time."

"So have her parents."

"Did they mention her to you?"

"Not a word, not even when I had a heart-to-heart talk with her father."

She nodded, put the basket down on a hay bale and pulled her buggy out of the back corner from among the lineup of the big carriage, sleigh and smaller carts. She saw *Daad* and Gabe had already taken the work wagon out. Trying to stay calm near Nate when she didn't know what was coming next, she went out to fetch her buggy horse, Sally, in the side field. Although the horses were often out in this mild weather where they could graze, she still took the mare's feed bag with her so Sally would get her grain and vitamins. She saw three of the family's work team of big Percherons were still grazing in the field. She whistled and her smart former harness racer came right over to the gate.

Again, she was grateful that the Eshes' horses had not been in the barn when it caught fire. Could the arsonist, if there was one like Nate evidently thought, be Amish and know how important the horses were? No, not if he'd burn a precious barn.

She fastened Sally's feed bag on, brought her through the gate, past Nate, and backed her up to the double-seat buggy.

Most Amish women, unless they were unwed, didn't have their own vehicle. Despite the fact it marked her as an unwed *maidal,* she loved her freedom and kept the horse well-tended and the black fiberglass buggy clean and shined. Although Nate was usually full of talk and questions, he came closer and leaned against a stall rail just watching.

"I have to have these half-moon pies at the Dutch Farm Table before they open at seven," she explained. "It's a real challenge in the winter, but I like the time alone to observe everything just waking up, any season of the year."

"I guess the speed of a buggy gives you time for that. I keep learning about things I thought I had answers to."

She wasn't sure if he meant about his investigation or the way they lived here, but she just nodded as she put the crupper under Sally's tail and the breast strap between her forelegs, then took the feed bag off so she could get the bridle on.

"When your father and brother opened up the barn this morning," Nate said, "I really looked around in here to get an idea of the preburn layout of the Esh barn. Then I searched German bank barns on VERA's laptop."

"Searched?"

"Oh, yeah, sorry. On my computer. I studied up—a crash course on barns with three levels like yours and the Eshes'. I couldn't believe how your barn exteriors are misleading. I mean, there's so much more space inside than what I expected. It's like, don't judge a book by its cover, I guess, like with people, too. Sarah, I don't want you to get the idea I'm prejudging people, Hannah or Jacob or anyone else."

Over Sally's back, their gazes locked and held again, the way they too often did. She always felt a funny fluttering in her lower belly she'd never had with Jacob. This man made her blush, too, but at least her complexion usually hid that.

"I had to ask your friend those questions last night, get her info," he added in a rush.

"You're really barking up the wrong tree with her."

"You said that about Jacob, too."

"She loves her parents, but they wanted her back in the nest under their roof and rules, and it led to harsh words. She was crushed to see the barn was gone."

"Sarah, she's still bitter about all that. She's chosen to be about as far from Amish as she can get, despite the fact she's still dressed in black."

"She would never burn the barn!" she exploded at him, then put her hand up over her mouth as if she'd cursed. This man brought out all kinds of emotions in her she'd never known were there, or at least ones she'd never let out before. Why couldn't she just be like other Amish women, content with her lot in life? Why did she have to yearn for the forbidden—to paint pictures, that is?

"Okay, thanks for that testimony about Hannah," Nate said, his voice clipped. "You're starting to sound like an expert witness, but I guess I asked for that. See you later. I've got a long day over at the site of the burn."

As he strode away, she was upset she'd lost her temper. Patience and humility, not anger and pride, were what she needed. She went back to harnessing Sally but turned her head to watch Nate walk away. The man was too lanky, and she'd like to feed him up good. His head was down while he punched something into a little cell-phone type thing with both thumbs. He headed toward the back lane where he had VERA parked. She might have just kept staring, except Sally snorted and stamped her foot.

Just as she was heading out of the end of the lane onto the road, Sarah heard the purr of the big engine behind her. Nate in VERA, of course. Was this driven man, who needed some speed bumps in his life, as edgy as she? Was he annoyed to be slowed down by the buggy, impatient with their ways? May the Lord forgive her, but sometimes, Sarah had to admit, she was impatient with her people's ways. But right now she hoped Sally didn't leave any horse apples for his fancy vehicle to drive through. At least he knew better than to honk like some moderns.

As Sarah headed toward town under real horsepower, she craned her neck to watch VERA as Nate went the other way, toward the Esh farm.

Because a TV reporter with her cameraman and several tourists had been standing out in front, Ray-Lynn Logan had opened the Dutch Farm Table a half hour early. She was already there with a couple of her Amish waitresses, anyway, and her profits had been down lately. So she was glad to see Sarah Kauffman coming in the back door with the day's supply of half-moon pies, which sold much better than doughnuts. Full-size schnitz and shoofly pies and other Amish desserts like date-nut and carrot cake came in from area bakers.

"Not late, am I?" Sarah asked. She was out of breath and looked as rosy-cheeked as she did in bitter winter.

"Not our heroine of the day," Ray-Lynn told her, taking the basket from her hands and handing it to Leah Schwartz, who took it through the swinging doors into the kitchen. "You should see the special edition Peter put out. Got a real nice ad for the restaurant in it, too, but then he'd better, since he owns part of it. There's a copy on the counter. Oh, by the way, he'd like a more in-depth interview with you, and I'll bet the outside media coming in would, too. Two of those critters just left."

"No. It's a blessing I just happened to spot the fire first and I don't want to sound prideful. Someone else made the call."

"And he's got a lot to say—Jacob, that is," Ray-Lynn said, tapping her index finger on the middle paragraphs of the article under the large photo of the flaming barn behind the dark silhouettes of firefighters. "He kind of makes it sound like you were working together to call the fire in."

"Oh, rats," Sarah said, and leaned over the paper on the counter. "I did not tell him directly to make the call, but I figured he'd have a phone on him, even if half the other *rumspringa* kids did, too. I have refused more than once to see him, and we are not in cahoots of any kind."

In cahoots, that's a good one, Ray-Lynn thought, pouring Sarah a cup of coffee, then reaching in her quilted apron pocket for money to take back to her mother and sister. The Amish had a fresh way of saying some things. Sarah Kauffman might not want to be in cahoots with Jacob Yoder, but she'd sure like to get Sarah to be in cahoots with her about doing some paintings Ray-Lynn could sell for her. The girl was extremely talented, and Ray-Lynn was willing to risk a lot to bring her Amish art to the world.

"I see there's a big interview here with Fireman Getz," Sarah said, obviously trying to shift the subject. "It says he has a broken arm but he doesn't regret going in first to try to put out the flames."

"More fool he, and that Levi Miller, too. Levi's cousin to my waitress Anna, you know, and she says both men got released from the regional hospital. Well, I bet I know why

Mike Getz played the hero. He and his gal, Cindee what's-her-name—"

"Cindee Kramer. She works in the hardware store where I buy my paint."

"Right. Anyhow, they're not married but been living together—"

"I know. That takes extra nerve around here."

"They got into a real tiff in the restaurant last week, something about she didn't look up to him anymore, but I'll bet she does now. She had a real conniption at table eight in the back room. I was afraid he was going to start throwing things, but I'll bet he could run for mayor after those heroics," she said, pointing to the picture of him, smiling, no doubt, prefire, all decked out in his fireman gear. "What? You're frowning again."

"Nothing. I will just give the devil his due."

Ray-Lynn wasn't sure what that meant, coming from an Amish girl, but she saw outside what she'd been looking for and muttered to herself, "Speak of the devil..."

The sheriff's shiny black cruiser with that bold light bar had pulled up to parallel park in front. The restaurant door opened, and Sheriff Jack Freeman came in, hanging his hat on a wooden peg, his sharp gaze scanning the room as if he'd find a robbery or kidnapping in progress in this little burg.

"Morning, Ray-Lynn, Sarah," he said matter-of-factly. He passed them with a nod and his version of an official smile, then sat in his usual spot at the curve of the counter facing the door with his back to the wall so he could keep a good eye on things. Ray-Lynn used to scurry to pour him coffee and take his order—even when she knew what he'd order already—but she'd decided on another tactic now. No falling at his feet, just take it easy, a bit hard to get.

While Sarah scowled over the newspaper, Ray-Lynn saun-
tered down behind the counter and nonchalantly poured Jack
his coffee during their usual chitchat about the weather. She
was up for that much of their old routine, at least. She knew
darn well he'd want sausage gravy on buttermilk biscuits and
two eggs over easy, but she asked, "What will it be today,
Sheriff? I'm sure you've got a busy day ahead with the extra
folks in town, so I'll send someone right over to get your
order."

She left him staring wide-eyed at her while she went over
to fill other people's cups at the tables.

Jack Freeman was a few years older than Ray-Lynn but he
was holding up better than most men his age. No paunch,
very few gray hairs, just enough to make his auburn hair
looked frosted at the temples. Unlike the bearded Amish
men, he was clean-cut, something he'd never changed from
his former marine days. He always looked slightly tanned,
which set off his clear, brown eyes and white teeth. His black
uniform was military clean and crisp-looking, pretty surprising since he'd been divorced for years and Homestead's one
dry cleaner had gone out of business. It annoyed Ray-Lynn
that she got kind of shivery around him. The man exuded
authority and control, both of which she was itching to dis-
mantle, at least in private, with her Southern gal feminine
wiles. But he seemed to put up a big wall when she came on
soft and sweet, so her new strategy was worth a try.

She ignored him but made a big fuss over seating four
tourists from Columbus, chatting away to them, while
Anna Miller took the sheriff's order. Good—she could tell
he didn't like the lack of personal attention. It was another
risk, but she'd decided some things were worth it.

She walked back to Sarah while Jack took out his own

copy of the special edition of the *Home Valley News*. It was only about eight pages this time—a lot of ads, about half of them for businesses Peter had his finger in, even the Buggy Wheel Shop, which had only Amish customers who would go there to buy new buggies whether there was an ad or not.

"The rest of that fire article's not so bad, is it?" Ray-Lynn asked Sarah. "As I've told you a hundred times before, you're a fabulous artist and should be aiming higher than just quilt squares on barns. I know you're yearning to do more than copy patterns even if you do choose the colors."

"I wish he hadn't put my age in here," Sarah whispered, looking as if he'd written that she was a serial killer. "It sounds weird that a twenty-four-year-old woman still has her maiden name. 'Sarah Kauffman, age twenty-four, from the Kauffman farm next door.' Why do papers think they have to tell stuff like that, and who told him my age?"

"Listen to your friend Ray-Lynn, my girl. At twenty-four, you are still what the big, bad world would consider a young chick, believe me. Now, I know Amish women your age are usually wed by now, but it'll happen. Besides, not to sound like a broken record, but you've got other talents, and I'm real sorry to see that first pretty quilt square you did got burned up with the barn. You've got to branch out, so my offer is still open for you to paint an Amish scene on that long wall right there instead of that old-fashioned wallpaper. I'll never forget those beautiful drawings you showed me from your sketchbook."

"Thanks, Ray-Lynn. I haven't shown anyone but Hannah, Ella and you those drawings, so I guess we're keeping each other's secrets, right?"

"And secrets they will remain for now," Ray-Lynn said. The thing was, Sarah had eyes like a hawk. Maybe all artists

did. Though Ray-Lynn had tried to hide it, her Amish friend
had picked up on the fact that she was smitten with Jack
Freeman. "You just keep that offer about the mural in mind
now," she urged Sarah. "I'd pay you well for your time if
we can just get permission from your powers-that-be around
here."

"Can I take this copy of the paper to show the arson investigator?"

"Why, sure. But if you don't want to be interviewed,
better steer clear of the Esh place. I think a camera crew
and a few others went out there to talk to him—oops, more
customers to be seated."

"I'm supposed to take some things to the Eshes, a chicken
dinner when *Mamm* and Lizzie get it ready."

Though Ray-Lynn knew the Amish rarely showed affection in public, she gave Sarah's shoulders a quick squeeze. As
she passed Jack, heading to seat more folks who'd come in
the front door, she said, "I'll have Anna refresh that coffee
while you're waiting for whatever you ordered, Sheriff."

# 5

IT WAS ARSON. BY NOON, NATE KNEW FOR SURE. He'd been interrupted more than once by curious Amish or others. Bishop Esh had said he trusted Nate's judgment so, with two of his sons, he was planting a cornfield to the south.

Nate had stonewalled the Cleveland reporter and her cameraman, though they still hung around by their van which read News Live at Five. He'd phoned the state fire marshal from the privacy of VERA. It was going to be an interesting case file. He hoped he wouldn't be recalled until the area supervisor returned from his daughter's wedding in Hawaii. He'd told Mark he had some leads already, though he hadn't told him he was convinced that there'd be another arson. He had nothing to back that up but his instincts, and Mark was a just-the-facts guy.

As he left VERA, Nate saw Sarah driving her buggy into the lane. His insides flip-flopped—probably, he told himself, because the reporter had asked him if he knew where Sarah was and he'd said no. He hadn't exactly lied. She could have been anywhere on the three miles of road between here and the restaurant in Homestead.

"How's it going?" she asked as she reined in.

"Arson for sure," he told her. "I'm going to point out the evidence to the bishop when he comes back for lunch."

"We call it dinner," she said, "and I've got it right here all packed up in my buggy. A lot more food than you moderns are used to, I bet, but we've all been up early working hard—you, too."

"If I ate like your people, I'd gain more than evidence about an arson around here."

"You could afford to gain some weight," she said, then blushed. "I mean, someone who jogs and walks all over like you do, even though you drive your truck, too."

"VERA's a gas hog, but I still call her my home away from home. But I'm now as much of an expert on banked, three-story barns as I am on VERA."

Twice he'd spent late hours online and learned that banked barns were also called German barns—no surprise there. What was banked was the slanted, hard-packed earth leading up to the broad double doors. The only other entry was in the stone-constructed lower level. Originally, that was where the barn animals had stalls, though he'd observed that the local Amish kept their horses in stalls and their buggies stored on the second level called the threshing floor. A haymow or loft was on the third level under a peaked roof with a cupola on top to aerate the barn. Windows were small and minimal but threw enough light inside, especially if the double doors were open.

The most important thing he'd learned was that the window or windows were all on the third level. So the arsonist had to have been up in the loft or on a ladder to get lit trailers to go through a window. Sarah's wooden ladders and scaffolding had been burned from outside the barn—but had they been used by the arsonist first?

"So how is VERA as a home?" she was asking.

"Cozy, maybe too cozy. I'll show you around, and then you'll see what I mean."

He didn't say so but he found the confines of the VERA's high-tech combination of lab/office/storage/bathroom/bedroom a little claustrophobic, especially out here in the wide-open Home Valley surrounded by rolling hills. If the weather stayed mild and dry, he planned to keep sleeping out under the stars. It brought back the best memory he had of his dad when they used to camp out in Southern Ohio down by Old Man's Cave, before his whole childhood went up in flames.

"By the way," he said when their mutual staring in silence stretched out a bit too long, "you'd better stay in the house if you don't want to be interviewed. As you can see by their vehicle, the TV folks are still here." His BlackBerry tone sounded, and he looked down to see if it was his boss again. "I've got to take this," he told her. "It's my foster mother, and I always take her calls."

"Foster mother?"

"I'll explain sometime."

"I'll head straight in with the food and come out with the Eshes when you announce the arson," she said with a snap of her reins. "Unless someone tells the TV people who I am, they won't notice me separate from the others at all."

But even as he took the call, he couldn't help thinking that Sarah somehow stood out. Even among the Plain People, she didn't seem plain at all.

★ ★ ★

Everyone ate before hearing Nate's verdict, maybe, Sarah thought, to fortify themselves for what was to come. Then, too, though no one said so, it was possible the bishop was hoping the media outside would leave them alone to hear about the autopsy of the barn fire in private. That's what it felt like, Bishop Esh had said, an autopsy of his dead barn, with the burial and then, hopefully, the resurrection yet to come.

At the Esh table the number of guests swelled, but then *Mamm* and Lizzie had sent over enough fried chicken, biscuits, gravy, applesauce, chowchow, dandelion salad, schnitz pie and rhubarb crunch to feed an entire work crew. Churchwomen were taking turns sending a noon meal to the bishop's family for a while. The Eshes had insisted that Sarah, Nate and Mike Getz, who showed up and had just done an interview with the Cleveland TV station, join them. Also, two church elders, Reuben Schrock and Eli Hostetler, who both had Sarah's squares painted on their barns, dropped by in time for dessert and coffee.

Sarah saw that Nate ate like a field hand, after they'd just had that talk about his gaining weight. And she also noted that Nate watched Mike Getz like a hawk.

"I know now it was a bad move," Mike, a big guy with a shaved head and goatee, admitted. "I shouldn't have rushed inside to try to pull some of the buggies out, but the barn looked like a goner and I wanted to save something."

He ate with his left hand since his right was in a cast. Sarah could see the clean, white plaster had writing on it already, including in pink ink, "Love Ya! Cindee" and a large heart. Mike's head seemed to sit directly on his broad, slanted shoulders—a man with no neck, and not, she thought, a lot of sense.

"But a broken bone's a small price to pay," he went on, his mouth partly full, "to help a neighbor."

Strictly speaking, Mike wasn't a neighbor of the Eshes but lived much closer to Elder Reuben Schrock and his family, over on Fish Creek Road.

"Have you rushed into other buildings on fire?" Nate asked. The entire Esh family, along with Sarah and Nate, had eaten first and it was mostly men at the table now, with Sarah and Esh daughter Naomi clearing dishes and serving more pie and coffee. Naomi was betrothed, and Sarah knew how badly she missed having her older sister Hannah here to help plan for the big event next autumn. Well, Sarah thought, maybe she and Ella could somehow convince Hannah to attend that day—if Sarah could talk Ella into building bridges with Hannah.

"I've always done what I could," Mike Getz was telling Nate. "I've been working with the volunteer department since I was twenty—for six years. Man, I think your job must be really fascinating, Mr. MacKenzie."

"It is," Nate said, "and I'd be happy to talk to you about it. I always like to meet dedicated firefighters."

Mike Getz just beamed. As she stood in the doorway to the kitchen, Sarah wondered if Mike had just gone to number one on Nate's list of suspects.

"We have something to announce," Reuben Schrock said, and cleared his throat. "Bishop Esh, we would like to hold a barn raising soon as possible with an auction of goods even sooner to raise some cash for the project and to build up the alms fund for the rebuilding and other needs."

"We are grateful," Bishop Esh said, his voice quiet, his face

serious. Sarah could hear his wife, Mattie, standing beside her, sniff back a sob.

The other elder, Eli Hostetler, spoke. "Date for the raising to be determined, when we can clear the space and order the wood and all. But we'll be announcing the auction for next weekend at the schoolhouse, lest it rains."

Sarah knew her family and others would donate quilts and that outsiders would snap them up. For once, she almost wished she liked quilting bees, but she never had, standing out like a black sheep among the other skilled-at-stitching Amish sisters. At least some of *Daad*'s birdhouses would be for sale, a few things she had decorated. She wished she could contribute some painted quilt squares on wooden wall plaques, but her father had said he didn't think it was a good idea for her to be branching out too much.

When everyone rose from the table—still not hurried— and Nate passed Sarah, he whispered, "So is that alms fund like Amish insurance? Will you explain later?" He kept moving, not waiting for an answer.

They all gathered outside where Nate, standing knee-deep in the black bones of the barn, took over. The TV reporter, a blonde woman, scribbled notes while her cameraman held out a microphone on a long pole. The bishop had asked them not to film, and they'd agreed. It wasn't so much, Bishop Esh had explained to the reporter, that the Amish saw still or moving pictures as making graven images, which the Bible warned about, but that having one's picture taken or being featured in a magazine or newspaper story could make one prideful—that is, feel better than or separate from the community.

Sarah thought again of her interview with Peter Clawson, who had just come roaring in in his truck. *Had* she been

prideful to speak to him and to be so pleased with the printed color pictures of her quilt squares adorning Amish barns? Community oneness was everything to her people, their essence, their very survival. So why couldn't she squash her desire to paint entire pictures of the Amish? Defiant independence to chase a personal dream fueled by a God-given talent had ruined Hannah's life so far.

Word really must have spread that the arson investigator was going to give his verdict. Most of the Lantz family from the third adjoining farm buggied in, including Sarah's friend Ella, her parents and four of her siblings. Sarah noted that Barbara, nearly sixteen, went over to stand by Gabe, but he shook his head at something she said and shifted a few steps away. Ella came over to stand by Sarah, linking arms with her as Nate's voice rang out in the hush. It was disturbed only by the spring breeze turning the windmill, birdsong and the occasional snorting of the buggy horses tied to the fence rails near where Hannah and Sarah had stood together just last night. She should be here, Sarah thought, and whispered that to Ella.

"*Ya,* Hannah should be home with her family and you and me, just like in the old days," Ella whispered as Nate's deep voice rang out.

"Arson is often proved by investigators finding a path of foreign accelerants that ignited, then spread, the flames. Accelerants can include grease, kerosene, gasoline and paint thinner, but I've been able to eliminate the accidental spillage of those or even the presence of those. Besides finding a bunch of matches—unlit—outside of the barn, I found evidence of accelerants within, so let me explain and point that out."

His cell phone tone sounded. Sarah noted he ignored it.

"The front door frame," he said, pointing to a big, tumbled beam with a blackened metal handle on it, "shows what we call alligatoring—shiny blisters." Several people leaned closer. The Cleveland reporter and Peter Clawson scratched away on their notepads.

"This indicates a rapid rise in temperature of the blaze, so nothing really smoldered. Evidence here," he said, continually moving through the debris and pointing things out, "indicates it spread unusually fast, which eyewitnesses corroborated. These beams were from the roof—third or loft floor. Also, the fire seems to have started in more than one place, one at the back of the barn near a window, another near the east side window. Multiple V-pattern burns are also major clues pointing to arson.

"But how did someone reach those high windows to get the fire going in the loft where hay was stored? I'm surmising that the arsonist used one or both of the ladders that were on the ground outside the barn, which were then destroyed in the fire. In that respect, the arsonist either knew the ladders were available or stumbled into being able to use them. It meant he or she could stay outside the barn rather than going in and climbing the built-in ladders within to start the fire."

The arsonist had used her ladders! Why hadn't he told her that—warned her he'd say that? At least no one but Mattie Esh so much as glanced her way, but it made her sick that her equipment might have been a part of this—and that Nate had not confided that to her earlier when he told her it was arson.

"What might this accelerant be?" he went on. "I'm still running some tests in my mobile lab, but kerosene residue can be recovered from beneath floorboards, which it permeates. It can be found under the ash-and-water pastelike substance a hot, fast fire leaves behind. That was proba-bly the case here, especially on the third floor or loft level, which was the ceiling of the threshing floor level. Bishop Esh reports that no kerosene was in the barn, not even an old lantern, and no gasoline in the farm equipment. No green hay to give off methane to cause spontaneous com-bustion, the latex, water-soluble paint cans were sealed." A few heads turned Sarah's way. "So my report, sad to say, in such a helpful, concerned community is criminal arson by a fairly primitive incendiary device lit from at least two points through small window access on the loft level."

"Any way to catch the firebug with what you got?" Mike Getz spoke up.

"Arsonists have a way of being caught in a trap of their own making," Nate said, staring at the big man. "The Esh fire is a crime and will be severely prosecuted by the state fire marshal's department in the state courts of Ohio. The penalty for such is long prison time. So spread the word that arson is never, never worth the risk."

Sarah noted that the portly, ruddy-faced Peter Clawson kept nodding fiercely, as he stood a few people in front of her. Sarah pulled Ella off to the side before he could turn around and ask her more questions. But she heard him tell the Cleveland reporter, "You can't say the guy isn't eminently quotable. You got some great sound bites, and I got another great article for the *Home Valley News,* and you can quote me on that."

The next day an Amish work crew of young men—overseen by Nate—removed the remnants of the barn. They hefted the ruined debris out of the stone basement level where a lot had fallen and hauled it away in their work

wagons with Nate keeping an eye on every piece for more
clues. Then the Amish scraped and raked the place flat, down
to the stone foundation on which the new barn would be
erected.

It was hot and sweaty work, even just mostly doing the over-
seeing. Nate needed a swim in the pond near the woodlot—
who needed a shower when the old swimming hole was
there?—and some coffee to keep going. The test on the com-
position of the residue from under the old barn boards had
proved to be kerosene, but that was in full supply around here
and didn't necessarily point to an Amish arsonist.

He drove VERA back past the Kauffman place, wishing
he'd see Sarah, but no one was out for once—just laundry
flapping on the line, blacks and pastels, men's and women's,
big and small, the daily life of an Amish family, all hung
tight together.

He parked VERA and stripped to his underwear and
waded into the pond. When he saw the water was deep
enough, he dived. It felt fantastic, cool, refreshing. Like a
kid he swam on his back, splashing. He should have brought
some soap out. He floated, then treaded water in the center
of the pond, listening to the sounds of the wind through the
maples and oaks, birdsong. He stared up at the blue sky with
cotton clouds for he didn't know how long.

Suddenly a voice called out, "You shouldn't swim alone,
you know. It could be dangerous."

# 6

"DANGEROUS HOW?" NATE ASKED. HE SPUN AROUND to see Sarah with a large package in her arms.

"This just came for you at the house—FedEx," she called to him. "Now that you've announced it was arson and you're going to find the arsonist and send him to jail, what if he tries to hurt you?"

Nate swam toward her side of the pond, his muscular arms lifting from the surface at each stroke. When he was close enough to talk easily he stopped and treaded water. "You startled me, though I was expecting that package. It's my fire protection hood. It wasn't packed in VERA when I left. And thanks for worrying about my safety, but arsonists are usually cowards about confrontation. The arsonist wants my attention, not to get rid of me, but I'll be on my guard."

You won't if you're splashing around like a kid and not paying attention to who's approaching, she thought, but she just nodded. As he remained fairly motionless about twenty feet away, she could see a lot of skin through the water. What if he was in there buck naked, because why would he have brought an *ausländer* swimsuit?

"So you fight fires, too?" she asked, hugging the package to her breasts. She'd come out here barefoot, a common practice among her people in the warm weather, especially on their own property. She fought the desire to sit down and dangle her feet in the pond. Though she'd done that a hundred times and her family shared ownership of this woodlot with the Eshes and the Lantzes, it suddenly felt like forbidden, foreign territory.

"I don't fight fires if I can help it, but I don't hesitate to go into a partially burned building or even one on fire if it will help me trap an arsonist. If you wouldn't mind turning around for a minute, I'm not exactly clothed in here, and I'll get out."

"Oh, sure. Right," she said, and sat down facing away with her back to the pond. Beneath the shade of her bonnet, her cheeks flamed. She stretched out her legs. Her toes barely peeked from under her moss-green skirt. "I'll bet it feels good in there," she said, hoping he didn't think she was fishing for an invitation to join him. His voice had faded a bit, and she heard the water rippling as he evidently swam away.

"Sure does. I've got a washbasin and head—sorry, toilet—in VERA but no shower."

"I'll bet *Daad* will let you use ours if you want. I was going to send Gabe out with this package, but he took his buggy over to see his friend, Barbara Lantz, two farms over."

"I take it your family's close to them, but no quilt square on their barn yet?"

"It was decided first the bishop, then two elders, then the Millers wanted one. I've done those, but since then, no one

else has come forward to ask for another. But your mentioning the Lantzes reminds me there's a second reason to
be careful in this pond. There's a strange, cold current in it
sometimes," she said, still talking toward the trees. "I think
there's an underground spring that flows through it, especially after a rain. When we were teenagers and swimming
here, Ella did a little jackknife dive and just kind of stayed
under. Hannah and I about went off our beans—panicked,
you know. We dived and found her and pulled her up but
we could feel the colder current pulling us deep down, very
scary. We had to almost pump the water out of her. She—
well, she changed after that, got very rigid and strict with
herself and others, always followed every rule."

"So Ella Lantz owes you two her life," he said, his voice
coming closer until he stood in front of her. He'd pulled his
jeans on over his wet legs and his black T-shirt stuck to the
muscles of his chest and his flat belly. His short black hair
looked even darker all wet. For a second she couldn't recall
what he'd just asked.

"Oh, we don't think of it that way," she told him. "It was
the Lord who saved her, and we were just His way of doing
it. No thanks needed, and we didn't even let outsiders know,
though someone blabbed, and it got into the *Home Valley
News*."

Nate reached down to her, and she gave him his package
before she realized that he had meant to give her a hand up.
His skin was cool from the water, or else hers was hot. Both
barefoot, they walked back around the pond where he had
VERA parked beside two big oaks. The vehicle had a tall,
thin tower projecting upward from the back, and from that
sprouted a five-branched antenna.

"Peter Clawson's really got his ear to the ground around

here, doesn't he?" Nate asked. "I need to interview him about any leads he may have."

"He keeps a lot of Amish employed in businesses he at least owns part of—the Dutch Farm Table, the Buggy Wheel Shop, a bunch of others. But his paper is his pride and joy."

"Can I show you around VERA?" he offered with a sweep of his hand toward his big, worldly buggy.

"I'd like that, but better not right now. I have to get back. Gabe wants to see it, too, so can we come out later? And, oh, *Mamm* says come to supper—evening meal, not half the amount we eat midday, in about two hours."

"Tell her thanks. I'd love to."

She wanted to throw caution to the sweet breeze that had begun to dry and ruffle his hair and go into the back of VERA with him—it was cozy there, he'd said—but she knew she shouldn't. She was already too attracted to him, like he had some kind of magnetic field and she was a compass needle.

"Before you go, then," he said as he walked her back a ways toward the farm, "will you explain the alms fund one of the elders mentioned? It sounds like private Amish insurance, but I thought that was forbidden."

Forbidden, *verboten,* danced through her mind as she darted another glance up into his intense, blue-sky gaze. Again, she had to unscramble her thoughts to grab for the right thing to say.

"Not forbidden if we keep it within the Amish community," she explained. "We do not pay into worldly insurance companies or the American government's Social Security or ever use such funds, because health is a gift from God and that would be gambling against that in a way. But we do collect a percentage of everyone's wages on a regular basis and use that to support those in the group who have big medical bills—or something like a house or barn burned. The church deacon collects and puts the money in a savings account until we need it. No big corporations profit. The family in need does pay a small part of their bills first, before our fund is used."

"Like a deductible," he said, nodding. "It's really a private, small group insurance. Very smart—amazing..." He looked at her closely and he drew out the last word so it almost sounded like Ray-Lynn's drawl. His gaze caressed her as he peered within the dim shelter of her black bonnet.

"I've got to get back," she said, quickening her steps. "See you for supper and then Gabe and I can take a look at VERA later, if it's okay."

She didn't want to seem like she was running away, but in a way she was. Standing so close to him, both of them in their bare feet, had made her think of Adam and Eve in the Garden, and look at all the trouble they'd got into!

If the bountiful Amish evening meal was what Sarah described as less food, Nate was as astonished by that as he was by his crazy attraction to her. It was probably just the fact she was so different from any woman he'd ever known, he tried to tell himself—bright but naive, stubborn yet humble, plain yet stunning, modest yet sexy without even trying. Man, he had to keep his mind on the food and the conversation, because her father, Ben Kauffman, had been drilling him about some things and here came another calmly couched but key question. At least he'd waited for this one until they were on the coffee and fabulous strawberry shortcake with home-churned vanilla ice cream. How Nate could put this dessert away after chowing down on sauerbraten, homemade bread, German potato salad and noodles with gravy, he wasn't sure, but maybe he was about to pay the price for this great meal.

"So far, Mr. MacKenzie," Ben Kauffman said, "have you found any proof, even hints, that the barn burning might be someone upset by Sarah's painted quilt square?"

"No, sir, I haven't. But it's something I've considered and will stay aware of. I realize that such a work of art is to be useful—not just decoration."

"In that case," Ben Kauffman went on, "I will allow—ask—Sarah to paint a square for our barn. I ran it by Bishop Esh. I want to stand up for the earlier decision that she be allowed to paint her patterns on Home Valley barns to bring more visitors in. Amish businesses are slow. Orders for my gazebos, kids' playhouses, birdhouses and other items are down. And I want everyone to know that I believe her painting was not and should not be a target of arson."

Nate could see Sarah was surprised and elated. Her amber eyes filled with tears she blinked back. *"Danki, Daad,"* she said. Darn, Nate thought, if he wasn't actually catching on to some of the German they used. Sadly, he hadn't been able to speak to her elderly grandmother at all. She rarely spoke English anymore, and seemed pretty afraid of him, not to mention confused about things. She sat at the other end of the table, eating, but with her eyes on him as if he might leap at her. Sarah had introduced them, then whispered something to the old lady about him being here to help and that he could be trusted. Also at the table were Sarah's mother, Anna, Gabe and Martha.

It really impressed him how the Amish generations stuck together. When he'd lost his parents in the tragedy, how he'd wished he'd had a grandparent or even an aunt and uncle to take him in. At least his childless neighbors down the street, Jim and Mary Ellen Bosley, had been willing to give him a foster home. But living so close to where it all happened had been hard. In a way, that empty lot where what people called "the death house" had sat haunted him all through his youth—and yet today.

"I'll have to replace my ladders," Sarah said.

"While you paint here, you can use the barn one and only buy one," her father said. "And those planks for the long tables you can stand on."

"I have a ladder in my truck Sarah can use," Nate offered, "at least while I'm here. And a safer scaffolding than planks— if you don't mind the suggestion. I won't need them—unless there's another blaze to investigate, and I hope not."

"We pray not," Anna Kauffman said.

"If the man in black comes back, there will be more fires." The old lady spoke for the first time and in English. "I heard Sarah tell Martha the fire burned the barn like a beast devouring it. That's what it will be like again if that monster keeps sneaking around my house at night."

Nate could see Sarah was embarrassed by the outburst. "If you mean Nate here," Sarah said, leaning toward the woman and taking her hand, "he's only in the neighborhood for a while to help. And maybe you just dreamed the man in black."

"No, I saw him with his horrible, glowing eyes when I got up to go to the bathroom. *Ya,* I did!"

Sarah's parents just looked at each other as Sarah helped the old woman away from the table. She was obviously demented. On the other hand, if she had seen someone, Nate wondered who, because it hadn't been him.

★ ★ ★

Ray-Lynn knew Peter Clawson was a bit of a loner, but she couldn't argue his generosity to others. Whether it was large tips for her Amish waitresses or his funding of local businesses, the man was magnanimous to a fault. And, if she thought she managed to catch all the local gossip, she was a rank amateur compared to Peter, who seemed to know almost everything about everyone. Why, if it wouldn't be frowned on around here, he'd probably run something called the *Home Valley Enquirer.* She sometimes shuddered to think that he probably knew what kind of toilet paper she used at her house, though at least she'd stopped his just dropping in.

"I suppose you're really going to talk up the Saturday auction to benefit the barn raising," she said to him as she rang up his evening meal at the cash register.

"If not talk up, print up. You bet I will," he said. "And not only for a broader distribution of the paper. The regular Thursday edition will have a full-page spread on it. The layout is already done. Lots of folks far and wide will come in for Amish goods at an auction, especially the cooking and the quilts."

"I just heard about the auction and chicken barbecue from one of my girls," she admitted as she handed Peter his change and watched him take a peppermint and a toothpick from her counter. "But then you always have your ear to the ground when it comes to business."

"That's right, Ray-Lynn," he said with a wink as he smoothed his straight brown hair back from his forehead. "And, let's face it, you are one of my most important business affairs."

She could have kicked him, but it seemed no one else had heard. She didn't like the suggestive way he'd worded that, because she'd done a good job holding him at bay. A good business partner, yes, but not a partner for life—no way. He was single, but he didn't seem to look at women—that is, besides her.

Peter, at age forty-five, was balding and it obviously bothered him. Why his being overweight didn't, she wasn't sure, if he was so doggone concerned about his appearance. At least with his hair, he wasn't to the stage where he'd tried a comb-over, but he was always messing with it. "Even if it's monkey business, I'm on top of it, so don't get too close to our illustrious sheriff, you hear now," he added with a smug grin.

For one moment, Ray-Lynn was at a loss for words. Now how had he found out about that? Surely, Sarah hadn't talked, so it must have been her own falling all over Jack that Peter had seen. Well, ding-dang. He was kidding her, of course, yet there was a strange edge to his voice. Surely, as well as Peter had seemed to take it that she wouldn't date him, he wasn't jealous.

"Monkey business?" she countered, hands on hips. "You'd better keep your mind and newspaper on the serious stuff around here, and there's plenty of that lately."

"I don't like to show off my extensive knowledge of newspaper trivia, my Southern belle, but monkey business was what brought down presidential candidate Gary Hart, not to mention John Edwards. I suppose you don't remember the details, but Gary Hart dared the press to follow him around, and they did…and found that married man—pillar of American morality—with a young mistress aboard a yacht called *Monkey Business*. Do you remember that?"

"No, Peter, actually, I don't. I must have been too busy

serving up mint juleps and sitting on the veranda with Scarlett O'Hara that year."

"My point is, the newspaper people Hart dared to find out
his business brought him down, just as the *National Enquirer*
torpedoed John Edwards. Goodbye presidency, goodbye
power. Ah, the power of the press. I'll see you tomorrow,
Ray-Lynn," he concluded, speaking as usual almost in one
breath as he went out and let the wooden door swing closed
behind him.

Ray-Lynn wouldn't have minded a bit if it had swung
closed faster and hit him in his big rear end.

There was still a good hour of daylight left when Gabe
and Sarah accompanied Nate to see VERA and to check if
his ladder would suit for the quilt square she planned to paint
on her own family's barn. Though she would have preferred
to have painted the entire, realistic scene of the farm, Sarah
was thrilled to have another pattern to paint, one she was
being allowed to select this time. And she was touched that
her father believed in her work, especially when he'd been
reluctant at first. More than that, she was excited to see
VERA's insides at last. Gabe was, too. He kept chattering
about wanting to sit in the driver's seat, no doubt dreaming
about driving the big truck, whatever was in the back of it.
As for her own dreams…

"Gabe, I'd like to ask you a question about the night of
the fire," Nate said as the three of them walked along the
farm lane toward the woodlot. "On the level now, I take it
some of the kids in their running-around years try smoking
cigarettes."

"Some," Gabe said, nodding so hard his bangs bounced on
his forehead under his straw hat. "A few even try pot. We're

allowed. I know it's not good. Some kids have problems giving it up later, even tobacco cigs, I mean. You know, after they join the church, but, yeah, it's kind of common, like maybe having a coupla beers."

"So is there any chance someone could have sneaked across the field, maybe been around the Esh barn the night of your party but, because the party, at least inside the barn, was chaperoned by your mother and sister, wanted more privacy?"

To Sarah's dismay, Gabe cheeks went as bright as a polished Red Delicious apple. She bit her lower lip to keep from either trying to help him out or questioning him herself. She recalled how out of breath and red-cheeked he'd been when he'd rushed into the barn to tell her Jacob was outside. Could he have come from way across the field and not only been outside their barn?

"I don't think so," Gabe said. "A coupla guys were smoking regular cigs outside behind the buggies—not me—but I have a time or two."

"I'm not blaming anyone for smoking or accusing them of being an arsonist," Nate assured him with a pat on his shoulder. "As I said, a single dropped cigarette or match in the hay was not how the barn fire started, but if some kids were over there, maybe they saw something—something they don't even know was important for my investigation. I'd love to talk to them. I need all the help I can get," he added as they approached VERA. "And I can keep things confidential. You know that word, Gabe—confidential?"

"*Ya,* Mr. MacKenzie. I can ask around and keep my ears open."

"Good man," Nate said, and this time hit his shoulder lightly with a balled fist.

Sarah and Gabe watched as Nate took a small bit of metal and plastic out of his pocket—not quite a key—aimed it in VERA's direction, then pressed something. They heard a double click and VERA's lights blinked once as if in welcome—or warning.

"Like a magic lock," Gabe said as he climbed up into the high cab next to Nate while Sarah sat by the passenger's side window. "Way cool."

Sarah kept silent while Nate explained and demonstrated the various dashboard instruments. He showed them how the GPS worked and how the computer could perform other tasks. But Sarah sensed that it was just being in the big truck cab that impressed Gabe most. He kept touching the outer edge of the steering wheel and glancing out through the windshield. So her brother had a good imagination, too, just different from hers, that's all, she thought.

"Do you want to see the magic techno-cave in back now?" he asked the wide-eyed seventeen-year-old.

"Maybe later," Gabe said, his eyes aglow. Barbara Lantz, Sarah thought, might be jealous if she saw how her brother lusted—yes, a sin, but so human—after this big, polished, black truck cab.

"Then while I show your sister," Nate said, "why don't you slide over in the driver's seat?"

"Nate!" Sarah blurted.

"Don't worry," he said as he got down and closed the door on the rapt boy who now had his hands on the steering wheel. He came around to help Sarah down. "He can't start it, can't go anyplace."

He gestured toward the back of the vehicle, and she went with him. She'd been tempted to see VERA up close earlier today and now she would. After all, as entranced as Gabe was up front, he was here as a kind of chaperone. So what could happen while an *Englische ausländer,* however entrancing he was, introduced her to his sleek, brilliant, mechanical partner?

# 7

AT FIRST, NATE SHOWED SARAH THINGS INSIDE VERA she'd expected to see, like firefighting gear and an ax and shovel he'd used to examine the ruins of the Esh barn. He explained a scene light and demonstrated the neat collapsible ladder he said he'd loan her. She figured that was all to break her in easy when he began to show her the array of amazing instruments and machines neatly stowed inside VERA. But she was even more amazed by her feelings being so close to him. Despite Gabe nearby and the back doors being wide open, she felt so alone with Nate as it went from dusk to dark outside.

Nate's tour of VERA's marvels with brief explanations of their uses blurred by: a thermal imager, a digital camera, a laser range finder. He showed her handheld, wireless phones. Several years before she'd heard Peter Clawson call them walkie-talkies when he used them with his reporter, before times got tough and he started doing everything at the paper himself, except for some volunteers. Nate showed her his laptop computer and his printer, copier, scanner and

O

fax machine. He said he had a fingerprinting kit but didn't show it to her. VERA had what he called a camcorder and a fourteen-inch color TV with a built-in DVD that played flat silver disks and worked off a generator or the truck's batteries.

"The antenna system you've seen on the roof is invaluable in the rolling terrain around here," he went on. "The tower retracts into a rear compartment—here, see—and is raised and lowered by a single switch to go thirty-four feet into the air. Five antennae then pop out so I can get signals for communication."

*Signals for communication*—his words echoed in her head. She hoped he didn't know how his closeness was getting to her, as if his occasional light touch on her elbow or back, the scent of his hair or skin, was giving her body silent signals.

He was right about it being cozy in here. Besides a narrow counter for lab work on both sides of the truck, a skinny central table with newspapers open on it took up some space. She saw the *Budget,* the latest issue she'd been reading to her grandmother, and the special edition of the *Home Valley News* spread out with some things underlined or circled in red ink.

"Any clues in there?" she asked.

"Just trying to learn more about the area and the people. You've been very helpful with that."

"Good. We all want to help you find who did it. You told my father you didn't think the fire had anything to do with my paintings. I appreciate that."

"I think it's more likely someone's out for revenge against Bishop Esh. But I'm glad you'll be working at home for a while, because I don't want to imply you don't have to be careful painting your patterns. That's what I'm looking for, a pattern. I'm just hoping—praying, as your mother put it—that I can find something that makes sense and leads to the arsonist. I can tell how much those painted quilt squares mean to you."

"What I'd really like to paint are entire scenes of Amish life," she blurted, though she was usually so guarded about sharing that. "Ray-Lynn Logan at the restaurant, Hannah and Ella are the only ones I've told. To my people, it would be too personal, too prideful, even if I didn't sign my name on them. Ray-Lynn said I have a folk style, kind of primitive, but that it would suit my subject matter. She said it would be something like a woman called Grandma Moses used to paint. She told me that several months ago, but I remembered the name."

"So you'd risk being a rebel to paint like that?"

"No, I'm fine doing the barn art. That's a big step for all of us."

"Your work might be like Grandma Moses, huh?" he said, leaning over the keyboard of his laptop. He tapped something, and the screen came alive, a picture of a group of men, including him, together under the sign Fire and Explosive Investigations Bureau. Then he typed in the words *Grandma Moses* and *art,* then another screen lit up with a series of paintings. He enlarged them one at a time while she stared at them in awe.

"Oh, yes," she said, her voice shaky, "if those rural hills and farm scenes were Amish—*ya,* I could do that, only with my own touches, in my own way." They leaned toward the screen together, so close her bonnet bumped his cheek. "Well, good for Grandma Moses," Sarah said with a huge sigh, "and that nickname probably means she was elderly, too."

"She took up painting very late, it says here, leaving the

art of embroidery to follow her heart toward a new kind of art."

To follow her heart... Sarah suddenly felt almost as close to the long-gone Grandma Moses as she did to her own *grossmamm* Miriam. The Amish didn't embroider—too fancy—but she'd long ago given up stitching quilts unless she absolutely had to, and she'd suffered socially for that. Still, she did not want to be elderly when she got the gumption to try entire paintings, not with the latex paint she used on the barns but in oil paint on stretched canvas like she'd seen for sale in the back corner of the hardware store in town.

Nate left a big painting on the screen, one called *The Old Oaken Bucket,* with horses in the field, barns and hills, women in long skirts, even an Amish-looking man in the lower left corner of it. As much as Sarah was impressed with VERA's insides, that picture perked things up, almost as if it were hung on the wall. It seemed like a gift Nate had given her.

She meant to move away, but they were suddenly wedged in close. Her breasts brushed his chest as she sidestepped.

"Okay," Nate said, as if he needed to agree to something or was warning himself. "You know, I don't mean to pry, but I smell lavender perfume or something really nice on you."

"Not perfume," she told him, blushing. "My friend Ella Lantz has a great lavender garden and makes soaps and sachets to sell. That's just my—her soap. If you have a special someone, you might want to buy some of her Lavender Plain products, a gift from Amish country to take home."

"Ah, no. I mean, there's no special someone at home."

She nodded. Their eyes locked again. She felt his intense stare clear down to the pit of her stomach.

Wiping his palms on his jeans, he moved away and peeked

out through a small front window at Gabe as he had several times already, then back at her. "He's still entranced," he said, tilting his head a bit as if to peer inside her bonnet brim. She had the strongest urge to take it off, but she tried to concentrate on what Nate was saying now. He seemed as desperate to get back to business as she did, so he showed her his firefighting gear and explained how it went on, piece by piece.

"In those storage bins," he said, pointing, "are PPEs—personal protective equipment—for a chemical or biological incident, coveralls, gloves, overshoes and a filter mask, some overlap from the fire gear I showed you. I'm a first responder in case there's a terrorist attack. VERA's equipped for Homeland Security, too."

"Like 9/11 or a chemical attack, but I feel like there has been a terrorist attack on our Homestead area, too—only, thank the Lord, no one got seriously hurt."

As he reached past her to show her the tiny fridge and microwave, they were standing too close again. "I can heat up my supply of MREs—meals ready to eat—in here," he said. "But the food everyone's been so kind to share puts those to shame, so I won't even show you. I keep a cot in there, but prefer my sleeping bag outside."

"Staking out the Esh barn."

"I haven't seen any sign of activity since the other night. The arsonist usually returns quickly to the scene. Sarah, I'm going to interview Hannah tomorrow. I know—you think she's innocent, but I have to follow every lead. I was hoping Mike Getz would come to me for another fellow fireman chat, but I'm going to check him out, too. And Jacob. But I don't want you warning anyone, tipping them off I'm coming or that they're on my list."

For once, he wasn't looking into her eyes but at her lips. That made her aware she had thrust out her lower lip, pouting over his still suspecting Hannah. He lowered his head just a bit. She could feel his breath, warm and strong. She tried to relax her mouth, but she was tense all over. She had the definite feeling he was going to touch her—kiss her. She almost swayed into him.

"Oh, what's that?" she asked, like a coward, pointing at a pair of strange-looking binoculars hanging above his head.

He looked up, then turned around. "Night goggles so you can see in the dark," he said. "Things look kind of greenish and grainy, but these can come in handy. I'll show you sometime, but we have to get you and Gabe back with the ladder before it gets too dark."

"At least, when it looks dark, peering out from a lighted place, it's always brighter outside than you think," she said, feeling both relieved and regretful her private tour was over. "But you're right. We'd better get back. I'll see if I can pry Gabe out of the driver's seat." She beat a too-hasty retreat out the back of the truck, stepping down on the flat, back bumper.

But she jolted when a pulsing sound emanated from inside, like when Martha accidentally walked out of Wal-Mart with something she hadn't paid for.

"What? What's that?" she cried, but Nate was already snatching up his cell phone.

"Where? Yeah, I can find it. Sarah," he shouted, jumping out of VERA and slamming the back doors, "get in the front seat and put Gabe in the middle. Sheriff Freeman says the Schrock barn's on fire, and I want you two to show me the fastest way there."

★ ★ ★

Nate lowered the antenna, swung VERA around and started down the lane, driving fast. He turned on his brights in the deepening dusk. Gabe was going to get his ride. "Sarah, how far to Schrock's?" he asked.

"Maybe four miles—other side of town. Turn right on Oak Ridge."

"Is he the church elder who was at the Eshes?"

"Yes, Reuben Schrock, the auburn-bearded man who announced the barn building and the auction."

"And he has one of your paintings on his barn?"

*"Ya,"* she said as her voice caught. "Tumbling Blocks."

He bit off a curse. As they roared past the farmhouse, he saw Anna Kauffman walking toward the *grossdaadi haus.* She stopped to stare at them. He rolled down his window and shouted, "Barn fire at Reuben Schrock's! Sarah and Gabe will show me where."

In the rearview mirror, he saw her run back to the house. He turned right on the road, heading toward town, toward what he knew in his bones was going to be another arson. It was exactly what he'd sensed and feared—a serial arsonist working under cover of night in an isolated area. Another Amish barn owned by another church leader. Another of Sarah's painted patterns—oh, yeah, he knew he'd find a pattern now.

"Nate, be careful," Sarah said as he looked both ways, then went through the single Homestead stoplight—which was red. The place looked dark and dead, but for lights in Ray-Lynn's restaurant and the little newspaper office. And, he noted as he accelerated again, in the two fast-food restaurants and what must be security night-lights in the Citizens

Bank. The self-serve gas station was open, one of the few in the state, he figured, where you didn't have to pay before you pumped. According to his research, the town claimed about four hundred residents, but that had to include some outlying areas.

"The fire truck's still in the firehouse," Sarah reported, "but two cars are there already. We're going to beat them to the fire."

"Where do we turn?" he asked as he accelerated.

"About a mile yet, left on Fish Creek Road, but I can't remember if there's a sign. Nate, Mike Getz is a neighbor of the Schrocks."

"Bingo," he muttered.

Gabe, wedged between him and Sarah, was wide-eyed and mute either with fear or excitement. When Nate had questioned him about kids being in the Esh barn, he'd had a gut feeling Gabe had seen something the night of that fire.

"There!" Sarah cried, pointing. "On the horizon at about eleven o'clock. It looks like the sun's setting there—see?"

"The barn's not fully engulfed yet, so someone spotted it early. And it's not burning top to bottom but low. So much for that pattern."

"It's also a different kind of barn, not like ours or the Eshes'. Only two floors, a real sharp slanted roof to shed the snow, second-floor haymow doors that look like they're open."

"That will fan the fire—suck it upward, too. Okay, we beat the fire truck here," he shouted as he roared up the lane past the Schrocks' house and outbuildings. "No lights on in their place."

"Maybe they're not home, either. That's a pattern."

"Gabe, you go pound on the back and front doors of their house," Nate ordered. "Sarah's going to help me suit up."

"Suit up?" she cried. "You're not going into that inferno?"

"I'm not some amateur, volunteer firefighter!" Nate shouted, for the roar of the flames was enough to muffle their words. "Just to take a look. Gabe, go!"

The moment Nate got out, the boy slid over and sprinted toward the house. "Sarah!" Nate yelled. "I can do it myself, but you can help get me in there faster!"

He dragged his equipment out of the back of VERA and threw it on the ground. The Schrock barn was gray with black trim and a high-gabled roof, shingles over planks. He couldn't stay inside long because Sarah's ruined quilt pattern called Tumbling Blocks was probably going to be the fate of this proud structure. And then he saw her running toward him.

Sarah saw the fire truck, its red-and-white lights pulsing, but without the siren, streaking down the dark road toward them. She wanted to stall. No way she wanted Nate going into a flaming barn. Look what had happened to Mike Getz and Levi Miller. With a quick glance at her still-intact painted square, she realized her entire world might be falling apart. And then she rushed to the back of VERA to help him pull on the protective gear he'd showed her about a half hour ago.

She tried to remember how it all went. Nate had it laid out on the ground, and was already into the thick pants and suspenders. She helped him jam his feet into his oversize, steel-toed boots. Then she held his bulky, beige jacket so he could get into it. He yanked on the fire protection hood that had arrived in the package she'd delivered before supper.

It encased his head and neck but not his face. Her fingers weren't used to the oxygen mask he pointed toward, so he ended up pulling it on and tightening the straps himself. She helped him put on the heavy fire gloves and handed him his hat. It looked scorched and smelled of smoke.

Meanwhile, all around her, volunteer firemen were hauling lengths of hose out of their truck. Sarah knew Nate wanted to beat them inside. She wondered if Mike Getz was among them, but surely not with a broken arm. Then she saw him off to the side with Cindee Kramer. Their faces, lit by orange flames, seemed to glow with excitement.

Nate nodded to her and headed toward the barn door. The firemen were still dragging out two hoses, one from their truck and one to draw water from the pond, as Nate walked toward the flaming hell.

Talk about VERA being claustrophobic when he slept inside, Nate thought as he lumbered into the burning barn. Until the oxygen started flowing through his mask, he always felt a moment of drowning panic. If he breathed in before the flow was good, his eardrums seemed to suck right into his head, but he was fine now. Somehow, it was always otherworldly. He couldn't hear anything but his own breathing, couldn't talk, could hardly see, plodding under seventy-five pounds of gear.

At least he had hopes no one was trapped inside. He'd seen burned bodies, curled in a fetal position—black, unrecognizable, flesh and fat gone right down to the bone, smelling like charred meat on the grill. Thank God, it seemed no one was home at the farm again. The arsonist was clever and careful. But Nate couldn't afford to be careful right now. He had to look in the guts of this structure to see if he could pin anything down. Already, even with two internal points of combustion observable from outside, he saw it was a different M.O. But it had to be the same person setting these, didn't it? A copycat arsonist was rare, no doubt especially in a rural area where harmony apparently ruled.

He didn't mind that this blaze brought back his fire training—it was the other memories he tried to fight. That night when he was eight and the roaring inferno of their home engulfed him. His mother screaming his name, coughing, gasping, crawling on the floor through the pall of choking smoke to where he huddled near his bed. The last time he saw her, her nightgown was ablaze. And then his father rushing in—too late....

This barn—again, the horses were in the field—had a large central bay and two side bays, one with stalls, one with stored grain. The flames were so fierce, he figured he could almost hear some of the corn popping, when he actually couldn't hear a thing. Popcorn—that's what Sarah had said while she helped him get suited up. The Schrocks had harvested a huge crop of popcorn last year, sold most of it to the Orville Redenbacher's company.

Just about six feet inside the barn, he was dazzled by a burst of flames and sparks—a small explosion in amazing hues, violet, magenta, chartreuse. Was he hallucinating? Chemicals this time?

When the flare-up spread away from him, licking at the wooden beams that supported the inner bay and stall walls, he shuffled toward the source of the colors, prettier than the sunrise had been that morning as he watched Sarah hitch her horse to her buggy. It almost mesmerized him. And it must be something incendiary, because it was at the tip of one of the V-burn patterns the firemen were trying to douse.

A stream of water from a hose bounced before his eyes, throwing something against his boots. Grunting, he stooped to picked up a remnant. He had a hunch what it was and it wasn't kerosene this time.

Sarah and Gabe stood off to the side, beyond the reach of the heat belching from the blazing barn. Once again, observers gathered as they saw the flames or the word spread. Nate was still inside, but then several of the firemen were, too, so they must figure the structure was sound enough right now. The flames were consuming her bright pink, green and brown tumbling blocks on the stark-white background. She imagined she could hear it crackling in protest. The Schrocks had picked the design because it looked like it was moving both up and down, depending on your point of view. She watched the paint curl and blur, making blocks seem to tumble like the barn beams and roof would if they couldn't get the fire out soon.

Sarah tried to stem the tears that prickled her eyelids, but she couldn't keep from crying. Her vision blurred to make the barn fire seem like Armageddon with the entire world aflame. Her quilt squares, now the barns of two families who had trusted her to paint them there, were under attack. Who hated the Home Valley Amish? Did someone blame her for something? Sure, there had been hate crimes against her people from time to time. Some *Englische* blamed the Plain People for being pacifists, for their slow buggies, for just being different. No way it was smooth sailing in this life she'd been born into and then had chosen.

She wiped tears from her cheeks with both hands. And then she saw something glint from the darkness beyond the barn. She couldn't tell what—who—because it was as if she'd been looking into the sun, but she was suddenly sure someone was there watching, standing back a ways, not joining the others. Despite drifting smoke, had it been eyeglasses or sunglasses or binoculars that had reflected the flames? Surely not just a distortion from her own tears. A big meadow stretched into the darkness, so why would someone stand in the middle of it?

Sarah hurried back to VERA, climbed inside and took down Nate's night goggles. She got back out and moved into the shadow of the big vehicle. She fumbled to get them on, had to end up holding them over her eyes. But her view was so blurry, just a sea of eerie green flecked by shifting, speckled grays, kind of like swimming underwater.

Yet she glimpsed a figure, someone moving away, apparently from watching the barn burn. Man or woman? *Grossmamm's* man in black? Should she race across the meadow in pursuit, at least to see up closer?

But at that moment Nate emerged from the inferno, stumbling, unsteady, and she ran toward him instead.

# 8

SARAH COULDN'T TELL WHAT NATE WAS CRADLING so carefully in his gloved hands. He walked around her and deposited something on VERA's wide, back metal bumper. Embers? The small mass, looking like a smashed piece of wood, was glowing as if it had a life of its own. It suddenly sparked pink and purple.

He pulled off his helmet and mask, sucking in air, out of breath.

"Stay back from that!" he told her.

"What is it?"

"Not positive yet. What are you doing with my goggles?"

"I saw someone in the back meadow but it was blurry. Someone hurrying away."

He pulled off one of his gloves and wiped his sweaty face with his free hand. "Amish?" he asked.

"I couldn't tell."

"Male or female?"

"Not sure. I noticed at first because of a glint from the fire, on glasses or binoculars, I think."

He shrugged out of his jacket and, still wearing his protective pants held up by suspenders, took the goggles from her and put them on. He walked away and peered into the distant darkness for several minutes, then returned and handed her the goggles.

"Is there a road or another farm back that way?" he asked.

"A road and a farm, but way over the hill. Levi Miller's place, the Amish man who had his ribs broken when he and Mike Getz went into the first fire. He's the church deacon who has one of my painted squares on his barn. Other than Bishop Esh's barn and those of the two church elders you've met, Levi Miller's is the only other one I painted—so far, now that I'm going to do one on our family barn."

He frowned. "I need to run a test on that material," he told her, nodding toward the remnant on his bumper. "I'm going to smother it so it doesn't burn further." She watched as he put the glove he'd removed over it, pressing it down.

"But won't that hurt it, if you need to find out what it is?"

"I'll be testing the ashy residue, the chemical contents. I'm betting on oil-treated sawdust from cedar with a copper-based coloring compound. In other words, what's left when you break open and ignite an artificial fireplace log."

"I've seen those!"

"In town?"

"It must have been in the hardware store. I'm going there tomorrow."

"Don't you be asking who bought some. I'll take care of that."

They both jumped as a white light nearly blinded them, but it wasn't from Nate's evidence. Peter Clawson had arrived and was taking pictures of the scene with a strobe. At least Sarah could tell, if he'd shot a picture their way, she had her back turned to the camera. He probably wanted ones of Nate and VERA.

"Can you stay here with this—not touch it, guard it—until I see how the guys are doing with the fire?" Nate asked, peering closer at his prize.

"*Ya*—yes, sure."

"Where's Gabe?"

"Over there with some friends," she said, pointing.

"I'll be right back."

She watched him talk to the two firemen who were holding the hose that was drawing water from the pond. It actually looked as if they could keep this barn from tumbling down, although her tumbling blocks pattern was a goner. Peter Clawson approached Nate, and they spoke for a minute. Sarah saw Ray-Lynn, who had just driven in, and was standing near the sheriff's cruiser. Ray-Lynn didn't see her standing beside Nate's truck or she would have come over. Nate made a beeline toward Gabe and his friends, bending toward them in earnest conversation. Next, he huddled in private with Sheriff Freeman, who had arrived while Nate was still in the barn and had been keeping the growing crowd back.

To her dismay, Peter Clawson came over to her, but at least he kept his camera at his side.

"Another of your pretty paintings gone, Sarah."

"The barn is what matters."

"Of course. It's starting to look as if someone's holding a grudge—a big one—against Amish church leaders, doesn't it?"

"I pray that's not the case."

"Right. God's will."

"Do you doubt that, Mr. Clawson?"

"The thing is, the devil's loose on the earth, evidently with God's tolerance or permission. So, I see you're helping Nate MacKenzie."

"Not exactly. He had dinner with my family, then Gabe and I came along to show him where the Schrock barn was when the call came in."

"So what's that stuff on the bumper of his truck?"

The man wasn't taking notes as he had when he interviewed her about her quilt squares, but she didn't want him quoting her and she didn't want to give anything away that Nate wanted kept quiet for now. Yet she totally shocked herself when she looked straight into the man's eyes and told a lie. "I've decided to keep a burned piece of each barn where I had a painting, just to remember how kind the families were to let me do it."

"A quaint idea," he said. He squinted at her, then rubbed his eyes, probably stinging from the pall of smoke. The breeze wasn't blowing this way, but the entire area— including her clothes and hair—hung heavy with the smell. He started to say something else, then, to her relief, thought better of it and hurried away, taking pictures again.

She stayed right where she was, guarding Nate's evidence as she saw him leave Sheriff Freeman to walk over to Mike Getz and Cindee Kramer. To Sarah's surprise, Nate slapped Mike on the back as if they were old pals. Right then her parents buggied in and got out with Bishop and Mattie Esh.

Nate spoke to the four of them, pointing her out to her parents before he walked back to her and stared at his ashy evidence again.

"Peter Clawson asked what that was, but I told him it was mine," she blurted.

"I appreciate that or he'd be after me with more questions.

I don't want those or my answers in his paper. And to keep that from being a lie, I'll give you a bit for a dirty souvenir. But guess who phoned this fire in?"

"Not Mike Getz?"

"I knew I should hire you as my assistant. We've got another arson here but between you, VERA and me, one way or the other, we're going to nail someone soon. We have to before this happens again."

The next morning, after delivering her half-moon pies, Sarah had breakfast in a booth at the restaurant, waiting for the hardware store to open at nine so she could buy paint. While she ate, Ray-Lynn came and went to greet or cash folks out, but she sat across the table from Sarah when she could.

"So you're going to go ahead and paint a quilt square on your barn?" Ray-Lynn asked as Sarah finished her blueberry pancakes and sausage patties. "After two of them just went up in flames with their barns?"

"Shh. I discussed that with my parents and Nate last night, and we decided yes."

"Easy for him to say—and it's Nate now, is it?" she added with a wink. "Well, if he's camped out back of your barn like you said, maybe he wants to set a trap for the arsonist—or for someone else."

"Now, Ray-Lynn, no teasing. It's not that way and it's impossible."

"I thought all things were possible with God. But, okay, okay. Still, aren't you scared for your own barn?"

"The point is, we mustn't give in to fear. 'Yea, though I walk through the valley of the shadow of death, I shall fear no evil.' Barns and quilts are part of our way of life, and we have to stand up for that. What's happening here is hardly the valley of death."

"Not yet, anyway. I'm not a good ole Southern Baptist for nothing, my girl, so I reckon I could quote a thing or two from the Good Book myself. But the thing that keeps coming to mind right now is something my daddy used to say. 'Are we still ahead of the hounds?' And I'm not sure we are. But never you mind my rambling. You're a strong woman, Sarah—talented, too. Even if this attack on your people has something to do with your paintings, my offer for you to do a big mural here still stands. So I'm standing with you all no matter what."

"I'm grateful, my friend. Oh, by the way, I saw you at the fire last night, too."

For a moment Ray-Lynn looked upset. "Oh—yeah, when I heard the sirens, I let the girls take care of the restaurant and drove over, following the light in the sky. I didn't see you there. I didn't stay long. I decided it was time for me to get back here, fire or not, so I could close up."

"Not to change the subject but guess who just came in?" Sarah whispered. "No, don't even turn around if you're putting up fences between you and him."

"Good thought to keep giving him the cold shoulder, but unfortunately, I need to run this place," Ray-Lynn said, and reached over to pat Sarah's hand. "Talk to you later."

Sarah had to admire how Ray-Lynn handled the sheriff. Nice but cool as a March breeze. Polite but that was all. Sarah bit back a little smile as she slid out of the booth and took her purse with her money in it to buy new paint. *Grossmamm* always used to say that you catch more flies with honey than with vinegar, but Ray-Lynn's vinegar seemed to be working wonders right now, because when she did what she called her sashay away from him, Sheriff Jack Freeman was all eyes.

Nate fidgeted and stared at his computer screen, waiting for the chemical assay analysis reading to come up. Yes! A copper-based color compound in the ash residue. He'd only heard of one case where the arsonist started a fire by breaking open an artificial log and igniting it to burn the house of his former, remarried wife, but the story had been picked up in the media and he'd just happened to catch it. Now where had that case been? Out in L.A., maybe—but how long ago?

He jumped up and stretched. Such a chemically treated log made for a fast, hot and colorful flame and would eventually burn away completely, leaving no evidence, so his risking going into the blaze was well worth it. This arson was a far cry from the wick-and-accelerant approach of the Esh barn fire, yet it surely must have been started by the same person. Two barn burners using double ignition points and choosing buildings with Sarah's paintings was too similar to be a coincidence. Both incendiary devices used materials that were readily available in Amish country or anywhere. As soon as he talked to Mike Getz and Jacob Yoder—who were neck-and-neck as his top suspects, with Hannah running a close second—he'd stop by the hardware store in Homestead and see if he could get someone there to recall who had bought artificial fireplace logs. The problem was that purchases of those could have been made last winter or even in the fall. He was pretty sure the few Amish homes he'd been in didn't have fireplaces, but then Jacob wasn't technically Amish anymore.

★ ★ ★

The moment the bell over the hardware store door rang and Sarah stepped inside, Cindee Kramer called to her from behind the checkout counter. "Hi, Sarah! Boy, oh, boy, wasn't that fire something last night? Mike was so upset he couldn't help put it out, but at least he spotted it and called it in."

"Much appreciated, too," Sarah said, and stopped to talk. "That quick call probably kept it from burning to the ground."

Sarah knew she was supposed to leave all the questions up to Nate when he came by later, but with that lead-in, she couldn't help but ask, "So what was Mike doing when he noticed it—I mean, was he outside or something?"

"He ran inside from where he was grilling burgers out back and called 9-1-1. Even one-armed, he's great at bar-becuing, great one-handed at a lot of things, tell you the truth," she said with a little snicker. "I'm so proud of him lately, picture in the paper and all, helping with these fires. But our burgers burned to a crisp," she added with a tight grin. "Could have started our own fire, I guess, one way or t'other."

Cindee had naturally curly black hair, and lots of it, in a kind of big halo around her head. Her thin face got lost in it, but that was the only skinny part of her because she had a real full figure, chest and hips. She'd been helpful picking out paint in the past, and maybe she was being helpful today, too, and just didn't know it. After all, Nate had only told Sarah not to ask who bought artificial fireplace logs.

"So is your barbecue pit right where you can keep an eye on your broken-armed wonder, in case he needs help jug-gling all of that?" she asked Cindee.

"Not really. It's out behind the shed, 'cause I don't like the smoke drifting into the kitchen and that keeps sparks away from our big woodpile."

Their woodpile? Then, did that mean they didn't use artificial logs? On the other hand, Cindee hadn't had Mike in view while he was outside, so he could have slipped away to start a fire practically next door.

"Wow, the entire neighborhood smells of smoke," Cindee went on. "Now that you mention it, I did go out to help him use the electric fire starter, but he said he could handle that by himself and he did, too. So, you in for more paint? Since some of the Schrock barn's still standing, will you redo your block quilt piece when it gets fixed?"

"I'm going to do a quilt square on my own family's barn— Ocean Waves pattern. Do you remember I showed you that one?"

"Sure do. You said it was your favorite, 'cause you'd love to see the ocean. I remember it kind of seemed to shift and move."

Sarah could hear Mr. Baughman, who owned the store, talking to another customer down one of the aisles. She and Cindee walked toward the back of the store, where the paint samples always intrigued Sarah. Little paper squares laid out by color and hue, she wanted to arrange them into a painting right on the spot. Although it was not a big store, it seemed to have everything packed in, items for both English and Amish customers. They passed kerosene lanterns and kerosene, then an array of battery-powered kitchen gadgets, since electricity, unless provided by a generator, was *verboten*.

"Exterior latex, couple of contrasting blues and a white, right?" Cindee asked.

"Right, but I'll have to decide which blues. I really

appreciate your help. I'll drop you off a couple of half-moon pies when I take some to the Schrocks. My mother and sisters are making and freezing huge batches of them for the auction at the schoolhouse on Saturday." And that, Sarah figured, would allow her to take a look at their barbecue area. Could the burned barn really be seen from there?

"Can you believe the Schrocks missed that whole thing?" Cindee asked. "Told us they were going to hire a van driver to take the whole family to see relatives near New Phila-delphia, coming back later today, so I bet they don't even know, with no telephones and all. Poor people when they get driven in and see that."

So, Sarah thought, Mike Getz knew ahead of time that the Schrocks would not be home last night. She had to report all this to Nate when she saw him again.

When Mr. Baughman peeked around the corner and said a quick, "How you ladies doing?" Cindee hightailed it back to the front checkout desk. Sarah had always liked Cindee. Anybody who liked and knew paint colors the way she did was fine with her. At least Cindee hadn't brought up the fact that artist's tubes of oil paints, canvas and easels were on sale again, because Sarah could hear them practically calling her name from the other side of the store.

That night Sarah lay on the hideaway bed in the living room of the *grossdaadi haus,* unable to sleep. So much was happening so fast. Nate had not come back as far as she knew, but she'd left him a note about what she'd learned from Cindee, stuck in his sleeping bag he'd left on the ground. A nice way to spend the night, she thought—that is, him sleeping under the starry sky. She assumed he'd done a lot of interviews today, maybe even driven to Cleveland to talk to

Hannah and her employer to see if she had proof of where she'd been during the barn burnings—an alibi.

She sure hoped it wasn't someone Amish or even former Amish doing this, including Jacob. Enough outsiders thought the Amish were a little crazy, or quaint. Quaint—that's what Mr. Clawson had called something she'd said.

She and Martha had kept the news of the second arson from *Grossmamm*. She'd gone to sleep pretty well tonight and hadn't stirred—at least, Sarah hadn't heard her in the bathroom. Strange how the old woman was so afraid of Nate, but then it might be best if Sarah was, too, because he really intrigued her...really made her want to...

Sarah gasped. She heard gravel against the big window right over her head. Was Hannah here again? What if Nate was right to suspect Hannah, and she had come to look at the second barn she'd burned? Or had Nate questioned her today, and Hannah had come to tell her to keep away from him? Or it could be Nate himself, wanting to talk to her, even though she hadn't heard him drive in. Yes, she'd mentioned to him that Hannah had thrown gravel against the window the night after her family's barn burned.

She heard a handful of dirt or gravel again. Sarah sat up and pulled the bed quilt around her cotton nightgown like a shawl before she cracked the dark green curtains to look out. No one—she saw no one.

She tiptoed to *Grossmamm*'s door and didn't hear her stirring, so at least Hannah—or Nate—had not wakened her. Sarah hurried across the small living room, turned the single lock on the front door and stepped out into the warm, windy night, walking to the edge of the small porch.

"Hannah!" she called. "Hannah?"

Silence. Nothing moving but tree limbs. The hoot of a

barn owl sounded so lonely. The familiar squeak of the porch swing pushed only by the wind grated on her nerves, scraping along her spine to make the hair on the nape of her neck stand on end. The thick hair she let down at night moved back and forth across her shoulders like a ghostly caress.

Too late, Sarah realized she should not have stepped outside and no way was she going farther. Besides, last time Hannah had showed herself through the window, and Nate probably would have knocked. After all, *Grossmamm* had said she'd seen a man out here…unless it had been Nate looking around to be sure everything was quiet that night.…

She felt fear nibble at her, but when had any of them been afraid to go back and forth between the farm buildings even at night?

Her eyes adjusted to the darkness, but she still saw no one. As she turned around to hurry back inside, Sarah felt gravel under her bare feet on the porch. So it hadn't been her imagination. If it was Hannah or Nate, it wasn't one bit funny.

She gasped. A note was stuck to the front door with a basting pin. It must have been there when she came out.

She took it inside with her, locked the door behind her and lit the kerosene lamp. She read, in large, handwritten, black printing, words from the Bible: "For wickedness burns as the fire; through the wrath of the Lord of Hosts the land is burned up, and the people shall be as fuel for the fire."

# 9

SARAH WISHED SHE COULD JUST RUN TO NATE
with this note—this threat—but it was too late and too far
to go alone.

After checking on *Grossmamm* to be sure she was all right,
she paced the floor in the small living room, back and forth,
skittish at her own shifting shadow, peeking outside now
and then. She circled the note, not touching it as if it would
burn her. At dawn, she'd run to the house to show the note
to *Daad,* talk him into going with her to take it to Nate. For
once in her life, she wished they had telephones here at the
farm, or that she had one of Nate's handheld phones so she
could call him.

But had this note been left by the arsonist himself, or was
someone else horning in? Recalling how Nate had put the
evidence of the bundle of matches in a plastic bag, she went
to the small kitchen and got a gallon-size bag and sealed the
note inside. Nate had a fingerprint kit in VERA. Maybe
if he eliminated her prints from when she tore it off and
brought it inside, he could find other prints. But then he

couldn't go around making people give theirs, could he? Especially her people. They would mistrust him then— government intruding on personal privacy.

Each time she paced past the table, she glared at the message through the shiny plastic. Just regular, letter-size, white paper. Nothing special to identify that. Who wrote in such heavy, big print, or was that to show defiance or anger? And the fact it was a Bible quote—from someone Amish?

Was she to be the messenger of this threat to the church leaders or the entire Amish community? She did not want to cause panic or have the news media get hold of this. But how did the sender know she was in the smaller house and not with her family in the big one? Someone had been spying on her—or, again, it was someone Amish, someone they knew, who knew her family's ways, her ways. But someone Amish would have written in German, not English, wouldn't they?

Worst of all her agonizing was the implied warning that people would die, that the arsonist might burn more than barns. "And the people shall be as fuel for the fire." Did the barn burnings with her quilt squares mean that someone was angry with *her?*

Near three in the morning, she finally got hold of herself. She'd fight back—well, not really, because her people never did that—but she would not just let someone terrorize her or her community. She'd asked Cindee questions today. Now she had to learn more about this, not just let it destroy her confidence and faith.

Sarah tiptoed into her *grossmamm*'s room to borrow her Bible to look for the exact location of the verse. Out in the living room, as she bent close to the single lamp, her hands shook, rustling the well-worn pages. As if she heard *Grossmamm*'s shrill voice again, Sarah kept recalling the etchings of her people being burned alive from the pages of the *Martyrs Mirror.* That one picture of a young woman tied to a ladder and being tipped into the flames flashed before her eyes. She was perspiring, but a chill snaked up her spine.

Sarah knew to look in one of the prophets for this quote. Finally, she found it early in the big book of Isaiah in the Old Testament. She whispered it in the sonorous German, Isaiah 9:19. What followed were other predictions of a dreadful future for those who worshipped idols—or had this quote been plucked out strictly for its mention of fire?

Curled on the couch, she eventually fell into a fitful sleep, slogging from dream to dream. A fiery beast was trying to burn VERA, flames licking at the truck, devouring it while she huddled inside with Nate, holding on to the ladder he said he would loan her. They were both barefoot and had been swimming, but even water from the pond was not enough to put out the inferno that burned them, burned her....

She woke to find she was uncovered and shaking with the predawn chill. After looking out from every window, she ran to the big house to talk to her parents and fetch Martha to sit with their *grossmamm,* so she could take Nate what might be his best clue yet.

Nate was surprised to see Sarah and her father on VERA's back doorstep even before he took a quick swim in the pond or shaved. But then he'd been surprised to find her note in his sleeping bag last night with all the helpful intel about Mike Getz. In a way, that had saved his day, because it had been one frustration after the other.

He'd made the hour-long drive to Cleveland and managed a quick interview with Hannah's boss, Myron Jenkins.

Jenkins couldn't provide Hannah with an alibi for either night of the barn burnings, but of course, that didn't necessarily imply guilt. No one was home at Hannah's apartment, where she lived with two other women, and the neighbor he'd talked to had no clue where Hannah's boyfriend lived so he hadn't been able to question him.

When Nate returned to Homestead, he'd also struck out trying to trace where Jacob Yoder was living, so he was going to visit his previous place of employment in town today to ask some questions or even interview Jacob's parents. He'd also made an appointment to talk to Peter Clawson since the newspaper man was aware of all that went on in the area. The owner of the hardware store and Mike Getz's girlfriend, who worked there, couldn't recall who might have purchased artificial logs and certainly no one had lately. They were boxed away in sets of four—which could mean the arsonist had two more to use—in the back storeroom until autumn.

But one look at Sarah's face, and nothing else mattered.

"What happened?" he asked before either she or her father said a word. He wanted to touch her, hold her, but he didn't so much as move at first. Her pretty face looked ravaged; at the very least she hadn't slept or was sick.

Sarah extended a bagged note to him, and he scanned it. "Where and when was this found?"

"Last night on the door of the *grossdaadi haus* where I stay with my grandmother. Someone wanted me to find it right away and threw gravel against the window to get me outside. I thought it was Hannah and went out...."

His insides lurched and not just at her admitting the note could have been left by Hannah. This could mean Sarah's paintings—she herself—was the target of the arsonist. But it did mention "the people," not an individual.

"You've got to be more careful," he scolded, much too loudly. Even Ben Kauffman startled. "You could have been hurt!"

"Danger and fear—it's not how we think around here," she protested. "I wasn't hurt. It just made it hard to sleep. That's a biblical quote from the prophet Isaiah."

He fought to calm himself, to think and not just react. "And you thought to bag the note for me. Sarah, you're priceless. I assume you touched it."

"Yes, but I thought you could take my fingerprints. *Daad* says it's all right as long as you don't send them to the government, just use them to see if there are others on the page you can trace. If it would have been stuck to the door with a thumbtack, I would have brought that for the same reason, but it was put there by a basting pin—a long one, sometimes used for quilt making, really common around here."

Man, Nate thought, this girl is bright. Bright and shining in his eyes. But maybe the arsonist also knew she was bright and bold. Nate had thought her painting a quilt square on her own property would keep her safe, but would it? And that person her maybe-delusional grandmother had spotted—odds were now that the person was real and could be the arsonist. But he or she was also clever, probably too clever to get caught returning to where the note had been left.

"I'll also see if there are footprints or anything dropped near where you found this," he told her.

He tried not to frown, but this biblical reference backed up a possibility he didn't like, just as the kerosene and fake fireplace log—and now the basting pin—did. Such as maybe he was going to end up arresting someone Amish, not that others couldn't cite scripture for their own purposes. He was starting to realize what Sarah feared most was probably true. The arsonist was not some random outsider or even a "modern," as they put it, with a grudge against the Amish. It was someone right here in this tightly-knit community, maybe even one of their own people.

"Sorry," Sarah said, interrupting his agonizing. "But I think I—Martha, too—have made a mess of the gravel there, walking in and out, so you won't find footprints."

"That's all right. You've done really well. I pretty much struck out yesterday asking if anyone recently bought artificial fireplace logs at the hardware store, so now, with this and the note you left me about Mike Getz, we have something to go on. Let's just hope the perp—perpetrator—made a mistake and has his, or her, prints on this page."

Finally, her father spoke. He had looked pretty upset through all this, though Nate gave him credit for letting Sarah talk. He called Nate by his first name for the first time. "Nate, there's no way we can just keep Sarah to home, and that doesn't look like a refuge now, anyway. She said you have little handheld phones—no wires attached. I'll ask Bishop Esh, but since all this—" he gestured toward the note in Nate's hand "—I would say her idea you might let her borrow one when she goes into town and back could be a good idea."

"It would for sure. I'll show her how to use it, and she can call me if she sees anything strange. The only thing is, when I need to drive somewhere, I have to put my antenna down so a tree limb overhead doesn't damage it," he explained, gesturing up at it, "and that might play havoc with our signals. I was going to ask, anyway, Mr. Kauffman, would it be permissible for Sarah to take me to see the other two barns that have her paintings—in her buggy? I passed one on the road coming in, but I'd like her to tell me something about the patterns she's painted that may relate to a pattern with the arsons. Besides, I don't want to be seen driving VERA there, in case the arsonist thinks I'm daring him or her to strike again. Of course, you or Gabe or Martha could go along."

Nate realized he'd said too much, but he'd really wanted to explain himself so he didn't alienate Sarah's family or hurt her reputation.

"With plans for the big auction Saturday and buying the wood and hardware for rebuilding the Esh barn," Ben Kauffman said, "we're all pretty busy. But if you sit behind Sarah's seat in her buggy, so you're not real obvious, I say okay."

"Great. Would you like to come inside VERA, Mr. Kauffman, while I take Sarah's fingerprints? We won't be long."

"I'll just sit right here on the back, then walk her home. You two can make plans about seeing the other barns."

Nate rolled Sarah's prints as fast but as carefully as he could. Her fingers were delicate but strong. Talented hands, he thought. They sat, of necessity, very close together. Her hair smelled of that seductive lavender scent again. Was her friend Ella Lantz's making and selling lavender soap and sachets so different from Sarah's being able to paint scenes of Amish life? All three of the best friends—Hannah, Sarah and Ella—seemed to have special talents that didn't fit the mold around here.

He'd thought this assignment would be a piece of cake, but that old Amish saying was really hitting home right now. Sarah sometimes said quilts instead of cakes, but he was learning the hard way that dealing with the Amish was not all cakes and pies.

When Nate found no prints but Sarah's on the paper with the Bible quote, it only drove home again that the enemy was careful and clever. Would Hannah, Jacob or even Mike Getz have thought to keep the paper clean of their prints? Maybe Getz watched the forensic tech shows on TV. And both Hannah and Jacob were living out in the world where they could think of that, too.

He glanced at his watch. He had time to go into town for breakfast at the Dutch Farm Table, then to visit the Buggy Wheel Shop where Jacob Yoder used to work. That would give him plenty of time to get back here to go with Sarah—and guard Sarah, truth be told—to the other two barns with her painted patterns. If the owners were home, he was tempted to tell them to stay home after dark every night. He didn't want to panic them, but an empty house seemed to be part of the arsonist's pattern. So how, then, were "the people" going to be "fuel for the fire"?

As he drove past the Kauffman barn, he saw Sarah up on a ladder, chalking out the perimeter of the square for her painting. He stopped and unloaded his ladder and metal scaffolding, then set it up for her, so she had more stability. Since the barn burnings were at night—cover of darkness and more spectacular for the arsonist, he figured—he'd just take these back each evening when she was done in case he needed them. It would give him more excuses to see her, and not, he admitted to himself, just because she was proving to be such a help to him.

"Thanks," she told him. "I'll really need those when I start painting. I think it might rain this afternoon, which may wash my chalk marks off, but I needed to do something on this today."

"The threat of rain won't stop us from going out this afternoon, will it?"

"This fiberglass buggy and even the Amish woman who

drives it won't wash away in a little rain—or a swim in a pond, Nate MacKenzie," she told him, her voice teasing, almost flirty. His wanting to respond to that, but realizing he should keep this all business, made him almost tongue-tied as they looked into each other's eyes a moment too long.

"So what's this pattern?" he asked.

"It's my favorite, because I'd like to see the Atlantic and Pacific oceans someday. I've seen Lake Erie and just imagined it was the ocean. It's called Ocean Waves. A lot of triangles close up, but it looks like rolling waves with whitecaps from farther back."

"Like an impressionist painting."

"What's that?"

"Just what you said. Up close you can't see the images, only the pieces, but if you stand back a bit, the impression of the big picture becomes clear. I think most of the impressionists were French. I'll show you some on the laptop sometime."

"There's sure a lot I don't know about art and artists."

"That makes two of us."

"Maybe finding out who's behind the burnings will be like that," she said. "You know, we're so close to things—to people—we can't see the big picture. Nate, what if it's someone right under our noses?"

Nate finally got to meet Sarah's friend Ray-Lynn Logan, and was surprised to hear she had a soft Southern drawl. She gave him a good looking over, even a bit of a quiz about whether he'd left a girlfriend behind in Columbus—which he truthfully denied—so he had to wonder what Sarah had said about him. He also ran into Peter Clawson, who said he ate most of his meals there.

"Ray-Lynn tells me you own a piece of the Buggy Wheel Shop," Nate said to Peter as they walked out of the restaurant together. "So you're even into investments that sound as if they're Amish-owned."

"A couple. I like to put my money where my mouth is, so to speak. Some of these ma-and-pa businesses around here have taken a hit in the stale economy. It doesn't just affect the big boys on the Wall Streets and Fifth Avenues of the country, you know."

"So you're a local philanthropist."

"I never thought of it that way, more like a practicalicist—and I know that's not a word. For instance, I'm offering a five-thousand-dollar reward for information leading to an arrest of the arsonist, and I thought you should be the first to know. Besides the Saturday benefit auction information, the reward will headline today's edition of the newspaper. I have no doubt the media flocking in to cover this second barn burning will have to quote the lowly *Home Valley News* on that. Now let me take a guess, Nate," he went on before Nate could thank him for offering the reward. "You're looking for information on the Yoder boy at the Buggy Wheel—well, not a boy by Amish standards."

"Did you know him well? I assume he left the Buggy Wheel Shop when he was shunned."

"Right on that. For someone Amish, Jacob was really volatile. Low tolerance for criticism, and I'd say shunning—their so-called *meidung*—is the ultimate criticism from his people. The boy got way out of line messing with a car theft ring and who knows what else. Not sure what Sarah Kauffman saw in him—an independent spirit, maybe."

"Volatile," Nate repeated, not responding to the who-knows-what-else or the comment on Sarah. "You don't have a forwarding address for him, do you?"

"I doubt if even his parents do, but I'll give you their address, in case you want to chat with them, too. Of course, you can always ask Sarah Kauffman more about him."

Not biting on that, either—Nate was starting to think Peter was quite a manipulator, but then a lot of what he called media mavens were skilled at spin—he took the page Peter ripped off a small spiral notebook. In taut back-slanted script—the man was left-handed—he'd scribbled an address on County Line Road.

"Thanks," Nate said. "And I'll see you tomorrow morning just to chat about how you see this whole barn-burning situation. You're obviously a great pair of eyes and ears around here."

"That I am. Eyes, ears—and mouth," he said with a little laugh. Despite the lack of traffic on Main Street, the portly man looked both ways before he crossed toward his newspaper office. On the glass windows of the brick building was marked in big, bold print—black shadowed with gold—Home Valley News, Peter Clawson, Owner/Editor-in-Chief.

# 10

IT WAS A REAL PARADE OF INTERESTING MEN today, Ray-Lynn thought as she had a cup of sweet tea when the crowd slowed around ten-thirty, before the lunch rush. Not that Peter was intriguing to her, but he was a mover and a shaker and, despite lower subscription numbers for his newspaper, he evidently still had money to burn with that reward for information he was putting up. At last she'd gotten a close-up gander at that good-looking-in-a-kind-of-rough-and-hungry-way Nate MacKenzie. And now, here came Jack.

"Morning, Sheriff," she greeted from the front booth where she'd been sitting by herself to catch her breath, now trying not to be breathless at the fact he was here, for once off his precious schedule. Why, you'd think the man was still a marine drill sergeant. "A second breakfast or just coffee?" she asked. "Your usual counter spot?"

"If you don't mind, I'll just sit with you—coffee only."

When she nodded, he slid in across from her. Fortunately,

Leah Schwartz came over with the coffeepot so Ray-Lynn didn't have to get up to wait on him.

"Everything okay?" she asked, trying not to sound concerned. If nothing else, she'd love to get something out of him about the arson investigation he and Nate MacKenzie were working on. "I'm sure you're busy with the second arson and more news media in town."

"Yeah, well—thanks, Leah," he told the girl when she poured his coffee. She widened her eyes at Ray-Lynn and beat a quick retreat. "The thing is, it's a case, and one that means so much to the Amish, of course—and so to me. They're the backbone of this community and, like you, I admire them a lot, so I want to catch the firebug fast, before he does more damage."

Ray-Lynn sat still as stone, her mind racing. As many times as they'd chatted, he'd never opened up to her like this. Here he was admitting his deepest frustrations, trusting her with his problems. Should she let up on the purely professional facade she'd erected toward him lately—the fence, as Sarah had put it?

"I'm sure you and the arson investigator will solve this. You—are you thinking the arsonist might be Amish and that will upset the Amish?"

"Don't know. Could be. I know the crowds that are coming in are good for your restaurant and other businesses, but I'm having to spend too much time on PR and riding herd on traffic to focus on helping MacKenzie."

Her jaw could have dropped into her tea. Jack Freeman admitting he was upset? That he was anything but in total control? And unburdening himself to her as if he wanted her opinion or support?

"Do you or Nate have any leads?" she dared to ask,

wanting to reach over to cover his clenched hands with hers. He hadn't taken one swallow of his coffee. "You know— thinking the arsons are hate crimes against the Amish or something like that. There was a rumor that even the FBI might be sent in. Surely, you and Nate MacKenzie can han- dle things without that complication."

"They won't be called in unless the arsonist causes fa- talities. Interesting that he or she—it's usually young white males, from what I've been reading up on it—hasn't even caused the death of a farm animal."

"Oh, great, an arsonist with a heart, with a soft spot for the Amish whose livelihoods he's ruining."

"Yeah. Well, sorry I dumped all this on you. I know you've been extra busy in here lately. I could tell."

He looked up from the coffee cup he'd been studying as if he could read the future in it. She glanced down into her tea—no tea leaves to read.

"I'm really glad you stopped by when it wasn't so busy," she told him. "And that you told me how you feel. It will be just between us, and that's a promise. However many folks I talk to every day, I'm good at keeping confidences."

She watched him drain his coffee cup in a couple of quick swallows. When he went for his wallet, she shook her head and reached out to stay his hand.

"It's on me," she said, wishing her voice didn't catch so it sounded as if she was upset or hesitant. "You do so much for all of us, make us and me feel safe."

He cleared his throat. "I really appreciate it, Ray-Lynn, appreciate you," he said, his voice gruff as he slid out of the booth, retrieved his hat from the wall peg and went out the door. But he did give a quick look back.

★ ★ ★

Nate's frustrating lack of progress continued at the Buggy Wheel Shop. Despite learning a lot about how they actually customized the buggy interiors for Amish buyers, he hadn't learned much about Jacob Yoder. Maybe that was because he'd been shunned, maybe because he'd kept to himself and had worked hard despite getting in with the wrong bunch of "moderns" after work—he got that much out of Jacob's former coworkers.

Since that didn't take long, Nate decided to drive out to see if Jacob's parents could throw any light on things. He was so used to having Sarah tell him where to find something around here it took him a minute to remember to just use his GPS to find County Line Road. When he got there, he found a long, hilly road with lots of mailboxes bearing the same names—Miller, Garber and Yoder—but he had the exact address.

Despite that, he drove past the place at first. Unlike the Amish properties he'd seen nearer to town, the small, gray frame house looked run-down. No barn, no outbuildings, no *grossdaadi haus*. But then it had no electric or phone lines running into it, either, no lightning rods. A buggy was almost hidden out back by the small garage that could house a horse. He never should have assumed that all the Amish around here were prosperous farmers.

It reminded him not to stereotype anyone he met here or anywhere else—including the typical profile for an arsonist, one he knew so well. Young, white male, age seventeen to mid-twenties; poor relationship with his father; an overprotective mother; weak social skills; employed in low-paying jobs; possibly above-average intelligence but only poor to fair academic performance.

He turned around in the next driveway and went back to the house, parking on the driveway in front. He saw a white-capped woman glance out through the green curtains, then disappear. A bearded Amish man came to the front door, even before he knocked. At least they were both home, a break he hadn't had lately.

He introduced himself and showed his credentials, but they seemed to know who he was. After all, VERA always announced him. The Yoders—he had a feeling they both looked older than they were—sat on their sagging maroon couch, facing him as he sat in a wooden armchair.

"I realize your son, Jacob, is not part of the community right now, but I was hoping you could give me an idea where to find him. As you know, he phoned in the first barn fire and was a witness to it, so I'd like to get his description of it."

"What you know about Jacob, I'm not sure," his father said. "But in a shunning, even the family doesn't have any-thing to do with him."

"I understand that. But he could be living with friends you might have known or maybe you've heard where he's employed right now."

Mr. Yoder shook his head. "He phoned the fire in from the Kauffman farm. He was at the Kauffman farm that night." His expression didn't vary from a stony frown.

"Yes, he had stopped there either because he saw a lot of people at the party or perhaps wanted to see Sarah Kauff-man."

"He shouldn't bother her. She broke it off before he was shunned."

Jacob's mother spoke for the first time. "It might have been one of the things that made him angry—then he made mistakes, hanging out with the wrong sort. Made the sheriff get after him."

"I understand the sheriff went to bat for him, though, didn't file charges that could have meant prison time."

Mr. Yoder nodded. Mrs. Yoder began to cry silently, blinking back her tears but not wiping them away. "He was a good boy," she said. "Worked hard. He is—was—our only child, you see."

That really surprised Nate. He hadn't come across a small Amish family yet. So, the only child would have been especially treasured by the mother. Maybe his father had been strict with him and the boy had resented it, but he was reading into things here.

Feeling he had walked into another dead end in a maze, Nate excused himself and got up to leave. Mr. Yoder accompanied him out onto the front porch.

"Mr. Yoder, a fairly good source told me that Jacob was volatile. Did he have a temper?"

The man sighed and glanced out at VERA. He closed the door behind him and led Nate away from the house before he spoke. "When crossed, *ya*. His mother—God help us—she spoiled him some. I guess Sarah did, too, at first. I pray you can find him and get him help if he needs it, Mr. MacKenzie—help for his head. I been trying to decide to come see you or not."

Nate's heart rate jumped. "About what, Mr. Yoder? Do you know something that might help protect your fellow churchmen's barns?"

"Only that the boy used to like to burn the trash in the big barrel out back. And lit our cellar door afire with matches once when he didn't get his way and—" he gave a big sniff and wiped his nose with his sleeve "—carried around with him in his buggy one of those fancy fireplace lighters you just hit a button on and a flame comes out. We been a'praying it's not him, Mr. MacKenzie."

"The red car he drives—do you know its license plate number?"

"No, but I bet you can find out."

"I will and hope to find Jacob, too. Thank you for your honesty, Mr. Yoder. I can tell you love your son."

"The prodigal," he said. "But if he comes home, can't say I'd kill the fatted calf for him. I also been a'praying I wouldn't want to kill him instead, putting his mother through all this."

What an admission from an Amish man, Nate thought. Finally, he had a solid lead and prime suspect.

Nate texted an ASAP request to his office in Columbus for Jacob Yoder's license plate number before he drove into the Kauffman driveway. Despite the graying sky that Sarah had mentioned might mean rain, she had finished chalking the outline for her quilt square and had drawn some diagonal lines through the space.

As efficient and prompt as ever, she had her horse hitched to the buggy, so he parked VERA behind the barn instead of driving way back in by the pond. He'd been agonizing over how much to ask her about Jacob. Both Peter Clawson and Mr. Yoder had suggested he should, so why had he been hesitating? Was it the fact that she must have once cared deeply for Jacob that bothered him? It was a battle to keep things professional around her.

"Here," he said, getting his thinking back on track. He produced a handheld two-way radio that looked more like a cell phone. "Let me show you how to use this, in case you need to call me. But as I said, if I'm on the road with VERA, I'll have to put the antenna down that receives, so it might not work then—unless there are none of these beautiful hills between us. At least this is a broad valley."

*Hills between us...a broad valley...* There was so much that stood between the two of them. He had to stop thinking of her in personal ways, he lectured himself again as he demonstrated how to use the two-way, then walked back to VERA and took a practice call from her. Needless to say, she caught on right away as she did with almost everything.

"I've got chicken sandwiches and some lemonade," she told him as he came around the barn to join her again. "They're in a basket on the backseat, so you can serve while I drive. That's one thing about a horse and buggy. You can safely eat and drive."

She sounded nervous and her cheeks were flushed. Maybe it wasn't a good idea for him to go out with her like this, but he needed her help—talk time alone—and her father had okayed it. "Sounds great. Which barn first?"

"I was going to start with the Hostetler barn farther out, but considering the darkening sky, I think we should go to Levi Miller's first. Besides, that's closer to where I saw someone in the dark with your night glasses in case we want to look in that meadow. Upteyup," she said to Sally.

They pulled away, then slowed as her sister Lizzie ran out with a small sack of fresh-baked half-moon pies for them. She and her mother were still baking as many as possible to sell at the benefit auction the day after tomorrow. Maybe Jacob Yoder would show up for that, he thought. Surely, it would be a mix of the Amish and the English. But if he could get his license plate number, he could ask Sheriff Freeman to keep an eye out for him in this entire area. Nate and the sheriff had plans to join forces but, of necessity, they'd both been checking separate leads on this case so far.

Nate was really impressed with the interior of Sarah's buggy, as customized as those he'd seen being made in the Buggy Wheel Shop. Hers had roll-down leather curtains, a polished splashboard where a dashboard would be in a car, a hand brake that would rub against the tires, battery-operated front lights and turn signals and an emerald-green, crushed-velvet front seat.

"So how do you like the eight-to-ten-miles-per-hour pace of the buggy compared to racing around in VERA?" Sarah asked between bites of her chicken sandwich. Nate sat behind her as her father had instructed, but he was leaning forward and, despite the rising breeze, she could feel his breath and smell that clean, pine scent he always had on him. Would it linger in her buggy after he was gone?

"It sure gives me time to take in the scenery. Beautiful."

He no doubt meant outside the buggy, but she felt herself blush, anyway. "So, any luck with finding out who wrote that note?" she asked.

"Do Amish kids learn to print and write cursive in school?"

"*Ya*—yes. Because of the Bible reference, you think it was written by one of my people?"

"Or former people."

"Not Hannah again!"

"Probably not. Can you tell me anything about Jacob's personality?"

"A good worker but ambitious for more and fast. Maybe," she admitted, "that's one thing that drew us together at first. But, like I said, he got in with some bad people."

"So I heard. I talked to his parents."

"Oh. Can you locate him?"

"Nope, though I'm hoping to trace him through his license plate if I can get it from the Bureau of Motor Vehicles in Columbus."

"I have a better idea. You can get it from Gabe."

"Gabe?"

"He has a real talent for remembering numbers, working with numbers. All the *youngie liet rumspringa* boys were in love with Jacob's red car—bet you know what I mean. Gabe will know."

"I should have known to ask you first, Sarah, my Amish translator."

"So you feel like a foreigner here?"

"Less and less, thanks to you."

"Even with our technology gap? My people do use technology when it suits them, when it allows us to keep the family together, which things like TVs would not."

"Keep the family together— A worthy goal."

"Do you have family, other than your foster mother?"

"No, so I envy you that, the big, close families. My biological parents died in a fire—an arson—when I was eight."

"Oh, Nate! So that's why—"

"Yeah, I guess so. The thing is, my own father set it."

"No! I'm so sorry," she cried, turning to face him, so close her bonnet hit his cheek, their noses almost bumped, their lips nearly brushed. "I'm so very sorry," she repeated.

"Yeah, me, too, for my loss of them, my mother, at least. My dad was a murderer, actually, though he didn't intend to be. I'm sure he meant to save us. He died of smoke inhalation. A fireman pulled me out, but my mother was burned too badly and died at the hospital. So, even setting the fire, my father didn't know what the heck he was doing. He set it up all wrong, trapped himself and us inside, waited too long to get us out—an insurance scam that went wrong. I don't know, maybe I'm trying to make up for him as much as I'm trying to fight arsons for myself.

"A childless couple," he went on, "Jim and Mary Ellen Bosley—I call her M.E.—who lived down the street, took me in. They were very loving, but I was bitter, really a brat at times. They stuck with me, wanted to adopt me but I said no, and now I regret that."

His voice broke, but he continued. "Jim Bosley passed away a few years ago, and I still see M.E. often and call her when I can. I should see her more than I do, but she still lives on the street where I grew up, so I get her to come to me or to meet me at a restaurant or somewhere. Once I left I never wanted to go back because I still can't bear to see the vacant lot where it all happened.

"Sarah," he said, almost leaning his chin on her shoulder when she turned away to watch the road again as they neared a stop sign, "I had a doting mother and a distant, thoughtless father I resented—my real parents, I mean. That's often how an arsonist is made. Not me, obviously, but do you think that could be the case with Jacob's parents, him being an only child and all?"

"Could be," she whispered. "I'm regretful that was the way it was for you, and I'd say that was true of him."

The minute they turned onto curving Orchard Road, the traffic picked up. Despite the road's picturesque name, it led to the interstate. Though Sarah kept the buggy well over, partly on the berm, Nate got really nervous as cars came close, then roared past, usually with people craning their necks to see who was in the buggy. Most drivers were respectful; however, a few honked. One yelled, "Get a life! And a car!" At least Sarah and Sally seemed to be used to that. The slow pace, which he had begun to savor, now put him on edge. No wonder buggy-car crashes were another cross the Amish had to bear.

"There it is," Sarah told him, waiting for several cars to pass so they could turn left. "The Miller house and old barn."

Yeah, Nate thought, it was the barn with the quilt square he'd seen when he first drove into town, and he'd been so intrigued by it he hadn't noticed how run-down the place was.

"It would make a great moody painting with that cloudy gray sky behind it," Sarah was saying, "a study in soft, muted grays with only the bright quilt square standing out, but I'd like to put some people and horses in it, too."

*Moody* was putting it kindly, Nate thought. To him, Levi Miller's farm looked like a scene from an old Alfred Hitchcock movie, almost a replica of the Bates house from *Psycho*. An old Victorian peeling paint, an antique barn that hadn't been kept up, though that was highlighted by Sarah's bright square painted in glowing blue, green and gold. How unkempt the property was, even to an uncut lawn and scraggly bushes. This was the second lesson he'd had today that the Amish were not all prosperous or industrious—in this case, not even good farmers.

As if Sarah had read his mind—a dangerous precedent— she said, "He doesn't have much land, and he's not really suited for farming like some of the men. The square is painted on this barn not only because he's a church deacon, but because it's on this road, which is busier than most. Tourist buses come this way from I-77, and it's the first square they see in Home Valley and on a traditional barn, though it's seen better days. I've heard tell tourists don't even notice the house or condition of the barn when they see the square."

"I can attest to that," he said. It was the closest he had ever heard her come to praising her own work, though she was just stating a fact. "So what's the name of this one?" he asked. "It's a beauty."

"Crown of Thorns. You know, like the Lord's enemies put on His head before they crucified Him."

"Let's hope that's not a bad omen. I keep thinking how your Tumbling Blocks design was painted on a now tumbled-down barn. Do you think there's any connection between the patterns painted and what's happened, though I don't exactly get Robbing Peter to Pay Paul on the Esh barn."

"I've thought about that, but I just don't know. As I said, some of my people think my work is too showy. But burning barns for that reason? It's too far-fetched."

"You'd be surprised what is and isn't far-fetched when it comes to investigating a sick crime like arson. It looks like no one's home, and I was hoping to tell Levi Miller that he needs to at least stay home after dark. So far, *that* is part of the pattern, that the arsonist strikes when the place is deserted, but probably just so he won't be seen and stopped."

Sarah reined the horse in by the barn door, but when Nate gestured her on, she pulled around to the side so they would be hidden from the road. "If the Millers aren't here," he said, "let's look around, anyway, and I'll leave them a note."

They got out and walked around the barn, just as it began to rain. It was as if the gray sky, even the faded gray barn, were crying on them, he thought.

"Hey, what's that?" he asked, pointing at three, small,

furry bodies on the ground—without heads. Tiny pools of crimson blood indicated the little animals had bled out. They seemed to be arranged in a trail, leading around the next corner of the barn.

"Dead voles, I think. Barn owls or hawks sometimes be-head them," she said, her voice shaky as she backed up into him, and he put his hands on her shoulders to steady her.

Together, they peered around the corner at the back of the barn. Suddenly, Nate needed steadying, too. A few more small, headless vole bodies were strewn there. And some-one—sure as heck not a barn owl or a hawk—had scrawled in red on the back of the barn the bold, printed words Mack—Keep Away!

# 11

"IS THAT BLOOD?" SARAH ASKED AS THEY STARED at the writing, which was already starting to smear in the rain. Despite getting wetter, they both bent close to study it. "That much blood couldn't come from those dead little animals," she added, her voice shaky.

Nate touched a letter and lifted his fingers to his nose to sniff at it. "It's not clotting and there's no copper smell. It's paint. Fairly fresh."

"It's probably latex, like I use, but I avoid red, the color—" her voice faded as she thought again of Jacob's red car "—of martyrs' blood."

They straightened, both glancing behind and around, but the rain had closed them in like a curtain. When they retraced their steps toward the front of the barn, Sarah couldn't see the Miller house or the woodlot nearby, where someone could easily hide. They both jumped when a bolt of lightning flashed and thunder cracked too close.

They hurried toward where they'd left the buggy. Sally neighed and tugged at the traces. The whites of her eyes showed as she tossed her head. Sarah felt that frenzied, too. Despite the cover of the rain, she had the feeling they were being watched, but she didn't want Nate to think she was a coward or didn't have faith in the Lord's protection. "Sally doesn't like lightning," was all she said.

"Neither do firefighters. First that Bible warning to you and your people. Now this one looks aimed at me. Mack must mean MacKenzie. The writer must know darn well I'm not going to keep away. But keep away from what? Let's get the buggy inside the barn."

"Right. The Millers won't mind. If the arsonist left that message, he—"

"Or she…"

"—seems to know your schedule. He must have figured you would check the two other barns that have paintings. I wonder if there's a similar message on the Hostetler barn in case you went there." A rolling rumble of thunder shuddered through her as she led Sally inside.

"Or did he or she follow us, pass us on the road and paint it just as we drove up? We couldn't see the back of the barn from the road. The bastard—pardon my French—"

"That's English. Strong English."

"I was going to say it looks like the arsonist has been watching me—or you."

Nate's voice was clipped, and he looked tense and angry. That made her feel even more afraid. He was supposed to be the strong one with the answers, to be in charge here.

Nate glanced around the dim barn and rubbed his palms on the front of his jeans. "Being stalked gives me the creeps," he admitted, "about as much as knowing he or she is out there waiting to ignite another barn. We wouldn't be inside this one if it wasn't pouring hard enough that it would be

difficult to start a fire right now. But if the arsonist is following us, we may be able to set a trap later." He kept staring at
her as if waiting for something.

Sarah was suddenly aware of how she looked. Though
she'd shaken her skirts, they clung to her legs just the way
his shirt did to him. The only thing that was dry was her
hair and face under her *kapp* and bonnet. Sally stamped and
snorted even as the rumbling thunder grew more muted,
but the skies kept pouring rain. It drummed so hard on the
barn roof that it sounded like hoofbeats on a wooden covered
bridge. She had to say something to break the screaming
silence between the two of them. Her pulse pounded harder
than the rattle of the rain.

"Do you think my grandmother may have actually seen
someone lurking outside our *grossdaadi haus?*" she asked as she
brushed drops off her sleeves. "Not a monster with glowing
eyes like she said, of course, but I've been thinking we'd
better believe her about seeing someone since that Bible note
appeared. Still, she does imagine things at times. Nate, the
reason she acts afraid of you is that she's haunted by the per-
secution our ancestors faced in Europe, especially burnings
for our faith. It—it kind of haunts me, too, sometimes, all
of us. She thinks you're the government official coming to
take us away, to burn us out, burn us. I thought I'd better
tell you that."

"You've been tremendous through all this, helpful and
honest."

"Good," was all she could manage, when she wanted to
say something better and wiser. "Good."

He came close and put his hands on her wet shoulders.
She put her hands around his wrists, not only to touch him

but to prop herself up. She wanted him to hold her; she felt he knew that. Her lips tingled.

They had not closed the barn doors, so the wind whipped in, chilling their wet clothes. He let go of her and went over to slide the barn doors closed. At the grating sound—or at the idea of being sealed in here with Nate—she went all shivery with goose bumps.

Just before he slid the door shut, a whoosh and a swoop of air slapped them as a big-winged body swept past and out into the rain.

Sarah let out a shriek, and Nate ducked. "Oh," she said, "it's just a great horned owl flying out. She's probably the one that killed the voles, though she hardly lined them up that way. I'll bet she's feeding nestlings inside here."

"I'll leave the doors cracked for her, then. Speaking of which, my crackberry is vibrating."

"Your phone?" she asked, rubbing her hands up and down her arms. It was good to talk of something rational, something normal.

"Phone and more," he said, digging it out of his front jeans pocket. "Email, weather, global positioning, everything. I'll show you later. It's really called a BlackBerry, but it's so addictive that it gets the nickname crackberry—you know, from crack...cocaine."

She shook her head and shrugged as he answered the phone. It was a reminder to her that they came from two separate worlds. He had to talk loudly over the storm, so she knew it was his boss and something about Jacob's license plate. Could her former fiancé be doing all this? Yes, she was almost starting to think—to fear—he could. Surely, Jacob had seen Nate's name in the *Home Valley News,* and he might figure he was called Mack instead of Nate. Could that Keep

Away on the sign mean for Nate to keep away from this area or to keep away from her?

"That phone kind of runs your life," she told him when he punched a button and put it away. "It makes a crack in daily living, is that it?"

"Not exactly—kind of. Sarah, the Bureau of Motor Vehicles for the state says that there's no Jacob Yoder who has a license plate registered in this county or any other in Ohio. He must be driving with stolen plates, maybe ones he got when he was running with that auto theft ring. I'll take your advice and talk to Gabe when we get back to see if he knows the plate number."

To their amazement, the huge owl flew back in with a small snake in its beak, tilting to get through the door. They watched her glide into the side bay, then heard bloodcurdling screams.

"That can't be the snake! What in the—" Nate muttered, seizing her arm and spinning them around as if he would protect her from something.

"That's the nestlings, the baby owls," she told him.

He nodded. "Sarah, don't ever feel you don't understand my world—my tools of the trade," he said, patting his pocket where he'd put his phone. "I'm a babe in the woods when it comes to things you know, so—"

And then they heard the knocking.

But from where? Nate thought. What was that? Sure as heck not the owls. Outside or inside the barn? It seemed to be coming from the other side of the back wall where there was no window except high in the loft. His imagination ran wild. Was someone leaning a ladder against the barn, then moving it along? The arsonist had started one fire high, using window access. On the other hand, it could be a trap to lure them outside. He'd mentioned setting a trap, but could their enemy be one step ahead of them on that, too? Then again, it could be that the wind had shifted and a branch was knocking there or, in this ramshackle old barn, something had come loose to bang in the wind. The place had a hundred chilly drafts and strange fits of air movement.

He put his mouth close to Sarah's bonnet and whispered, "Close the door the rest of the way, but don't bar it in case we need to get out fast. I'm going up into the loft to look out that window, down toward where we saw the message."

"But what's that sound?"

"I hope it's a tree limb in the wind, but I'm not betting on it. Go."

She did as he said while he quickly climbed the rickety ladder to the loft. It was dark up here; the rain pounded overhead, closer, louder. As he felt his way along under the big roof beams, his eyes adjusted to the dark. Wan light seeped through the patched roof that had sprouted numerous leaks. The old floorboards creaked under his weight and once he felt the entire floor of the loft shudder. Cobwebs laced themselves across his wet face and snagged in his eyelashes. Half expecting he'd be peering out through the paned window into the face of an arsonist on a ladder, he pressed his nose to the glass, dusty on this side but running with rivulets of water outside. He turned his cheek to it, trying to look down, around.

Suddenly, the knocking stopped. The horrible shrieks had just been owlets, natural sounds, so maybe his tree limb idea was right. He'd scramble down, take a shovel or rake with him for a weapon and go outside to be sure. He wished he had the pistol he kept in VERA, but he'd locked it up there and had shown it to no one in peaceful Amish country.

Man, you're getting spooked by this place, he scolded himself. Creepy house, old barn, bad storm and then that bloodred message smeared on the barn that carried the implied threat Or Else! Did it mean to keep away from this arson case, the Amish or Sarah? And, if the latter, didn't that point to Jacob Yoder again?

He turned to go back downstairs and bumped into someone. It was Sarah, thank God. With the pounding rain, he hadn't heard her come up here.

"Did you see anyth— " she got out before there was a creak, a crack—and the floorboards under them gave way.

Nate grunted and Sarah screamed. He grabbed a beam, grabbed her. Slammed together chins to shins, they dropped partway through the floor, then stuck, suspended at armpit level. Her right arm was splayed along the floor where the rotting boards had given way. Nothing was in reach for him but her.

"Hold on!" he told her. "Hold on to me! Pull your arm in, 'cause we're going down."

As they fell, her black bonnet and cap were ripped away. They dropped amid dust, dripping rain and loose, splintered boards to land in a pile of hay, a tangle of arms, legs, her wet skirts and hair gone wild.

"You okay?" Nate gasped, lifting his head from their landing.

"In one piece, at least," she said, pulling her thigh-high, mussed skirts and slip down over her bared, white thighs and black stockings. She knew her voice sounded shaky, and it wasn't from the fall or their worsening situation with an enemy. Oh, no, she knew the enemy she struggled with right now was her own *verboten* desire for this man.

"Thank God for this pile of straw," he said.

"Hay. It's really hay."

"Sarah—you're beautiful. We could have been maimed or killed, but you're still teaching me...."

His voice faded and he looked at her intently. "And you *are* beautiful, you know," he whispered. "In lots of ways."

Still watching every move she made, Nate lifted himself on one elbow; his other arm was trapped under her, but he didn't move it. He looked at her, down, up, then deep into her eyes, that stare that always made her feel she was falling off a high ladder. She blinked to get some of the dust out of her watering eyes, which made a double image of Nate, his gaze devouring her.

The hay felt both prickly and soft beneath her bottom, back and limbs. He was so close—it was almost like being in bed with him. Suddenly she was aware of her body in a new, thrilling way. She was beautiful, he had said.... She should jump up, find her bonnet, repin her hair, which was splayed out under her head and shoulders with strands in her mouth that Nate gently drew out in a soft caress across her cheek.

Something was going to happen between them that should not, but she wanted to know and cherish each moment. She wet her lips, held her breath.

"My boss, your father and Bishop Esh would never approve of any sort of roll in the hay between us," Nate whispered, his face coming so close to hers that his breath almost burned her. "But I can't help this."

And then he tilted his face slightly to the side, lowered his head slowly, as if to give her time to turn away, and kissed her.

Smooching, her people called it. But this was entirely new, like nothing she'd had with Jacob. Spinning, swirling. Had the fall knocked her silly? She lifted her free hand to touch the side of Nate's face, the crisp, damp hair at his temples, his earlobe, the strong back of his neck as the kiss went on. She opened her lips for him and only moaned when his hand, trapped beneath her hip, moved, caressed the curve of her there, then slid slowly up her waist and rib cage, over her breasts to pause before coming up to cup her chin. His head had jerked a bit. He'd sniffed in a sharp breath. She'd bet he'd never known Amish women didn't wear bras—that is, not until now.

Every part of her seemed to come alive at his touch. And still the kiss went on, moving, deepening. He might be hovering on top, but she met him halfway until their entire bodies were pressed together as hard as their mouths. He rolled them over, her up and around until he was on top again. A roll in the hay, he had said. They breathed in unison, then she could hardly breathe at all, before he slowly—reluctantly, she could tell—came up for air.

"I should say I'm sorry, but I'm not," he whispered, his voice deep and raspy.

"*Ya,* me neither."

"I want to look around outside. We've got to go back."

"Right. This barn could have burned down around us and we would not have noticed."

He grinned, then chuckled. "I love an honest woman."

"Don't say that—love."

"You know what I mean. I just—what's that sound now?"

"A buggy."

"Going or coming? I've got to go look."

He brushed himself off as he got up, but she saw pieces of

hay clung to his back. He hurried past Sally and the buggy to the door. She heard him slide it open a little.

"It must be the Millers are home and going right to their house," he reported as she struggled to pin up her hair. He came back and watched her do it. She wished she was taking it down for him, not just stuffing it up under her *kapp* and the bonnet he retrieved for her and dusted off. Oh, why did this have to happen, because she felt doubly endangered now, by the arsonist and by her own feelings for this *ausländer* who would all too soon, unless there were more fires, take his VERA and go home.

After brushing all the hay off each other, they went to explain to the Millers some of what had happened in the barn. While Sarah waited in the house, in the lessening rain, Nate and Levi, and the Millers' oldest boy, Noah, went out to examine the broken loft floor and the back of the barn. They found the threatening words washed off and a maple tree limb that looked like it could have hit the back wall. When they returned to the house, Nate said they had seen the diluted, crimson paint along the edge of the barn's foundation. But Sarah had something to tell him, too.

"Nate, Mrs. Miller says when they pulled up just before we joined them, they found a note from Sheriff Freeman pinned to their front door."

His eyebrows rose. "From the sheriff? Pinned how?"

"Not with a basting pin—a thumb tack."

"Could I see the note?"

Sarah watched him stare long and hard at it, just as she had. It was in bold print, but not necessarily a match for the note she'd found. It was on lined, yellow legal-pad paper, not white letter paper. Besides, Sheriff Freeman as a suspect?

Too crazy. The note simply urged the Millers to be sure they stayed home after dark and kept a good eye on their barn.

"Which we would do, anyway," Levi assured them with a nod as he pointed at the written warning. "Got a good notion to sleep out there with my hunting rifle, broken ribs or not I got from fighting the Esh fire. But Noah's nineteen now, so he could take a turn guarding the place, too. The barn's broken down, but it's all we got now with no money to rebuild."

Sarah had once known Noah well, for he'd been a close buddy of Jacob's, but she hadn't seen him for months. She supposed Noah missed the shunned Jacob, because he'd really looked up to him.

"So," Nate said to Sarah as they took their leave and headed away in the buggy in what was now only light mist, "I keep getting surprised about the Amish. Levi might shoot at a person rather than turning the other cheek. Jacob's father said he'd struggled not to want to kill his son for what he'd done to his mother and…" he said, looking sideways at her with a little crimp on the side of his mouth.

"And I kissed you as good as you did me. See, Nathan MacKenzie, you're finding out the Home Valley Amish are not some kind of saints but human. That sign on the barn said you should stay away, but I'd be real sad if you did."

# 12

EARLY THE NEXT MORNING, NATE HUNCHED over his computer screen in VERA, parked out by the pond. He was searching for other possible arsons started by artificial fireplace logs, but he was having a hard time keeping his mind on his work. Surprised to hear a car engine close by, he glanced out and saw the sheriff's car. As Nate walked to meet him, Jack Freeman parked at the edge of the pond, got out, slammed the door and sloshed through the puddles toward VERA.

Nate had turned down an invitation from Sarah to join her family for breakfast. It wasn't so much that he couldn't face the Kauffmans after his passionate encounter with Sarah but that he'd already planned to eat at the Dutch Farm Table. He hoped to find Peter Clawson there so he could speak with him casually before they had their appointment. He had some things to bounce off that quick brain of his.

"Sheriff, I could have come in if you'd phoned," Nate said, extending his hand. "I know you're busy."

"That I am," he said as they shook hands. It was a firm

shake, almost too hard. He still wore the plastic rain cover over his wide-brimmed hat, though it had stopped raining sometime overnight.

"Anything new, Sheriff?" Nate asked.

"How about you call me Jack, Nate? Naw, nothing really new. I just thought we should touch bases again, 'cause I can't see much progress, especially with that second arson making us look bad. Thanks for the voice mail about that note left on the Kauffmans' *grossdaadi haus* door and the one on Levi Miller's barn. I'm keeping an eye out for Jacob Yoder's car, license plate number or not. A red sports car really sticks out around here. I took a look in the woodlot where he and his buddies had hidden those hot cars, but no sign of him there. We got to catch us a break somehow."

"At least we know the Amish aren't hiding him, not even his parents."

"You probably heard I covered for that boy, but I won't again. If he's the one behind this, I'll kick myself for getting him off scot-free, however hard his own people came down on him."

"I understand. When dealing with the Amish, it seems right to handle some things—well, differently," Nate said, wishing he hadn't touched Sarah and yet glad he did. It felt so good to have her holding on to him, her arms around him when they fell, her strong but soft body pressed against his. No question, he was falling for Sarah.

"By the way," Jack was saying, "I also hit the Hostetler house with a warning, but they were planning to do a night watch, anyway. So—Jacob still your number one suspect? He's mine right now."

"My interview with his parents indicated he has not only motive and opportunity, but the background for arson. I felt really bad for them. I'd suggest we don't both question them, if you're thinking of that. They're really agonized over this."

"See—you've learned to care about the Amish, too, and you've only been here a few days. So what's your next move?"

"I had a short chat with Peter Clawson at the Dutch Farm Table, but I'm going to pick his brain—definitely a close observer of things around here."

"Peter's not only an asset to the community but sometimes an ass, too. Nothing's privileged information with him, so don't trust him with any inside intel," Jack said, pointing an index finger for emphasis. "Just a word to the wise on that. See you later and keep in touch."

"Will do, Jack. Thanks!" Nate called after him as he got back in his cruiser and slowly drove out.

*Keep in touch,* Nate thought. He'd do that for sure because both Jack Freeman and, he hoped, Peter Clawson were great sources of information and support. He'd rather keep in touch with Sarah in more ways than one, but he knew he shouldn't.

As Nate looked off into the distance, he saw Gabe walking down the lane, carrying something in a sack. He realized he hadn't mentioned to Jack that Gabe might know Jacob's license plate number, or that he had a hunch the boy had kept something back from him about the night of the first fire. He could only hope that, like Jack had miscalculated when protecting Jacob, he himself hadn't screwed up by not grilling Gabe harder—yet.

After her usual Friday run to the restaurant to drop off half-moon pies, Sarah was on the road again. She was heading Sally back toward the Schrocks' house with potato salad and pulled pork sandwiches for them and, of course, some pies. She had given half a dozen little pies to Gabe to take to Nate so they could talk privately about Jacob's license plate. And, she'd grabbed a few extras to drop off to Mike Getz and Cindee Kramer. *Mamm* said she didn't mind since she'd made so many for the auction and the barbecue.

The little gift for Cindee was the perfect excuse to get a glimpse of their back area to see if the Schrock barn could be easily spotted from there. Sarah would be able to tell if Mike was home, since their garage was so full of junk that they always parked in their small front yard. And if his truck was there, she wasn't going near the place.

Truth be told, God forgive her if she was wrong, she was hoping the arsonist was Mike Getz, just so it wasn't Jacob or anyone Amish. She didn't like the way Nate kept insisting the barn burner could be a woman. It just couldn't be Hannah, and Sarah had to convince Nate of that.

Surely Cindee's comments about Mike being able to handle the electric grill starter one-handed and the fact he knew the Schrocks were away from home meant he could be the arsonist. If the Schrock barn could not be seen from the area where Mike claimed he saw it, she sure meant to tell Nate.

Sarah kept Sally going at a good pace, because she planned to get back home soon. Some other buggies were on the road, taking folks to work. Both Mike and Cindee should be at work, so she felt quite safe. No one was going to scare her away from doing her tasks and helping Nate, too. The arsonist was a coward, one who only did his deeds in the dark.

She saw Cindee's old car and not Mike's truck, so she pulled into their driveway. Cindee must be going into work

later. Rainwater sat deep in the ditches along both sides of
Fish Creek Road, but their raised blacktop driveway was
dry.

Taking out the sack of pastries, Sarah climbed down and
hustled around back instead of going to the front door. Because of their garage, she couldn't see the black skeleton
of the burned barn, but maybe she could farther on. But
no—the moment she stepped into their backyard, she could
see that either Mike had lied to Cindee, or he'd spotted the
fire from another position. Or maybe he'd gone over on
foot to start the fire and then came back to call it in. He had
called 9-1-1 quite early, and that saved the structure from the
complete destruction that had ruined the Esh barn. He was a
hero again. But shouldn't Cindee have known he didn't tell
her the straight story?

On the other hand, what beef could Mike Getz possibly
have against the Eshes or the Amish in general? Hopefully,
he wasn't one of those Amish bashers who resented that her
people were different. He might be a bit of what they called a
redneck. But maybe an arsonist who started and fought fires
for the thrill of it didn't need to hold any grudges against
those he harmed.

Sarah saw the grill was an old, yellow-glazed brick structure, not a pit and not a metal one like many of the moderns
and Amish used, the kind the Plain People would haul to
the schoolhouse for the charity barbecue and auction. But
she didn't see any fire starters here. Of course, he could have
taken them inside with all the rain.

"Lookin' for something?" came a loud male voice behind
her.

Startled, she spun to face Mike Getz.

★ ★ ★

"Sarah said I should bring you out some moon pies and that you wanted to ask me something," Gabe told Nate.

"You want to sit down in the front seat of VERA to talk?" Nate asked.

"Oh, yeah, sure."

"Want one of these moon pies?"

"*Mamm* said not to eat till dinner, but there's six of them in there."

Nate let Gabe sit in the driver's seat again while he got in the passenger's side. From his belt, he unhooked the two-way radio he kept with him in case Sarah called for some reason. He was wishing she would, not that she'd be in danger in broad daylight on her own family's farm, but just to talk. He put it on the dashboard, then opened the sack and let Gabe take a pastry before he did.

"That's not a tape recorder," he assured the boy. "It a two-way radio, in case your sister calls me."

"*Ya,* okay. I knew that."

They talked with their mouths half-full, just two guys, hanging out. Nate was pleased with the relaxed feeling, not only so Gabe would open up to him but because he really liked the kid. Actually, he hadn't met a Home Valley Amish person he didn't like, but then he hadn't seen Jacob Yoder yet.

Gabe kept his free hand on the steering wheel. Nate had never interrogated a witness here before, especially not one in the driver's seat.

"Sarah mentioned that you were really good at math—at numbers," Nate said. "You happen to remember the license plate number of Jacob Yoder's red car?"

Gabe nodded. "RGE 1297."

Nate took his notebook from his pocket and scribbled it down.

"You gonna drive VERA around to look for him?" Gabe asked.

"You got any ideas where I could look if I took you along?"

"Only what I heard."

"Which is?"

"It's not nearby. Just that he has a couple of English friends. Up I-77, halfway to Cleveland. I haven't been there, but I heard the general area." He told Nate the route to cut off from the highway, even the intersection where Jacob might have a friend.

"You're a big help, Gabe. Also, I was hoping there was something else—anything would help—that you might recall from the night of the first fire when you were near the Esh barn. I could keep all of it or some of it privileged information," he said, pointedly putting his notebook away. "But I'd really appreciate your help."

"Like you said before—confidential?"

"Absolutely."

Gabe sighed and wiped the hand he'd been eating with on his pants before he touched the steering wheel with it. He gripped it so hard his fingers went white at the knuckles.

"Well," he said, "Barbara Lantz and I were in the Esh barn that night, in the loft, but we didn't do anything wrong—not about the fire, I mean."

"I believe that. So can you help me out? Anything you saw or heard could give me a key clue."

The boy's cheeks had gone bright red again. "At first we weren't really paying attention—about what was going on outside."

Nate bit his lower lip and waited. He knew more was coming. It struck him that this boy was trying to express how he himself had felt when he was with Sarah in the Miller barn.

"But then I heard a car and thought it was funny—strange—so I looked out. And I saw someone get out, check the house first, then walk toward the barn. We heard the barn door open down below us and thought we were gonna get caught."

"It was Jacob Yoder."

"No. At first I couldn't tell who it was, in dark clothes and all. I peeked out through a crack in the haymow door. She was just standing, looking up at the barn, staring up at where—I guess—Sarah's painting must have been. Then she came inside."

"*She.* A woman? Gabe, I need to know who you saw. I won't let on who told me."

Gabe heaved another sigh that shook his shoulders. "When we saw who it was and that she'd know us, we got ourselves down the back ladder to the first floor and out that side door *schnell*—real quick. We ran across the field toward our barn and went in one at a time, so I don't know what happened after that, but I—I been wondering."

"Was it your sister's friend, Hannah Esh?"

He shook his head. "Mrs. Logan. You know, who runs the restaurant in town."

Mike must have just pulled up in front, Sarah thought as her insides lurched. She'd overstepped. She'd risked too much. She was so used to everything being safe around here. And she was so unused to having a phone in the buggy that she'd grabbed the pastry sack but had come back here without what she really needed. Not that she could have phoned Nate for help right in front of Mike Getz, anyway. She'd have to talk her way out of this without a call to Nate.

"I just wanted to see the place you were working about the time you spotted the barn fire," she said, forcing a small smile. "Cindee told me." She was amazed her voice sounded so calm, when he really scared her. He looked big and bulky with his bull neck and his fists clenched at his sides. "I told Mr. Clawson I don't want my picture in the paper for spotting the first fire, but I thought—if you had a good place for a photo somewhere around here—I'd tell him to just use yours for spotting the second one instead."

She knew she was saying too much, but she couldn't help herself. He had her blocked in by the garage, the big brick grill and a board fence. Yet if someone glanced back at the right angle from the road, they could be seen, so he wouldn't dare to hurt her, would he? And wasn't Cindee home?

"You know how my people are about photos and interviews," she rushed on, "but you gave those Cleveland TV reporters such good ones, I was hoping you wouldn't mind more. Only—I didn't want to just ask Mr. Clawson before I looked around to see if there was a spot for it."

"I think it'd be better over by the ruins of the barn," he said. He still frowned, but he shrugged his big, rounded shoulders and finally unclenched his fists. "Yeah, okay by me if Mr. Clawson says so."

"The other thing is," she said, extending her sack of half-moon pies toward him, "I told Cindee when I bought paint for another quilt square that I'd bring you both some of these, so she was expecting me."

"Yeah, well, she had car trouble so we switched for the day. She's at the hardware store."

"Then please give her these, and I'll be going to drop things off to the Schrocks. They're expecting me."

He took the sack. "The fire marshal know about this picture idea?" he asked, still blocking her way out.

"He does know you're a double hero now, so he will probably be glad to also be interviewed for the story, if that's what you mean. I guess you know, Mr. MacKenzie was really impressed with you," she added, and dared to step closer to him, hoping he'd move back and let her pass. She figured showing indecision or fear was not the way to deal with this man, especially since she now had another piece of proof he could be the arsonist, at least on the second fire.

Sarah could almost hear the wheels of his thoughts grinding away in that big, bald head. Did he have enough in his bean to be able to write that note with the Bible quote? Surely, he and Cindee would not be working together, even though she had easy access to the artificial fireplace logs at the hardware store. But if Mike Getz was not guilty, why didn't he just let her leave?

He shuffled aside and she edged by, fighting to keep from fleeing. She didn't relish having to tell Nate that she'd taken too much of a chance here. In case Mike checked up on her, she'd now have to tell Peter Clawson, whom she tried to avoid, that he should get a picture of Mike. But, as he'd said, it should be near the ruins, because he couldn't have spotted the fire from this backyard.

"Let me make sure I've got this right," Nate said to Gabe. "Ray-Lynn Logan went to the Esh house and found no one home. Then she came over to the barn, looked up at Sarah's painted quilt square and then came into the barn. You two took off so you didn't see what happened after. You're sure?"

he demanded, realizing too late that his buddy-buddy tone had evaporated. "You didn't tell Sarah any of that, did you?"

"I didn't tell anyone and told Barbara not to, 'cause we were up there together when the barn dance was at my place."

"Sure. Sure, I understand that."

"Sarah will tell you I didn't say a thing. You can ask her if you want, but she went to take some food *Mamm* made with some of those—" he pointed to the sack on the console between them "—to the Schrocks. I heard her tell *Mamm* she took some for Cindee Kramer, too."

"To the hardware store?" Nate asked, but he knew better. Cindee lived with Mike Getz, so he could only hope Mike wouldn't be home on a Friday morning. Sarah obviously meant to drop them off en route to the Schrocks. And he didn't like that idea at all.

"Gabe, we've got to switch seats. I've got to go somewhere."

"If you arrest Mrs. Logan, don't tell where you heard that, okay? She's a friend of Sarah's and pays *Mamm* and Lizzie good wages."

"I'm not going to arrest Mrs. Logan. Move!"

As they changed places—Gabe would be sad to see that Nate was going to put him out at his house—Nate swore under his breath and, from the front seat, reluctantly lowered the antenna that would allow him to make or receive calls on the two-way. He might be overreacting, but letting Sarah in on so much—using her, really—had endangered her. Why hadn't she told him she didn't intend to stay on her family's property after what they went through yesterday? With that threatening note pinned outside the place where she slept, didn't she realize the rules in cozy Amish country had all changed? As clever as she was, his Amish sidekick had clearly not gotten it through her pretty head to be careful.

Sarah was nearly to the Schrock house when she heard a loud motor kind of clearing its throat behind her. VERA? Nate had said he would be coming out here after the debris cooled down with a search warrant to sift through the ruins.

She glanced in her rearview mirror. Her insides cartwheeled and not because it was Nate. She saw Jacob's bright red car following her pretty close. He was probably expecting she'd pull over when she saw him, but she had no intention of doing that. If Jacob was following her now, had he been following her earlier? Nate had mentioned they might set a trap, but she hadn't wanted to set one this way. She'd call Nate on this two-way radio right now and tell him exactly where Jacob Yoder was, assuming that was him behind the wheel. The sun still fairly low in the eastern sky glared off the car's front windshield and in her eyes.

Sarah figured she had about three minutes before she could turn into the Schrocks' driveway. Surely, they'd be home. She grabbed the two-way, and hit the quick-dial number Nate had set up for her. Could she keep Jacob here long enough for Nate to get here?

But unlike when they'd practiced, the radio didn't make a sound when she turned it on. Even when she put the number in again, nothing appeared on the tiny screen but the word *Searching.* Maybe Jacob had been searching for her, stalking her. But that note on the Miller barn had been addressed to Nate. This was even more of a nightmare if the arsonist was someone Amish—even former Amish.

The red car's horn sounded twice. She giddyaped Sally faster, while she struggled to punch in the number yet again.

Jacob's car bumped the back of the buggy. Once, twice, then hard enough to shove it into Sally and send both horse and buggy crashing into the water-filled ditch.

# 13

AS THE BUGGY SLAMMED INTO THE WATER, Sarah went flying, her hands still on the reins. She went under with a huge splash and came up sputtering and angry. Sally thrashed the surface into waves, trying to get up but was trapped in the traces. Before Sarah could scramble to her feet, Jacob leaped in, too. He grabbed her arm so hard it hurt.

"This is your fault!" he shouted, thigh-deep in the roiling water. "All you had to do was stop."

"Let me go! You could have killed me and Sally!"

She glanced back into the half-submerged buggy for Nate's phone, but it was gone. Yanking free of Jacob's grasp, she sloshed toward her struggling horse. Thank the Lord, the mare hadn't broken a leg. Though the road wasn't busy, surely someone would come along soon. Then she remembered that Nate needed Jacob's license plate number, so she glanced up and tried to remember it in case Gabe wasn't sure. Jacob moved behind her toward Sally. He helped Sarah free the horse from the buggy so she could stand. Sally floundered to her feet, making even more waves. "It wasn't my fault. It was an accident!" Jacob shouted.

"*Ya,* one you caused! You caused anything else you shouldn't have?"

"Something else I caused? What's that supposed to mean?" Jacob demanded, this time gripping her wrist so tightly her hand went numb. He shook her hard. "You don't think I had anything to do with the fires? I saw you with him! He's been turning you against me!"

"You've been following me, haven't you, maybe sneaking around at night?"

It wasn't like her to lose control, but since Jacob was guilty of this rash act, he could have left the note on the *grossdaadi haus* and burned the barns, too. She told herself she should talk quietly, not only to calm Sally but to keep him here until someone came along. She should find out where he was living so Nate could question him. But as if he'd read her mind, he said what she feared.

"We can't talk here. Get in the car," he ordered, pointing at it. "Sally and the buggy will be all right."

"No. I need to get the buggy towed out. Can you help with that?"

He lunged at her and pulled her so close she could smell garlic on his breath. He hauled her to the side of the ditch, then dragged her, clawing his way up like a wild animal. She saw he had red splotches on his hands but no visible cuts. Paint. Red paint from that threatening note to Nate.

"Jacob, you're hurting me. Let go!" She realized he'd left the car engine running; the driver's door stood open. "You want to talk, fine," she forced herself to say. "We'll talk right here."

Seizing her upper arms, he pulled her to him, nearly lifting her off her feet. Up this close, she really looked at him for the first time in months. His flushed face was unshaven, and gray half circles shadowed his wild eyes. A frown furrowed his brow. He lowered his voice, but he sounded so menacing. She smelled something else on his breath—alcohol?

"We're not staying here. I don't want that nosy *ausländer* MacKenzie or one of my former Amish brethren to come along." His already-bitter tone turned mocking. "'Oh, there's Jacob Yoder, under the curse of the *meidung*. We all know he's evil, must have started the fires.' That's what you're thinking, isn't it, Sarah? And you're the one who once said you loved me, trusted me! Now you're listening to him, trusting him."

He loosed her arms only to seize her wrist and again drag her toward the open car door. He pulled hard, but she twisted the reins she still held around her right wrist so she was anchored to Sally. Her attempt at another calm command of "Let me go," was drowned by his shout, flecked with spittle.

"I said, get in the car! I'm innocent, and you have to help me. I know who lit the fires, and I'll tell you if you go with me. We'll call the sheriff, explain things to him to get MacKenzie off my back. Sheriff Freeman helped me before, but you'll help me now, won't you, for all we once meant to each other?"

"Stop hurting me. Violence is not our way."

"Our way!" he exploded again. "There is no 'our' anymore! I've been banned, banished! You don't think that's a kind of violence? And you're hurting me, too. Now get in this car, or I'll—"

Giving up all attempts at calm, Sarah tried to buck away

from him and screamed once, again. Someone might hear her, help her, maybe the Schrocks or even Mike Getz.

Then, roaring down the road toward them, came VERA. The square shape of the dark vehicle was unmistakable.

When Jacob turned to look, he shouted at her, "Judas! Jezebel!" He shoved her away.

She staggered back to the edge of the ditch, rolled into it and hit the water again, bottom first this time, next to where Sally stood. Despite heavy, soaked skirts and a curtain of drenched hair in her face, Sarah dropped the reins, got to her feet and clambered up the bank again only to see Jacob's car speed away. Realizing Nate might stop for her and lose him, she waved her arms and pointed as Nate slowed.

"It's Jacob. Go! Go!" she shouted.

VERA roared away in pursuit.

Nate stepped on the gas pedal and gripped the steering wheel hard. He was livid with Sarah for going out without telling him, for getting in this situation, but she had flushed Jacob out of hiding. He hadn't wanted to use her as bait, but had she done that deliberately? And he was furious with himself for not making her promise to stay home. At least he had Jacob in sight, but the car had a head start, and it was faster than VERA. A car chase was definitely not in his job description.

The red car—some kind of sporty one—must be doing eighty down this two-lane road. What if either of them hit a car or, worse, a buggy? People were out on the roads. He'd lose the trust the Amish had offered him. Police vehicles, even an occasional fire truck rushing to emergencies, sometimes hit and killed innocent civilians. He'd be pulled off the case; a crash investigation would take precedence over stopping the arsons.

As the red car crested a hill ahead and disappeared, Nate cursed the beautiful terrain again. It screwed up long-distance vision, communications and safety. He should call the sheriff, but he'd left his phone in the back of VERA. As he reached the top of the hill and saw a farm wagon pulling out ahead between him and Jacob, who must have just missed it, he knew the chase was over. He slowed, turned around in a driveway and went back. He wanted to check to see that Sarah was all right, find out what she'd learned.

"You didn't catch him." Sarah stated the obvious when he got back to where she was waiting. People he didn't know— a man and woman in a buggy—were with her and they'd managed to get Sally out of the ditch.

"I'll get the sheriff after him," he assured her. "I've got his license plate, and Gabe gave me a lead on where he might be staying. VERA wasn't built for high speed."

She looked like a drowned cat for the second time in two days, but beautiful nonetheless. Even her hair was wet this time. He was glad the others were there or he would have lost his temper over her endangering herself. She was definitely coming off this case, because if she got hurt he would never forgive himself.

"I'll be fine," she told him as if she'd read his mind. "These are the Rabers, and they can help us get the buggy out."

He thanked the couple, then gently pulled Sarah off to the side. "After this," he told her, "I'm not leaving you alone off your property—maybe not even on it."

"I had the phone with me but it didn't work—that is, before it went for a swim here."

"That, at least, was not entirely your fault. Let's blame the hills, or the fact I put the antenna down after I talked to Gabe and he mentioned you were going to stop at Getz's. But I see it was Jacob I should have been worrying about."

She petted and sweet-talked the horse while he got a rope out of VERA and, with Mr. Raber's help, tied it to the buggy. Reuben Schrock came along the road and together they got the buggy righted and out of the ditch.

Though he could tell Sarah wanted to argue with him, Nate asked Mr. Schrock to take Sally and the buggy to his place and said they'd retrieve them later, because he had to take Sarah to the sheriff to report the incident.

"*Ya,* sure," the bearded church elder told him. Then he added, "You think Jacob Yoder burned the barns, Mr. MacKenzie?"

"We're going to find out and stop him if he did," Nate promised, then thanked everyone again and hustled Sarah, who was starting to shiver, into VERA. As he went into the back to get a blanket for her, he realized whatever had just happened between Sarah and Jacob meant he had to keep her off the case for her safety and his sanity.

Sarah wrapped herself in Nate's blanket. The water quickly soaked it, but he must have known the seat would get wet. Ditch water from her hair and smashed bonnet dripped down her back. Though it was quite mild outside, Nate closed the windows and turned on the heater, but he kept glaring at her as if this was her fault—and, of course, Jacob's desperation aside, it was. And he hadn't even heard that she'd misstepped with Mike Getz today.

"Your career as assistant arson investigator is over," Nate said, his expression tense and his voice harsh. "He could have drowned you back there. It's my fault, too. I should have told you not to leave your farm—not that that wouldn't keep someone from coming onto it."

"I will not be kept a prisoner on or off the farm, even if the arsonist is targeting the barns because of my painted quilt squares. But I don't think Jacob meant to kill me. He was trying to make me go with him."

"Oh, fine. Abduction. And then when he got you alone, what?"

He darted another hard look at her, then hunched over the steering wheel. Though he was chasing no one now, he was still driving too fast.

"I was so angry I wasn't thinking that he could have hurt or killed me," she admitted. "Actually, when he shoved me into the ditch water, I recalled the horrible time Ella almost drowned."

"Don't change the subject."

"But I need to tell you about something else. I may not have found out whether Jacob was guilty of arson, but it might not be him who's lighting fires. I found out Mike Getz couldn't see the Schrock barn from where Cindee said he did, unless she was confused. So someone lied, and why?"

"I knew it! I hope Getz wasn't there when you trespassed."

"Unfortunately, he was, but I covered for why I was there. I told him I was going to ask Peter Clawson to take a picture of him again, and he fell for it, not to mention I had a sack of half-moon pies for them."

Nate muttered something under his breath. "Sarah!" he said through gritted teeth, "you've been a big help to me, but you've got to keep clear of all this so you don't get hurt. You have not been trained or sworn by the fire marshal's office!"

"Sworn? Sworn *in,* you mean? No, only sworn *at* by Jacob and now you. Nate, I'm scared the barn burner's targeting not only my people but my paintings—me somehow. But I'm in a good position to find things out."

"No way. You let me do that. So did Jacob say anything about resenting your paintings on church leaders' barns?"

"No, but he wanted to talk more. He was very upset that I've been working with you."

Nate muttered under his breath again and she was just as glad she didn't hear. "Did he say anything that could tie him to the arsons?" he asked. "He no doubt blames you and your people for what he's done to himself."

"Well, if I'm not helping you anymore, I guess I shouldn't say, but *ya,* he called me a traitor and more. Still, his being desperate to talk to me and angry at me for helping you doesn't mean he's guilty of arson. He denied he had anything to do with the fires but said he knew who did. That's possible, isn't it?"

Nate kept flexing his fingers on the steering wheel, opening them, then gripping it hard. She wondered if he wished he had hold of her neck instead.

"Isn't there a saying," he demanded, "'With God, all things are possible'?"

"So Mr. Nathan MacKenzie can quote scripture, too. I wasn't sure you had a religious bone in your body."

"You think I'm some sort of heathen? My foster mother took me to church. I'm a believer."

"But not a believer in accepting help from anyone."

"Sarah, why are we arguing?"

"Because you know you need me—for helping solve the arsons, I mean—and you don't want to admit it."

"I just can't stand it that you could have been hurt."

"You were thinking of setting a trap for whoever wrote that note on the Millers' barn. That's what happened, only I was almost trapped instead of Jacob."

"I refuse to use you as bait. But did Jacob admit to that much—painting the note on the Miller barn?"

"He didn't have to. He has dried red paint on his hands. But I suppose, unless you do some kind of chemical test on it, he could say he was just painting over scratches on his red car and spilled a bit of it."

"I admire the way you think things through. But I'm expecting the sheriff to go right out to arrest Jacob for assaulting you at the least, and we can keep him locked up that way."

Sarah kept noticing the way fields and trees, farms and woodlots, raced past so much faster than in a buggy. But that's the way she felt her life was going now, kind of out of her control, and it scared her silly, as did what she had to tell Nate next. He had accepted the Plain People's form of insurance, even their lack of lightning rods and fire alarms, but would he understand her refusal to help him with this?

"Then," Nate went on, "he can be detained so I can question him. Also, I'll want a complete statement from you of everything Jacob said."

"You can arrest him for assault, but I won't accuse him or testify against him. We don't do that. The government courts are not for us. We settle things our own way, in the church, among ourselves."

"Sarah! You say you want to help but you won't testify to the fact he even roughed you up?" Then to her amazement he lowered his voice. "Okay, okay," he said. "We'll get him for speeding and an illegal license plate, then. Anything to hold him for a while, until he can at least be questioned. You don't want to accuse him of assault, I get that, but the barn burnings are an assault on your people. I'm going to nail whoever's guilty, and I'm betting on Jacob, though I now have another lead I haven't had time to check out."

"Another possible arsonist besides Mike Getz? What happened? You're not thinking it's Hannah again, are you? You said most arsonists are men."

"Let it go for now. It's nothing you need to be concerned with."

"Of course I do, and you can't stop me. Or were *you* planning to abduct me and lock me up somewhere?"

"To keep you safe—I'd do it. I'm thinking maybe you shouldn't even paint that new quilt square on your own barn."

"My new painting is agreed on. I'm honoring my father's faith in me by doing it. He knows the risk. The decorated barns draw more tourists in, and the people need that to survive and prosper right now. The Lord will help us through all of this, and you should rely on Him, too."

"But that doesn't mean we should put ourselves in harm's way. The world can be an evil place, Sarah, obviously even your sheltered Amish world."

Of course, stubborn outsider that he still was, Nate was right about that. She had never actually argued with a man, the give-and-take like this, and it was strangely exciting. But if Nate MacKenzie thought she was some shy, sweet Amish woman he could question, kiss and then command to keep quiet, he was dead wrong. She wasn't saying so right now, but she was in this arson investigation with both feet.

Nate brought VERA to a stop in front of the small sheriff's office on the only cross street of the main one through town. Sarah had heard the building had only one cell. She hoped Jacob Yoder would soon be in it and tell them who the arsonist was. At least, if it was him, it would stop the fires, the ones in the barns, though not the ones in her body and heart for this stubborn *Englische* man.

After the sheriff heard what they both reported and headed out to arrest Jacob, Nate took Sarah home to dry off and change clothes before he formally deposed her in her kitchen. Sarah wore her hair in a damp, thick braid down her back. After Mrs. Kauffman fed them both, she hovered in the background, putting pastries into boxes and sacks. The sacks started crinkling a whole lot louder while Sarah told him about Mike Getz confronting her. It just proved to Nate again that however much he needed Sarah, he had to keep her out of the loop of the investigation.

"So," Mrs. Kauffman said after he took Sarah's statement, "somehow that modern, two-way phone didn't work for her. Sarah shouldn't get too involved with all your things, Nate."

The woman's words rang in his ears: Sarah shouldn't get too involved.... Was it obvious, especially to a watchful mother, that he and Sarah were getting too close to each other?

As if to emphasize her mentioning a modern phone, his cell buzzed.

"Good info on Yoder's location," Jack reported. "We're getting to be a good tag team. I'm bringing him in. You can have first crack at him, then he's mine."

"I appreciate that. The only eyewitness won't testify against him, and he probably knows that. But I've got some other ideas."

"Bet you do. See you there."

"He arrested Jacob?" Sarah asked.

"Yes, but we won't have to hold him for assaulting you, so don't worry about not testifying."

Still hovering, Mrs. Kauffman said, "The sheriff helped Jacob once, but even our shunning did not bring him back. He has been taken over by *hochmut,* puffing himself up, putting himself first."

"Like the old saying 'Pride goeth before a fall'?" Nate asked.

"*Ya.* Exactly," Mrs. Kauffman said with a firm nod. "In his heart, Jacob is no longer Amish. *Hochmut*—pride—is what some of our people thought had misled Sarah when she began to paint the big quilt squares, until Bishop Esh spoke up for her. Now we have decided she should paint one on our barn to stand up for her, too. But Jacob may be a lost soul."

"I feel bad for his parents," Nate told her. Even in the dim light that always seemed to characterize an Amish home, he could see where Sarah got her looks. Mrs. Kauffman's face seemed a faded, plumper portrait of Sarah's, and both women moved with a purposeful grace. "I don't have a wife or children to worry about," Nate went on, "but I can grasp how it is to agonize over someone you love who has gone astray, like the Yoders for their only son." He almost said something about his father, but he had things to do. Knowing Sarah, though, she knew what he meant.

"You take care of yourself, Nate," Mrs. Kauffman said. "Sarah will be right here with me or taking care of her *grossmamm.* She and Martha can both sleep in the *grossdaadi haus* tonight."

Looking into the woman's clear blue eyes, Nate nodded. "I value Sarah's help in this and yours, too," he told her. "Everyone here has been very kind. Thank you for your hospitality and support." He almost added, *And for keeping an eye on Sarah.*

Nate fought to keep from meeting Sarah's stare as he made a hasty exit. But as he pulled away from the Kauffman house, he noted the big, bold lines with which she'd sketched her quilt square. The rain had erased some of it, but he had no doubt she would draw it right back there again. And though he was going to try to steer clear of her for both their sakes, he felt her drawing him in again, closer and closer.

# 14

"I HAD NOTHING TO DO WITH THE LOCAL BARN burnings. That's all I have to say, Mr. Fire Marshal Mac-Kenzie!"

"Why don't you just call me Mack?" Nate countered. "Make that *M-A-C-K* and paint it on the side of a barn and line up a bunch of beheaded little voles pointing to it. You're in serious trouble here, Jacob."

Jacob shrugged and shook his head to get his bangs out of his eyes—he still sported an Amish haircut—but refused to meet Nate's glare. At least Jacob didn't deny knowing what he meant. He must have been following Sarah around and figured out that she was helping him with the arson investigation. Had Jacob hoped that barn burnings targeting her paintings would force her to go to him for help, but Nate got in the way?

Jacob cleared his throat and said, "It's Sarah's paintings on the barns that got her in trouble, not me."

"Got her in trouble how?"

"Whoever's starting the fires must be angry with her for

being prideful, no matter what the bishop says. It's got to be someone Amish, but I'm not part of that anymore."

"Being prideful. *Hochmut,* you mean?" Nate asked, using what he'd learned from Sarah's mother. Jacob looked surprised. "It's sad," Nate went on, "but I don't think Sarah can be proud of her former fiancé, running with thieves and being shunned. Then he knocks her buggy off the road, threatens and roughs her up."

They sat facing each other across a small, bare table in the only cell in the Eden County sheriff's office. Nate tried to read the young man's body language as he stayed slumped in his chair, hands thrust in his jeans pockets, one foot tapping against the table leg so it vibrated in a regular beat.

The sheriff had wanted to book Jacob for stalking, aggravated assault and attempted kidnapping, but he knew those charges wouldn't stick without Sarah's cooperation. He'd been through that before with the Amish, he'd told Nate. But charges for speeding, for DUI—Jacob had failed a Breathalyzer test when he drove in with the sheriff waiting at his place—and for driving with an illegal license plate would hold him for a while. The sheriff had read him his Miranda rights, but Jacob had still been eager to talk to Nate. If Jacob had really harmed Sarah, Nate wasn't sure he could have kept control, but he was trying to set a certain tone here—tough but fair.

"I know I shouldn't have got caught up by that car theft ring," Jacob said, frowning at the table. "But they don't give a guy a chance."

"They?"

"The Amish, especially the church leaders. Sarah and her family, either."

"I have the understanding that they'll take a penitent back."

He looked up, then away again. "A penitent?"

"Someone who's truly sorry and wants to mend his or her ways."

"They should stick with the person, not throw him to the dogs in the first place."

"What dogs have they thrown you to?"

"I never would have been taken in by car thieves if I'd been treated right, even before I was shunned. Sarah broke off our engagement and everyone supported her, not me."

"So none of this is really your fault. It's hers, right? I can tell you're angry about it."

"Not really, but it just isn't fair."

"Let's go over your statement again, then. The night of the first fire in Bishop Esh's barn, even though you were not angry with the unfair Amish, you just happened to be in the area and decided to visit some of them, specifically Sarah's family."

"This is America, freedom of choice and all that!"

"I've got to agree with you there. Maybe because the Amish give their young people freedom of choice to become Amish or not, you wanted to hang out with Gabe Kauffman and his friends."

"Those *rumspringa* gatherings—you know, our...their... so-called running-around time—have outsiders dropping in. I just thought I could see some people I used to know. But when Sarah spotted the fire, I was able to call it in, then ran over there with the rest, that's all."

"So before you showed up at the Kauffmans' that night, you were doing what and where?"

"Just driving around. Thinking about how I missed some

of my old friends, trying to decide to see my parents or not. The others might not talk to me or eat with me, but my mother would. To tell the truth, I knew some of the kids at that party might not shun me, and I guess I needed that. But what I don't need," he said, sitting up straight but still looking down, "is some worldly fire cop coming in here and conning Sarah into helping him, overstepping with her."

Nate decided to ignore that. Jacob hadn't gone for his challenge about "Call me Mack," and he wasn't going to react to the overstepping with Sarah accusation. Instead, he said, "So you decided to follow her until you could get her alone, even painted a message on at least one barn for me to stay away from her." Using the same calm conversational voice, he added, "Was the Miller barn third on your burn list, Jacob?"

He sucked in a sharp breath. "N-no, but I'll admit something. Yeah, I painted that message to you there, but I didn't burn any barns."

"I've done your case study and you fit the profile of an arsonist. Look, Jacob, this is going to go a lot easier on you and your poor parents, especially your mother—yes, I've met her—if you just confess, come clean and get this all over with. Your mother, Sarah and her family, let alone the entire 'unfair' Amish community, will think more of you if you tell the truth and ask for forgiveness than if you keep up your lies."

Jacob's hands came out of his pockets, fists clenched. He banged them once on the table. "I can't afford a lawyer, but I want one."

"Sure, we'll get you a lawyer in here for free," Nate said, leaning closer to him. Man, it was difficult to deal with someone who wouldn't look you in the eye. He had to be lying. "And I won't question you anymore without him or her being present. Only, to your former people, who don't trust lawyers much more than they like government officials—"

"You're government and seem to be doing just fine with Sarah!"

"Lawyering up, as we say, won't win you much support with the Plain People you've already let down and hurt. And in your head and heart, they are still your people, Jacob—you know they are," Nate said, rising and going to the door, even lifting his fist as if to knock for the sheriff or the deputy he'd called in from Wooster to spend the night here at the jail.

"Think about it carefully, Jacob," he said. "The arsonist has been clever and careful with the two fires. Frankly, I'm in awe of him and Sarah is, too. No one hurt, probably not even a barn owl, so the arsonist's prison time would not be as long as it would be if he kept telling lies or lit a fire where someone got more than just financially and emotionally hurt. I'll get that lawyer for you now."

"Wait! I—I'll plead to harassing and stalking Sarah, to painting that warning to you on the Millers' barn and Hostetlers' in case you went there, but I am not a barn burner. I told Sarah I knew who it was but I don't—honest!"

The man looked distraught, but he finally met Nate's stare when he'd seemed so shifty and scared before. Naw, Nate thought. He'd bet the farm—if he had one—that this was the arsonist, but that didn't mean he wouldn't keep looking. Mike Getz still needed to be questioned, as did Hannah Esh and even his new possibility, Ray-Lynn Logan.

"You want that lawyer now?" Nate asked.

"Changed my mind. Don't need one, 'cause I didn't burn those barns."

★ ★ ★

Late that afternoon, Sarah helped her mother place stacks of boxed half-moon pies in the big family buggy, then helped her father load the wagon with birdhouses he was donating to be sold at the alms auction the next day. She liked the flourishes and designs she'd done on these so-called condo birdhouses for purple martins with their multiple entry holes. She wondered if those beautiful birds lived like the Amish with the generations together. Would one of these holes be a sort of *grossdaadi haus*?

She wished she had her buggy here and, for her dona-tion, a collection of paintings of Amish life on stretched canvas, maybe framed, or even small quilt squares painted on wooden plaques, but that would really set everyone to talking about her painting pretty—her *hochmut*. But was it so prideful to wish she had painted birds or flowers, all parts of God's grandeur, on those birdhouses instead of circles and swirls? And to yearn to create on canvas or wood the scenes that paraded through her head and heart that would portray the Plain People in all their simple yet busy lives?

But she didn't have paintings or her buggy. At first Nate had said he'd take her to pick it and Sally up at Mr. Schrock's, but he'd later set it up with her mother, while she was drying off and changing clothes, that *Daad* and Gabe would go get Sally and the buggy after they packed these things for the auction tomorrow.

Her stomach twisted tighter. What if Nate really meant it that he would work on this arson investigation without her now? She sighed and went to the barn to stare up at the spot where she would paint her new quilt square, Ocean Waves. She and Sally and the buggy had made waves in that water-filled ditch today. If Jacob was the arsonist, at least they had him confined now.

She walked to the *grossdaadi haus* where both she and Martha would spend the nights together because of safety in numbers. Pretty soon *Daad* might even say Gabe should sleep out here, too, with his hunting rifle. Or he might put Gabe in the barn the way Mr. Miller had said his son, Noah, was guarding their ramshackle one. Tonight, hopefully, there would be no more notes with terrifying Bible verses tacked to the door, no more gravel thrown against the window, though that would be worth it if Hannah would only come back, even just to talk the way she did the night after the first fire.

As Sarah went into the living room, she could hear Martha reading to *Grossmamm* from the *Budget* in the bedroom before her late-afternoon nap. They'd had a family conference and decided that the *Home Valley News* was all right to read to her, too, but not the extensive coverage dedicated to the fires, because that might set the old woman off again, just as the tales of burning Amish from the *Martyrs Mirror* had.

In his most recent editorial, Peter Clawson said the arsons could be hate crimes against the peaceful Amish and that the state fire marshal's office must find out who was guilty and root out the perpetrators. She'd heard the newspapers were selling like half-moon pies around here lately.

Sarah shook her head and shoved back her dirty hair. She had to wash it tonight, get the ditch water out of it. A mirror. She wished she had a mirror out here, even the small one they had in the house. No need for mirrors among her people since beauty was all on the inside of a person, but with Nate around, she sometimes wondered how she really looked to him. She sighed again.

Suddenly overcome with exhaustion, she slumped on the couch, not even taking time to open the hideaway bed she or Martha would use tonight, while the other took a turn in a sleeping bag on the floor. Nate liked to sleep outside in a sleeping bag. She'd left him a note there about Mike Getz and had stroked the deep marine-blue of the soft flannel lining of his outdoor bed....

She forced herself to think about the hues of blue paint she would use for the triangles of her ocean waves. Tomorrow was the auction and then Sunday was a church day—the Hostetlers' turn to be hosts. But on Monday, after she took the pastries to Ray-Lynn in town, she would set up the ladders and scaffolding and begin to paint. She would use Nate's ladder and his scaffolding, not shaky, but firm. No fear of being tipped off...tipped off into the fires...falling from pride into the fires...

*They pressed her against the wooden ladder on the ground, ripped off her bonnet and prayer kapp. The crowd was screaming for blood, those who insisted on plain ways, who would not bow to the rules of the government's church. The flames grew higher, hotter, close, so close....*

*"For wickedness burns as the fire!" someone shouted as she was tied to the ladder. "The people shall be as fuel for the fires of hell! Burn them! Burn them for the fires of hell!"*

*The screams of others being burned—her friends, her family, her people—shredded her courage. She wanted to beg for her life. She wanted to struggle, but it was not their way. Accept. Forgive. Forgive them, Father, for they know not what they do. Much better to drown in the pond or the dirty ditch, ducked to death like a witch than this terror.*

*More men with angry faces came closer, bent over her, lifted her high on the ladder, tied her hands and waist and feet. If she could*

*only fly up to heaven, not have to face the fire! The heat seared her*
*already, burned her with desire for an outsider, an Englische aus-*
*länder, a man she could never have. Her precious paintings flamed*
*to pain and ashes as the fires lit her skirts, her skin and…*

Sarah heard someone scream, someone close. Was it *Gross-*
*mamm* afraid again?

"Sarah. Sarah! Wake up!"

Martha was kneeling by the sofa, shaking her shoulder.
"You had a bad dream. You screamed. *Grossmamm* nearly
jumped out of her skin and asked if the beast was outside
again."

"The beast? Oh, sorry. Get back to her."

"We're just all on edge. It's all right," Martha soothed with
a squeeze of her shoulder before she hurried back into the
bedroom.

But it wasn't all right, Sarah thought as she hugged herself
hard, then staggered to her feet and went into the kitchen
to wash her hair. She leaned over the sink, her hands on the
counter, propping herself up. Nothing had been right since
that first barn went up in a blaze, taking her painting and
her Amish turn-the-other-cheek beliefs with it.

After Nate filled in the sheriff about Jacob's claims of in-
nocence for the arsons, he went outside and, exhausted, just
sat in VERA's driver's seat. It was late afternoon, the time,
he'd heard, Ray-Lynn Logan went home for a break before
the evening rush. He knew which house was hers just outside
of this little one-cross-street town with its two rows of com-
mercial establishments and then a scattering of houses. He
intended to keep an eye on things at the auction tomorrow,
and he was sure she'd be in the thick of things there, too, so
he'd probably never get any private chat time with her then.

Yeah, he'd phone her just before going to her door. He had to check out the lead Gabe had reluctantly given him. Even if she wasn't somehow tied to the arson, she might have seen something. But why hadn't she come forward?

Before he could start the engine, someone knocked on his window. He jolted in surprise, then saw it was Peter Clawson. He turned the key so he could run the window down.

"I'd like your statement about Jacob Yoder's arrest," Peter said without any ado. "I'll get one from the sheriff, but you're still 'the Man' on this arson case."

"I've been wanting to talk to you for a couple of days," Nate countered. "Walk around and climb in."

"I'd rather have you come to my office. I have something you'll want to see."

Nate got out and locked up, then followed Peter across the street. "Working hard?" Nate asked as Peter held the front door of the newspaper office open for him. It amazed Nate that this was a one-man shop except for distribution, but with a small paper in the digital age, it was obviously possible and profitable.

"Always. To use a cliché—which I hate to do—I like to strike while the iron is hot, and these arsons are making things hot here."

"So what is it you wanted me to see?"

"Before I show the sheriff or write it up for the next edition—this," Peter said, and pointed to a piece of white paper with large, block hand printing on his cluttered desk.

Nate saw he'd placed the paper in a stiff plastic envelope, so it shone in the overhead lights. Nate read, "A fire goes before him, and burns up his enemies round about."

The handwriting looked the same as on the note pinned to Sarah's door, but to be sure, he'd have to scan and send both to a handwriting expert the bureau consulted with in Columbus. But the expert didn't like photocopies or faxes because the pressure of the pen point on the paper could reveal things, too. He was quite sure this handwriting was different from what Jacob had done on the Miller barn, even though the materials were so different.

"I checked," Peter said, sitting in his high-backed leather desk chair which creaked under his big frame. "It's a quote from the Bible, Psalms 97, verse 3—the Revised King James Version to be exact."

Nate began to sweat. He'd opted to keep the Biblical quote from the Kauffman *grossdaadi haus* privileged information, to avoid causing panic and undue speculation and so he could use it to be sure he arrested the right person. Besides the Kauffmans and the sheriff, only his boss knew about it. But if this man discovered he was withholding information from the public, he could skew it to look bad. He'd already written an editorial suggesting Nate should get on the stick—to use a cliché. Peter's pompous manner rubbed him the wrong way.

"What are you implying about this note?" Nate asked. "That it's somehow tied to the arsons?"

"Put through the mail slot of the newspaper that's been crusading to have the arsons solved. Don't you think so?" Peter demanded, thumping the desk with his index finger. "Fire...burns up...enemies. I'd bet my Phi Beta Kappa key that this is from the arsonist. He or she wants more notoriety, wants to stir things up even more, to cause fear and panic if I print this, but I can't see not printing it. You think I should?"

"As you said, only if you want to stir things up more. I suppose it would sell more papers if that's your main goal."

"It isn't. Absolutely, the truth matters, but I care deeply

about this community. I've got money and years of my life invested here, but I can't sit on something like this. However, if I had a strong interview about your questioning Jacob Yoder today—you did, didn't you?—I wouldn't have room to include the note, because I need to save big layout space for coverage and photos of the charity auction tomorrow."

Nate sat down in the wooden armchair at the side of the big desk. He was uptight, but he tried to look calm. He leaned back and put his arms on the wooden arms of the chair. "That almost sounds like a bribe. Or even a threat, Peter."

"Not at all. I'm willing to let you take that piece of evidence to see if you can get fingerprints off it, though I admit I touched it before I knew what it was, so you'll have to eliminate mine. Do we have a deal?"

"You can print that both the sheriff and the state fire marshal's arson investigator questioned Jacob Yoder, but he is only being held for DUI, speeding and driving with an illegal license plate at this time."

"You don't think the firebug is Jacob Yoder?"

"Do you? I respect how you seem to have your finger on the pulse of this place."

"I'd say the odds are good for Yoder. Motive—in spades. Proximity, at least to the first burn, ditto. To the second burn, hard to prove. But then, Mike Getz, maybe. Hannah Esh, possibly."

"I'm impressed."

"The power of the press—and the brain behind it."

Talk about pride and *hochmut,* Nate thought as he looked up at the framed certificates and famous newspaper articles on the walls of the office. Then, taking the plastic envelope, holding the note with him, he stood and walked over to read several of them.

"A Pulitzer for powerful reporting is my inspiration, my goal in life. It's what keeps me going in this little place I have come to cherish. And I think we're either up against an arsonist who is Amish—or one who wants to appear Amish—or a religious nut who hates the Amish. By the way, did I leave out anyone on your lists of possible perps? You can tell me that much, at least."

Nate turned to face Peter. He'd risen from his padded chair and sat on the corner of his desk. Wouldn't Peter be shocked to know that his own partner in the restaurant had been on the scene of the first fire just before it ignited?

"See you at the auction tomorrow," Nate said. "If you notice anything fishy there, let me know. When I nail the arsonist, I'll be sure you have the complete story before the big boys in the heavy-hitter papers in Cleveland or Columbus get a thing."

At that, Peter's chubby face lit in a smile that made him look like a Christmas cherub.

Ray-Lynn was hoping that Jack might be calling when her phone rang during her break at home, so she took her time answering it. But it wasn't him.

"Ray-Lynn, it's Nate MacKenzie. I know this is your downtime from the restaurant, but I'd like to stop by for a few minutes and ask you a couple of questions. It's important."

She gripped the phone hard. "In person? Not on the phone?"

"No, ma'am. I'm only a few minutes away."

"Don't you 'ma'am' me, Nate, because it makes me feel

older than I am and more old-fashioned than I'd like to be. All right. You just drop on by," she said, trying to sound cheerful.

She poured him iced sweet tea and fed him lemon sponge cake while they talked about the auction. He seemed interested in her *Gone with the Wind* collectibles—porcelain statues of Scarlett O'Hara, Miz Melanie and Rhett Butler, with a collection of china painted with scenes from the movie behind them: Tara before and after the war, Rhett carrying Scarlett up the stairs, the burning of Atlanta. She chatted on about it all, wondering if this investigator knew she had her net out to catch a cop—the head honcho around here. And then, the other shoe dropped.

"I'd like to ask you where you were the evening of the first fire, about 7:00 p.m. on Saturday, May 22," Nate said, looking up from her small painting of the Tarleton twins with Scarlett on Tara's portico from the opening scene of the movie.

Ray-Lynn's stomach flip-flopped. Could he know somehow? She hadn't seen anyone else there that evening. What if Jack found out that she hadn't told him? What if the Kauffmans, Sarah, got wind of what she had planned?

Slowly, she swirled the tea in her glass. "I suppose someone saw me on Bishop Esh's property," she said, trying to sound matter-of-fact. "I was fixing to ask him if I could get permission to have one of Sarah's quilt squares painted on the front of the restaurant, but he wasn't home, so I just admired her painting there on his barn. I could use the extra oomph of the publicity, you see, and I'm not afraid I'd be an arson target here in town near the sheriff's office. Don't you think the arsons are targeting Amish leaders rather than her lovely art?"

When he didn't comment but just studied her, she rushed on. "I've already asked Bishop Esh if Sarah could paint a mural inside the restaurant. I didn't get anywhere with that but thought I would try my luck with a quilt square."

"Sarah mentioned you encouraged her art, even thought she had a style like Grandma Moses."

"She's very talented. I have a friend who runs an art gallery in Columbus in the Short North area, specializing in naive art—that is, paintings by untrained but talented artists, often rural, often somewhat primitive in style. Since you're from there, you surely know how arty that area is. If you saw Sarah's sketchbook she's kept for years—drat, I forgot it's supposed to be a secret—but you'd be amazed."

"So you looked at her quilt square on the barn and left."

"Oh—I did open the barn doors and glance inside to see if someone was there, just in case. It seemed dark, but sometimes you can't tell when they just have a lantern. I swear, Amish eyes are more used to darkness than ours."

"And was someone there?"

She hoped her voice sounded steady. It wasn't working to just try to charm and chatter at this man. She was afraid that part of what she was going to admit would get her the wrong kind of attention from Jack as well as from Nate. And if her ultimate plan came out, she could lose everything she'd worked so hard for.

"It was pitch-dark inside, but, as far as I could see, no one was stirring, not even a mouse," she said, and forced a smile. "I hope to talk to the Amish powers-that-be about Sarah's art again, but with all the dreadful goings-on, I just haven't had time, not with packing things to donate for the auction tomorrow and all. I didn't want to bother you or the sheriff since I'd seen nothing amiss there before the barn burned.

I must have just missed the arsonist, though, and that gives me the absolute willies."

His eyes bored into hers.

"I—I'm sorry," she went on. Was she even making sense anymore? "It's just I didn't want any bad PR for the restaurant. I realize I shouldn't have held back, but I didn't want Peter—or Jack Freeman—all upset with me. I was afraid Bishop Esh would resent my request to act as a sort of agent if they'd let Sarah paint—get her in trouble, too, as if she were in on it—but my timing was terrible to go there, and I just figured I should keep quiet."

"You should have come forward. Next time you hear or see anything that could help, don't just say you'll 'think about it tomorrow,' got that?"

"I do—and you've seen the movie."

"My foster mother loves it."

"And you love her, so you sat through it more than once."

"I repeat, next time you know anything about anything, let me know and no stalling. It looks bad."

"Yes, yes, I understand. Thanks for all you're doing for all of us, and keeping an eye on Sarah, too, a close eye."

She wasn't sure if he got the hint that she knew things about him, too, that hadn't been shouted from the rooftops, but he simply nodded and went out. She leaned against the door with shaking knees until he pulled away in the big black vehicle, then went over to clear the table. On her way to the kitchen with the plates, she saw that he must have turned her Scarlett doll to face the china plate of Atlanta burning. Now what in heaven's name was that supposed to mean?

# 15

AS THE AMISH WORKED TOGETHER TO SET UP the auction early Saturday morning, Sarah hurried over to her friend Ella Lantz's Lavender Plain products table to buy several things before the crowd swelled. Already people were parking cars in the adjoining fields, and a sea of black buggies surrounded the scene. Blessedly, the weather was lovely, crisp and clear. The fact that this was the first day of their Memorial Day weekend gave moderns an extra Monday away from work and they might be more eager to shop. Sarah wondered if the arsonist would be here—if it wasn't Jacob.

"I'll take some more shampoo and some of the sachet," she told her longtime friend after a hurried chat. She helped Ella unpack and lay out some of her goods. "Hmm," Sarah said as she picked up a small quilted bag of the sweet-smelling sachet, "I see you've included a note here that this can keep moths away. If I was a moth, it would draw me right in."

"You probably can't tell, but I've mixed in some rue," Ella explained. "I just didn't want to be selling things that weren't purposeful."

"Oh, right," Sarah said. It was back to that again, she groused silently, but perhaps Ella hadn't intended it as a criticism of her barn paintings. No, she was just getting too sensitive about that, but what if the arsonist was targeting her work? As she hurried back toward the table with her father's birdhouses, which she had promised to mind for a while, she felt she was being watched. And then she saw she was.

Nate had arrived and was looking her way, though he just waved and didn't come over but kept pacing at the periphery of the activities. She saw him walk in, then out, of the schoolhouse like a security guard, which, of course, her people would never hire. Well, she told herself as she settled in with her box of coins and small bills for change, she and Nate weren't the only ones nervous today. Sheriff Freeman had been here from the beginning, talking to the Amish men who would guide the cars in, looking around everywhere as if he could spot some criminal in the crowd. Even the Amish, who trusted all things to the Lord, were on edge. This was an important day, one that should make them all joyous instead of jumpy.

*Daad* had left a disappointed Gabe behind in the house with a loaded hunting rifle, though he promised to relieve him just after noon. Mr. Miller, who was unloading sacks of rhubarb next to their buggy, had said he'd left his boy Noah in their barn with orders to repair the loft floor and keep an eye on the place, even though it was broad daylight. Mr. Hostetler, too, who had a painting on his barn, had someone watching it during the night since the arsonist had struck in the dark. It was sad and scary, Sarah thought as she made her first sale of a birdhouse, that her quilt squares were starting to serve as hex signs, not ones that kept disaster away but attracted it.

★ ★ ★

Nate had surveilled the entire area, amazed at the variety of things for sale, everything from baked goods to beautifully crafted oak, cherry and maple furniture pieces, which he'd expected, to farm machinery, which he hadn't. He walked the rows of plows, spotted an antique-looking McCormick-Deering tractor and two types of machines he didn't recognize. Reuben Schrock told him they were corn binders and manure spreaders. Yard tools, new and used, were propped along the east side of the schoolhouse, some with prices, the rest waiting for bids to be written on their tags. Buggies, four wagons and a sleigh vied for places with bales of hay—or was it straw?

Meanwhile, both men and women prepared booths or tables that would sell every kind of what the Amish called "eats," such as ice cream, popcorn balls and submarine sandwiches, not to mention preparations for lunch—no, Sarah had said they called it dinner. Five hundred pounds of chicken would soon be cooking on smoking grills that were being set up. He'd only had half-moon pies and coffee in VERA this morning, and his stomach rumbled.

The hand-lettered signs that boys were pounding in the ground promised dinner starting at 11:00 a.m. It would consist of chicken, noodles or mashed potatoes, green beans, dressing, gravy, coleslaw and dinner rolls with a piece of either rhubarb cream pie or oatmeal pecan pie, iced tea or pop included. Rather than a price being posted, the meal was available for "a kindly donation."

Random items for sale included Ben Kauffman's birdhouses and made-to-order gazebos, various handcraft goods and even Ella Lantz's lavender items, which wafted out a cloud of fragrance that reminded him of Sarah. Strangely, the scent made his mouth water more than the sight of the food. Cute little kids toddled freely around, most barefoot, dressed like miniatures of their parents, while kids of elementary school age clustered around the playground's volleyball net, swings and slide.

Nate had also checked out the interior of the schoolhouse. It was hard to believe that at the end of the first decade of the twenty-first century, the school was a one-room building with a cloakroom and a potbellied stove. Not a TV screen or laptop in sight. It made him feel even more that he'd stepped back into pioneer days. The schoolroom was hung with quilts on clotheslines along the four walls, stretched from blackboard to blackboard or just hung over dowels between stacks of cinder blocks.

He'd talked briefly to the sheriff as he made his rounds. Jack reported that Jacob had paced in his cell most of the night but had eaten a good breakfast. They were awaiting a visit from Jacob's parents this morning, so Mr. and Mrs. Yoder were probably the only people from the area not coming today.

Many Amish nodded to Nate, said his name in passing or gave him a smile. Strange how that warmed him, not only to be accepted but to feel somehow included. Since he didn't want to call attention to himself, he slipped out back behind the two school outhouses and the rented Porta-John facilities to make a second phone call on his cell. Earlier, he'd talked to his boss, Mark Lincoln, to give him an update of Jacob Yoder's arrest. He told Mark that Jack Freeman was getting a search warrant for Jacob's car and single rented room in West Salem, a small town where the sheriff had made the arrest.

Mark had asked him how sure he was that Yoder was the

arsonist, and he'd told him truthfully, "On the evidence, about seventy percent. On my gut, about twenty percent."

Mark had urged him to pull out all the stops to solve the arsons, which were getting higher profile by the day, thanks to news agencies and online servers picking up some of Peter Clawson's headlines and photos. Amish Barn Arsons Could Be Religious Hate Crimes was sure to bring in more outsiders to this auction today as would Plain People Targeted by Barn Burner. Was there a Pulitzer Prize for Peter Clawson in the future? Maybe.

"M.E., it's me," Nate said when his foster mother answered her phone.

"Nathan, so good to hear from you. You're all right, aren't you? Did you catch that barn arsonist? There are lots of stories about it in the newspaper here. Are you taking time to eat all right? I still think you're too thin."

"Are you kidding? I'm gaining weight the way everyone feeds me here, and you should see the spread they have today."

She had a hundred questions of concern. He usually called her on Sundays. She was seventy-four, and her health had not been the best lately. After seeing how tenderly the Kauffmans looked after their matriarch, Nate felt guilty he didn't see her more.

"As for the arsonist," he told her, "I'm still working on it, but you know what they say about all work and no play. I'm at an Amish sale and auction, and I just saw your birthday gift—a handmade quilt, but I'm not sure what colors you'd like."

He knew he'd better not tell her how much the quilts were likely to go for. A factory-made quilt from Wal-Mart or Sears was more her style. He thought he'd like to buy one of those beautiful pieces for himself, too—well, he'd rather have a painting by Sarah, but he didn't dare ask—and he wanted to contribute to the rebuilding of the Esh and Schrock barns.

"Blues, greens and golds would be lovely," M.E. said. He'd never been able to call her "Mother," and she understood that. So Mrs. Bosley had become Mary Ellen and then M.E. over the years. "You know," she went on, "I'd like for you to take me up there someday to see the area, after your work there is done—I mean, if you would just take a few days off."

"I hope we can do that. Okay, blues, greens and golds. I'll keep that in mind."

"Nathan, what are we going to do when I can't get out as easily to meet you somewhere? I know you don't like coming here, but what will we do? Even with this knee replacement, I'm just not as spry as I was when Jim and I were chasing after you."

"I'll talk to you later about that. It will all work out."

"I'm not moving out of this house I love. I've told you that before and I mean it. My married life and rearing you, my dear boy, all happened here, and they'll have to carry me out feetfirst."

"I know. I—I gotta go, but I'll talk to you soon. I—I love you, M.E."

He returned his cell to its case on his belt and went back into the schoolhouse to see if there was a quilt with blues, greens and golds.

Sarah saw that Peter Clawson had a camera with a huge lens. It must be one of those cameras where the photographer could stand back a ways yet get close-up pictures. When her father came from where the men were barbecuing chicken for the big feed—picnic tables were being set up near the playground—and took over selling his birdhouses, she went a roundabout way to where Peter was taking long-distance shots from the side field.

"Sarah, how's the birdhouse biz?" he asked when he saw her coming.

"Doing fine. How's the newspaper biz?"

"Hate to say it, but the arsons and the Amish make fascinating reading both here and outside the Homestead area."

"I happened to be talking to Mike Getz and thought, since he spotted the second fire, you might want a picture of him from where he saw it."

"I already used one of him with the lead article on the first fire."

"Just a thought. It's terrible to sound as if we're numbering the fires, isn't it?"

"You mean, like we're waiting for the next one—third time's a charm? You see, Sarah," he went on, crossing his arms over the top of his big-lens camera, "that's the thing that's pulling people in to read about these crimes. The contrast between the charm of Amish country—including your quilt paintings—and the obscene outrage of burned barns. You have to admit that your artwork might be helping some sicko decide which buildings to burn. I'd bet on it. Though now that your family's going to have one, too, you must not agree you're tempting fate."

"You know the Amish don't believe in betting or in fate, Mr. Clawson," she said, and went back into the crowd to help set up the tables for dinner. But what he'd said scared her more than ever.

Sarah saw that Ray-Lynn was helping set up, too, opening folding chairs. Way before eleven, a line of folks waiting to eat wound around the grills and serving tables. Sarah ended up dishing out a choice of mashed potatoes or noodles while, with clear plastic gloves on her hands, Ray-Lynn added a dinner roll to each plate as people passed down the line.

Mike Getz and Cindee Kramer passed through as well as numerous other locals she knew, but lots she didn't. Both Amish and *Englische* seemed to see the women serving as part of a fast-food machine, because time after time, they discussed things as if they weren't there.

"Do you believe these fires around here?" one woman asked another. "Wasn't there a Hallmark Hall of Fame TV special with Patty Duke that had something about Amish fires? You know, the actress that played that deaf and dumb girl, Helen Keller?"

"They must think we're deaf and dumb, the way they carry on," Ray-Lynn muttered as the women moved on to the dessert table.

"Welcome to being Amish with outsiders discussing your ways in front of you as if you only understand German," Sarah whispered. "Potatoes or noodles," she asked the next person and dished out potatoes.

"It's just like in the restaurant," Ray-Lynn said. "You wouldn't believe the things I sometimes overhear. We live in an in-your-face world, Sarah, not to say people don't still have deep, dark secrets. So, does Nate think Jacob's behind everything?"

"I haven't spoken to Nate since he interviewed him. Potatoes or noodles?"

"Ever think you'd like to paint this busy scene?" Ray-Lynn asked. For once Sarah wished she'd just shut up and serve. It was too much to keep her mind on this work, listen to Ray-Lynn, skim the crowd for Nate and worry about someone possibly coming through the line who burned barns.

Wishing another server would step up to take her place, Sarah didn't even bother looking up anymore. "Potatoes or noodles?" she recited.

"Noodles, please, Sarah."

Her hand jerked, and her heartbeat kicked up. She almost put a heaping spoonful of noodles on Nate's coleslaw instead of next to it.

"How is your day going?" Sarah asked him as Ray-Lynn popped a roll on his plate.

"I hope to buy a quilt for my foster mother," he said. "Thanks. You, too, Ray-Lynn."

And he moved on. He ended up sitting with Bishop Esh, no less, but it made Sarah nervous that he could look straight at her, which he did. Whenever she could grab a glimpse between moving heads in the line, it seemed he was staring at her.

"He cares about you," Ray-Lynn said out of the side of her mouth.

"Not a possibility. He cares about solving the arsons. And speaking of caring, how is your I-don't-care campaign going with you-know-who?"

"Better, but he's married to his work, too."

On it went in a blur—plates, people, food and worries… and disappointment when Nate left the table where she could see him and disappeared into the crowd again.

Nate could not believe the bidding for the quilt he had his eye on was going so high. Five hundred and twenty-five bucks already with four people still holding up their hands off and on. At least it was going to a great cause.

Reuben Schrock himself was the auctioneer, and he was good at it, his voice rolling along in rhythm like a stick stuck in the spokes of a wheel. It was ironic that some of the money earned here today would go to help the Amish rebuild Schrock's barn, after enough was taken out for the Esh barn.

Ray-Lynn was one of the bidders upping the ante on the quilt, so she was obviously finished with dishing out food. That meant Sarah might be free, too. He'd been tempted to seek her out, but he should save it for later. Why be seen talking to her here with hundreds of people around?

"Five hundred fifty!" Nate called out.

The quilt was amazing with its cream background and interlocking rings of blues, greens and golds. When it was introduced, he'd learned the pattern was called Wedding Ring.

He figured M.E. would like that name. She'd really loved her husband and still missed him. To have a love like that... but to be able to include a foster son in her life. Nate seldom thought of having kids of his own, but he wanted that, didn't he? It's just that he'd never found the right woman, especially since he'd buried himself in his work....

"Six hundred from the lady over in the corner, Mrs. Logan from the restaurant. So do I hear six hundred fifty? An-a do I hear six hundred and fifty for this Wedding Ring quilt, a-going once, a-going twice..."

Nate looked over at Ray-Lynn. Was she hanging tough with this because he'd caught her holding back information? Her gaze caught his and she frowned as if to dare him to bid more.

"Six hundred and fifty for a beautiful quilt and a good cause!" Nate called out.

That seemed to bring the bidding to an end. The crowd buzzed. He heard his name once or twice and the hissing sounds of the whispered word *arsons*. He went toward the front to write a check and get his quilt, when he had a crazy idea. Maybe he could get Sarah to paint this same design and give M.E. both the painting and the quilt for her upcoming seventy-fifth birthday. Women liked decorations in their house to match and go together, didn't they? Besides, if he was going to keep Sarah safe from involvement in the arson case—and involvement with him would only hurt her—he needed some excuse to have a little time with her. Or was that really dangerous thinking?

After Nate stowed his plastic-wrapped quilt in the back of VERA, he stood and watched a game called eckball. Kids stood in corners of a laid-out square about half the size of a baseball diamond and tried to hit people milling around inside with something they called a mush ball. Evidently, anyone who got hit had to get out, until only the winner was left.

That's what he had to do, he told himself. Keep tossing lobs at possible perps until only the arsonist was left, and he had to do it before disaster struck again. At least he had a good handle now on who the candidates for the arsons were, unless it was someone from out in left field. If he could not discover who it was, he had to find ways to eliminate who it wasn't, but he couldn't lock up everyone until the arsons stopped. Sarah had helped him get to know people here, introduced him to the culture during the one week he'd been here, but he had his feet on the ground enough now that he didn't need her. At least, that's what he kept trying to tell himself.

He went back to the eating area; Sarah, her older sister, Lizzie, and Ray-Lynn were among the women wiping off the tables nearby now that the food line was closed. He hoped the "kindly donations" requested for the hearty and delicious food brought in a ton of money. He'd put in twenty bucks for his meal, amazed at the Amish attitude that people would give more money than if charged a specific price.

"I'd like to help clean up," Nate told Levi Miller, who seemed to be heading up the men's work.

The man nodded and handed him a wooden brush with metal bristles. "Pitch right in a'scraping, then dump water on it. Promised to go relieve my boy Noah, so he can come for a bit, but think I let him down. He's upset today 'cause Jacob Yoder was a buddy of his, and he heard he tried to hurt Sarah Kauffman and got locked up for the arsons."

News sure traveled fast on the Amish grapevine, Nate thought. "He was questioned about the arsons, but he's being held on lesser charges right now," he explained.

"I'll tell Noah. And take him a good if cold dinner and hope he got some of those repairs on the loft floor done."

"Since I fell through, I'd be happy to help pay for supplies."

"No need. Real glad you weren't hurt and aren't trying to sue us like some moderns would."

A modern, Nate told himself, feeling as if cold water had been thrown in his face. He might feel a certain camaraderie with these people, but he was a modern, an *ausländer,* or outsider as they liked to say. And suddenly that made him very sad.

Nate kept a good eye on the heaped pile of silvery, glowing embers discarded from the grills as he helped scrape stuck meat and sauce from them, then poured buckets of water on some if they had to be loaded back in buggies right away for the trip home. Some grill owners had chores to do, especially the dairy farmers who had to see to milking. Mike Getz, even one-handed, came over to pitch in, which impressed Nate until he saw why. Peter Clawson was starting to take photos of their efforts to put the grill fires out. Like the Amish men, Nate turned away from the camera and bent over his work. Mike maneuvered to get his face in the shot.

The next grill was really black and hot; the water Nate poured on it hissed and sent up smoke, gray and wispy against the clear blue, late-afternoon sky. The plume of smoke seemed not to stop but drifted and curled into distant clouds.

No, that was not this smoke he saw.

His stomach tightened. He grabbed Levi Miller's arm as he walked by with a box of food, no doubt for his son.

"Mr. Miller, see that smoke in the sky?" he said, pointing. "Could someone be burning trash? What could that be?"

The horrified look on the man's face said it all.

"My place!" he cried as others came to look and point, too. "Have the sheriff call in the volunteers! Someone find and tell my wife!" Levi thrust the box into Nate's hands and was off at a run toward the buggies.

"Wow, where there's smoke, there's fire," Nate heard Mike Getz say.

But not an arson, please, God, not an arson in broad daylight, Nate prayed as he ran toward VERA while others ran to find the sheriff. Not with Jacob in jail and the rest of his suspects—except for Hannah Esh—right under his nose.

"Mr. Miller!" Nate shouted. "Your buggy's too slow. Come with me!"

# 16

SARAH WAS WATCHING NATE WHEN HE AND THE men spotted the distant smoke. When she saw Mr. Miller run for his buggy, she moved away from the schoolhouse so she could see the sky. Oh, no! If not at the Millers' place, near it. At least there was not much wind today to fan the flames. And a fire in daylight—not at night?

She got to Mrs. Miller just after Reuben Schrock told her about the smoke. "But, if that's our place, Noah's in the barn!" she cried, then pressed both hands over her mouth. She looked as if she'd collapse.

Sarah held her up by one elbow. "If we can't catch your husband, you can go with me," she told her as Mr. Schrock supported her other arm.

"Where is Levi?" the woman asked.

"Somewhere in the line of buggies and cars heading out," Sarah said, scanning the area. "I don't see him now, but I do see a way."

She let Mrs. Miller lean on Mr. Schrock and ran to the schoolhouse lane just as Nate pulled VERA out of the field still crowded with departing, slow-moving buggies and cars. Four cars and several buggies blocked him from being able to get out on the road. Suddenly, from VERA came a rhythmic, loud croak like the honk of a goose. As the buggies pulled off to the side to let Nate through and the cars tried to get out of the way, Sarah and Mr. Schrock hurried Mrs. Miller toward VERA.

Once they were close enough, Sarah saw that Mr. Miller sat in the cab with Nate. As they hustled Mrs. Miller closer, she seemed to drag her feet until she saw her husband in the big black truck.

"Mrs. Miller's going, too!" Sarah shouted to Nate through his open window.

"Make it fast and secure the door once you're in!"

Her heart pounded. She was going to this fire with Nate, too. The sheriff's car, which had been parked along the road, sped away with its lights pulsing and shrill siren sounding loudly enough to drown out VERA's lower one.

Peter Clawson appeared, out of breath, red-faced, still toting his big-lens camera. "What's that smoke from?" he shouted at Nate, then saw who sat next to him. "Millers? Can I go, too? You owe me big-time, MacKenzie, and turnabout's fair play!"

She didn't hear what Nate told him, but Peter ran around in back, too. It seemed an eternity to Sarah as she and Mr. Schrock got the trembling woman in the back of the vehicle and both climbed in with her. Peter managed to get in without help. While Mr. Schrock closed and latched the back doors, Sarah ran to the small front window to the cab and rapped her knuckles on it. "Go! Go!"

The traffic ahead must have cleared, because they careered out onto the road. The four of them in back grabbed for handholds. Sarah sat Mrs. Miller down in the single chair at the narrow table. Sarah and Mr. Schrock sat on the floor, wedged in, while Peter put his equipment on the floor but stood looking around inside VERA.

Sarah was soon back on her feet, propping herself up between the table and the counter. No wonder things inside here were all bolted down or stowed away. The once-familiar roads outside the front windshield she could peek through between Nate's and Mr. Miller's heads went by in a blur.

It annoyed Sarah that Peter began to question Mrs. Miller, so she told him, "Have a heart."

With a little shrug, he said, "But I have a head, too, and you know this fire doesn't fit the pattern. The decorated barn does, of course, but not the timing."

When no one answered him, he went back to eyeing the carefully labeled drawers and shelves. No doubt, Sarah thought, there would soon be a newspaper article on Nate's vehicle. But what did Peter mean that Nate owed him big-time and turnabout was fair play? She didn't like the way he'd called the barn she'd painted "decorated."

At least in the rush of things, Nate hadn't had time to argue about her going along. He'd said he wanted her off the arson case, but here she was, of course with her own finagling. If it was the Miller barn, if it was arson, didn't that prove Jacob wasn't the arsonist?

"Can you see the smoke through that little window, Sarah?" Mrs. Miller asked. "It can't be our place, our barn. Not in broad daylight, not with Noah there."

"Noah?" Peter said. "You mean someone was supposed to be protecting the barn?"

Mr. Schrock spoke, his voice shaking, but he addressed Mrs. Miller, not Peter. "Levi said Noah was doing repairs in the loft. Was it so dark he'd take a lantern up there? Is there hay or straw around?"

"Hay and lots of it," Sarah said, before she realized she should have let Mrs. Miller answer. "We're on your road now," she reported. "I see the sheriff's car way ahead, but we're going to beat the firemen."

"Minus two of them," Mr. Schrock said. "Mike Getz is on leave and Levi's with us. We'll do what we can."

Sarah could see now that it was the Miller place—and the Miller barn. She wasn't sure whether to tell Mrs. Miller or let her see it for herself when she'd have her husband to comfort her. But better forewarned, she thought. She'd want to know to prepare herself for the worst, if it was her family's barn.

"We're almost to your house, Mrs. Miller. I see a lot of smoke but not many flames coming from the barn. Let's pray Noah is waiting outside the barn to help fight the fire, too."

Nate was furious. He had not been sure he had an arsonist locked up, but he had been sure he had definite suspects, knew a profile of the criminal and had figured out his M.O. But this—if it was arson, and the barn and painted quilt square said it was—blew all his work away. Once he checked out Hannah Esh's alibi for this blaze, if she had a solid one, he had nothing. Yoder was in jail and everyone else was at the auction, including Ray-Lynn Logan, his long-shot possibility. He'd thought solving these Amish arsons would be a walk in a pretty park. What an idiot!

"I don't see Noah," Levi said as Nate turned into the yard and parked close to the house. Sheriff Freeman was there, his light bar blinking as red as the few flames that were visible. He was walking around the barn with his gun drawn.

Nate didn't hit the digital electronic siren again but laid on

his horn to see if that would bring Noah from the house or
barn. The sheriff probably didn't know there was a missing
person here. Levi was out of the truck, running for the burning barn. Nate jumped out as Peter Clawson climbed down
from the back, then Reuben Schrock and Sarah climbed out
with Mrs. Miller between them. Nate knew he'd broken
protocol. No civilians in the way during an active fire, certainly none packed in the back of VERA, but the Amish had
changed him. He saw Mrs. Miller hurry toward the house
while Reuben ran over to fill in the sheriff.

"Do you want your fire gear again?" Sarah shouted to
Nate. "I can get it ready."

"Yes! Good!"

She turned back toward VERA. What would he do without her—ever—a voice in Nate's head shouted at him.

Both of the Millers were screaming, "Noah! Noah!
Noah!" Mrs. Miller was yelling into the front door of the
house, and Levi toward the barn. Nate could see he was
heading to slide open the big front doors, which were,
strangely, both closed. Sarah's Crown of Thorns painting
in blue, green and gold—M.E.'s colors—seemed to writhe
behind the pall of drifting smoke.

"Don't open those doors, or the air will fan the flames!"
the sheriff shouted at Levi before Nate could. "Right now,
it looks contained at the back, high up, maybe still mostly
smoldering."

"Wet wood and wet hay from leaks in the roof," Nate
shouted. "I checked it out on Thursday. But when the flames
eat down to the dry stuff, it will really go."

The fact the fire was high up, Nate thought, was like the
first fire, and this barn was built somewhat like the Esh one,
despite the fact it was much older and run-down. And, like

at the Esh fire, a ladder lay on the ground, next to the barn that he hadn't seen there two days ago. He had to get geared up and go inside to see if Noah had been knocked out or was down from smoke inhalation. That could be as deadly as the flames.

"Is there a first floor door in back, like the Esh barn?" Nate asked Levi and the sheriff as he held the Amish man's arm to keep him from lunging at the doors. Once he and Sarah had seen that painted note and the torrents of rain began, they had not made a complete circuit of the structure, nor had he when he came out with Levi. He knew now he should have.

"*Ya,* a door, but it's got years of vines all over it, sealed shut. What if he fell and bumped over a lantern while he was working? Fell in the loft like you did? Noah! Nooo-aaaah! I should have stayed with him! Nooo-aaah!"

Sarah was dragging Nate's fire gear over to the edge of the yard just a few feet from them, laying it out in order just as he had learned to do in fire school. The woman was amazing.

Then, they heard someone scream.

They all froze, looking at one another, listening for the muted sounds over the increasing crackle of roof flames. "Those great horned owl nestlings?" Sarah asked, cocking her head. But then the scream became not an *eeeeeee* sound but *"Help meeeee!"*

The sheriff ran back to his vehicle for something. Levi lunged for the barn doors, and Nate let him as he dragged his heavy fire pants up, pulling the suspenders over his shoulders. On her knees before him, Sarah untied his running shoes and yanked them off and shoved his boots toward him, so he could jam his feet into them. She thrust Nate's heavy jacket at Reuben Schrock; he held it for him as he shrugged it on.

As Nate moved under the weight of it toward the barn, Sarah held out his hood, then his oxygen mask, for him.

Levi had one door partially open. The heat blast from the barn smacked them, even thirty feet away. Smoke belched out, blinding them as Reuben grabbed Levi to keep him from running inside. Like a harbinger of doom, the barn owl flew out past them with a whoosh of its huge wings. Mrs. Miller lifted and clasped her apron to her face, not to stop the stench of smoldering wood and hay, but to wipe away tears so she could see.

Nate jolted as a deep, loud voice behind him said, "Noah Miller, are you inside the barn? Noah, this is the sheriff. Where are you?"

The sheriff had brought out his bullhorn.

"Help me!" Noah called weakly from within.

Nate adjusted his oxygen mask and turned on the flow. He heard only his own breath. His Amish superwoman handed his hat and gloves to him. As Reuben held Levi back from plunging into the heat and smoke, Nate took the big flashlight she held out to him and walked into the burning barn.

Sarah moved and talked as if something within her had taken over. She blinked back tears from fear as well as from the stinging smoke. How could Nate so much as see in there? He'd said sometimes firemen found victims by crawling on the floor or by stumbling over them. The place where they'd kissed and caressed had become an inferno, and if Noah was trapped in there...

She remembered how Noah used to follow Jacob around. He was younger, but somehow they'd hit it off at school—or had that been at Lizzie's wedding? Jacob had the answers for everything then, and Noah had been thrilled when Jacob gave him attention, got him a job sweeping up and greasing axels at the Buggy Wheel Shop. She was grieving to think that another Amish barn with one of her paintings was going up in flames, but a life was much more precious.

Then she remembered the window high up. Nate had tried to look out of it during the storm, hoping to see what was making the knocking sound or even get a glimpse of someone who'd left that note on the barn.

The sheriff had gone back to his car. Sarah left the Millers and Reuben Schrock as they waited and prayed for Noah and Nate. Around the side of the barn, she saw the flames, and the worst of the black smoke roaring through the broken roof seemed to be on the other side. It was probably too smoky inside to see much, but she could try looking in through that high window.

When she ran around the barn, she saw the sheriff had driven out on the road and had left his car there with the light bar blinking. He was jogging back toward the barn after setting up orange cones to stop traffic coming from the direction of the freeway, but he'd left open the way from town. Peter was standing back a ways, photographing the burning barn. The flames from the roof reflected in his huge lens as if his camera was on fire. Where were those firefighters? It seemed she'd been here hours, but it was probably mere minutes.

Because she didn't want to pull the Millers away from their vigil, nor have Mr. Schrock tell her she shouldn't try this, she picked up only the far end of the ladder and dragged it around the corner and under the window. She was good at setting up ladders against barns, at managing her skirts as she climbed the rungs. She beat down horrible memories of her nightmare of being burned, tied to a ladder. She had to try this without the others seeing her.

When she got up to the level of the window, she saw her idea was useless. Smoke boiled inside, bubbling to get out. But when Noah screamed again, he sounded so close, as if he was just on the other side of the glass. That meant Noah was in the loft! If she could break this window, could he crawl out here? Firemen on ladders made rescues from windows. Nate surely couldn't climb that flimsy ladder they'd used inside to get to the loft, not in that heavy gear of his.

"Help me!" she screamed. "Back here!"

Peter hurried around and began to take pictures of her up on the ladder. Sheriff Freeman ran around the corner of the barn right behind him and yelled, "What in the Sam Hill are you doing, girl! Get down from there!"

"I can hear Noah close to here! I think he's trapped in the loft. If you have something to break the window, maybe we can pull him out here!"

Mr. Miller came, too, and started to climb the ladder, before the sheriff pulled him back. "Get down, Sarah, and I'll try to break the glass with this gun handle. Get down and let me up!"

Something inside the barn gave way and the few flames eating through the roof roared higher, slapping them all with heat and light. Sarah scrambled down and the sheriff climbed up, quickly shattering at least one windowpane with the butt of his gun while Mr. Miller and Sarah held the ladder and Peter's camera clicked madly away. Mrs. Miller watched in horror.

Sarah saw the sheriff duck as smoke roiled at him like a black fist. If anything happened to Jack Freeman, Ray-Lynn would probably kill her. But if anything happened to Nate, Sarah could almost see killing herself.

"Noah! Noah Miller, you hear me?" the sheriff shouted.

Despite the gush of smoke, he yelled directly in the window, then called down to them, "Says he's trapped, half hanging down from the loft! Scared to drop down. You go tell Nate! I think he was coming back out."

"He can't hear a thing with that oxygen mask on!" Sarah shouted. "Tell Noah he has to let go before the hay under him catches fire! Nate can help him if he'll just drop to the first floor!"

The sheriff relayed what she had said back to Noah. She knew Noah didn't have long before the hay in the ground level would be aflame and roast him to death, like chicken on those grills today, if smoke didn't kill him first. It seemed to be chokingly thick even out here as she ran around to see if Nate had come out yet. Maybe when someone was being burned, the best to hope for was smoke suffocation. Maybe those Amish martyrs years ago could breathe in the smoke and not have to suffer from the flames. She pictured herself and Nate, hanging, caught halfway. No fire then, only the one between them.

Yes, thank God, Nate was outside. But now she'd have to send him back in. Finally, she heard the wail of the distant fire truck sirens coming closer. Should she wait for them and not tell Nate? But Noah could be dead by then.

She got in Nate's face—his mask, that is—and tried to gesture to him about Noah. Noah in the loft, caught, just like us. Noah's father almost ran inside before his wife held to him hard. Again, she ignored Peter's camera almost in their faces.

Sarah thought Nate nodded. At least he lumbered back

inside and, in what seemed an eternity, came out dragging Noah with his shoes and trousers tattered and mostly burned off. The skin from his torso looked blistered and his legs blackened and—and loose. Hefting him by his arms so only his feet dragged, Nate and the sheriff laid him gently on the grass, at least forty feet back from the barn. He screamed once as they set him down, twisted in agony, then lay still.

Sarah and Reuben Schrock had to hold the Millers back from touching him, even his head and upper torso, which didn't look so ravaged. Sheriff Freeman got on his phone; Sarah could hear him telling someone at his office to call for MedFlight and talking about the Cleveland Clinic. Noah started hacking up black spit and gasping for air.

Nate pulled his head gear off. "No—don't cover him, either!" he told Mrs. Miller as she took off her apron and knelt next to her son. "Don't touch him, or his skin will come off. It's bad enough I had to drag him, but the hay was going to go."

The barn suddenly roared as scarlet and orange flames battled with the billowing smoke. Nate knelt next to the burned boy and put the oxygen mask over his nose and mouth. "Breathe, Noah. Breathe, breathe," he recited as Noah started to suck in the air. Sarah knew his lungs could be damaged.

Sheriff Freeman finally told Peter to get away, and he did, turning his attention to the firemen fighting with the flames. Though the volunteers worked feverishly to douse them, those around Noah Miller hardly looked away as the boy fought for his life.

# 17

AN ENDLESS HALF HOUR WENT BY AS NATE kept Noah breathing rich oxygen and the volunteer firemen fought the blaze. Nate could recall vivid details of the moments the Columbus firemen had pulled him from his burning house. One of them had put his oxygen mask over his mouth and nose that day until the emergency squad arrived. He tried to shut out those haunting memories, but concentrating on the here and now was terrible, too.

With whispered prayers, the Millers and Sarah knelt around them in a little circle, as if to protect Noah when that wasn't possible anymore. They could see he was suffering, gasping for breath, even with the flow of oxygen. He moaned but did not move. Nate knew that third-degree burns over fifty percent of the body would be fatal. Noah's legs were definitely third-degree with peeling flesh, but his torso seemed second degree with blisters. The smell, not only of smoke, but of burned flesh was stomach-churning.

Nate sent Sarah over to the sheriff, who was helping the firefighters, to suggest he put up more orange cones to stop traffic both ways on the road. "Tell him to signal the medical helicopter to land there, instead of near the barn. We can't have the fire fanned by the wash from the chopper's rotors coming too close."

A few minutes later, the helicopter landed out on the road in a whirl of air and noise. When the two flight nurses—one man, one woman—rushed toward them, pushing their gurney up the dirt lane from the road, Nate identified himself and helped them lift Noah onto it. He followed along to the helicopter and watched as they switched Noah to their oxygen supply and started IVs. It helped to learn that one of them was a burn specialist. They said one person could accompany the patient. The Millers decided Noah's mother would go.

As frail as she looked, Nate admired how Mrs. Miller had held up in the face of all this, even better than Levi. He felt for them, felt he knew them, after all he had been through with his own family. Sarah had said Mrs. Miller had nearly collapsed at first, but he'd seen her come through strong when Levi almost lost control. His mother would have been like that—if she had lived.

"Nate, you okay?" the sheriff asked. "Soon as I get this traffic moving again and not just gawking, I'm going to get someone to drive Mr. Miller and Reuben Schrock to the hospital in Cleveland."

Nate nodded. He should volunteer, because then he could go directly to question Hannah Esh again, but Levi and Reuben would need someone who could stay with them for a while. Exhausted, he blinked back tears he wiped away with his filthy hand, realizing for the first time how his eyes watered and stung from the smoke. That was it, wasn't it— just the smoke?

Sarah came up to him with a wet towel. He hadn't seen her for a while, but he realized she must have been helping Mrs. Miller get some things together. As the chopper took off, turned tail and flew away to the north, Nate realized an Amish woman and her son were taking a forbidden airplane ride. When it was necessary, the Amish adapted. If he sided with Ray-Lynn to try to get Sarah a chance to paint, would she be willing?

"Thanks for all your help—again," Nate told Sarah as he wiped his face and hands with the towel.

"You've seen things like this before, Noah's injuries, I mean," she said, her words barely discernible over the noise of the departing chopper. "Do you think he'll make it?"

"I hope—pray—so, but I'm not sure." But he was sure he wanted to question the boy as soon as he could, right after he had a chat with Hannah Esh.

After the fire had burned itself to a tumble of black, charred barn bones, Sarah knew she should leave with some of the Amish who had finally arrived from the auction in buggies. But she left the Miller farm as she'd come, in the back of VERA with her mother with her and no one in the front seat with Nate. She was grateful to have someone Amish here instead of Peter Clawson.

As far as she knew, he was still asking questions and taking pictures back at the Millers'. She, like Nate, had noted that Mike Getz had arrived and was helping fight the fire, one-handed. Ray-Lynn had appeared, too, and was handing out coffee and doughnuts, just as she had the morning after the first fire.

"Isn't this VERA something?" *Mamm* said, looking around wide-eyed. In the deepening dusk, Nate had lit the interior for them, and the chrome and white walls shone. "Looks like a modern kitchen. Oh, I pray Noah will be healed. Did you hear anything those rescue people said?"

Sarah responded to that and *Mamm's* other questions, but nothing seemed to stick in her brain except that three times someone had targeted barns with her paintings on them. It scared her to death that she'd overheard Nate tell the sheriff he was going to question Hannah again. She prayed silently that all this could somehow help bring Hannah home, but the right way, not charged with arson by the man Sarah wanted so to help.

Nate drove up their lane to drop them off at the house, but he turned VERA out toward the road, not the pond, before he got out. Sarah's stomach knotted tighter. Was he going back to the fire or after Hannah right now?

Martha ran from the *grossdaadi haus* and Gabe from the farmhouse to meet them, both full of questions until *Mamm* said that *Daad* would be back in the buggy soon and they would all talk then. Sarah knew Nate was going to drive away before she could talk to him, but his so-called crack-berry sounded and he took the call. As he listened, he looked at Sarah. Everyone stopped talking. Sarah feared Nate might tell them that Noah Miller was dead.

"Okay, just a minute," he told whoever it was.

"Sarah," he said, "Hannah Esh wants to talk to me and insists I bring you along. Will you go with me?"

"*Ya,* but clear to Cleveland?"

"She's parked by the cemetery, just down the road. She says she's been in the area all day."

Sarah gasped and clapped her hand over her mouth. Hannah here all day when nearly everyone else was at the auction? Was she going to confess to the arsons and surrender to Nate so she wanted her old friend there to support her?

Just a week ago, Sarah would have asked for permission to go off with Nate in VERA, but she took her hand down from her mouth and squared her shoulders. "Sure, I'll help—hopefully help Hannah and you."

After Nate told Hannah to stay put and they'd be there soon, *Mamm* told Sarah, "See if you can bring her back here. Tell her we all want her to come home. She can stay here if she needs—you know, needs a place to live halfway home."

Sarah nodded and climbed up in the passenger seat of VERA while Nate got in and closed the driver's side door.

"As I said, I'm really grateful for all your help today, especially after I came down so hard on you before. I just don't want you to get hurt," Nate told her as he drove out of the lane and turned onto the road.

Her voice snagged with emotion. "I want to help." It was unspoken and that simple, but somehow she knew they were working together again. But what would she do without him when this was all over, one way or the other?

"When I was inside the Millers' barn that first time today," he said, "I could see the fire was set from inside, probably from spilled—or poured—kerosene or gasoline, far back in the corner near no windows or doors. That keeps up the pattern of a different incendiary method for each barn burning, but it's hard to believe our clever, careful, after-dark arsonist would set a fire in the lower part of the barn while Noah was using a hammer and saw in the loft. If I don't get a confession here from Hannah…"

"Then you will have no suspects left?"

"We'll see. By the way, Ray-Lynn tells me she's approached you about doing some paintings, not to be sold

around here, but through an art dealer friend of hers in Columbus. She let slip you have a book of sketches she admires."

"*Ya*—yes to both things. But I can't take that step yet and
she knows it."

"Yet? Then you've considered it?"

"Only in my wildest dreams, but I dream about a lot of
things that will never be. Why did you bring that up now?"

"As different as these fires are, besides the common link
of the barns belonging to church leaders, your paintings are
what they all have in common."

"I know. Someone hates me, you think? Nate," she said,
turning in her seat belt to face him, "you don't think that
Ray-Lynn... I mean, I suppose if all my barn paintings were
ruined or I couldn't do more of them, I'd be more ready to
try paintings of Amish life. Or are you thinking the arsonist
might want to draw big-time attention to my art instead of
ruin it? But—"

"Okay, okay, we'll let that go for now, but I'm getting
desperate enough to set some sort of trap at the Hostetler
barn and stop your work on your own barn."

"No, I won't stop. I can vouch for Ray-Lynn just like I
can for Hannah, if you think someone who cares about me
is trying to draw outside attention to my work."

"Some people are not what they seem. I've learned that
the hard way. Besides, you can't vouch for either of them.
You weren't there, weren't with them."

"I know my friends! And that fire demon from hell is not
going to scare us or stop us, not me, not the brethren and
sisters. Let's set a double trap, one at the Hostetlers' place
and one at ours. I know that's what my *daad* is starting to
think now, Bishop Esh, too. There—up ahead, see?" she said,

pointing through the windshield into the deepening dusk. "There's Hannah's car."

As they got out, Hannah appeared, hurrying down the hill from among the simple Amish gravestones. Sarah knew she used to visit her *grossmamm*'s grave a lot. They had been very close, just the way Sarah was—had been—to hers. In VERA's headlights, Sarah could see Hannah's hair was still spiky and red, her black leggings, skirt and top slashed and torn, but she'd toned down the dramatic makeup.

"Wow, that thing's quite a ride!" Hannah said, pointing at VERA. Her light tone surprised Sarah. She didn't sound like someone who was about to confess to arson.

Hannah hugged Sarah, emanating that same incense-smoky smell—not cigarettes—then extended her hand to Nate to shake it. Sarah had to remember to tell Nate that Hannah had smelled like that for over a year, so it was not barn smoke, but her insides twisted tighter. What if Hannah was to blame?

"I was hoping you two would do a big favor for me," Hannah told them. "I don't know who else to ask or trust here, or who would agree."

"Talk," Nate said as Sarah held her breath. She could tell how tense he was. His muscles seemed coiled, as if he'd leap at Hannah.

"I was trying to get up the nerve to come to the auction today," she admitted with a big sigh, "but I just ended up here, walking all over, waiting for you to be free, driving around some. I tried your cell number you gave me a couple of times late afternoon, Mr. MacKenzie, but you weren't answering, and I didn't want to leave voice mail. I even drove past the auction twice, but when I came by a third time, everyone was peeling out. I have one hundred and thirty-five

dollars saved up and I want to donate it—anonymously—to
the fund to rebuild my family's barn. I thought if you took
some of it and Sarah donated some, they'd never realize or
question the source."

"That's why you were hanging around here all day?" Nate
asked as Hannah dug a wad of bills out of her black leather
purse. "Don't you know about the fire at Levi Miller's?"

"I—no. Not another fire!"

"Or that Jacob Yoder's in jail for questioning for the arsons?" he went on, his voice hard. "But unless he lit Miller's
barn from behind bars, it has to be someone else."

For one moment, Sarah thought her friend would turn
and run.

"I—I haven't been online or seen a paper, not even the
*Home Valley News,*" she said, looking panicked. Her gaze
darted from one to the other. "It's not me, if that's what
you're thinking!" She thrust the roll of bills at Sarah. "I came
for this and that's all. I told you before I did not burn my
parents' barn. I came to donate to help rebuild it and I have
nothing against the Schrocks or Millers. All I know about
the Millers is that Noah used to be a friend of Jacob's—you
knew that, Sarah. What? Why is Sarah crying?" she asked
Nate instead of Sarah herself.

"Noah Miller was badly burned in the blaze today and
may not make it," Nate told her.

Hannah gasped. This whole thing was a surprise to her,
Sarah was sure of that. She couldn't be hiding all that guilt,
even though Sarah had seen her hide things from her parents.

"And," Nate went on, "if there's a death from an arson,
that can bring in the FBI and that will make everything
around here ten times tougher—not easier, believe me—for
the Amish and my investigation. Sarah, take your friend's

money so we can donate it for the cause, but we're all going to step inside VERA right now for an in-depth interview about everything you did today, Hannah."

"I didn't do it—anything! And don't start thinking that was a bribe!" Hannah shouted as Sarah took the money in one hand and squeezed her friend's hand with the other.

"Look, Hannah," Nate said, stooping to get right in her face, "I just need answers. I'm not accusing you of anything yet."

*Yet,* Sarah thought. She could feel Hannah trembling, and it vibrated clear through her. Nate showed Hannah a badge he carried in his wallet and explained he had the right to question her either here or at the police station if she preferred to do it there.

Sarah was soon shaking, too. How had this happened that she was helping a government authority, and worse—one she was afraid she was coming to love?

After nearly an hour of what Sarah considered harsh questioning, the same things asked, over and roundabout, from every direction, Nate finally let Hannah get in her car and leave. Her alibis—Nate's word—could not be verified with anyone she'd been with. But Hannah had spoken as passionately as ever, Sarah thought, and she was certain she was telling the truth—she just had to be.

They had tried to talk her into spending the night with Sarah at the *grossdaadi haus,* but she wanted to go home, though Sarah had noted when she said the word *home,* her voice had wavered.

"You know where your home is, really, don't you?" Sarah said to her in German as she hugged her hard. "You come back, stay with us for a while in transition. *Mamm* said so, like the Kauffman place can be your halfway house to really going home. Besides, Seth—"

"Don't talk about him!" Hannah insisted, also in German. "I just can't. Please, Sarah, if you don't have to, don't tell my people Mr. MacKenzie thinks it might be me, because it isn't!"

"I know. I'll work on him."

"I can see you already have," she said. She got in her car and pulled away. Sarah watched the red taillights, like two feral eyes, fade into darkness.

In VERA, going back to the Kauffman farm, Nate said, "Sarah, I'm just trying to clear her, honestly. When you two spoke German, did she say anything that would help?"

"Not help you, nor me and her family because we want her to come home. I trust her, Nate."

"And that goes a long way with me—really. I think your instincts are good."

But a mess lately, she thought, because she wanted to throw herself in his arms the moment he stopped VERA near the *grossdaadi haus*. Leaving the motor running, he hurried around to open the passenger's side door for her this time.

"I heard her say my name in German, but who's Seth?" he pursued. "You mentioned a Seth."

"You have good German ears, *ausländer*. He's the man she thought she'd marry. He—he married someone else."

"He or his wife don't belong to any of the families with the burned barns?"

"No! No. It's a long, sad story."

He walked her to the porch steps. She got the key out from under the pot of newly planted geraniums. Maybe it was because she was just remembering how much Hannah and Seth had once loved each other, but this reminded her of what a come-calling friend would do, walk a *maidal* to her door. And then, there would be a good-night smooch, of course, but she wasn't expecting that now, only wanting it badly.

"Sarah, would you trust me enough to let me see your sketchbook?"

"Sure. I'd be pleased. It's just inside, and I can get it back from you tomorrow."

"I'll need to spend time at the Miller barn, then I'm going to the Cleveland Clinic, hopefully to interview Noah, but I'll see you get it back safe and sound. I know the drawings are wonderful."

While he waited on the porch, she unlocked the door and slipped inside. Deeply touched by what he'd said—it was as if he'd embraced or caressed her with those words—she stood for a moment in the dark, her hands clasped between her breasts. Hannah and Ray-Lynn believed in her work. Now, perhaps Nate would, too.

Her eyes adjusted to the deeper darkness. Martha was asleep, breathing loudly, on the hideaway bed in the living room. Tiptoeing around the bed, Sarah retrieved her sketchbook from the back of the end table drawer where she kept it under her Bible. As she took it out to Nate, she realized she hadn't looked at it for months, maybe since she'd showed it to Ray-Lynn, then refused to show it to that art dealer friend of hers from Columbus. Yet how much it meant to her, precious memories, a dream deferred, the outpourings not only of her hand but of her head and heart.

She gave the book to Nate and leaned back against VERA's warm hood next to him, so close their arms touched. The motor was still running, so she knew he didn't mean to stay long. They were not in the headlights, but enough light reflected that they could see.

"I'll take good care of this," he promised. "My face and hands are the only clean part of me. Time for a dip in the pond."

"You be careful, swimming alone at night."

"Come with me, then."

"I'd better not," she said, but she wanted to go really bad. She watched him open the book to the first sketch, then went to the next, then another. Why was he looking at them so fast? Oh, maybe because she'd not only sketched people but had dared to draw their faces, when that was forbidden. But she couldn't help herself, for that was part of her art. Truly, her love of this place included the faces of those she knew and loved, smiling faces, serious faces, worshipful faces—

"Sarah, I can tell you didn't do these flames, these fires— did you?" he asked.

"Fires? What fires?"

She leaned closer, squinting to see. With a gasp, she grabbed the book from him and bent into the glare of VERA's headlights, flipping through faster, faster, clear to the back of it. On every drawing, in what looked like dried blood, someone had scrawled leaping, streaking flames burning buildings, barns and—and her people.

# 18

SARAH'S KNEES BUCKLED. AS SHE STARTED TO slide down VERA's hood, Nate grabbed her and held her to him, her shoulder under his arm.

"No. No, I never... Who would do this?" she whispered, still fanning through the pages, then just pressing the sketchbook to her breasts as if to comfort all the people inside it.

"And why?" Nate demanded. "Do you think someone could have broken into the *grossdaadi haus,* looking for something else, then saw this? When did you see it last?"

"A couple of months ago. It was hidden. It hurts for me to look at these sometimes."

"Because you want to draw or paint more than that?"

She nodded jerkily.

"It looks like blood."

"I know. Quite a bit of it. I—now I'd have nothing to show an art dealer, anyway."

"Did Jacob ever see the sketches?"

"No."

"Martha or Gabe? Your parents?"

"As far as I know, only Hannah, Ella and Ray-Lynn, but…"

"What?"

"Well, you know my grandmother gets off her bean sometimes over how our people were persecuted and martyred in Europe, burned to death among other torments. It's the reason the Amish came to America. She fears we'll be burned out again and she keeps trying to warn us. What if she found this and did this?"

"I take it she's not working with knives in the kitchen anymore. Does she have any cuts on her?"

"Cuts and bruises. You've seen her, Nate. We try to keep sharp things away now, and she doesn't quilt anymore. But she still dresses herself and we close our bodices with straight pins."

He looked at her breasts, squinting as if to see the pins. She went on in a rush, "I guess a pinprick could make drops of blood to smear like this, but she must have done it time after time."

"Or we're back to someone else who found your art and wanted to warn or punish you because he or she knew it was *verboten*. The art itself and drawing in the faces—right?"

Sarah nodded. As distraught as she was, it touched her that Nate was not only recognizing German words but using them now. And that he'd come to know her people well enough already to realize images of Amish faces were as frowned upon as prideful drawings.

"So you can't ask her if she did this?" he asked.

"I could, but these pictures would upset her. Her copy of the *Martyrs Mirror* has some etchings of Amish being burned, and those haunt her."

"Who knows about that book?"

"All the Amish. It's second only to the Bible for us, and we have a hymnal of song lyrics passed down, too, the *Ausbund*."

"Your grandmother never goes out and around on her own, does she?"

"You don't mean does she wander the nearby fields to ignite barn fires!"

"I mean, if she found this book, wherever you had it stashed, what if she showed it to that person in black she thought she saw."

"I don't think she imagined that anymore, not since I saw someone through your night goggles in the field when the Schrock barn burned. But show it to a stranger while he defaced it—no."

Suddenly, she couldn't keep the sobs inside. Holding the ruined sketchbook to her breasts with one hand, she pressed the other over her eyes. As she sucked in air and her shoulders shook, Nate took the book from her and put it on the hood, then pulled her into his arms. She clung tight to him, crying, shaking both of them. Then, suddenly, he picked her up and sat down on the grass with her sprawled across his lap.

It was dark, though the gold streaks of VERA's headlights still stabbed into the night beyond. She shifted in his lap, turned to him and clung, lifting her face toward his. She meant to tuck her face under his chin, but suddenly his comforting turned crazy, his hands everywhere, his lips on hers, soft at first, then strong, demanding.

Thinking she would explode inside, she met him kiss for kiss, opening her lips to his. Nothing else mattered but his touch, his strength, his need battling with hers. These runaway feelings—*ya*, she'd never known herself before this.

"Sarah, Sarah," was all he said, and then they kissed again, longer and deeper as her arms around his neck held him to her. They sprawled on the soft grass, already wet with dew. Everything bad seemed washed away, all her fears. She would not have cared if the entire world was lost right now, flamed into the fires she was feeling. Dizzy, dazed. Nate. She wanted Nate MacKenzie even more than she wanted to paint.

They jolted apart as they heard her *daad*'s voice, probably from the farmhouse porch, but too close.

"Sarah? Nate? *Mamm* wants to know did Hannah say she'd come back?"

Suddenly bereft of Nate's touch, Sarah stood, settling her skirts. How she found a steady voice she wasn't sure as she walked around the front of VERA where he could see her in the headlights and called to him, "She left. I think she's missing everything here, though."

"A lot can be learned from your old friends Hannah and Jacob," *Daad* called to her, not coming closer. She heard the porch swing. How long had he been sitting there? "They both wanted something away from our people outside the Home Valley and both are unhappy and in real trouble."

Was that a clever warning to her about Nate? About her painting? Did *Daad* think Hannah could be guilty of the arsons?

"I'd better get going," Nate said, keeping his voice low. "Can I take the sketchbook to look at it carefully, maybe run a test on the blood?"

"*Ya,* it's no good to me now—ruined."

"Anyone looking at it carefully could still tell a lot about the artist, the skill, the potential."

"You don't think someone would look at it and think the artist is a pure maniac?"

"Pyromaniac?"

"That's it."

"I think your raw talent shines through. This book would have to actually *be* burned before someone wouldn't see a unique artist at work here."

He walked around the truck cab and got in. Sarah stepped up on the *grossdaadi haus* porch, feeling the lack of him—physical, sure, but emotional, too—the moment he drove away. She could not bear to go speak to her father now, so she went into the *grossdaadi haus* and locked the door behind her.

She tiptoed into the bathroom, hearing her *grossmamm*'s gentle snoring in the next room. Could she have defaced the drawings? It must have been her. If not, since the sketchbook had been hidden, she'd have to start believing in a demon who left damning notes around, where she was sure to find them.

On the way out of the Home Valley the next morning, Nate saw the buggies of Amish families as they headed to church. Services were held in homes or barns every other Sunday, and the Hostetlers were hosts today. All those people—about thirty local families—would gather in the Hostetler barn with Sarah's painting on it with an arsonist loose, one he couldn't catch. He pictured Sarah's sketch of buggies parked around a barn for a church service and the bloody flames someone had smeared across it all.

He wondered if the arsonist would be at church. If so, it wasn't Jacob Yoder, though he was back in the mix of suspects again at least for the first two barn burnings. Could the third have been a copycat arson? At dawn this morning, Sheriff Freeman had served the search warrant to go through Jacob's rented room and car in West Salem, a small town about a half hour away. Nate had just met with the sheriff at his office.

"That third fire makes it look like Jacob's not guilty, but I've got to show you what I found on his bedroom wall," Jack had said, and pointed to a folder he shoved toward Nate across his desk.

Inside were at least ten newspaper articles about the first two fires—pieces of tape still attached—roughly ripped from the *Cleveland Plain Dealer* and the *Home Valley News*. One of them had printing in small block letters up the left margin: "Serves them right for treating me wrong" and another had "God's Justice!"

"I guess he's back on the list of possible perps for the first two arsons," Nate admitted. "First tier."

"You got a second tier?"

"Just people of interest. Not counting Hannah Esh, two other females on the fringe of things. Women involved in something like this are rare. But Cindee Kramer for one. I talked to her about an hour ago, got her out of bed while, luckily, her charming friend Getz was still asleep. She claims she was confused about where she told Sarah that Getz was standing when he saw the second fire. She has easy access to artificial fireplace logs. Maybe she's working with Getz or just covering for him. And I found out only recently that Ray-Lynn Logan was at the Esh place just before the first fire ignited, even opened the barn doors."

The big man jerked back in his chair as if he'd been slugged. "Ray-Lynn there then! You gotta be kidding me!"

"One of the Amish kids told me so I talked to her. She said she saw nothing and didn't want to get involved. She was there to ask Bishop Esh if Sarah could paint a quilt square for the restaurant. Let's just say she's been encouraging Sarah to branch out with her painting."

"Ray-Lynn should have told me that and told me you talked to her."

Nate thought Jack looked as if he'd chew his desk apart. His ruddy complexion had gone bright red.

"Jack, you okay?"

"Yeah, sure. Just surprised about Ray-Lynn, though it proves nothing except she needs a good shaking up for with-holding evidence. Anyhow," he went on, though Nate could tell he was still steaming, "about Jacob. I found nothing but those articles in his possessions to implicate him. Thing is, his parents want to get him out on bail. Don't know where they'd get the money, though. I can stall them until tomor-row, but, after that, I think he's sprung unless we got more than these articles. Anger at the Amish does not an arsonist make."

"The printing doesn't look like a real match for the two threatening notes, either."

"I gave Clawson a bad time for not bringing that note he got at the newspaper office straight to me, but then you're the one he really wants info from. Let's just pray there are no more fires and that you get information out of poor Noah Miller. He might have seen something before that barn blaze."

As he'd left the sheriff's office, despite being hungry, Nate avoided Ray-Lynn's crowded restaurant. Jack had said she usually kept it closed on Sundays in deference to Amish be-liefs about no Sunday sales. But he'd also admitted he knew that she'd been ticked off at the Amish lately for forbidding Sarah's artistic talent to blossom and that Ray-Lynn needed the money. Nate wondered if she could also want money from helping Sarah sell her art. And if Sarah's barn paintings were destroyed...or got her more publicity...

Sarah was at the center of things again. Nate agonized as he passed more buggies. Sarah, his helper, his distraction, his passion. He sighed, and tried to force his mind back to business. She'd said that after the long church service of preaching and singing, the Amish shared a simple meal. He'd been invited to both and would have liked to attend, but he'd called the Cleveland Clinic and—since he was an official on the arson case—was told he would be allowed a few minutes to speak with Noah Miller. His condition had stabilized but was still serious.

Driving past the burned Miller barn, which he would examine more closely when the ruins cooled, Nate left Eden County and turned north on busy I-77. The pace picked up. Lately, he'd gotten used to slower driving, and he had to force himself to keep up to the speed limit. He needed to push this investigation. Funny how the Home Valley area seemed so sheltered by gentle hills, yet a serpent had gotten into paradise.

Partway to Cleveland, he got a call from his boss. He put him on speakerphone so he could drive with both hands.

"I got your message, Nate. Have you talked to the burn victim yet?"

"On my way right now. They stabilized him, some second-degree burns, some third."

"He dies, and we get the FBI in on this."

"The Feds will come in strong and that won't work in Amish country. I've been learning the hard way there are special dos and don'ts around here. At times I still walk on thin ice, even though the Amish have embraced me."

Nate wished he hadn't used the word *embraced*. That

sounded strange. He knew Sarah was never far from his thoughts.

"By the way," Mark said, "Peter Clawson called me for a phone interview Friday."

"A real go-getter, that guy."

"He insists there's an estranged daughter of the family from the first fire you're not looking at, maybe because she's a neighbor and friend to Sarah Kauffman, the one you said is helping you."

Nate gripped the steering wheel harder. He'd mentioned Hannah to Mark, but what was with Peter Clawson horning in?

"I've interviewed Hannah Esh twice," Nate explained, "once just last night. Her alibis are vague but plausible. She's on the list and is getting cut no extra slack."

"Glad to hear it. Well, you know the big-fish-in-little-pond syndrome, and I suspect Peter Clawson has it in spades. I've read his paper online. After you interview the fire victim, let me know if you still think the third fire is atypical."

"Roger that."

"One more thing. Are you going to publicize those two threatening quotes from the Bible or still sit on them? Clawson's pressing to publish the one he got."

"For now, unless Clawson blows it, I'd like to keep them quiet. We don't need more upheaval around here. But if a third one shows up, I might change my mind."

"It's your call. You know what you're doing. Talk to you soon."

And he'd talk to Peter Clawson soon, Nate thought. He would get on his case if he kept meddling. How Ray-Lynn, whom he hadn't mentioned to Mark as a person of interest but maybe should have, put up with Clawson as a partner was beyond him. Of course, if she could act as agent for Sarah's art, maybe she'd earn enough to buy full control of the restaurant and get Clawson off her back, too.

Sarah was glad that church was in the Hostetler barn today instead of the house. Not only did it allow the nearly one hundred and fifty Amish in their district to sit in the same room—men and women on separate sides of the aisle on backless benches—but their presence seemed to bestow a blessing on the only barn left with one of her quilt squares. The painting was Sunshine and Shadows, with its contrasting pattern of yellow, white, gray and black. *Ya,* she thought, life was like that, too. Much joy but much sorrow.

She stood with everyone for the first hymn, led by the deep-voiced *vorsinger,* or song leader. As usual, it was Seth Lantz, Ella's brother, the man Hannah should have married. Sarah remembered how beautifully their voices had blended together. For sure, Seth's sin was part of the reason Hannah left home. Sarah's rejection of Jacob didn't help him, either, but what he got into wasn't her fault—was it?

The barn had been swept and scrubbed. She loved being in it, feeling its strength over and around them. Her eyes took in the rows of her people all dressed up for the service as the chantlike first hymn began. Like some of the others, it had been penned by imprisoned Amish martyrs in Europe awaiting their torture or deaths. No wonder *Grossmamm* had fears buried deep inside her, despite the fact that was generations ago and they were safe here in America.

But lately, not safe enough. Noah Miller might die and was horribly burned. Someone was waging war on their barns, someone still hated and persecuted the church leaders—perhaps her, too—for her prideful art. Tears in her eyes, she sang the traditional hymn in German.

*We wander in the forests dark,*
*With dogs upon our track;*
*And like the captive, silent lamb*
*Men bring us, prisoners, back.*
*They point to us, amid the throng,*
*And with their taunts offend,*
*And long to let the fire or ax*
*On heretics descend.*

After a hymn of praise, Bishop Esh began to preach, gesturing broadly, walking back and forth before the congregation. Forgiveness and turning the other cheek were his first topic. He shared passages from the Book of Psalms that promised protection even in the hardest of times, which, as far as Sarah knew, was right now, the worst since the old days of death and burnings.

"'I called on the Lord in my distress...I will not fear, for what can man do to me,'" Bishop Esh recited.

He was much heartened she knew, by the thousands of dollars raised at the auction that would go toward his new barn and some toward the Schrocks'. Now there would be huge medical bills for Noah. The local lumber mill had donated part of the timber for the new barn, and it had been announced this morning that the raising would be this coming Saturday. Nate had said he wanted to help. She hoped he had the arsons solved by then but she still wanted him to be around to be part of that. His completing his work here was something they all hoped for, yet something she dreaded.

As the congregation knelt in silent prayer with their

elbows on their benches, Sarah prayed extra hard for her own weaknesses and sins. But she prayed, too, for the *Englische* man she would never have but would never forget.

Nate followed the Cleveland Clinic burn unit nurse down the hall into the sterile area of private rooms. The nurse had said they'd worked hard to stabilize Noah, to keep him from going into shock. This afternoon he would have a hyperbaric treatment in an oxygen chamber, the beginning of months of painful but necessary healing and rehab.

Like her, Nate wore scrubs and booties and had been warned not to touch Noah or anything in the room. "The third-degree burns on his legs are, in effect, an open wound," the nurse told him.

*An open wound.* The words stuck in his mind. Once you lost someone in a fire, there was always an open wound, even when your body healed, even when someone gave you a good home and the years passed. But you always longed for your own people and place.

"His mother's sitting with him, and I believe his father and two friends who came with him have gone to the cafeteria," the nurse said as they stopped at one of the closed doors. "If you'd like me to have her step out, I will."

"Yes, I'd appreciate that."

She put her hand to the door but didn't open it. "Did the young man start those Amish fires?" she asked. "I've been reading about those in the *Plain Dealer.*"

"That's what I need to talk to him about."

The room seemed bare with just the raised bed, a bank of blinking monitors, the IV stands—Noah had two tubes snaking into his arms—and minimal furniture. Mrs. Miller rose from a chair and came over to them.

"I can't thank you enough for pulling him out of the barn, Mr. MacKenzie. I thanked Sarah Kauffman, too, for her quick thinking. And the sheriff. We might have lost Noah, sure could have."

"Has he said anything about the fire?"

"Just that he's sorry, very sorry. I'm sorry he didn't see whoever set it to help you out, but he must have been so busy in the loft when that person sneaked in, that's for sure."

Nate nodded, thinking how Hannah had kept repeating that she was sorry the night she came back to see her family's newly burned barn. He regretted that Mrs. Miller might not be so grateful to him when she learned why he was really here. After a brief talk with the nurse and another peek at her son, she left the room.

Nate approached the bed quietly. Noah's legs were un-covered and looked horrible. His torso, where he had more shallow burns, was covered with white gauze. He hated to wake him because the pain must be awful, despite the meds they were pumping in him, but it had to be done.

To Nate's surprise, Noah opened his eyes. They were bright blue, feverish above the breathing tube attached to his nostrils.

"Noah, you know who I am?"

"*Ya.*"

"I need to hear what happened in the barn to start the fire. I know you'll tell me the truth. I don't think the arsonist was anywhere around. Did you accidentally spill that kerosene and ignite it somehow?"

His eyes widened in surprise. He grimaced slightly. Nate could see even that movement hurt him as a deep frown fur-rowed his brow. Tears tracked from the corner of each eye into his hairline.

*"Ya,"* he whispered.

"I thought so from the burn pattern. Was it an accident or not?"

"I—it's an old barn. We need a new one."

"That's not what I asked. After the kerosene ignited, why did you go back into the loft?"

"I left *Daad's* tools up there—forgot. Expensive."

"Exactly how did that lantern spill and ignite downstairs?"

"Needed more light up there. You remember, *ya?* Dark up there."

"Noah, I know you're in pain, but you know your people are, too, fearing the arsonist will strike again, so I have to find him."

"It's not me."

"I know it isn't. I asked your father last night where you were during the other two fires. So maybe it's still Jacob Yoder."

"He wouldn't. Can't say more. Sorry, that's all," he said, and closed his eyes.

"All right, then. I'll tell you a true story, since you won't tell me one. The reason I am so dedicated to my job is because my father deliberately lit our house on fire when I was a boy, much younger than you."

Noah opened his eyes and fixed them on Nate as he spoke. "He wanted insurance money for the house because he was going into debt—didn't have as much money as some of his friends and neighbors. I know the Amish don't have insurance, but they have donations and barn raisings."

More tears ran down Noah's cheeks.

"But my father made a mistake. He didn't know the flames would spread that fast. He used an accelerant that got out of hand. He was going to be a hero and get us out. But my mother was burned so badly in the fire she died, and my dad got trapped, too, and died. The fire got out of his control and trapped him. Is that what happened to you? You lit it so you'd get a new barn and so your friend Jacob wouldn't look guilty? You ran back up to the loft for the tools, but fell through the hole in the rotting floor and got trapped, right? I'm trying to help your family and your people, Noah. I need the truth. Is that what happened?"

Noah closed his eyes tightly; his lips moved. Nate could barely hear the response, one he wanted yet dreaded because it would make a bigger mess than he was already in with the Amish in this case.

"*Ya,*" Noah said. "I did it."

# 19

AFTER THE CHAOS OF THE WEEKEND, SARAH was glad to get back to her normal Monday morning schedule, even if it was the Memorial Day holiday for worldly folk. As she carried her basket of half-moon pies through the back door of the Dutch Farm Table, she saw the place was already full of *ausländers*. She peeked in all three rooms but didn't see Nate. He'd driven VERA past the *grossdaadi haus* toward the pond late last night and had left early. Though she longed to see him, she had her whole day planned. After having breakfast with Ray-Lynn, if her friend had time to sit down, she was going to begin to paint the pattern on her family's barn.

Sarah wanted to get a start on it before Bishop Esh and other church leaders called on *Daad* this afternoon to discuss whether setting a trap for the arsonist would be permissible. Despite her belief in forgiveness, she couldn't see why they would even hesitate. The arsonist was a dangerous criminal who needed to be caught and that was that.

"You didn't get any sleep, did you?" Ray-Lynn greeted

her, took the basket and handed her the money right away. She looked upset and rushed.

"Not much, but how about we tell each other we look and feel great?"

"Ah, the power of positive thinking, though even little lies are not very Amish. Here, sit at the far end of the counter, and I'll be back to chat if I have time. We're full of gawkers and media-types this morning, so hide under that bonnet if you don't want to be bothered. In other words, try not to look like your picture in the special edition Peter put out this morning. He must have been up all night, too. I'll be back in a sec," she promised, and darted away.

Her picture in the paper? That's all she needed after the comments and looks she got about the feature on her painted barn squares, Sarah thought as she climbed into one of the tall-legged, wooden chairs and slid a copy of the paper down the counter.

"Oh, no. Oh, no, oh, no!"

The story about the fire had bumped coverage of the community auction off the front page with the headline Amish Heroine Helps Save Man Trapped in Barn Fire. Arson #3?

She forced herself to read it slowly, whispering, her lips moving.

The antique Levi Miller barn on Valley View Road went up in flames at approximately 3:30 p.m., May 29, the third Amish barn in the Home Valley area to be ignited under mysterious circumstances. The Miller son, Noah, 19, was medevaced to the Cleveland Clinic with life-threatening burns after being trapped in the barn. He was rescued by the heroic efforts of Sarah Kauffman, 24, the Amish artist who painted the quilt patterns on the Miller barn and two others that have burned; Nathan MacKenzie, 30, State Fire Marshal Arson Investigator; and Eden County Sheriff Jack Freeman. MacKenzie has been investigating the Amish barn arsons for a week and is "the best the state has to offer," according to State Fire Marshal Mark Lincoln of Columbus.

Although the target of the fire fits the pattern of the previous Amish barn arsons, some of the circumstances do not, such as time of day and the fact this barn had a person working inside, who evidently did not see or did not stop the arsonist. The old edifice was well-known in the area not only as a historic building but as one of the first barns to bear a painted quilt square.

Wide-eyed, Sarah studied the largest of the three color photos. It was her all right, a full, clear profile of her face because she'd shoved her bonnet back to see better. She was up the ladder. A distraught Mr. Miller and the angry sheriff were standing below her. Right under that, two other photos were almost as large. The one on the left was of Nate in his fire gear, emerging from black smoke and flames, pulling Noah after him. The one on the right was of her half-burned quilt square on the barn with two streams of water from the pumper truck crisscrossing in front of it.

"I'm not an Amish heroine," she told Ray-Lynn, who bustled up and poured her a cup of coffee. "I'm just trying to help."

"I know you feel that way, and this doesn't help with the humility I know you all value. But you *are* a heroine. Listen, Sarah," she said, leaning close and putting one hand on her shoulder. "I don't want to see you scolded or persecuted by the people you love, but you have got to realize that your painted squares make you special. If you'd ever agree to draw and paint the Amish daily life scenes you've shown me, the sky's the limit."

"I just want us to catch and stop that arsonist. None of us need this kind of publicity," Sarah said with a nod and glance that encompassed the entire restaurant.

"I can't argue how good it is for business," Ray-Lynn admitted. "So, are you still fixing to help Nate?"

"He's got his feet pretty well on the ground now, but when I can."

"You should let him see your sketchbook. Maybe when he goes back to Columbus, he could show it to my friend for us."

"I can't think about all that now." She sighed and took a sip of the coffee. She almost told Ray-Lynn Nate had already seen the sketchbook and about her sketches being defaced with blood and flames, but something held her back from sharing that.

"Gotta go," Ray-Lynn said, "but I was just wondering if Nate has said anything about other suspects, if Jacob Yoder doesn't pan out."

"You'd better ask him," Sarah said. For once the pancakes with strawberries Leah Schwartz placed in front of her didn't look good at all. If she'd lost her appetite, things were getting to her really bad.

Sarah had a good start on her Ocean Waves painting when the church leaders—minus Levi Miller, who must still be at the hospital with Noah—arrived in separate buggies. Bishop Esh, elders Reuben Schrock and Eli Hostetler, and two deacons went into the house to meet with her father. To her surprise, Nate drove up in VERA, parked on the lane, then jogged back to her house and, with a wave, went inside, too.

Was he invited to let them know how Noah was doing or was he going to plead his case for staking out Hostetlers' and this barn? No doubt the Amish leaders weren't happy with the newspaper coverage. Sometimes, she had to admit, it would be nice to live in a community where the women could sit in a gathering of leaders making big decisions, but that just wasn't their way. The home and children were the woman's realm, and that didn't include painting pictures of people on barns or anywhere else.

Nate saw that the meeting was going to be around the Kauffmans' big kitchen table. That was fine with him, except the seat they'd left gave him a view of Sarah out back, up the ladder, which was distracting. Every time she leaned or stretched to paint, her raised hem flaunted the edge of a white slip and her shapely black-stockinged legs. It was incredible that a glimpse of stocking could be arousing in this day and age, but she always got to him that way.

He fought to keep his eyes on the eager, bearded faces as he told them Noah's condition had stabilized but that he faced a long, painful battle for full recovery.

"We'll need more money raisers, another auction and dinner," Bishop Esh said. "Let's hope the women can go back to quilting soon. We have some money in reserve to help the Millers with the hospital costs, but we have three barns to rebuild now, not two. Anything else about this third arson before we discuss plans for stopping the arsonist, Nate?"

"Yes, there is something I need to go over with you. The Miller fire was an arson, but not by the arsonist who set the first two. I suspected that from burn patterns I saw in the barn. Noah confessed that he set the blaze, and he asks for forgiveness."

They sat in silence until Bishop Esh's fist hit the table and rattled his sugar spoon against his coffee mug. The Amish men looked at one another, then at Nate. No explosions, no swearing, no name-calling or accusations. Finally, the bishop spoke. "He's paid a steep price for that sin, as all must for theirs."

"At least he's confessing," Reuben said. "It was an old tinderbox of a barn. He must have hoped for help rebuilding."

"That," Nate said, "and he thought another barn fire while his buddy Jacob was in jail would get him freed. Like others I spoke with, Noah believes however distraught Jacob was, he would not burn barns. Noah had no idea that Jacob was locked up on other charges. But the circumstances of this third fire make Jacob's guilt possible again, and Sheriff Freeman says he will probably be released on bail soon."

"Government law is sometimes not God's laws," Ben Kauffman said. "Will you, Nate, as the government's official here, charge Noah Miller with arson, even if he's not the arsonist we really want to stop? Just to be clear, he isn't, is he, maybe working with Jacob Yoder?"

"After interviewing him, I believe it was a naive attempt at what we call a copycat crime. Since I've returned from Cleveland, I've checked out Noah's alibis for the other two fires and he was not involved. When I told his parents what he'd done, they, of course, refused to bring charges. I'm willing to let your church deal with him. Under the circumstances, I can't see prosecuting him, if you'll handle things. He's already facing years of pain and rehab and may be crippled the rest of his life. Besides, prosecuting Noah would distract, in town and in the local paper, from finding the one we still need to capture. But can we agree to set a trap for the other arsonist?"

"Would you mind stepping into the living room for a minute or two?" Bishop Esh asked. "This won't take long."

"Sure. I understand," Nate said, and went into the neat, sparsely furnished living room. He could hear their low voices, but of course, they were speaking in German now. Looking out the window toward the road, he wished he could see how Sarah was doing from here.

He began to pace back and forth across the hardwood floor. Mark Lincoln trusted him to handle this delicate investigation. Nate had broken a minor rule or two, like hauling civilians around in VERA while heading for a fire. He was about to break a bigger one if he didn't arrest Noah. But the Amish had to be handled differently, didn't they, or was that wrong, too? His offer to let Noah Miller off scot-free from prosecution was a breach of ethics, but worldly ones. This was a different world here, and the Amish would see that Noah was punished and rehabilitated. But the worst—and, somehow, the best—thing he'd done here was falling in love with his Amish aide.

He stopped pacing and shook his head. He was sweating but a shiver snaked up his spine. In love? Was he crazy? In eight days he was in love and with an Amish woman? No way. He was just grateful to her, fascinated by her and under such pressure he wasn't thinking straight when he absolutely needed to.

"You can come in now, Nate," Ben Kauffman said, interrupting his thoughts. He went back to the kitchen and sat down at the table again.

"About your deal that we should set a trap for the arsonist, we don't make deals with the government," Reuben said.

"Whatever the crime, is entrapment of the criminal fair and moral?"

"The government has made deals with Amish ways before. You know that. Being able to run your own schools, for example," Nate argued, keeping his voice calm and leaning forward over his clasped hands on the table. "The fact the U.S. government agreed that the Amish need pay no Social Security taxes because you refuse to accept Social Security benefits. Again, I think we need to work together for the safety of your people. So let me explain my plan, and then we can all seek the advice and permission of a higher power to get it done."

"Can I see you in private, Ray-Lynn?" Jack asked as he stepped in the back door of the restaurant.

Why the back door? she thought. What was going on? It was nearly time to run home for a while, but she'd been so busy this morning she was thinking of skipping her break.

"Why sure. Can't you come in for a cup of cof—"

"Right now, out here, if you wouldn't mind."

She told Leah and Anna she'd be right back and went out the door he held for her. The sheriff's car was parked behind the restaurant. No one else was in sight. Her heartbeat kicked up as he took her upper arm and steered her around to the other side of his car, almost as if he was going to put her in it, arrest her.

"So what is this ab—" she got out before he interrupted.

"I learned something yesterday that teed me off, Ray-Lynn. I was gonna let it slide, but I just can't. Our state fire marshal investigator and I had a debrief about first tier and second tier suspects for the arsons, and I recognized a name I knew real well on the second tier. Now why in Sam Hill didn't you tell me you were at the Esh barn right before it went up in flames?"

She'd sensed that question was coming, but it didn't help. Although her stomach twisted, she was angry, too. "Because I didn't see anything suspicious, as I hope Nate MacKenzie told you. And, with the restaurant and all—as a partner to a man who puts every ding-dang thing in the paper he can find and manages to make everyone look guilty—I didn't want to get involved!"

"Didn't want to get involved?" he exploded when he'd been almost whispering before. "You should have told me, told MacKenzie right away, at least. He got it out of some kid who spotted you and then you confessed! Not get involved? You and I are involved, aren't we? You should have told me so I knew, so I could question you—protect you if it came to that."

"Protect me? And no, we aren't involved in any way other than I bring your food and pour your coffee and provide a sympathetic ear once in a while. Is that your idea of involved?"

He looked shocked either at the fact she'd shouted back or just maybe, hopefully, at what she'd said.

"I thought we were...friends," he said, looking hurt, almost like a little boy. Yet he was still Jack Freeman, former-marine hard-as-nails sheriff, standing there in that sharp uniform, six inches taller than her with his macho gun belt. He was a bright man but dumb as a doorknob when it came to soft feelings, to emotion. She had to keep remembering this was a man's man, her own Rhett Butler, not an Ashley Wilkes. But she was no Scarlett O'Hara, who didn't know what man she wanted.

Before she could stop herself, she blurted, "Us being just

friends is for sissies, Sheriff, and I didn't think you were that. If I'm not under arrest for wanting more, I'm going back inside where I'm needed for something, at least."

She stomped away without looking around and slammed her own back door.

To Sarah's surprise, Nate was the last to leave the farmhouse after the others pulled away in their buggies. Perhaps he'd been speaking with her mother again. They seemed to get along pretty well.

He walked out slowly toward where she was stirring a can of marine-blue to paint the dark triangles she'd laid out on her chalk grid. Even before Sarah returned from the restaurant this morning, Cindee Kramer had been kind enough to drop off the last two cans of the lighter paint she'd need. Called Wedgwood blue, they were still in a sack just around the corner of the barn in the shade.

She turned to face Nate, hoping she didn't look as giddy to see him as she felt.

"So you've got the pattern all laid out," he said, looking at her instead of above. He crossed his arms and tucked his hands under his armpits. He looked like he was hugging himself.

"Did you get your plans settled, about how to trap the arsonist?" she asked, still holding her paint can between them. "Three fires, one in broad daylight, but then he picked a good time when everyone was busy, and probably just never figured Noah would be in there."

"Sarah, I don't want this to become public knowledge—or get in the paper for obvious reasons—but Noah intentionally set that fire."

She stopped stirring. "In his own barn? To draw attention to how much it needed to be rebuilt?"

"More or less. Also, he figured if a barn went up while Jacob was in jail…"

"In other words, Jacob could still be guilty of the other two arsons. I was so sure he'd never do something like that. I'm still positive about Hannah, though. Is Noah's guilt going to stay private information, or are you going to arrest him?"

"I'll have to eventually explain things to my boss, and it sure would go a long way if we can catch the serial arsonist. But I'm going to let the church leaders handle Noah—if we can keep Peter Clawson from discovering and printing it, like he does everything else. Just before our meeting broke up, Reuben Schrock showed us a copy of today's paper."

"I saw it, too. But as for your handling of Noah," she said, blinking back tears, "Nathan MacKenzie, we're rubbing off on you."

"Someone is," he said with such an intense look she was glad she held the paint can between them—or maybe not. "So did the church leaders say you could try to trap the real arsonist?"

"I think we've come to an agreement. Stan Comstock, the state fire marshal supervisor for this region of Ohio, is back from his daughter's wedding. I'm going to bring him up to speed on everything and have him stationed in the Hostetler house with night goggles to watch their barn, while I camp out here with the same gear."

"But the first two fires happened when no one was home."

"Here's the way I explained it to the elders. I think the arsonist is feeling invincible, wanting to up his game. He's had two successful fires, and it hasn't been announced that

the Miller fire wasn't set by the same person. He probably
wants to reestablish himself. About now, serial arsonists get
not only bold but careless. And how better to prove what
they think is their brilliance and power than by a barn fire
when the people are at home? It's the ultimate challenge,
even if word may have gotten out that someone might be
inside the barn or house on guard. Besides, I don't think this
particular arsonist would fall for it if we put out the word
your family or the Hostetlers were leaving their houses and
would be back late. From my experience interviewing other
serial arsonists and studying this one, I think we've got a
good chance at this."

"But you and Mr. Comstock will stand out among us."

"We're going to dress Amish, try to blend in, and our
vehicles won't be anywhere in sight. Your father has given
me permission to use both your farmhouse and *grossdaadi
haus,* since views from those windows will cover your entire
barn."

"The *grossdaadi haus,* too? It will upset my grandmother
to have you around."

"I think your mother's going to move her to a bedroom
in the farmhouse—you and Martha, too. Your part in this
will be to keep painting that square. I would hate to have
it be a target, but my goal is to save it, the barns—and get
whoever tries to harm it or the Hostetlers' quilt square."

"I want to help. You can't be two places at once here. I
could be in whichever place you're not at night. You'll need
to sleep sometimes."

"We'll see. By the way, I guess they're going to get my
Amish clothes from Lizzie's husband, Sam. I haven't met him
yet."

"He's sinewy like you, but you're taller. I bet his trousers come above your ankles."

"Sinewy, huh? So anyway, what I actually came over here to ask is, do you still want your sketchbook back?"

"I can't stand to look at it. But yes, I do."

"The blood is type AB. Do you know what your grand-mother's is?"

"No, but I can probably have my mother find out the next time *Grossmamm* sees her doctor."

"How about you get me the doctor's name and number, and I'll check it out?"

He walked to VERA and came back with the sketchbook. As if it were evidence, he had it in a clear plastic envelope. "Did you dust it for prints?" she asked.

He grinned. "No, but I tried to remove the blood from the last page in the book, and it smeared your lines, so I quit trying. I just wanted you to know that was me and not someone else tampering with it. And about my putting my hands all over you last night..."

"Yes?"

"I'm apologizing for doing that during your weak and emotional time. That's what I feel around you, too, weak and emotional. But an apology in this case doesn't mean I'm sorry."

He handed her the sketchbook; their fingers touched. She would have sworn a lightning strike crackled along her arm and ended up in the pit of her stomach. Despite his heartfelt admission just now, she wondered, with this other investigator coming in and with all the group activities and planning, would they ever really have the chance to touch again? She sensed that Nate was taking a huge risk, even needed courage, to admit deep feelings for her. Weak and emotional—not what a strong, take-charge man like him would easily admit.

In the moment of awkward silence, he thrust his hands in the pockets of his jeans, then said, "By the way, I also got permission to help with the Esh barn raising on Saturday. I hope we'll be celebrating the arrest of the arsonist by then. Word's going out about the raising. I can't believe how quickly everything came together for it, but the timber was all ordered already and partly donated. They say workers will show up in droves."

"But as soon as you catch the arsonist, you'll be leaving. If there's ever any need for a fire marshal here again, it will be Stan Comstock."

She felt her lower lip quiver. Surely, she wasn't going to cry.

"I'm planning to bring my foster mother to see Amish country," he told her. "I'll stop in here, show her this quilt square and the one on Hostetlers' barn. She'd love to meet you and your family."

"Sure. That will be real nice."

"Sarah, I want to grab you again, press you up against that wall or carry you into that barn and make love to you. But what would that get us except more pain—and trouble? We need the goodwill of your family and your people. I just can't see any way—"

"Neither can I," she said, turning away from him and climbing the ladder with her paint can. "Better take your VERA back to the pond and go swimming with her!"

The second it was out of her mouth, she was ashamed of such nonsense. It sounded like she was jealous of that truck.

She was acting like a spoiled child, not a mature and proper Amish *maidal*. But this man did strange things to her.

Muttering under his breath, Nate walked away and drove off toward his usual parking spot.

Once Sarah had the marine-blue paint on one triangle, she knew she didn't like it, didn't like anything right now. Why did Nate have to come and ruin things for her here in the first place? It was bad enough she was tempted to take Ray-Lynn's offer to consider painting entire pictures. Truth was, she wanted to paint people's faces, too, and that was one step more *verboten* than painting just for pretty. And why did that Stan Comstock's daughter have to get married right now so it wasn't him who came to solve the arsons? Once Nate left, even if Sarah eventually wed, she knew she'd never quite be content anymore, not with memories of him, not here in Amish country, however much she loved the place and her people. It was a big, fat lie that it was better to have loved and lost than never to have loved at all!

Deciding to mix this dark paint with a bit of the lighter shade Cindee had dropped off, she hustled back down the ladder. It would take more time, but it would please her more—if anything could right now.

She set her can of paint down and went around the side of the barn and lifted the sack with the two cans of Wedg-wood blue. She saw there was a receipt for it inside or maybe a note from Cindee. Putting the sack down, she reached in and pulled out the letter-size piece of paper and gasped. In big, bold, familiar print, it read: "He performs great signs, so that he even makes fire come down from heaven on the earth in the sight of men. What a revelation! Unlucky 13:13."

Unlucky 13:13? Nate was right. The arsonist was getting

bolder, even adding things to the note that weren't from the Bible. She read it again, then, lifting the cans from the sack, dropped the paper back in it and ran down the back lane to show Nate.

# 20

SARAH SAW NATE WAS SWIMMING IN THE POND. She could tell from the waves that he had just dived in. Out of breath, she ran closer. He saw her coming and waved.

"You're going to take me up on the swim?" he shouted.

"A third note! Someone left a third note in the sack with the paint Cindee Kramer dropped off for me early this morning. It was sitting out by the barn! I just looked inside it."

He swam over to the edge where he'd left his shoes, shirt and jeans. Bare-chested, he got out, wearing nothing but his underwear, dark green-and-blue plaid, which clung to him. She knew she should turn away but she moved closer, extending the sack.

"Except for the second note," he said, "they seem to be coming to you, and I don't like that. But the fact this one was in that sack doesn't mean Cindee or Mike left the note, not if it was sitting outside for a while."

"I agree. Mike and Cindee wouldn't be this obvious," she told him. "Maybe someone wants us to think it's them or else just dropped it in a place I'd find it without knowing Cindee left the sack."

"Can you read it to me without touching it again?" He used the T-shirt he'd dropped on the bank to dry his face and upper body. Black, curly chest hair tapered down over his stomach and pointed below his navel. His hair was plastered tight to his head.

Grateful to have a chance to look away, she tipped the sack so that the printing on the note was visible without pulling the paper out. "It's in that same printing again," she told him. "It's a quote from the Bible, the Book of the Revelation. I'm pretty sure this section is about the beast, the evil one who serves the Antichrist. So here it is— 'He performs great signs, so that he even makes fire come down from heaven on the earth in the sight of men. What a revelation! Unlucky 13:13.'"

"'What a revelation' and 'Unlucky 13:13' is not in the Bible, is it?"

"No. So our beast is adding things, making a joke about his own revelation. Do you think the fact it says *he* makes fire means the arsonist is a man?"

"Not if he or she is just picking Bible quotes about fire. Let's check it out online—on the laptop."

"The Bible is in there, too?"

He nodded as he sat on the grass, struggling into his jeans, which stuck to his wet legs. "This means the writer of the Bible notes," he said, "who is probably the arsonist, is starting to get cute, sarcastic, maybe frustrated. That's what I was hoping for. He's itching to burn another barn and he's going to get careless. I hope he or she resents that we're holding the other notes without publishing them. You know thirteen is supposed to be an unlucky number, right?"

"Superstition, yes, but I'll bet that's the chapter and verse of the quote, too."

"Let's look it up," he said, pulling on his bright blue shirt without putting his wadded, wet T-shirt back on.

In VERA, he slid the paper out of the sack onto the narrow table, then, with a quick glance at the sack, set it carefully aside. He leaned stiff-armed over the writing, studying it from every angle, then turned on what he called his laptop. It sat on the countertop in a little frame, probably so it didn't slide around when he drove. She watched, wide-eyed, as he hit keys to bring up different screens, and there it was, the Holy Bible, then the Book of the Revelation, then the exact verse, 13:13.

"So tell me more of what you know about this section of Revelation," he said as he intently scanned the surrounding words.

"This part is prophecy about the coming of the Antichrist, the ultimate evil, Satan's tool. And, in turn, there are two so-called beasts who serve the Antichrist." She leaned close to him to skim the section from the note.

"It says this second beast who uses fire rises up, and people worship him. In this case, the arsonist probably means people are in awe of the fires. Most arsonists are egomaniacs—extremely prideful—one way or the other," Nate said.

"See where he makes war with the saints?" she asked, pointing to the screen.

"In the arsonist's perverted mind that could mean his battle with the Amish. It also says that he persecutes God's people during a time of tribulation. Sarah, this is someone who knows the Bible and hates the Amish—but that doesn't mean he or she is not Amish."

"But you just proved anyone can look it up," she

challenged. "Is there a way to somehow search to find a word like *fire,* or would the person who wrote the note have to have read and know the entire book?"

"You're right—as usual. It's easy to do such a search. I guess I'm remembering only the comforting parts in the Bible, not scary stuff like this."

"At least Jacob's not the one who sent it, since he's in jail."

"He isn't," Nate said, straightening. But just as she was starting to feel relieved that at last he believed her, at least about Jacob if not Hannah, he added, "I mean he isn't in jail. His parents somehow raised bail money for him. But the sheriff called me to say an *Englische* friend picked him up in a car about an hour ago. Legally, Sheriff Freeman couldn't hold him if we didn't formally charge him with the arsons, and we don't have enough evidence for that. I'm hoping, if we give him some rope, he may hang—or at least snag—himself."

"Oh," she said, feeling deflated.

"You still care for him?"

"Not that way. I told you, I just don't want it to be someone Amish."

He took her hand and they both stared down at the paper on the table, then at each other. "These notes I've tried to keep secret," he said, "are like a ticking bomb. Since Peter Clawson knows about only one of the three, I've made a deal with him that, if he doesn't print it, I'll give him some early, exclusive information when we catch the arsonist. I've told my boss about the notes. But now, not releasing the information—I'm not sure. I don't want to cause more panic than there already is, however your people accept the Lord's hand in what is happening. It's touchy when pacifist civilians start guarding their barns with hunting rifles. This has to end soon."

"I think you're right that releasing these notes would only foster fear."

"Speaking of which, I'm also starting to worry it could be someone random, someone we don't know. It's happened with serial murderers—serial arsonists, too. Peter Clawson may be right that it could be a hate crime against the Amish. Someone who resents Amish ways or beliefs—I don't know. But I do know you've been invaluable to me in all this, what-ever happens. Wait—did you hear that?" he said, cocking his head. He dropped her hand and moved toward the open back doors.

"Sounds like Gabe's voice," she said. "I just ran off, so maybe they're worried."

"Good. I hope they keep an eye on you if I can't. Don't you laugh at me tomorrow when I turn Amish for a couple of days. Yeah, it's Gabe," he said, and stepped out and waved to him.

"She's here, going over evidence with me!" Nate called to him. "Sarah," he added, speaking quickly as he climbed back inside, "when you drop off the half-moon pies at the restaurant tomorrow morning, I'd like to ride back to your house in your buggy—hidden. I'm going to put the word out I've gone back to Columbus for something, then try to look Amish with your dad's help and live undercover that way at your house for a couple of days. Your father's going to explain everything to your family tonight."

She stood, amazed at all Nate, her father and the church leaders had agreed on. *"Ya,"* she said, "I can bring you back from town. I think *Grossmamm* will like you much more dressed Amish, but I kind of like you in green-and-blue plaid."

Just before Gabe popped around and peered up into VERA at them, Nate whispered, "Sarah Kauffman, you are a tease."

The next morning, Nate drove VERA to the sheriff's house—a nice brick ranch two miles east of town—and parked in his double garage, which the sheriff closed and locked. Hoping he didn't need more than the communication equipment he'd put in a pack with some personal items, Nate got on the floor in the back of the sheriff's car and rode into town with him. When the sheriff gave him the okay, Nate got out behind the office. After hiding his backpack behind the Dutch Farm Table under a bush, he walked around to the front door of the restaurant and went in to sit at the counter.

"What will it be?" Ray-Lynn greeted him. "Breakfast or more cleverly worded accusations?"

"Not much time for either today," he said, glancing down at his watch. "I'm heading back to Columbus for a couple of days—lab work, debriefing, but I'll be back in time for the barn raising."

"I'm sure someone around here will miss you," she said, her tone tart.

It was interesting, he thought, that she'd turned so cold to him when he thought they'd parted amiably after he'd questioned her. He'd figured that, no matter how upset she was, she'd be charming at the restaurant. The flip tone of "What a revelation!" in the note danced through his mind. Sarah had said that Ray-Lynn was raised a Southern Baptist. If anyone knew the Bible, they did.

"I had to tell our mutual friend, if that's what you're upset about," he told Ray-Lynn when she glared at him.

"If either of you really think I could be behind something like that, you can just eat elsewhere, both of you," she muttered, and flounced away.

One of the Amish waitresses came up, poured him coffee and took his order. Peter Clawson ambled in, looking rumpled and sleepless, like some absentminded professor, but Nate knew he was hardly that. Those comments on the last note—"What a revelation!" and "Unlucky 13:13"—sounded like something Peter would say. Of everyone he knew around here, Peter fit the egomaniac description best, but what would be the motive? Increased paper sales? That Pulitzer Prize? But then, why would Peter have cooperated with and even agreed not to publish evidence at the request of an arson investigator? Naw, this guy was pompous but he only had time to cover the arsons, not start them.

"Nate, my man," Peter said, and plopped down on the next stool. "How's Noah Miller?"

"Good news for you to print for once. Despite facing a long, hard haul, he's going to make it."

"I called the Cleveland Clinic, but they read me the patient privacy act. How in the world did the arsonist start that fire with the boy in the barn?"

"Noah was trying to repair the hole in the loft, which he then fell through and was trapped. I haven't had time—nor have the charred remains cooled-off enough yet—to confirm evidence. Meanwhile, I'm heading to Columbus until Saturday morning, but I'll be back for the Esh barn raising."

"While the cat's away, the mice will play."

"Isn't that a cliché?" he tweaked him.

"One that's apropos. Doesn't it worry you to be leaving right now?"

"Sheriff Freeman's on alert, and the Amish are much more aware now. Speaking of the Amish, I wish you'd quit featuring Sarah Kauffman in the paper. You know they don't like their faces photographed—or to have a public focus on them."

"She's a huge part of this story. Besides, Ray-Lynn is really impressed by her art, thinks she could have a good career in the big, bad world. I'm just giving that a boost. Besides, I think she's covering for a close contact, and I want to shake them both up."

Nate's head jerked up. "Jacob Yoder?"

"You're the investigator here. Let me just say I'm sure I saw Hannah Esh standing a ways back in the newly planted field between the Esh and Kauffman farms, watching that first fire—her family's barn."

Nate's stomach knotted. He stopped pouring maple syrup and looked at Peter. The man didn't blink but added, "Here comes another cliché, but they were thick as thieves, Sarah, Hannah and Ella Lantz. It's obvious Sarah is willing to buck the Amish establishment to a certain point with her art. I know, the bishop et al finally approved it, but only those copy-the-quilt-design paintings, when Ray-Lynn says she can do so much more. But I think Sarah would defend Hannah at any cost. Again, not to turn a cliché on its head, but I hope you're not so enamored with one particular tree that you're missing the entire forest. And one more thing. I'm going to have to print what was in that note dropped off at the paper. I can't sit on that anymore. The public has a right to know."

Though he was still trying to process Peter's information

about seeing Hannah at the fire—why didn't he share that before?—Nate said, "I thought we had a deal on your holding that."

"It's too important to let slide. Besides, it might give you a lead if someone comes forward with info on it. It's a unique note with the threat, the Bible language. I intend to print it in full in the issue that covers the barn raising unless there's a reason to do another special edition first. If you're going to Columbus in the midst of all this mess, check out the paper's website to keep up with things."

Did Peter smell a rat with his leaving at a time like this? "If you print that note," Nate said, intentionally filling his mouth with a three-tiered bite of pancakes and chewing slowly before he went on, "and it triggers another arson, I'll hold you accountable. And be sure to print that the state arson investigator mentioned another Bible quote, Exodus 22:6— 'He who makes fire shall surely make restitution.'"

Peter looked impressed, so Nate hoped he'd recalled that right. After Sarah had left with Gabe yesterday, he'd done the obvious, searching the entire Bible online for quotes about fire.

He and Peter ate side by side, not saying much more, while Ray-Lynn went past, glaring darts at both of them, though Nate had no idea why she was ticked off at Peter. He saw Sarah come in and tried to ignore her. She sat in the rear booth where Ray-Lynn flitted back to talk to her now and then. He had to make his move now.

Nate said he'd see Peter on Saturday at the barn raising, paid his bill and, when he saw Mike Getz come in, chatted with him and just happened to mention he was leaving for a few days. Before Peter could pay and catch up, Nate walked down the street and ducked back behind the buildings. He retrieved his backpack and, looking both ways, tried to get himself settled in the narrow, short space behind the driver's seat of Sarah's buggy.

Lying down with his knees bent, he used his hard backpack for a pillow. Besides some personal items, it was jammed full with his satellite phone, three two-way radios—Sarah had lost his fourth one in the ditch—and night goggles. Stan Comstock would supply anything else needed, and they'd use only dedicated channels to speak to each other. If something needed to be sent back and forth between the Kauffman and Hostetler farms, however much they prided themselves on being cutting-edge investigators, they would rely on Amish help with a horse and buggy.

As he tried again to get comfortable—where was that woman?—he shook the buggy. Sally merely snorted once, as if she expected strange things from him.

He figured it was about ten minutes later when Sarah came out. The buggy rocked under her weight as she settled in. "All set?" she whispered. "I've felt more worldly while you've been here, Nathan MacKenzie, and now, I guess, you're going to get a little taste of what it is to be Amish—at least wearing the clothes and walking in our shoes a bit."

She blew a kiss to Sally, and they pulled away. The clip-clops and the sway of the buggy could have lulled him if he wasn't so upset that Peter had claimed to see Hannah at the first fire and suggested that Sarah was probably covering for her. Of course, Sarah had defended her friend tooth and nail. Man, he wished Hannah had a decent alibi for the two arsons. And she'd looked so shocked to hear about the Miller fire—as if it really annoyed her that someone else had dared to set one. Hannah knew the area. Like Sarah, she could easily walk the fields to get to barns she'd known all her life.

He tried to calm himself. Peter had withheld that information, so what else was he holding back on? "We're going to be passing other buggies so I'm not talking to you." Sarah interrupted his agonizing. "But it's okay if you talk to me."

"Maybe I'm taking a nap or just enjoying the view," he said. He reached out under the seat toward her ankle, but withdrew his hand before he touched her. He had to fight his need for her. The only thing he should be concentrating on, he told himself, was catching the arsonist before one more barn burned.

Sarah was moving *Grossmamm* and some of her things into the farmhouse when they crossed paths with Nate in the living room as he came down the stairs. That is, she met Amish Nate, dressed in her brother-in-law's trousers, white shirt and dark coat. Clean-shaven, he looked like an unwed Amish man except for his short hair, but the straw hat hid that.

Gabe and *Daad* were with him. They nodded and both patted Sarah's and *Grossmamm*'s shoulders and said their names, but they went to the kitchen, and she heard the screen door bang closed. For a moment, she stood in awe at Nate's transformation, but before she could figure out quite what to say, her grandmother asked him in German, "Are you Sarah's come-calling friend?"

At least, Sarah thought, stifling a laugh but turning bright red, the old woman wasn't afraid of him now. "This is Nate, *Grossmamm,* a friend of the whole family," Sarah said in English.

Switching to English, *Grossmamm* retorted, "Well, even if

he's just one of the cousins from Pennsylvania come to help in the fields, he should be your come-calling friend. He's handsome. And," she said to Nate, "our Sarah is a lovely, loyal young woman. I'd miss her if you took her away, but she would make a good wife." Looking back at Sarah, she asked, "You never married that other one, did you?"

"*Grossmamm,*" Sarah said, wishing she hadn't switched to English, "let's go upstairs."

"At least up there, it will be harder for that man in black to look in my window," the old woman said, not budging. "When I saw him outside, I pulled up the window and told him to get away. He terrified me, though, because I think he was one of them—the burners."

Sarah got goose bumps. When she should have just passed over it and gotten her grandmother settled to avoid upsetting her, she asked, "What did he say? What did he look like?"

"He said nothing. He knew I'd caught him. Or maybe it was a woman. I can only say the person looked like a demon with huge eyes that stuck out like a grasshopper's. I wasn't dreaming. I was right on my knees, looking out. I've always told the truth. I'd tell the truth even if they tortured or burned me like is happening now. And I didn't want him to come in and burn your *verboten* drawings, so I put bloody fire on them before he could...."

Sarah gasped, shocked at the demented twists in her *grossmamm*'s mind. But at least the arsonist hadn't targeted her sketchbook.

"Sorry, Nate," Sarah said, and put her sacks down to take *Grossmamm*'s elbow to lead her toward the stairs. "I shouldn't have asked her."

Nate picked up the sacks and followed them up the stairs. At the bedroom door where the old woman had slept for many years—*Mamm* and *Daad* were putting her in there since it faced the front and not the barn—Sarah thought she would balk. But entering her old room seemed to calm her. She went right in, then broke Sarah's heart when she said, "Your *grossdaad* will be back from the fields soon. You two just enjoy yourselves, and I'll be fine, just waiting for him here."

Sarah caught Nate's gaze. There were tears in his eyes, too.

# 21

"YOU READY TO PULL AN ALL-NIGHTER?" SHERIFF Freeman asked over the satellite phone Nate had provided for him.

"Hope I can stay awake after the supper they fed me here. Between the Amish and Ray-Lynn's restaurant, Jack, I'm tanking weight on."

"Yeah, it's all good home cooking from scratch," Jack said with a sigh. "I should appreciate it more than I have."

From the darkened room, Nate glanced out the upstairs bedroom window toward the Kauffman barn. Sarah had a good start on her quilt square. He hoped, if that "beast" of an arsonist was targeting this barn next, he or she wouldn't wait until the painting was completely done. If the arsonist wanted to burn a completed one, then Stan and the Hostetlers would have to be the ones to react.

Though it was barely dusk, Nate had stationed himself at the back window of the big bedroom he had learned Lizzie, Sarah and Martha had shared when they were younger. Now that Lizzie lived nearby, it belonged to the two younger

Kauffman daughters, though they usually alternated nights with their *grossmamm* in the *grossdaadi haus*. It felt strange to be setting up a stakeout in Sarah's bedroom, and, if he took a break for a catnap, that it could be in her bed.

"Ray-Lynn's really mad at me for mentioning her visit to the Esh barn to you," he told Jack.

"At you? Wouldn't be real surprised if she starts seasoning my food with arsenic."

Nate arranged his gear on the floor around his chair while they talked. He had borrowed Ben Kauffman's binoculars and would soon don his own night goggles. Ben was stationed in the *grossdaadi haus* tonight, since it would be better for him than for Nate to be seen traversing the yard between there and the farmhouse if necessary. Gabe and Sarah would take short shifts here at this window to give him some breaks, and Martha was out with her father. Mrs. Kauffman was in the master bedroom with her mother-in-law.

"I just talked to Stan Comstock," Jack went on, "so his satellite phone's working, too. First hint of trouble, you call me."

"Copy that. But we need to be sure we have the arsonist here before the Jack Freeman cavalry comes charging in. We don't want to spook him."

"He is like a spook, isn't he—or she? Like a specter that comes and goes at will, but we're gonna nail the bastard. Listen, I'll be moving around some tonight, not just sitting in this office, not going home right away, but I'll keep this phone with me. I'm gonna check out the ruins of the Miller barn, be sure no one's around there admiring his or her fine work."

"Jack, one more thing—and I'm trusting you with this,

trusting you to understand why I did it and to keep it quiet, especially from Peter Clawson."

"I don't like the sound of that. You did what?"

"Kept something secret, with the agreement of the Amish leadership. The Miller barn was an arson fire, but not by *the* arsonist."

"Say again."

"The Amish are going to handle this just the way you handled Jacob Yoder at first, in an understanding and humanitarian way."

"What? Besides, that blew up in my face."

"Noah Miller lit that fire hoping to get his dad a new barn and show us his old buddy Jacob wasn't the arsonist. He's confessed, and the Amish are going to deal with him."

The curse out of Jack's mouth did the ex-marine proud. Nate realized he'd given up swearing since he'd been here. In Amish country, a *yes* or a *no* were emphatic answers that didn't need any kind of dramatic emphasis. He steeled himself for an argument or attack from the sheriff.

"So you got the idea from the way I handled Jacob at first?" Jack asked. He sounded touched, almost wistful. "I agonized over that, but it was worth a try to help a kid and the Amish. Living here for a while, when guys like us are used to hardened criminals, is a real revelation, isn't it?"

The word *revelation* jolted Nate more than Jack's surprising reaction did. It was, no doubt, just chance that he said it that way, but could he be behind those threatening notes? He didn't sound or act as if he had some serious grudge against the Amish. Although they tolerated professional soldiers and government law enforcement, their mistrust of officers was well-known, so did he secretly resent that? Jack had freedom of movement, access to information, probably knew who was away from their homes and barns....

No, there he went again, acting paranoid, Nate scolded himself. Pretty soon he'd be thinking Martha or Gabe was the arsonist.


"Are you managing to stay awake?" Sarah asked Nate as she came quietly into the room around midnight. "I'm going to take the first watch for you, then Gabe will be in about 3:00 a.m."

"I'm drinking a lot of coffee, but that means trips to the bathroom, so I'm glad you're here. You remember how to put these night goggles on?"

"I remember how strange everything looks through them, like swimming underwater."

"They're invaluable here," he said as he got out of his chair and she sat in it. He helped her adjust the goggles. "In the first place," he told her, "to us worldly moderns, it's strange to see an area so dark at night. No interior glowing electrical or digital gadgets, no exterior house lights, streetlights, city lights."

"Moonlight isn't much tonight, but at least we have the stars outside."

"I haven't been star-gazing in years. Be right back."

He hurried to use the toilet and wash his hands. A shower would feel really good right now, but then it might make him sleepier, too. He was usually good with just several hours of sleep, but, despite chasing an arsonist here, it seemed as if his interior clock had slowed down in Amish country. Besides, he hadn't done an all-night sting operation in a long time. He wiped his hands and face with one of the fluffy towels Mrs. Kauffman had laid out for him. He was still amazed by the modern look of the bathroom with all the amenities and had scolded himself for thinking it would be primitive. Even the kerosene lantern hissing gently on a small table gave enough light to see everything and probably had a calming effect—but not tonight.

He should have splashed his face with cold water, but he went back and stood behind Sarah's chair in the dark room instead of stretching out on the bed.

"So," he said, "do you miss this room, staying out in the *grossdaadi haus* so much?"

"Strangely, except for the comfort of the bed, which you'd better try out," she said, without turning her face away from the window, "I don't. I guess when a woman gets to a certain age, she's ready to move out, move on, have her own home."

"I can understand that. So you've considered that, too. Ever thought of living with Hannah for a while?"

"Not that. No goth friends who talk music all day long for me. I'd have a place with a room to paint, one sunlit in the morning."

"Sarah, can't you have that here? If everyone could see some of your sketches—new ones, so vibrant with Amish life—"

"You're starting to sound like Ray-Lynn."

"On that, I agree with Ray-Lynn. Surely, your family and your people care about you enough to give you a chance to try painting more than birdhouses and barns."

"It's a different world here, Nate. You've seen that. I'd have to leave them, leave the church, move away to the modern world. It would be too individual, too prideful, considered too 'just for pretty.' I'd be painting images of people and that's *verboten*. Yes, they love me and that's why they'd shun me. That's the real decision I would need to make, if it's worth leaving what I know and dearly love to follow my dreams at the cost of being shunned. Individual dreams aren't important here, community, sharing—that's reality."

"Jack Freeman and I were talking about Noah possibly being shunned. Can you explain it to me? I can sit back down there with the goggles while you talk if they bother you."

"All right," she said. "Then, I'll take them back while you get some rest."

He helped her take them off. The strap snagged in her prayer cap and pulled it off, freeing the heavy pinned-up braid that fell across his arm and down her back. The fact she didn't try to fix either was strangely moving. He sat down and put the goggles on, wishing he could see her instead, though she'd just given him a glimpse into her heart.

"Okay," she said, sitting on the floor beside his chair with her back to the wall, "our words for what is commonly known as shunning are the *meidung* or the *bann*. Believe it or not, it usually works to bring the erring or sinning person back into fellowship."

Nate heard the bedroom door creak. Maybe Sarah's mother was bringing more coffee or Gabe was here already. He turned away from the window for a quick look.

A woman screamed. Sarah scrambled up beside him.

"That's him! That's him!" Sarah's grandmother shrilled, pointing at Nate in the goggles. "The barn and people burner, the man in black with the big eyes!"

"Am I formally under arrest this time?" Ray-Lynn asked as she answered her front door and saw Jack standing there, hat in hand.

"I just wanted to talk, and I was afraid if I called ahead you'd tell me not to come."

"Very astute. Talk about what?"

"I'd like to step in just for a few minutes, as I'm making rounds. I want to apologize."

Not knowing what to say and feeling she was all out of sass, she moved aside and let him in. She wished she hadn't changed her clothes after work. She'd washed off her makeup and thrown on a comfy pair of jeans and a sweatshirt. Her hair was a tousled mess. And the way he was looking at her right now, half whipped puppy and half hungry wolf, really sapped what strength she had left.

"Please sit down," she said, leading him into the living room and gesturing toward the couch. He sat on its far end, turned toward her as she settled on the other end, tucking one leg up under herself. When he dropped his hat on the coffee table, he just missed her bobblehead Scarlett O'Hara who nodded at him. "Go ahead," Ray-Lynn said. "This is your party."

"Wish it was. I just want to say I know I overreacted to you not telling me you were at the Esh place the night of the first fire. But you should have told me, told me why and that would have been fine. Topic number two, I know you're gung ho about helping Sarah Kauffman paint more than geometric designs on old barn wood, but you better lay off. Not only because you'll upset the Amish community, but because she seems to be the focus of our arsonist."

"You want the truth? So far, this sounds like true confessions, so here goes. Yes, I want to help Sarah. And on a practical level, she'd be able to pour money into this economically hurting community, hurting at least until this big bump in visitors we've had from the arsons. But I want to help her for myself, too, partly because it would give me great satisfaction to bring her talent to others, partly because if I could act as her agent, maybe I could dig my way out from under my partnership with Peter Clawson. He owns seventy percent of my business, not fifty, like most people think."

He turned more toward her. "That right? Maybe you could get some local investors, buy out his share."

"No one I know has that kind of money, especially in these tough times, and he'd refuse unless I took him to court—where he'd defend himself brilliantly. I just don't like him telling me what to do, thinking he can control me in other ways."

"What other ways?" Jack demanded, leaning forward and frowning. "He been coming on to you in ways he shouldn't? Making passes?"

"Not for a while. Not since I told him off. You know, like in the old days, 'Unhand me, you cad!' and 'I'm not that kind of girl'?"

Jack threw one arm on the back of the couch and leaned toward her. "Ray-Lynn, you just say the word, and I'll see he never so much as orders anything at the restaurant again, let alone orders you around."

"And then you'll do what when he fires me? Technically, he can. Besides, he already resents you because you're the other big man on campus around here, not counting our fire marshal boy wonder."

"Nate's a good man for this job."

"I know he is, and I think he's a sort of silent partner on my side about Sarah daring to take control of her life and talent. Now, please, don't you go roughing up Peter, either verbally or physically, because it will all come back on me. I don't want to get you involved, but, I swear, I'd do about anything to get that man off my back!"

"So how much money's involved for you to buy him out?"

"I don't think he'd let me buy him out. Jack, I'm sorry I've been so rude and inhospitable," she rushed on. "Every proper Southern lady I ever knew is spinning in her grave because I haven't offered you something to drink or eat and here we are in food-for-all Amish country."

She got up and started toward the kitchen, but he snagged her wrist in his big hand and pulled her down, close to him on the couch. "Ray-Lynn, listen. I meant to say this the minute I stepped through the door, but I figured you might brain me with one of those painted china plates if I didn't work up to it. I'm not real good at soft or sweet words, but since you're a Southern girl—lady—let me put it this way, then you can toss me out on my tail if you want."

Her eyes widened and her lower lip dropped. She forgot to breathe.

"I'd like—I want," he stammered, "well, to court you, date you, see you, if you could just put up with a guy who's loved only once, ended up with a wife divorcing me. I've lived alone too long, married to my job, and I'm so upset about these arsons I can't see straight."

For the first time in her life, Ray-Lynn Logan could not find her voice. So she nodded, kept nodding, until she realized she must look like her Scarlett O'Hara bobblehead doll. She gave him a hard hug.

Sarah tried to calm *Grossmamm*. Her *mamm* ran into the room. Since it was so dark with only wan hall light reflecting here, Sarah's first instinct was to get a lamp so the distraught woman could see it was just Nate. But they didn't want light here so that someone outside could see in.

Nate had turned back toward the window obviously not wanting to stop looking out or else to help calm *Grossmamm*.

"She was just sitting in the rocking chair," *Mamm* told them. "I just stepped out for a second. Come with me," she crooned in German to *Grossmamm,* taking the old woman's arm. She didn't budge. "Sarah, help me," *Mamm* said.

They tried to move the old woman out into the hall, but she kept shouting, "Burner! Burner! Leave my people alone!"

"Those are just special glasses so Nate can see in the dark," Sarah said, though she should have known it was foolish to try to reason with her. She turned *Grossmamm* toward her and held her cold, fragile hands between her own. "That's our friend you met downstairs, remember?"

"But he's been sneaking around in the dark. Have you been meeting him secretly outside?"

Finally, Sarah and *Mamm* managed to get *Grossmamm* back in the front bedroom and settled. *Mamm* kept talking to her quietly, got her going in the rocking chair, which usually calmed her, while Sarah waited a moment in the doorway, hastily pinning up her braid and putting her *kapp* back on.

"I'm surprised all that shouting didn't bring your father or Gabe running," *Mamm* said over her shoulder, "but the window was closed."

"Don't you believe me?" *Grossmamm* said. "That is the man I saw from my window at the *grossdaadi haus*."

Sarah hurried to her and knelt by the rocking chair. "I believe that you saw someone in night goggles like Nate is wearing," Sarah said. "But it surely wasn't Nate. He's our friend."

"That is how they used to arrest us, send a spy, someone trusted who told them where we were hiding. Then the torment, the ax and the fire."

"Go tell Nate we're sorry, Sarah," *Mamm* said, putting her hand on her shoulder. "You and Martha—I didn't really know how much you do out there at night. Go tell him. I'll be fine."

Sarah closed the door behind her and hurried across the hall and into her bedroom. How unreal it felt to have Nate sitting there in the window. After this was all over and he went home, she would always picture him there, not looking out but in.

He turned his head as she sat down on the floor again, her legs stretched out next to his chair, her back to the wall near the window. "*Mamm* says to tell you she's sorry that happened."

"It's all right, except I regret your *grossmamm* is haunted by a past she didn't even live through. But she gave us a piece of information I should have figured out on my own when she said the person in black had eyes like a grasshopper. She saw someone sneaking around the barn with night goggles, probably the same person who left that first note on the *grossdaadi haus* door. Probably the beast of an arsonist."

"But who would have access to night goggles? Didn't you say they are for soldiers and law officers? What about someone like the sheriff?"

"Anyone could buy them if they knew the right place, including online."

"*Ya,* it seems everything's online, from Grandma Moses paintings to the entire Bible. Being online is *verboten* to my people without permission, and yet those things are good. You—you still want to hear about shunning? I'm afraid you're not getting enough sleep."

"Now you sound like my foster mother, M.E."

"Is her real name Emma and you just call her Emmy?"

"It's an *M* and an *E,* my nickname for Mary Ellen. I know she would have loved for me to call her Mom, but after losing mine—and so close to where the Bosleys took me in—I just couldn't. That's what I mean about hauntings, like your grandmother suffers from. It was years ago, and I'm a grown man who's seen too many other arson scenes, but I can't bear to see that one."

"I understand. I'm sure M.E. will be glad to see you've put a little flesh on your bones here," she said, hoping that wasn't an obvious attempt to change the subject. The man suddenly looked shaky.

"Yeah, she's always asking me if I'm eating enough. The thing is, I'm not getting my jogging in here, where it would be a great place to run. But I am getting too much exercise lifting fork or spoon to mouth." He yawned. "Okay, tell me about the *meidung,* then I'll take a little nap while you keep watch."

"Shunning is a fearsome thing among our people, because it removes us from the community that is the bedrock of our being," she told him. "It means the one under the *bann* cannot eat with loved ones, or sleep with them, if it's a marriage partner. The Amish may do favors for the shunned one, but he or she cannot do acts of kindness or favors in return— and giving as well as receiving is also the foundation of our church and beliefs."

"But if you make confession and change the behavior in question—"

"The sin in your life."

"Right. Then you can be taken back?"

"With confession and a restoration process. There is so much joy when a lost soul returns to the flock, the prodigal son or daughter."

"What are some of the things deemed shunnable?"

"Well, of course, aiding and abetting a car theft ring—that could have sent Jacob to prison. Adultery, of course. Pre-marital relations—which does happen, though usually the couple makes confession and weds and is taken back in good faith. We're not saints. That's a wrong idea *ausländers* have of us sometimes. Also, cheating in a business transaction, using banned technology without permission, marriage outside the faith, owning a car, flying in an airplane—anything that is jumping the fence of our *ordnung,* the rules."

"But Mrs. Miller won't be banned for going with Noah in the medical chopper?"

"No. The *ordnung* might sound strict, but it is open to interpretation, and mercy rules judgment at times, like with Noah. He might be banned for a while but when he's taken back, he'll be stronger for the separation."

"Isn't there any hope against shunning for someone who decided to pursue her artistic talent to paint pictures and then sell them?"

She hesitated a moment. "There is an Amish artist in Pennsylvania, Susie Riehl, but she does mostly still life, quilts or buildings and, if she does a person, she makes him or her faceless. And she stays at home, never goes to shows of her work or promotes her own work. Considering the challenge I had just getting permission to paint quilt squares, my guess is that the *meidung* would be pronounced on me. Nate," she said, her voice trembling and hurried, "I'd have to go live in the world, and that would mean shunning, too. It's almost like being dead to your family and friends—to be dreaded as much as…as much as being burned."

"Don't talk like that. You sound like your *grossmamm.* I believe your artistic talent is a God-given gift and shouldn't be hidden or stifled. Just remember that, if your own people ever try to bring you up on *meidung* charges."

Sarah had to smile at the way he'd put that, law officer that he was. He still could not grasp the impact of an Amish person being cut off. Good old American individualism and independence made it so hard for the *Englische* to really grasp their ways. She let him help her get the night goggles adjusted once again and settled in the chair. Without turning her head, she knew he lay down on her bed. But then—

Her heart almost leaped into her throat. A man out there! A man walking past the barn, looking up at it....

She saw it was *Daad,* coming back into the house for something, not hurrying. It must not be an emergency. It didn't seem as if he had seen anyone. If only one of them had seen who put that last note in the sack with the paint, but she'd asked the whole family. It would be pointless to ask Cindee. If she and Mike Getz wrote the note, she'd deny it. If they had nothing to do with it, the cat—like the note—would be out of the bag.

Grateful she hadn't scared Nate with a false alarm, Sarah leaned her elbows on the windowsill and stared into the darkness outside and that within.

# 22

"THIS BAD WEATHER IS GOING TO RUIN YOUR surveillance plan tonight," Sarah told Nate the second night of their vigil.

They stood inside the screened door of the farmhouse, watching the rain slant sideways so heavy they couldn't see the barn. The wind howled, and trees thrashed in the gusts. It was coming from the other direction, or they would have been soaked with just the screen between them and the force of the storm. But Sarah was so aware of another force of nature standing behind her, close but not touching her. She wanted to lean back against him but she stayed rigidly where she was.

"Bad weather is God's will, right?" he asked. "Maybe He thinks I need more than three hours' sleep, but I can't imagine sleeping during this."

"It's a good thing I didn't paint more today, or it might have washed away or been peeled off," she told him, hoping he realized she was joking.

She hadn't admitted that she was really torn about working

on her quilt square. The more progress she made, the more she felt she was endangering her family's barn, and yet they wanted to lure the arsonist out in the open. But on a night like this, they'd never even see him, let alone catch him.

"How do your people prepare for a weather emergency, if they don't know it's coming?" he asked. "No internet, no TV…"

"Sometimes word of mouth, but mostly battery-operated radios for weather emergencies. *Daad* has one upstairs, so I suppose that's where he's been since the others are in the living room."

Sarah knew Nate had been talking on the satellite phone to the fire marshal supervisor, Stan Comstock. From him, Nate had learned the storm was widespread.

They both jerked as a flash of lightning blinded them and a horrific boom of thunder resounded somewhere close. He put his hands on her shoulders, tight.

"All we need is lightning hitting the barn tonight," he said. "It's a good thing some of the trees by the pond are tall, because maybe they'd draw the strike. Stan says there are tornado warnings south of here, too, but you never know where those might hit."

"And that's why—" *Daad*'s voice came from behind them "—we trust in the Lord who giveth and taketh away. But I still agree we can call the arsonist the Beast now, since that last threatening note. You two get out of the doorway, 'cause I'm going to have to go on out to the barn and look around after that strike. Nate, you want to come with me?"

"Sure. With this storm, no one's going to start a barn fire tonight."

Although lately they had kept the horses in the fields in case the arsonist struck, they had been forced to move the four big plow team Percherons and the three buggy horses inside. Not only did the animals get nervous outside, but they could be struck by lightning or hit with flying debris.

*"Daad,"* Sarah said, "you know Sally always gets off her bean over thunder. I'll go, too."

"You've changed, my girl," *Daad* told her. "Just two weeks ago, you would have *asked* if you could go along."

Nate had taken his hands from her shoulders the minute they heard *Daad*'s voice. Her father looked at her, then at Nate. He turned and went into the living room. Sarah assumed he was talking to her mother there. When he came back, he carried three coats and two large flashlights, one of which he handed to Nate. Nate had to fuss with the backpack he wore. Since Amish clothes had no pockets, he carried his satellite and cell phones in there. Even if they'd had an umbrella, Sarah thought as they stepped out, it would be turned inside out or ripped away.

On the porch, they waited for a slight lull in the rain. Finally, after *Mamm* came into the kitchen to see if they had gone, *Daad* led the way out.

The wind hit them hard, ripping at their clothes and hair, whipping leaves and grit against their skin. They squinted their eyes almost closed and stumbled along through puddles. Nate pulled her to his side, and they bent into the blast together right behind her father.

"Forty, fifty miles per hour," Sarah thought Nate said, but she wasn't sure in the shriek of the wind. In the leeward shelter of the barn, under her partly painted quilt square, *Daad* and Nate worked together to slide the door open enough that they could dart in, then slide it closed behind them.

Within was a cove of quiet; however, the wind howled outside. Each rumble of thunder made Sarah think this vast building was clearing its throat or its belly was rumbling, giant that it was with them inside. In the drafts and wind, the entire barn seemed to gasp for air. It looked so different at night without the wan, golden glow of a lantern or two. The depths of darkness seemed to swallow their flashlight beams. As silly as it was of her, she almost felt she'd never been here before. How did the arsonist feel when he decided to murder a barn?

Nate and *Daad* played their beams along the floor so they could see as they made their way toward the snorting, stomping horses in their stalls at the back. Something was creaking, something else was banging, just as that day during a lighter rain in the Miller barn before it was burned.

*Daad* went to pat and talk in German to his work team, big, blond babies that they were. Sally tossed her head and showed the whites of her eyes in the reflected light of the flashlight Nate held.

"Will she be okay in the dark with you?" Nate asked as Sarah petted and crooned to the mare. "I'd like to go up in the loft and check around the interior perimeter—see and smell if that lightning strike hit anything. Something like that can smolder for a long time before bursting into flames."

Their gazes snagged and held. When he looked at her like that she could almost feel heat between them.

"Sure, we'll be fine. Won't we, girl?" Sarah said, and looked away.

Soon she could tell that her father also walked around the barn, darting a beam of light into corners. Sarah inhaled deeply, hoping she didn't smell smoke. No. She was just imagining things, letting the sounds outside shake her up as much as they had Sally.

It seemed an eternity before Nate and *Daad* came back to her. When they held their flashlights low, the shadows on their features made them look scary.

"Until it lets up a bit, I'm gonna stay out here. Nate, you want to go back to the house or the *grossdaadi haus?*" *Daad* said.

"I don't think any of us could so much as see the barn tonight from outside of it. We've learned the Beast is clever, so he or she must know it would be crazy to try an arson tonight. You want me to get Sarah in the house, then come on back? She can tell them what we're doing."

"How about bringing out some coffee and cookies or half-moon pies?" *Daad* said, and turned back toward the horses.

Sarah wanted to stay, too, and tend her horse, but since her father had made that earlier comment about her not asking for permission, she kept quiet. Besides, she still felt more skittish out here than poor Sally.

She and Nate waited for another little lull and, holding hands, made a dash for it toward the porch of the house. When they almost slipped in a mud puddle, she held him up better than he did her. She wanted to cry, to laugh. She wanted all the dangers to go away so she could just be here on a calm early June night with Nate. She wished he'd come calling, wished he was Amish—but then he wouldn't be Nate.

*"Mamm,"* Sarah called when she saw her mother's silhouette behind the screen door, *"Daad* and Nate are going to stay in the barn for a while, but can you put some coffee in a thermos and pack some snacks for them?"

Without a word, *Mamm* turned away. "You should get some dry clothes," Sarah told Nate as they stood on the porch. Hers stuck close to her skin, and, after she took off her jacket and shook it out, Nate kept looking her over.

"I only have one outfit—one chance to be Amish," he told her. "You tell everyone not to worry about your dad and me out there tonight."

He tugged her away from the door. Between it and the window, he pulled her to him, holding her tight. They pressed together knees to foreheads in a hard hug. They didn't kiss, just held each other up in the sweep of the storm, but it sent her head spinning as if he'd kissed her silly. And she had the strangest thought. Although Nate was the outsider here, she suddenly felt she was, too. At that moment she felt closer to him than to her family or her friends and community.

They jumped apart when they heard *Mamm*'s quick footsteps in the kitchen, then her voice, "Here, double-bagged."

"Get some sleep," Nate said, talking to both of them.

"As if, in this noise," Sarah told him.

He waited on the porch a moment, picking his time, then darted into the wet, devouring night.

*Mamm* held the door for her, and Sarah stepped inside, dripping wet. "We have to be strong," *Mamm* said, and put her arm around Sarah's wet shoulders, "but then not be too bold, either. Keeping on the straight and narrow, that works the best."

"Maybe so," Sarah said, "but that's pretty hard in a big storm, one I didn't ask for, one I can't see through." Did her mother know she was talking about Nate? That's what *Mamm* had meant, hadn't she?

*Mamm* looked like she'd say more. Little worry lines like birds' feet crowded the corners of her eyes. "Nate's a good *Englische* man, and I like him," *Mamm* said. "But he can't be for you, Sarah. I'd burn that barn myself and confess to the other burnings if it would make him leave," she blurted, and then fled the kitchen.

"I can see you and Sarah are getting close," Ben Kauffman told Nate as they sat on hay bales in the barn. The lightning and thunder were getting more distant, but now this—a talk Nate did not want to have.

"She's been a tremendous help. Because of her barn paintings, finding the arsonist is personal to her, too."

"But you two been getting that way—personal."

Ben's voice was not raised. It was barely discernible above the rain on the roof. Nate knew the Amish man would not confront him in a worldly way. Somehow, that made it harder than if they could argue or fight it out. He didn't even know how to confront himself about his feelings for Sarah.

"She's a very special woman," Nate said. "Bright and talented."

"And tempted by things she can't have, a worldly art career and an outsider, however kind a man he is."

"Her God-given talents to draw and paint—why can't she have that? Some Amish build barns, some quilt, some grow and sell lavender, some bake, some build birdhouses and gazebos and farm, too."

"I was hoping you could understand what keeps the Plain People going after all these years is unity of purpose, tradition and beliefs."

"I see that. But individual differences within the group are to be cherished and encouraged, too, aren't they?"

The older man took a gulp of coffee. He leaned over and put his hand on Nate's shoulder. "Once you've found the barn burner, we want you to leave with good memories of

the Home Valley and the Kauffman family, Nathan Mac-
Kenzie. But we don't want you to leave with our Sarah."

"If she leaves, it would be her decision, not mine. That
much I can promise you. You've let me put a lie out to the
community that I'm not here right now and for a good purpose. But I can't lie to someone who has been such a good
host as you, Mr. Kauffman. I care deeply for Sarah and can
promise only to support her decisions as best I can, whatever
she does or doesn't do."

"Then let's agree the decisions will be hers."

"Fine. But if not mine, not her parents' decisions, either.
Hers alone."

Ben Kauffman nodded, and they shook hands. It was quiet
between them after that and not because of the whine of the
wind and roar of the rain.


"You didn't have to stay at the restaurant until I closed
up," Ray-Lynn told Jack as he walked her to her car. She
didn't see his, so it still must be parked at the police station.
"I've driven home in bad storms before, and the worst seems
over. It's barely sprinkling right now. It sure smells fresh and
clean out tonight, doesn't it?"

"You get free bodyguard protection, you better take it,
Ray-Lynn. This isn't exactly a mecca for crime, except for
our arsonist, but you can't be too careful going to your car
at night. Unfortunately, the evils of society are creeping out
of the city and into the country more and more. Here, let
me hold that umbrella over both of us. You want to take a
little stroll?"

"Sure. It'll be like that old movie, *Singing in the Rain*. We'll
splash in the puddles and dance."

"We could go dancing some night if you want."

She took his arm, and he held it tight to his side. "You do a great job around here, Jack, but I can't believe Nate's left this all to you right now. He hasn't called from Columbus, has he? Shouldn't he be here, keeping an eye on things?"

It seemed to her he was going to say something, then thought the better of it. "He'll be back for the barn raising Saturday," he told her.

"I hope he's got some evidence or at least a good lead. Do you think he does?"

"Just don't you worry yourself about any of that. Now, if you would have gotten that quilt square painting of Sarah's done on the front of the restaurant or even a mural inside, I might have told you different. We can't tell if the arsonist is targeting barns of Amish church leaders or her art."

"I wonder if Nate knows about the storm, at least. I actually saw some of Peter's precious newspapers being swept down the street as if they were tissues. He'd have a conniption if he looked up from his work long enough to see it, and now he'll have to cover the weather as well as the arsons and the barn raising."

"Like I said, he so much as hassles you over his coffee getting cold, you let me know. Hey, see the light on in the hardware store? It's gonna do a land office business selling chain saws and such tomorrow to cut up fallen limbs. I wonder if Mr. Baughman's getting ready for the onslaught," he said, "'cause it looks like they stayed open late. For once, not just Peter's office but the hardware store's all lit up."

"But it's usually brighter than that when they have the store lights on," Ray-Lynn said.

"Good observation. That light's pretty dim. Mr. Baughman should have told me if he decided to start leaving a safety light on. I'm gonna get you back in your car and go check it out."

"Not when we're almost there, you're not. You just go peek in, and I'll wait here."

She stayed in front of the Amish Antiques Shop—some of their stock wasn't Amish and some wasn't antique—while Jack strode across the street. On the far edge of town she could see the lights from the McDonald's and the Wendy's that she once feared would ruin her business. Lately, they hadn't made a dent. Except for locals, the non-Amish eating places held little allure.

But she was starting to feel Jack's allure—no, not starting. For some reason, the man had gotten to her from the first, and it wasn't just the masculine marine aura or the spiffy police uniform. Maybe it was his deep aloneness, a soft side he tried so hard to hide.

She edged a bit closer to the hardware store. With all the visitors and strangers in town lately, she could see why Mr. Baughman would want it lit at night. Jack was right about crime creeping into rural areas, though that car theft ring Jacob Yoder got involved with was about the worst scandal they'd had in Home Valley—before the clever arsonist took to lighting barns.

She watched Jack peek in the corner of the front window of the store, then jump back. What? Surely not a robbery in progress? She pressed herself against the front of the Hair Port Barber Shop. She slid along past the Hole in the Wall— the pizza and subs shop.

If Jack was into something dangerous across the street, would he be all right?

She moved along until she could see inside the hardware store, which abutted the Homestead Pharmacy and Kwik

Shop. Gazing into the store where Jack had gone was like looking at a distant, dim TV picture.

She gasped. Jack was inside with his gun drawn!

Figuring that Stan Comstock was calling to report in, Nate grabbed his satellite phone when it sounded. Caller ID showed it was the sheriff. Nate kept petting Sarah's horse as he talked.

"Nate here."

"I'm at the station. I just arrested and booked Mike Getz and Cindee Kramer for B and E, even though she had a key—and for attempted larceny. I surprised them as they were loading up his truck with some stock items from the hardware store, which I think she was juggling in the store records. They probably thought the storm would keep folks off the streets so no one would notice."

"Good work! So instead of Jacob, we have another suspect off the streets and out of the fields and barns."

"Right. But let me tell you what they had loaded up. Some tools and camping equipment, including a package of artificial fireplace logs, like you said ignited the Schrock barn. But here's the kicker. They took a dual-burner Coleman stove and two cylinders of liquid propane to fuel it—or to burn something else."

"Bingo! The arsonist has been using a different incendiary device for each burn so far, and propane would sure do the trick. Be careful with it because even the slightest spill can give human skin severe frostbite."

"Frostbite? And it ignites fires? So anyway, you want to have a chat with one or both in the morning?"

"I'll come into town in the back of Sarah's buggy when she delivers Ray-Lynn's half-moon pies. Let's hope Getz is our man. I hope I can question him quietly so people don't know I'm back."

"You want me to have a go at him first? I didn't trust the guy from the git-go, always in the right place at the right time to play the hero."

"If it's okay with you, I still think I'd better do it, since we want to tie him to the arsons. With the fireplace logs and propane—you know in law enforcement coincidences usually aren't. After I question them, I'll have you get me back here, let me out somewhere near Kauffman's and I'll walk back in. I'm looking pretty Amish these days. But I'll bring my civilian clothes along for their interrogation. Those two aren't locked up together, are they?"

"So they can think up a cover story? No way. I had to put Getz in the storage room."

"Thanks for the good work. This may be the break we need. See you in the morning, and I hope they don't lawyer up."

"Haven't so far. It's gonna be a long night without a deputy here right now, but I can't see having one drive in from Wooster with debris all over the roads until tomorrow. See ya."

A Coleman stove and propane, Nate thought as he punched in Stan Comstock's number. Then he'd call Mark Lincoln in Columbus. Yeah, that propane in Getz's possession could have burned Hostetlers' or this beautiful barn into oblivion.

# 23

THE MORNING AFTER THE STORM, SARAH HAD to guide Sally around broken tree limbs and piles of wind-swept litter on the roads to get to the Dutch Farm Table with the half-moon pies—and get Nate to the sheriff's office. She had him hidden again, dressed Amish, but with his own clothes in his backpack. She'd been surprised that her parents had let her take him into town since it was obvious they realized how much she cared for him. Well, they were hardly going to elope in a horse and buggy. Or ever. Above all, *Mamm* and *Daad* wanted the arsonist caught, so Nate could leave.

At least Nate now had another strong lead, not Jacob, and, thank the Lord, not Hannah. Sarah hoped the sheriff's prisoners might be the guilty ones, even if she felt real bad for Cindee to have picked the wrong man to fall in love with.

Nate seemed all business now, so she concentrated not only on safety but speed. She let him out behind the sheriff's office before heading for the restaurant. She had wanted to say so much that wasn't arson talk. She sensed that he had, too.

Ordinarily, she thought as she headed for the alley behind the restaurant, a big storm would be the topic of conversation for days around here, but it would probably still take second place to arson talk. And word would soon be all over town that Mike Getz and Cindee Kramer were under arrest. Still, Nate had said, if they didn't confess, he wanted to keep what he called a sting going at her house.

"Oh, good, you're here," Ray-Lynn greeted her as she came in the back door. "I should have known that neither rain nor snow nor sleet nor gloom of night—that's a post office slogan, I guess, but it suits you and your people, too. I know about Mike and Cindee's arrest," she said, whispering now and leaning closer. "It's not common knowledge yet. I was with the sheriff last night when he spotted them in the hardware store. We were walking in the rain. And the night before last, Jack more or less asked me out. I meant to tell you yesterday when you were here but I was so busy."

"Oh, Ray-Lynn, that's great, on both counts—them getting caught and maybe Jack, too. So your hard-to-get plan worked."

"Something did, my friend," she said with a glint in her eyes and a funny wiggle of her eyebrows. "I only hope and pray our intrepid arson-fighting duo have the right suspects. Here, I saved the back booth for you because I want you to meet someone who came in from Columbus."

"Nate's boss?" she blurted, afraid he might have come to tell Nate he was recalling him.

"The state fire marshal? Why would he come here if Nate's not around? No, just a sec. Oh, here's the money for your mother and sister," she added, digging in one apron pocket and then the other. "Drat—it's still in the cash register. Be right back," she said over her shoulder as she broke into a half run around the counter.

Sarah sighed. She was happy for Ray-Lynn, the sheriff, too. But that just made her sadder about Nate, so close but yet so far. After the way *Daad* had given her his I-won't-say-it-because-you're-old-enough-to-know-better look and after what *Mamm* had blurted out last night that Nate was not for her, she felt all the air had gone out of her.

Ray-Lynn appeared, bringing a nice-looking *Englische* couple with her. She slipped Sarah the money and whispered, "These people could pay you a hundred times that every week."

So, Sarah wondered, was Ray-Lynn promoting *Mamm* and Lizzie's pastries to restaurant owners in Columbus? That probably wouldn't work since the pies needed to be fresh, and they'd have to pay someone to deliver them daily.

"So this is the quilt square artist," the woman said with a warm smile. She had smooth, copper-colored hair that looked great, not crimson and spiky like Hannah's, but not so natural as Ray-Lynn's, either. It blended beautifully with her creamy complexion, sharp brown eyes and the russet-and-olive outfit she wore. "We're honored to meet someone so talented and so modest about it," the woman added. "Most of the artists we deal with are overly entranced by themselves."

Uh-oh, Sarah thought as Ray-Lynn made the proper introductions of Ginger and Geoff Markwood.

"We've seen your barn paintings in the papers and in person—the Hostetler barn one," Geoff Markwood said. He was quite a big man, but not fat. Like Mike Getz, he was bald but he had an earring in one lobe. "Ginger's the eyes and brain, and I'm just the moneyman," he said with a smile.

"We both like your abstract work very much and hear you do primitive realism, also."

When Sarah simply nodded, Ray-Lynn said, "It must be great to have a marriage and a business partnership, even steven, like you two do. Sarah, Ginger and I were sorority sisters years ago in Georgia, and now here we both are, living in Ohio."

"Ray-Lynn has said you also do panorama work—scenes with Amish people and places," Ginger said. Sarah knew she had to say something. She didn't want them to think she was tongue-tied or dense.

"Only in sketches so far. The colors that would go with them are in my head."

"We'd love to see any sketches you could share with us," Ginger said. "We specialize in developing and launching emergent talent through our gallery New Horizons in Columbus, but we have a large online presence, also."

"Why don't we sit down here? I've been fixin' to get you all together for a long time," Ray-Lynn said, sounding more Southern than usual when Ginger didn't one bit. Ray-Lynn eased them into the booth across from Sarah, then squeezed in next to Sarah so she was blocked in.

"I have no sketches to share at this time," Sarah said, ignoring the fact Ray-Lynn gave her a little kick under the table. "My sketchbook's been damaged."

"Really?" Ray-Lynn asked. "What happened?"

"It's a long story. It was very nice to meet both of you, especially since you're Ray-Lynn's friends, but I really need to be getting back home."

"Oh," Ray-Lynn said, looking upset when Sarah thought she was the one who'd been penned in here without warning. Nate might call this a sting.

"Of course, we understand," Ginger said. "We hope you won't object if we drive past the painting you're doing now, and please keep us in mind at New Horizons if you do decide to look for funding to paint or need a studio space or a gallery outlet."

"Thank you. I sure will, and Ray-Lynn will remind me if I don't."

Sarah bumped hips with Ray-Lynn to make her scoot out of the booth. At the back door, Ray-Lynn caught up with her. "Sarah—"

"You set that up when you know temptations like that can cause me all kinds of problems."

"I didn't set it up," she insisted as she followed Sarah outside to her buggy. "They just appeared today, surprised me, and I couldn't pass up the chance to introduce you. Sarah, I promise I won't bug you again, but you know your painting career would make you happy and help your people. Your profits could rebuild a lot of barns, pay for a lot of hospital bills...."

"We do that as a group, Ray-Lynn."

"Oh, right. All for one and one for all. I'm sorry, but I think you're making a big mistake."

"I've made them before. But I hope not to make ones to lose me everything—including someone I've considered a trusted friend."

She climbed into the buggy and snapped the reins to make Sally move. Weak rebel that she was—yes, rebel, because she wanted to run back there and promise to paint for them right now at their place called New Horizons, because she longed for new horizons of her own—she began to cry. She dared not strike out on her own and she was going to lose not only that chance but Nate, as well.

★ ★ ★

Nate emerged from a two-hour interrogation of Mike Getz and a half-hour one with Cindee Kramer, feeling like a failure. The guy hadn't budged from the claim that—yes, he'd been "borrowing" a few things from the Homestead Hardware Store since Cindee began working there two years ago, but he didn't have anything to do with burning barns. Oh, no, he was a hero in that regard, always on Nate's side.

It was just, Mike had explained, that Mr. Baughman who owned the hardware store, didn't pay Cindee enough. They liked to save money on firewood in the winter, and they liked to go camping. So the logs and the Coleman stove and propane would be well used.

The fact they'd taken the camping stove as well as the propane made Nate half believe the guy, even though he wanted to throw the book at him. In a way, it was Jacob Yoder all over again. A criminal was under arrest but maybe not for the arsons.

And Cindee? She'd done nothing but sob and say how much she loved Mike. She knew nothing about a note in the sack of paint she'd left by the Kauffman barn for Sarah, and she and Mike knew next to nothing about the Bible. Even though they'd been read their Miranda rights, neither of them had asked for a lawyer. And wouldn't they have done that, Nate thought, if they were guilty of arson?

"So, you still think we don't have our man?" Jack asked as Nate almost collapsed in the chair on the other side of his desk.

"Or woman. Probably not."

They both sat silent for a moment before Jack spoke.

"Happy to say, I've got another woman, though, and I'm not talking arson. I believe Ray-Lynn's explanation of her being at the Esh barn the night of the first fire. But, on a personal note, I made up with her, too."

Nate glared at him. "Did you ever try to find out if she had an alibi for the Schrock fire like you said you'd do?"

"I said I believe her. You're getting punch-drunk, man. Go get some sleep. I'd arrest Bishop Esh—or Sarah Kauffman—before I'd think it was Ray-Lynn!"

Nate didn't want to get the man more upset than he already was. As soon as the rent-a-deputy got here from Wooster, Nate wanted Jack to drop him off near the Kauffman farm so he could hike back in as Amish. But he didn't know how long this charade would last. One person he wasn't fooling was himself. He wasn't Amish and yet he was falling in love with an Amish woman. She wasn't worldly and wasn't leaving her people. And he'd failed to solve an arson case he'd thought at first would be so simple.

The rest of that day did nothing to make Nate feel better. After the sheriff dropped him off near the cemetery and he hiked back to the farm, it was even more obvious that Sarah's parents were keeping her away from him. That evening, they insisted Sarah and Martha take care of their grandmother back out in the *grossdaadi haus* and keep watch on the barn from there. Gabe stayed in the barn while Nate had Ben with him in Sarah's bedroom.

Out by the front of the barn, absolutely nothing had changed, except that Sarah's painting was growing larger. He had stared at it so long that it actually looked to him as if the multicolored ocean waves were moving, cresting, breaking on the dark wooden sea of the barn. He recalled how Sarah had told him she and Hannah had rescued Ella from drowning in the pond years ago, how there was some cold current deep down that tried to pull them under. He felt like that was happening to him.

On Friday morning, the day before the barn raising, Nate helped Ben and Gabe haul chairs and tables over to the Esh property. They even let him drive the big team on the road between the two farms.

Meanwhile, Mrs. Kauffman and Lizzie baked half-moon pies for the Dutch Farm Table and the barn raising. Outside, Sarah kept painting the quilt square. Back in the Kauffman kitchen for noontime dinner, Nate stared at the battery-operated clock on the wall. He heard his own clock ticking, his thudding heartbeat. He had to catch the barn burner. His boss had to have VERA back soon. Sarah—would he get some time with her to even say goodbye? He'd found the woman he wanted and he could not have her without destroying her. The Bible notes he'd kept secret were more than a ticking clock. They were a time bomb in Peter Clawson's hands. Nate could be accused of secrecy, of betrayal. He'd blown this case, his first failure on the job he used to be more passionate about than anything else—before Sarah.

He almost refused to eat dinner with the family, but where else would he go without a car? He didn't want to insult them, but he couldn't bear to see Sarah across the table, because she might as well be across the continent. Once he was called back to Columbus and this continuing investigation was turned over to Stan Comstock—however much the man had hinted he wanted to retire—he'd never see her again. In this world, one just didn't text or call or pick up an Amish woman for a date. He was sure she cared for him, too, but that made everything worse. So when the family bent their heads before the noon meal and prayed silently as was their custom, he asked the Lord for help to know what to do—to stop the arsonist, to not have to give up the woman he loved.

Right after the meal, when Ben and Gabe had gone next door to help Bishop Esh with a big delivery of timber for the new barn, Ray-Lynn called Nate on the cell number Jack had given her. M.E. was at the restaurant with two of her friends to see Amish country and she wanted to see him, too, because "she knew very well he wasn't in Columbus like this nice lady who runs the restaurant said."

"I don't like being misled or strung along by you or Jack," Ray-Lynn told Nate over the phone, her voice sharp. "He figured he had to tell me you've been around here the whole time despite what you told me. Trying to trap me, Nate? And Jack went along with it, so he doesn't trust me, either. If you're still looking at me as a suspect, then the kind, sweet woman sitting in booth twelve did a lousy job of raising you! Jack said to tell you if you need to get VERA, he'll unlock his garage door. So if you're going to turn back into Superman instead of being Clark Kent again, you just stay away from Sarah because neither you nor Jack deserve either of us!" She hung up.

Nate explained to the Kauffman women that his cover was blown. "With Ray-Lynn and anyone in earshot of the restaurant, I'll have to give up the ruse of not being here and get to VERA so I can go see my foster mother. I'll let the word out that I've returned for the barn raising. I'll come back and park at the pond later, if it's all right with Mr. Kauffman, but it ruins my pretending I'm not here. Still, I'd like to help keep an eye on things around here tonight."

"Sarah, with us so busy," her mother said matter-of-factly, "you'll have to buggy Nate to get his VERA." Mrs. Kauffman and Lizzie were rolling out more balls of pastry dough

for their second big batch of half-moon pies that kept coming out of the oven like a production line. "Then you come
right back so you can finish the painting like you wanted."
Mrs. Kauffman gave Nate a narrow-eyed look as if to say,
*You behave now.*

He'd felt furious that M.E. had just shown up and ruined
things. But had she? He'd wanted a chance to talk to Sarah,
though he had not one clue what to say, and he'd been close
to tongue-tied when she'd taken him into the sheriff's this
morning because he couldn't bear to say a private goodbye,
or any goodbye to her.

Sarah pulled the buggy out of the farm lane onto the
road, heading for Sheriff Freeman's garage so Nate could get
VERA and change his clothes before he headed into town.
She knew he was real down about the arson case, and she
wished she knew what to say to comfort him. In case this
was their last time alone, she wanted to say so much, but
Nate spoke first. "I don't like riding around hunched down
like this—except for the view," he told her.

"How can you see where we're going down there at all?
Oh, you mean—"

He put a hand under the seat, gently grasped her right
ankle, then took it back. She fought to keep her hands steady,
but she jolted so hard she could have steered Sally right off
the road.

"We never got our swim in the pond together," she
blurted. "The twelve days you've been here have gone pretty
fast."

"Sarah, I think I'm going to be recalled to Columbus and
Stan Comstock will take over here."

"I was afraid of that."

"Being here with you, your family and the community has given me a lot to think about. My nightmare of losing my parents in the fire my father set—I realize in a way I've resented M.E. as much as I've been grateful to her. She could never be my mother, so I shouldn't have punished her for that. I was afraid to really let her in my life, to really love her, as if I'd betray my own mother that way."

"You just put it really well how I feel about my parents. I love them, respect them, but I'm resenting the ties that bind me to them. I feel like I'd be betraying them if I tried to paint these places and these people for a career, so that takes a lot of soul-searching and courage. Ray-Lynn introduced me to the Columbus people with the art gallery this morning at the restaurant. I practically ran away from them when I really didn't want to. Now I'm going to kind of run away from us, too."

"Your father talked to me during the storm about not getting more personal with you. I don't want to alienate them, but you and I have had something going from the first—curiosity, sure, but a powerful attraction. You've really changed me in a short time. I feel deeply for you. If you ever do decide to leave here, I could help. Loan you some money, get you a place to stay while you paint."

"I just don't know. It would be worse for my people than when Hannah left. She wasn't shunned because she was never baptized in the church, but I was—I would be put under the *meidung.*"

"I'd like you to meet M.E. After you let me out, will you buggy to the restaurant on your way home? I'll catch up with you and introduce you. I know your mother said to come back to the farm fast, but it would mean a lot to me if you'd come in to meet her."

"I'd have to face Ray-Lynn after how I ran from her friends, then argued with her this morning."

"You could wait out back. She's mad at the sheriff and me, too, for lying to her about where I really was. And right after she and Jack were flying high."

"Flying high—that's a good one. Not very Amish, at least if it means an airplane. Now if it's a bird—"

"Or a woman at the top of the ladder, reaching up to paint the ocean or the sky…"

Sarah didn't say so, but she didn't like that picture in her head of herself at the top of a ladder. The nightmare of being tied to one and burned still haunted her really badly. But she realized she was trying to change the subject now. She was afraid of her emotions, of having to meet Nate's foster mother, of being without him. Even of having the arsonist still on the loose. She pictured a farewell kiss coming when she let Nate out of the buggy, but Sheriff Freeman was home and came out to meet them by his garage.

Well, Sarah thought, perhaps it was all for the best. She'd break into a million pieces if she had to say a final goodbye to Nathan MacKenzie.

Nate parked VERA in the front of the restaurant—had to take a parking spot and a half—but figured he might as well let everyone know he was back. Had he actually cooked up the sting operation, he asked himself, just to be able to stay at Sarah's house for a while? No, it had been a viable idea, at least for someone who was desperate to catch an arsonist.

He hadn't passed her on the road into town after he'd changed his clothes and talked to Jack, who was fuming at Ray-Lynn for cutting him off after they'd just come to some kind of an understanding. "Women! Can't do with 'em or without 'em," Jack groused.

Nate could only hope Sarah had not gone right back to the farm but was parked behind the restaurant as he'd suggested. The only thing Ray-Lynn said to him when he walked in the front door was, "I'm not sure you deserve a mother—foster or step or whatever—as nice as that woman. Nice friends, too."

"Have you seen Sarah?"

"I told you to leave her alone. Yes, she's out back, although I warned her to leave you alone, too."

"Thanks, Ray-Lynn. I'm sorry and Jack is, too, but—"

She spun away and filled someone's coffee cup. He saw a lot of empty booths, but it was midafternoon. He hurried back to where he saw M.E. Silver-haired and slender, she was sitting with two chunky blondes, both on the far side of seventy. M.E.'s hair was straight and sleek with bangs that almost hid her eyebrows. She had a pug nose and pert smile.

"Nathan!" she greeted him, and stood for a hug. "You made Amish country sound so lovely that when I talked about it to Claire and Janet, we just had to come. I hear there's a big barn raising tomorrow, but we've got hospital volunteer work then."

He knew both of the other women, had for years, so he accepted their hugs, then perched on the edge of the booth beside M.E.

"Nathan," she whispered, "what's this about you being in Columbus when you really weren't?"

"I'll have to explain all that later. If you ladies wouldn't mind my taking M.E. away for a minute, there's someone I'd like her to meet. It's Sarah Kauffman, M.E., the Amish woman who's helped me here."

"Oh, well, yes, of course. I'd be honored to meet anyone important to you."

"It's not like you're thinking," he told her as he escorted her toward the back of the restaurant. She'd been matchmaking for years. But actually, he scolded himself, it *was* what she was thinking—only impossible.

"You don't know what I'm thinking, except that you look tired but a whole lot more healthy with a little more meat on your bones. And Ray-Lynn's food is rather filling, isn't it? Tasty, too, though I'm thinking Amish fare may be a little too heavy on the salt and sugar."

He opened the back door and escorted M.E. out into the alley. Sarah climbed down from the buggy, smiling but looking almost as shaky as he felt.

"M.E., this is my friend Sarah Kauffman, who's been such a help here."

"We're still not sure Nate has the arsonist under arrest," Sarah said, "but he's been a big help to us, too."

"I'm glad to hear that. I'd love to stay for the barn raising tomorrow, but my friends and I do volunteer work on Saturdays. The house feels a bit empty since my husband passed away and Nathan moved out and is so busy. You just come and visit me sometime, won't you, Sarah—I mean not by buggy, but somehow? You are always welcome."

"I've never been to Columbus—Cleveland, though. I'd like to take you up on that, but I just don't know."

Was she actually wavering about leaving here? Nate wondered. If she came to Columbus maybe M.E. could take her in. But then, to visit Sarah, he'd have to go past the barren lot where what some neighbors still called "the death house" had stood.

He gave Sarah a hand up into the buggy, though he knew

she didn't need it, probably, in the long run, didn't need him. He realized she was in a hurry to get back to the farm and her family, her real life.

M.E. waved as Sarah blew a kiss to Sally and headed out. Like some kind of adolescent, Nate pretended she'd blown the kiss to him.

# 24

"WHY DOES THAT WOMAN KEEP LOOKING OUT the window?" *Grossmamm* asked Martha, as if Sarah were not in the room and she didn't know who she was. Recognizing people came and went, but their grandmother had been pretty good lately on that. It was after dark, and the three of them had moved back to the *grossdaadi haus*. They had not lit a lantern so Sarah could watch the barn and not be on display herself.

"Just thinking about her quilt square she finished today, I guess," Martha answered with a helpless shake of her head when Sarah glanced their way. Martha, like Ella, was a stickler for not even telling what the world called little white lies, but she knew not to get *Grossmamm* upset again about barn burnings.

"When I was the age of you two," the old woman told them as she rocked in *grossdaad*'s old chair, "I was stitching entire quilts, not just one square."

"Let's go in the bathroom where there's a lantern, *Gross-*

*mamm*. You can get ready for bed, then I'll read to you from the *Budget* again," Martha said.

"I always did the family budget, especially the egg money," she told them, and got up with Martha's help. "I don't know why your father decided not to keep those good laying hens when we moved to this little place."

Well, at least she had those details right, Sarah thought. Things from the past seemed to stick if not the present. Still keeping an eye outside, she darted up from her chair and gave *Grossmamm* a quick good-night kiss on her paper-smooth, cool cheek, then hurried back to the window. Barely a moon tonight, just rising, but to eyes adjusted to the dark, it made enough light to watch the barn without the night goggles Nate was using. She pictured him sitting in her bedroom window, looking out with *Daad* right behind him.

She'd told Nate that she was ready to move on from that bedroom, but was she also ready to move on from this farm, this way of life? Ray-Lynn was right that painting made her happy and was purposeful. But would it be enough to carry her through if she lost everything here she had loved since she could remember?

Besides, Nate would haunt her heart everywhere she worked around here, everywhere she went after he was gone. At the Dutch Farm Table where she wanted to paint a mural for Ray-Lynn or a quilt square outside on the street. The pond—she'd always see him swimming there—the spot where he'd parked VERA. In the barn, the house, her own room and window and bed...

Something moved outside! Someone in black. Sarah shoved her chair aside, knelt by the window, hunched down. Someone carrying binoculars—*Grossmamm*'s grasshopper eyes! Could Nate see the man and would he come running? Her pulse pounded so hard she heard drumming in her ears.

She saw the intruder carried something. A sack? A sack with what kind of incendiary device this time? Because *Daad* was not a church leader, the arsonist must be targeting her paintings. Someone wanted her either to stop doing the quilt squares or to draw attention to them in the most horrible way.

She gripped her flashlight so hard her fingers went numb. Don't startle the intruder, she told herself. Wait. Wait. But don't let him run.

Maybe Gabe would spot him from the barn. Nate had given him the extra phone. She'd wondered if it was because she'd lost the other one in the ditch when Jacob hit her buggy or just because Nate could keep an eye on the *grossdaadi haus* but not the inside of the barn. If the intruder started toward the barn, she would have to confront him, then shout for Gabe and Nate. If a fire started, she could not let Gabe be trapped like Noah Miller.

Instinctively, she blinked and ducked as gravel hit the window.

Hannah? Could that be Hannah? The form seemed so shapeless she wasn't sure. She'd been relying on the fact that someone else—whoever had left that first Bible note—knew that signal would draw her out. Still, she wasn't stepping outside unless she saw Hannah's face. She'd trust her then, of course she would. None of this horror could be her fault.

When the person threw a handful of gravel at the window again, Sarah saw it was Hannah, the silhouette of spiky hair, the shape of the pale face. Still she hesitated, then started to open the window sash to speak before going outside.

But as she did, a second form appeared. Nate! He grabbed

Hannah, forced her to the ground as Sarah opened the window just in time to hear the confrontation.

"Ow! What? Lemme go!"

"Hannah? It's Nate MacKenzie. Just lie still."

Sarah rushed outside. Nate held one of Hannah's hands behind her back and had her face down in the grass. He was patting her all over as if she was hiding a gun—or a wick and matches.

"Nate, she was just throwing gravel against the window," Sarah protested. "That's how she always got me out to talk at night!"

"She's real good at night appearances near endangered or burned barns, isn't she?" he muttered, coming up with her car keys, which he dropped on the ground next to her bag.

"That's right," Hannah cried. "I just came to see Sarah."

With his night goggles still around his neck, Nate shone his flashlight first on Sarah's binoculars, then inside her bag.

"Amish clothes," he said, dumping the contents on the grass. "For an incognito getaway? And those are really big binoculars. Great for watching barn fires from nearby fields, I bet."

Sarah shivered. That person she'd seen in the field at the Schrock fire—she hadn't been able to tell if it was male or female, but in black... No, she knew Hannah as well as she knew herself. It could not have been her.

"I borrowed them," Hannah muttered. "You're hurting me."

Nate ignored that and kept pawing through the things he'd spilled on the ground. *Daad* and *Mamm* came out of the house, and Gabe came running.

"Gabe, get back in the barn," Nate ordered. "Mr. Kauffman, can you go with him? She could be working with someone. This could be a distraction, a diversion, while someone else torches the barn."

"I'm not working with anyone! You're crazy!" Hannah insisted.

As the men left again—looking reluctant but alarmed—Nate got up, pulled out handcuffs and put them on Hannah behind her back. He lifted her to a sitting position. She looked horrible, Sarah thought—stunned, furious, frightened, her heavily made-up face dirty. Her skin was ashen, a shocking contrast to her dark mascara running from tears. She almost looked demonic. Surely, Hannah was not the Beast who had written those threatening notes. For a moment Sarah wavered. No, she still had faith her longtime friend would not burn barns.

Nate was looking more frustrated as he kept playing his light over the items from the paper bag. As far as Sarah could see, besides Amish garments, the pile included a big bottle of water and snack bars. Nate looked hesitant, puzzled.

"Hannah, if I search the grounds near the barn, am I going to find something to light a fire?" he asked, his voice quieter now. He knelt beside her, looking closely into her belligerent face. Sarah sat down beside her and *Mamm* hovered over them. Sarah saw that Martha stood now on the other side of the *grossdaadi haus* window, but she didn't come out. Only her white *kapp* and apron showed, ghostlike.

"I have no idea what might be near the barn," Hannah said. "If you find something bad—incriminating—it's not mine."

"Let's hear why you're sneaking around here in the dark," Nate said with a frown at Sarah that clearly said, *Keep your mouth shut.* "This seems to be a habit with you—all the wrong barns, too."

"I know my family's barn raising is tomorrow," she said with a toss of her head. "Jacob told me."

Sarah let out a little gasp. She felt sick to her stomach at what might be coming next.

"I guess misery—and revenge—loves company," Nate said. "Nice of Jacob to keep tabs on the barns for both of you, but then you've been doing that for yourself, too, hanging around in dark nearby fields, right? Go ahead."

"I was going to ask Sarah if I could secretly watch the raising from the loft window of this barn, that's all. With the binoculars, I could see pretty well across the field. I know everyone will be there tomorrow at the crack of dawn and no way I was going over there to see it. You know I gave some money toward it, Mr. MacKenzie. I still can't—won't— go home, but I wanted to be near for this, at least. That stuff in the sack is the last of my Amish things, and I thought Sarah could use them—plus, some things for my breakfast if they let me stay here."

"Of course," *Mamm* said. "You can stay here, and we'll fix you breakfast, too."

"Mrs. Kauffman," Nate cut in, "Hannah Esh is only staying here tonight if she's under lock and key and if I don't find anything she brought to burn your barn around here or in her car."

"You're arresting her?" Sarah blurted.

"I'll tell you what. Since you're evidently so certain she isn't involved in the barn burnings, even though she's demonstrated an amazing amount of guilt over her parents' barn, let's just—"

"Of course she shows guilt for that," Sarah argued, "for leaving them. She's torn about that, not about arsons she didn't commit."

"Sarah, I'm not reading her her Miranda rights or calling the sheriff in—yet. How about you stop playing defense lawyer and let me handle this?"

"*Mamm* and I know her better than you do, that's all."

"Hannah," Nate said, "I have a witness who spotted you in the field watching your family's barn burn."

Hannah gasped for air like a beached fish while Sarah insisted, "I didn't say I saw Hannah through your night goggles that night!"

"Not you. Keep quiet or go back inside the *grossdaadi haus!*"

"It wasn't me!" Hannah cried. "Someone's mistaken or lying."

"Then that's enough from all of you right now," Nate said. "Here's the deal. Hannah agrees to stay in the house—handcuffed to you, Sarah—while I search the grounds and her car. Is it at the cemetery again, Hannah?"

She nodded.

"Do I have your permission to search it? If not, I'll get a search warrant."

"Yes, I don't care. Look, I can understand it looks bad. I know you've been bugged by my lack of alibis, but I did not harm our barn or any other, let alone watch them burn. I did not!"

He unlocked one of her cuffs and, without asking for Sarah's permission, snapped it on her wrist. "Let's go inside the farmhouse," he said, putting Hannah's things back in her bag and handing it to *Mamm* while Sarah and Hannah got to their feet, not only cuffed together but holding hands. "Mr. Kauffman and I have a lot of ground to cover out here in the dark," he said as they all trudged toward the farmhouse.

"Don't waste your time," Hannah told him. Her voice had slowly come to sound like her again, almost defiant.

"You going to tell me where your stash of fire starters is, then?" Nate challenged when Sarah had thought he might be softening.

"I've done a lot wrong in my life, Mr. MacKenzie," Hannah said, turning to face him on the back porch, so that Sarah's hand was yanked around and she faced Nate, too. "But you're the one who's wrong about this. Dead wrong."

It was nearly dawn when Nate finally had to admit he'd found nothing to incriminate Hannah Esh. A few cigarette butts in the ashtray of her car was the closest he and Ben Kauffman could get to anything having to do with fire, though the interior of the old compact model smelled of smoke—incense, Sarah had said once—the same scent on Hannah's clothes and in her hair. He could not see hauling her into the same small jail cell that held Cindee Kramer, because that would make three suspects locked up, none of whom he could prove were guilty of arson.

"Hard to believe anyone Amish or former Amish would do it, anyway, Nate," Ben said as they dragged themselves into the farmhouse just before dawn and slumped at the kitchen table. "We know how precious the barns are. In the old days, folks would build a decent barn before they built themselves a good house."

Mrs. Kauffman poured them both coffee and, without a word, pointed to her husband's grimy hands. He and Nate got up to wash at the sink while she got bacon and eggs going on the stove.

"I haven't heard a peep out of the girls for a couple of hours," she told them. "But I heard them talking for a long time last night, not what they said, though. Always tight friends, those two, and Ella Lantz, they sure were."

"I'd better go up and unlock their handcuffs," Nate said. "I can't see grounds for holding Hannah."

"Her watching the raising will hold her here today," Mrs. Kauffman said. "It's fine with us if she watches from the barn window. I'm going to take your *mamm* over with us, Ben. I think it will do her good, but if it disturbs her, I'll bring her back. She keeps muttering about burnings, so seeing the *sheierufschlagge* up close will do her good. As for Hannah, I'm just praying that Sarah will convince her to come home for good—and not the other way around."

Taking a quick swig of his coffee, then pausing at the kitchen door, Nate said, "Sarah told me she'd never go to live with Hannah."

Both of the Kauffmans looked at him. The silence, but for sizzling bacon, screamed at him. Were they still afraid he would take Sarah with him?

"I'm leaving after the barn raising," he told them. "VERA's needed in Columbus for other cases, and Stan Comstock's back now. I apologize to you and your people for stirring the waters without forcing the arsonist to the surface."

"We'll still be watching the barn today," Ben said. "Gabe and I will be taking turns, and we're real glad you're staying for the raising."

Nate nodded and went upstairs. He knocked on Sarah's bedroom door. "It's Nate." Like Siamese twins, bound together, when the door opened, both Hannah and Sarah stood there, looking tousled and bleary-eyed, still in the clothes they'd worn last night. Sarah wore no prayer *kapp* or bonnet, of course. Her long, thick hair spilled over her shoulders.

"Nothing was found," he informed them, "so either I owe Hannah an apology or I missed the other sack."

"There was no other sack," Hannah said. Her face looked ravaged by tears. Sarah, too, looked as if she'd been crying.

He unlocked their handcuffs. "The Kauffmans say you can stay in the barn during the raising," he told Hannah. "Either Gabe or Mr. Kauffman will be back and forth, and I might be, too. It's my last day here, and I'm honored to help rebuild your family's barn."

"I know you need to do your job," Hannah said, rubbing her wrist with her other hand. "I want whoever burned the barn found and stopped. Sarah tells me you're to be trusted."

Nate's stare slammed into Sarah's, just as it had that first time they'd met at the ruins of the Esh arson. "It's because I'm *trying* to be worthy of trust that I'll be leaving the Home Valley tonight."

He wanted to say much more, but it was best that he didn't. He hustled downstairs to eat breakfast with Sarah's parents, planning to head for a swim in the pond, then get over to the barn raising as fast as he could.

A new barn in a day—amazing but doable. Catching the barn-burning arsonist—difficult beyond belief. Forgetting the unique woman he'd come to love—mission impossible.

# 25

LIKE MOST AMISH ENDEAVORS, BARN BUILDING
was a community event—a miracle of cooperation and coor-
dination. Just after dawn, Nate stood in awe at the number
of people who appeared at the site of the old Esh barn. They
kept arriving through the morning mist in an army of buggies, and some *Englische* neighbors came in cars. Vehicles
filled the Esh side lot, lined the driveway and one side of
the road, clear to the Kauffman farm. Peter Clawson was
everywhere, taking notes and pictures, toting a big camera
bag around.

The women watched the children and kept busy in and
out of the Esh farmhouse, fixing what would be a big noon
meal. Nate noticed that the older women either sat outside to
watch or set the long tables that had appeared from wagons
and buggies. Sarah's *grossmamm* sat among them, seeming
subdued today.

"Can you handle a drill?" Ben Kauffman asked Nate,
and thrust a battery-operated one into his hands before he
could answer. "Over there, holes in the boards we'll pound

foot-long pegs through to hold things together later. Just
follow what the others do, teamwork."

Nate nodded and bent to his task. Eli Hostetler seemed to
be the crew boss for this swarm of laborers. He recognized
several of the other Amish men. They all seemed to accept him with a nod or a brief word. When directions were
given—perhaps for his sake—men spoke in English.

Nate looked up now and then, keeping an eye on the
Kauffman barn and Sarah, but also just trying to cherish the
moment, the feeling of acceptance, of working together. He
wished—he prayed—he hadn't failed them. Maybe when
the arsonist saw how the so-called Plain People accepted
tragedy and rebuilt from it, he or she would stop or move
on to someplace else. But he'd give almost anything to get
his hands on whoever burned the barns.

Later, he saw Sarah move among the men with a tray
of water in plastic cups. It was still early morning—coffee
time—but this was heavy, hot work, and water was best for
that. Besides, Mrs. Kauffman had fed them well this morning, and her coffee was great. Sarah had come in partway
through breakfast after delivering half-moon pies to the restaurant. Before that, Nate had been forced to try to make
conversation with Hannah, and they had gotten along pretty
well. As for Gabe, as ever, he had hung on Nate's every
word.

"Thank you," Nate told Sarah when she extended the cup
of water to him. "Thank you for everything."

"You too, *ausländer*," she whispered.

She moved on with a smile and a nod, blinking back tears.
*Ausländer,* outsider. Was he an outsider here but also in his
own world, not wanting to ever go near where his childhood
home burned? Never letting M.E. and Jim Bosley adopt him

or even get as close to him as they would have liked? To be so driven by his dedication to fighting arsons that he hadn't taken time for a wife and family?

His thoughts were nearly drowned out by the banging of hammers, the sound of saws. He watched men drive join-ing pegs with their big wooden mallets into the holes he'd helped make. The tall wooden framing pieces for the barn, called bents, were secured to the foundation. The sides of the barn now lay on the ground in sections, being formed before they would be lifted into place. Nate sensed the unity of the effort; they were raising a barn, but everyone's spirits, too.

How she would love to paint all this activity, Sarah thought, to capture the strength of her people, working to-gether, separate lives, yet united. *All for one and one for all,* Ray-Lynn had called it the other day when they argued. Ray-Lynn was her dearest *Englische* friend—before Nate, anyway—and Sarah felt bad to disagree with her. Actually, she didn't disagree, if she could just find the backbone, a sturdy one, like the beams of this barn, to go out on her own to paint precious scenes like this one.

She went inside to help peel potatoes, standing next to Ella. She longed to tell her that Hannah was home, at least as far as the next barn, but she'd promised to keep it a secret.

"I miss you," Ella told her. "You come over sometime soon, *ya?*"

"I will. Just like old times, right?" Sarah said, but she knew that old times could never quite be captured again. How had the three of them grown apart? Ella had never forgiven Hannah for taking off, so what if Sarah decided to do something more radical than painting on barns someday?

They bent to their work, only talking of distant cousins and other *maidals'* autumn weddings.

When other women had the potatoes boiling in big kettles on the stove, Sarah went outside and checked on *Grossmamm* again. She seemed to be entranced by the builders, but that was better than living her nightmares.

A sudden hush descended on the rumble of men's voices, then came the cry they all awaited from the master builder, Seth Lantz. "Take 'er up! Take 'er up!"

The women in the kitchen rushed outside to see the moment this big construction job was named for. Almost sixty pairs of hands seized one massive side section of the barn. It began to rise. Muscles strained, men grunted as it was lifted, first by hands, then by long poles while men sitting on the beams high above waited to secure the pieces and begin pounding them into place. Sarah's heart lifted, too, when she saw Nate among the men. She hoped Mr. Clawson would put a picture of him among the Amish brethren in the paper, because she would cut it out and cherish it forever.

Like the huge beams Nate had helped to lift earlier, shoulder to shoulder with the Amish men, the weight of the sides of the barn was tremendous, yet up they went. He got splinters in his hands, but he had splinters in his heart from loving—yes, loving—then losing Sarah, having to leave her behind so he would not hurt her, hurt these people.

Again, behind them, came the men with long, spike-tipped poles to push each section higher into the blue sky. Men with ropes pulled them upright, a span of eight-inch-square timbers and two-by-fours. Four times they groaned, lifted, pushed and pulled so that the men aloft, straddling the sections, could connect the entire frame by the hand-hewn joints and wooden pegs.

"Everything will fit perfectly." Peter's voice behind Nate emerged from the cacophony of other sounds. "Quite amazing. Plan and cut ahead and everything comes out *magnifico!*"

"You mind if I email you later for some of the photos?" Nate asked.

"Pushing your luck, asking for favors, aren't you? I'm still holding the story on that hellfire-and-damnation note, and you promised me some inside scoops I don't see coming my way. Not about Jacob Yoder this time, but about Getz and his girl's arrest."

"Once again, they aren't under arrest for ar—"

"Right, not for arson. Oh, there's Ray-Lynn. I was hoping she could get away for a while."

Nate watched Peter head straight for her, toting his camera bag and equipment. She was taking big coolers out of her trunk and clear plastic jugs of something pale like lemonade. Nate recalled that Jack had said she might start putting arsenic in his food. He hoped Jack and Ray-Lynn could patch things up.

As ever, Nate kept a good eye on the Kauffman barn whenever he looked up. He thought about Hannah over there, in self-made exile from all she loved, longing to come back, but unwilling or unable to. As much as he wanted to take Sarah away with him, he'd never put her through that. He also noted that every two hours, Gabe and Ben changed positions between guarding their barn and building this one. More than once, he saw Sarah glance over at their barn, too. At least with buggies parked as far as their property, a lot of eyes would be on that barn today as well as on this one. He'd heard her people admiring—or at least remarking on—the bold, newly painted quilt square there.

When the dinner bell rang, Nate was swept along with the men and wedged in at a long oilcloth-covered table— actually, several picnic tables shoved together—while the women served. It turned into a real gabfest with news of families, jobs, marriages and distant kinfolk the topics of conversations in both German and English. People kindly included him from time to time, but no one asked him how the case was going, maybe because they knew it wasn't going anywhere. He didn't see his replacement, Stan Comstock, though he said he'd try to come. Did Stan like the Amish as much as he did? At least he'd never been nuts enough to fall for one of their women.

Pulled pork sandwiches, roast beef, chicken and too many side dishes to count went by, served by the women or just passed down the table. There was coleslaw, beet salad, chow-chow, casseroles of corn and green beans, bean and fruit salads, homemade bread and rolls with a peanut-butter-marshmallow spread he'd come to like and, later, about ten kinds of pies and cakes. With bittersweet feelings, Nate tucked in to what he figured would be for him the Amish equivalent of the last supper.

After the men had gone back to work and the women had eaten, they cleaned up. So many hands made light work, so Sarah went out to check on *Mamm* and *Grossmamm* again. She need not have worried that her grandmother would be tired or upset, because she was asleep in her chair under the shade of a red maple tree. *Mamm* was nearby, sitting with others, a quilt stretched between them on separate hoops, stitching and chattering away.

Leaning against the tree trunk, Sarah watched the raising of the roof rafters while other men swarmed around
the foundation, nailing on the wooden siding. The din was
almost deafening, yet it was a good sound, steady and strong.
Amazingly, it did not wake the babies or the older women
who were nodding off in the early-afternoon sun. Such a
perfect day for the barn raising, a beautiful day for most
things, except saying goodbye.

That reminded her of Hannah again. Though Hannah denied it, Sarah had a theory that she would have tried coming
back home except for Seth. Hannah's come-calling friend
had gotten another girl pregnant, then married her. Sarah
could see him among those straddling the peak of the roof,
a big, muscular blond, hammering away. He was a widower
now, but that hadn't softened Hannah's anger at him. Seth
and Hannah, Sarah and Jacob—how had things changed so
much? With her binoculars, could Hannah pick Seth out,
too? Now that Sarah had come to love and want Nate—now
that he was leaving, though he hadn't let her down like Seth
had Hannah—she understood Hannah's rebellion even more.
Because today, more than ever, even amid this huge, happy
community effort, Sarah had to admit that she herself felt
like an *ausländer.*

Last night, Sarah had made Hannah promise that when
she was ready to leave today, she'd hang the apron she had
brought for Sarah in the loft window of the barn. Though
Sarah hadn't said so, when she saw it, she planned to rush
over to say goodbye. Too many goodbyes...

"Hey," Ray-Lynn said, startling her. "Sorry I upset you
the other day."

"Forgiven if not forgotten," Sarah told her as she accepted

a paper cup of lemonade from Ray-Lynn's tray. "It's my heart's desire to paint, but I'm needed here, too."

"I understand," her friend said. A long pause stretched between them. "I hear Nate's leaving."

"After this, heading back. His boss needs VERA and Nate."

"Not just a painting career awaits you in Columbus, but him, too."

Sarah sighed. "I do intend to do some drawings of this barn raising. I'm taking it all in. But don't mention that to anyone unless I decide it's time to."

"I've overheard a lot of talk about the new quilt square on your barn."

"Not all of it good."

"If they're not impressed by it, and still think it's like a worldly decoration, that's their problem. It stands out so you can see it from the road, the fields and hills. It's great."

Ray-Lynn bustled off, but her words snagged in Sarah's soul. Not only *it's great* but *it stands out.* That had probably been her problem from the beginning. Things she did stood out; she stood out, didn't fit the pattern, the people. *It stands out,* and she wanted it to. She longed to draw and paint pictures where individuals stood out and yet were part of the Plain People. She hated to be a fence jumper, but she had to admit that she wanted her art to reach out to others, *to stand out.*

And then she saw the small white square in the loft window of their barn. Hannah was going away, not coming home.

"*Mamm,* I'm going to say goodbye to our guest," Sarah told her, leaning over her mother's shoulder as she ran a line of even, tiny stitches through pale blue cotton, her hand amid the others working on the quilt, a Sunshine and Shadows pattern.

"Your *daad* came back from there, so it will be just Gabe and our guest. If you catch her, you remind her she can visit us whenever she wants, and we'll keep her secret she's been there today," she went on, whispering. "But she needs to think about coming home, all the way home."

"*Danki, Mamm,*" Sarah said, and squeezed her shoulder before turning away. She skimmed the crowd for Nate as she walked toward the field. She finally spotted him up on a tall ladder, pounding nails into the siding over the barn doors. It looked to be the ladder from VERA, the one he'd loaned to her for the painting and had just taken back. Would Bishop Esh ever dare to ask her to paint another quilt square there where Nate was working?

The workers started nailing down the sheet-iron roofing. If the siding made a din, this was a clamor. Surely that would wake the sleepers. Sarah could hardly think, and the sound seemed to echo off her own barn as she hurried toward it.

Tempted to put her hands over her ears, she picked up her pace through the field she'd run across the night of the Esh fire. Only two weeks ago, but so much had happened. At least Hannah's name had been temporarily cleared, she thought, even if Jacob's hadn't. She watched where she stepped because their plow team and buggy horses were grazing here today. It wouldn't be good to be tracking horse apples around. She barely broke stride to pat Sally as she came up to nuzzle her and walked along for a minute before stopping to graze again on the fringe of the field.

Sarah looked back at the new Esh barn. That gentle slope of land where it had been burned had seemed so naked without it, but there the new one stood, almost identical. The men atop and around it in their black trousers and white shirts with so many moving and bobbing straw hats made the barn look like a living creature now, a benign beast.

She rounded the corner of their barn and glanced up at her new quilt square in satisfaction. Not in pride or *hochmut,* not because it was "just for pretty," because it wasn't. It was a sign of Amish gifts to the world, a sign that the Home Valley was a good place to be, bad publicity of barn burnings or not.

The sliding door to the barn stood about three feet ajar. Gabe probably wanted the light and air inside. "Gabe, it's Sarah!" she called out as she stepped in. "Hannah, you still here?"

The distant hammering seemed muted inside the cool vastness. No air stirred and silence engulfed her. "Gabe! Hannah!"

Maybe one or both had gone into the house or *grossdaadi haus* to use the bathroom or get something to eat or drink, but Gabe should not have left the barn open. Even in broad daylight, it was dark in here with just the light from the loft window, muted by Hannah's apron, and the single shaft of light from the barn door.

And then, behind her, the door rolled shut and slammed, plunging the barn into deeper darkness. Sarah spun to stare in the direction of the door, but her eyes still had not adjusted.

"Gabe Kauffman!" she said. "This isn't funny!"

Something shuffled through the straw, across the wooden floor. She could hear it, feel it—something alien and evil. Instinct, self-preservation, fought with rising fear as she felt the hair on the back of her neck prickle. Whoever now stood in the corner of the barn near the door, behind the grain bin, was breathing heavily, even as Sarah was from her dash across the field. She had to make a run for the door. One more step back, around to the side, not straight for it.

She tried to tiptoe but a board creaked. Fear careered through her. Was there a beast, some sort of demon? Human, of course. Her heart nearly thudded out of her chest. Even if she escaped and screamed for Nate, for the others, they would never hear her with their noise. She had to make a break for it, run all the way back to her people.

But as she took another sideways step, she tripped over something and fell to her knees over it. In the darkness, she sensed more by touch than sight.

A body!

"Gabe?"

No answer came but the sound of someone's breathing and the muted din of pounding, pounding. *Ya,* it was Gabe! He lay unmoving, sprawled facedown, his hair and the floor sticky with wetness.

"Hannah! Hannah, are you still here?" Sarah screamed.

"She left," a whispery voice said. "Though she'll be blamed for this barn going up in the flames of hell."

# 26

WAS IT JACOB IN THE DARKNESS? SURELY HE hadn't been working with Hannah. Or was she here somewhere unconscious, too? But something about the voice—she was sure it wasn't Jacob.

She heard footsteps coming closer and backed away, hitting the ladder that led to the loft. Slowly, her eyes adjusted to the dim depths of the barn she knew so well. A form emerged to become the shape of a man holding two weapons. No, a canister with a spout was in his hands and a camera on a strap was slung over his shoulder.

For one moment she thought to play dumb, ask him to take pictures of the scene so the sheriff could find clues to learn who had hurt Gabe. But she knew the truth now.

"Nate MacKenzie is meeting me here in about two minutes," she lied, amazed that the words came out of her mouth before she could form a plan.

Peter Clawson laughed. "I knew you two were an item, and if I printed a scandal sheet, I'd lead with that story," he said, his voice taunting. "I have no doubt he'll be here, but too bad, too late. He's still pounding away over at the Esh place. This barn burning is my pièce de résistance, my masterpiece—you know, like a fine painting."

She made a move to bolt past him, but in one quick blast he shot fire from the canister in front of her feet. She gasped and jumped back.

"'He even makes fire come down from heaven on the earth in the sight of men'—women, too," he said, and she knew he was quoting from his own threatening notes. The flames scorched the barn floor but did not ignite the wood. Still she had no doubt what that fire thrower could do to the rest of the barn and to her.

She needed to talk to him, stall him. Obviously, this was a man prideful at his own cleverness. Since she and maybe Gabe knew who the arsonist was, he must intend to burn them with the barn. He might not have meant to at first, but he would have to now. If she played on his weakness, it might give someone time to come. Hannah might have second thoughts and return, Gabe would wake up—or, dear Lord in heaven, wouldn't someone notice she was gone or taking a long time and come help? No, no, she'd told *Mamm* where she was going, and she'd only been here a few minutes.

"But why burn our barns and my paintings?" she asked Peter, her voice quavering. "Just to get good stories?"

"Partly, but that's too obvious and shallow a motive. Ah, my dear, let me count the reasons. I need to keep Ray-Lynn in my control, and she has some wild idea of repping you to her artist friends and leaving me in her dust, so I was hoping to warn you off further painting. She'll come around, though, admit she belongs to me. Eventually, I'll find a way to get rid of the sheriff—make a fool of him as I have your gung-ho fire investigator MacKenzie."

Her mind raced. His words barely made a dent in her frenzy. She knew she had to try to escape soon, even if he shot that fire at her. Her skirts would catch. They would flame, and she would be burned like poor Noah. But if she could get outside, someone across the field might see her. Surely, Nate and *Daad* were keeping an eye on this barn, too.

"Why do you hate the Amish?" she asked. "Without us, what would make your paper special?"

"I would!" he shouted. "You could put me in the middle of a field, and I'd find something exciting to write about even if I had to create it. The *Budget*—that gossipy, amateur Amish paper you all read—is nothing compared to mine, and these barn burnings have proved that, so—"

She ran. She leaped past him and made for the door, but something hard hit her head from behind, and the world went black.

Nate scanned the crowd of women, searching for a glimpse of Sarah. When they all wore their bonnets and prayer caps, many looked alike, though he could distinguish the women he knew—and he was good at picking out Sarah. He could spot her mother and grandmother, her sisters, too, but saw no sign of Sarah. With all the clatter and pounding around and over him, he couldn't hear himself think.

He climbed down his ladder and moved it closer to the corner so he could help to nail the next section. He walked over to the trough filled with nails and stuffed more into the canvas work apron he'd been loaned before he climbed up again. Shading his eyes, he looked across the field toward the Kauffman barn. Everything looked normal, except for a white something in the single, high loft window. Hannah must have covered it for some reason. Maybe she'd done it to just look through a slit so no one would see her there. Or it could be the glint of sun off the windowpanes at this angle. Despite the fact there seemed to be a separation of the sexes here today, he headed down the ladder again and walked into the throng of women and bent to speak with Mrs. Kauffman.

"There's a white cloth in your barn loft window," he told her as some of the women turned their heads his way, lifting their eyes from the quilting.

"Oh, *ya,* I know," she said, and stood to walk away from the quilting circle with him. "Hannah told Sarah she'd put an apron there when she was ready to leave, so Sarah ran over to say goodbye. Gabe's there, too. Don't worry."

"I didn't see her go."

"I know you watch her good."

Their eyes met and held. A frown furrowed her brow. This woman—all the Amish—seemed to have a talent for saying so much with few words.

"Don't you worry about her," she repeated. "It's nice you are helping here."

In Amish-mother-speak, Nate thought, that meant don't go over there where you could have time to talk to Sarah alone, especially right before you are supposed to leave. He excused himself and went back to his ladder, wishing like a fool that he and Sarah had planned that she'd put a white flag of surrender in the window if she'd leave with him today.

Sarah regained consciousness in a haze of crushing pain. She tried to move her arms and legs. Could but just a bit. Couldn't talk, couldn't cry. Was she dead? Something in her mouth—gagged. Tied.

It all came back in a rush. The Beast was going to burn the barn.

She forced her eyelids open and saw she was tied to the ladder that went up to the loft. The dreadful nightmare of being burned with the Amish martyrs hit her hard. They tied her to a ladder and were going to tilt her into the flames. They had ripped her bonnet and prayer *kapp* off. She was going to die. The crowd was screaming for blood—no, that was the distant din of the pounding at the Esh barn. She was so woozy, but she heard a voice in her head, "For wickedness burns as the fire! Burn them! Burn them for the fires of hell!"

"I was hoping you would not wake up again, Sarah—really," Peter called to her, dragging her from her half-waking dream. He was quickly and methodically going around the edges of the barn floor, shooting flames from his canister until he had a ring of fire burning everywhere but near the front doors. Each blast of flame he threw illuminated his face as if he were one of those fright masks in the store windows at Halloween. Where straw or hay caught, flames leaped and smoke began to billow.

"Since you have such an inquiring mind," he went on, his words more muffled as he lit the empty horse stalls, "I'll tell you that my incendiary device of choice this time is a drip torch, used by men fighting forest fires for controlled burns. Controlled burns—that's one of my many talents."

It didn't matter what he said anymore. She had to get loose, get out. Gabe still lay sprawled on the floor, unmoving, almost at her feet. At least the outer walls of the barn would burn first. But then the flames would get to Gabe; though he was low enough the smoke would choke him after her, that smothering stench of this sick man's hatred and pride. She half prayed, half tried to send Nate a mental message. *Barn burning! Come now!* That other nightmare was nothing next to this, for this was real.

"Parting is such sweet sorrow," Peter called through the smoke and flames. "I'm sorry, Sarah, really. I didn't know either of you would be here but it's too late now. And Hannah's being here, then leaving—how perfect. I'll do all I can to see that she is prosecuted as the Amish barn arsonist. Now won't that be a fine series of articles? I can see the headline now Rebellious Amish Woman Turns Against Her Own People. Well, back to the barn raising. I'd better return before anyone notices I'm missing."

He coughed in the thickening smoke. She heard the barn door slide open, then shut, and the outer latch bang down.

The man was everywhere with his camera so no one would suspect him, blame him.... The Beast would no doubt just blend back into the crowd as he always did, or if found here, say he was taking pictures of her painting. Hannah... poor Hannah would be blamed. She had to stop him, to save Gabe.

The smoke thickened; the flames crackled. The gag in her mouth made her want to throw up. Surely someone across the field—anyone!—would see smoke or flames soon. But it was a wide field, and it would take time for the firefighters to come. All their worst fears, their premonition that this barn could burn... Coming true... Nate's VERA was still back at the pond, so his suit he'd rescued Noah in was out of his reach....

She began to cough. Her eyes stung with smoke. As she pulled against her ties, she saw they were reins for the plow team. Peter had tied them around her and the ladder but not tightly, maybe because she was a sagging deadweight in her unconscious state or he was in a hurry. If she could just get up a step, slide her backside and her bonds upward against the ladder, maybe she could reach the loft, break the window, get out, wave the apron. Maybe she could slide herself right off the top of the ladder. She had to get down to the ground, then back in the barn to try to get to Gabe.

Breathing through her nose only, gagging on whatever was in her mouth, trying not to take in smoke, she managed to slide the reins from around her thighs up enough that she could lift one foot, then the other. Yes, her knees could bend now. Lift one leg, get her heel on the next rung, then the other leg. It was so hard, grueling. If she could only scream Gabe's name again, try to wake him. Gagging, gasping, sweating, up another step, inching the cords around her upper arms up, too, then straining to take another step.

It seemed a climb up a mountain, higher, higher. But the smoke was thickening, and this took so much strength, so much time. This barn, her family's barn, was burning, dying. And she and Gabe were, too.

Nate kept watching the field, waiting for Sarah to return. She'd talked to Hannah all last night, so did she have to take so long? He didn't like it that she wasn't here when things were winding down. He couldn't bear to leave if he couldn't say goodbye to her, even if the entire Amish and *Englische* community was watching. Or was it her plan to stay away while he left so they would not have to say goodbye?

"Hey, Nate!" Mr. Kauffman called down to him from the roof. "Want to come up and see the view from here before you go?"

Before you go—another kindly worded hint, Nate thought. "Sure," he said, though he realized his ladder was not tall enough to get him up there. "But I've got to check something out first."

"How about me?" Peter Clawson called out from below. "Nate, can you at least take my camera up there for a shot of the crowd?"

Nate saw Peter was sweating and out of breath, but then he was lugging the camera and a big equipment bag. Before Nate could answer, Jack approached Peter and started jawing with him about something.

And then Nate smelled the faintest whiff of smoke. No barbecues here today. No bonfires for trash. Surely, no one was smoking. But that wasn't cigarette or cigar smoke.

He didn't even wait to assess the situation or go for the binoculars he'd brought, thinking he might just end up watching the action today. "Jack, with me!" he shouted, ignoring Peter's snatching at his arm. He broke into a run across the field with the sheriff right behind.

He wasn't even halfway across when he knew. The Kauffman barn had smoke seeping out under the front doors. It was ready to break into a blaze.

Sarah slid herself—torso, then legs—off the top of the ladder. The worst of this backward climb had been getting past where the ladder leaned against the edge of the loft, but she'd found the strength—the desperation—to drag the back of her bonds through that snag. Now, unable to break her fall, tipped backward, she fell about four feet to the loft floor where Hannah had been looking out today. Her eyes streaming tears, her hands still tied but with more leeway now, she scrambled to her knees, pulled her arms around in front and picked up the feed trough from *Grossmamm*'s old chicken coop. In a burst of panic, she rammed it into the window.

Nothing. She was too weak. No air. She felt faint. If she broke the glass, it would feed the flames below. No choice, no choice. But she did have a choice about painting what she longed to, about who she loved. She desperately wanted to live to make those choices.

She hooked the part of the gag that protruded from her mouth onto a nail sticking out of the loft wall and it snagged. She managed to pull it out of her mouth. It was her wadded-up prayer cap. Coughing as she sucked in air and smoke, she yanked the apron off the glass and hit at the window again with the old trough, wood against bare glass. Two panes shattered outward. Smoke seemed to grab at her, but she broke out the rest, both glass and wood.

She sucked in fresh air even as the smoke rushed past her. Then, through the gray-white haze, she saw salvation coming from across the field—Nate, the sheriff, others. She seized Hannah's apron and tried to flap it out the window.

Wreathed with smoke, she stuck her head out. Nate was below her, shouting, "Stay put. I'll get a ladder!"

"No— Gabe's lying on the floor of the barn! Help him!" In case she didn't make it, they had to know who did this. "Peter Clawson's the arsonist!" she shouted down, still coughing. She watched as Nate, the sheriff and her father raced around to the front of the barn.

Her eyes and nose were running. She wiped at them with her sooty sleeve and realized she was not burned.

Her mother and Martha emerged from the growing crowd, Lizzie and her husband, too. Ray-Lynn stood there, wringing her hands. "Get my paint ladder!" she shouted, and her sisters ran for it. She heard voices below her in the barn.

She wanted to scream down to ask if Gabe was all right, but her throat was raw.

With Ray-Lynn's help, Lizzie and Martha banged their father's ladder up under the loft window. It didn't reach, but Sarah didn't care. She was getting out.

She would have to dangle her feet to reach the top rung, but she knew this ladder, the feel of the rungs, how far it could tip. She saw that she would cut her hands hanging from the broken window, her artist hands, so she covered the jagged glass at the bottom with Hannah's apron, folded over. She hung there, smoke streaming past, clinging to her, billowing out. But just when she knew she'd have to let go, Nate was scrambling up her ladder to the very top, shouting.

"Hang on! I'll grab your legs and you can fall back on me!" She felt him grab her ankle, both ankles. It felt so good. So strong and safe.

"Gabe?"

"Alive but still out. Help is coming. I've got you! Let go! Trust me!"

His words pounded in her head. She did trust him. And she was going to have to learn to let go.

She fell against Nate and the ladder. Somehow he held on to her as the women below gasped, then cheered. Nate held her to him against the ladder. She put her arms around him and held on, even as he guided her down. She saw more of her people streaming across the field to help.

"Did you hear me say Peter Clawson?" she asked, coughing, her voice rough. It hurt to talk, but she had to.

"The bastard dared to show up first over at Eshes', then here, just business as usual—arson. I tackled him and Sheriff Freeman arrested him—with a drip torch in his bag."

"I'll testify," she insisted, hacking. "It would be wrong not to. I'm going to have to go against my people on that—on other things. Oh, Nate, *Daad,* not our barn, too!" she sobbed as he handed her down the ladder to her father.

They heard the shriek of the approaching siren. They wanted her to lie down but, holding on to both Nate and her father's arms, with trembling legs she walked around to the front of the burning barn. The scene reminded her of the night they saved Noah from the Miller barn as her mother knelt over Gabe's prone form.

Coughing up gray mucus, sucking in air, then breathing pure oxygen from a mask while the firemen and Nate fought the fire, Sarah sat by her brother, too. In the end, they saved only the front wall and doors of the barn, where Peter Clawson had not used the drip torch, no doubt so that he could escape, but he'd never escape justice now.

In the midst of praying women, Gabe regained consciousness and moaned. The ambulance came to take him to the Wooster hospital with *Mamm* going along. With her sisters by her side—someone, blessedly, must have kept *Grossmamm* over at the Eshes'—Sarah looked up at her quilt square painting. It was sooty, charred at the edges; some of the color had crackled and blistered, but it was pretty much intact. It had come through the flames, just like her.

She glanced over at Nate again, still busy with the firemen, then back up at her painting. Instead of an abstract pattern, she pictured there a panorama of a barn raising with the Amish brethren lifting the wooden sections toward the heavens, and the women bustling around the long tables to feed everyone, and the hills of the Home Valley under a brilliant sky with puffy clouds but no smoke—and, like the golden sun, with lots of love shining over everything.

# 27

*One month later*

IT WAS WORSE THAN WHEN SHE TOLD HER family she was going to testify against Peter Clawson in a Cleveland courtroom. Now Sarah looked at the dumbstruck faces of each of her loved ones around the breakfast table. She had waited until they were all together. Gabe was home from the hospital and had started to grow his hair out where they'd shaved his head to put in stitches. Plans were set to rebuild the barn. But she wouldn't be here. She'd just told them she was leaving for Columbus.

"Just for a visit?" *Grossmamm* inquired in the stunned silence. "That will be nice."

"Staying where?" Martha asked breathlessly. *Daad*'s fork had clunked down on his plate, and *Mamm*'s eyes swam with tears. Sarah knew it was what they'd been dreading.

"Staying with Nate's foster mother, Mary Ellen Bosley," she told them, gripping her hands in her lap so they couldn't see how scared she was. She'd agonized over this ever since the barn burnings had been solved. "She's a widow and has a spare bedroom and a nice glassed-in sunroom I can use to paint. I *have* to paint. It's part of me."

"And we aren't?" *Mamm* blurted. "You'll be put under the *meidung!*"

"I know. I've thought it all through."

"If you could paint here, more than decorations," *Daad* asked, his voice very quiet, "would you stay, or is there another reason you are going to Columbus?"

"I need to find out if there's another reason. Yes, I think there is, but I need to give that time, a chance."

"A chance?" *Mamm* jumped back in. "We don't live our lives by chance. And how will you get a hundred miles to the big city of your dreams?"

Sarah blinked back tears. She'd steeled herself for this, rehearsed it over and over, but she felt as if she was being ripped apart.

"I hired a car, the same driver we used when we went to see Lake Erie. Ray-Lynn offered to drive me there, her art gallery friends offered, Nate and his foster mother offered, Hannah offered, but—"

"All those people knew before us?" *Mamm* cried. "And Hannah? Her rebellion gave you this idea!"

"No, my own head and heart and hands gave me this idea," Sarah said, fighting to keep her voice under control. "I am so sorry that what I need to do cannot be accepted here. I know our people strive to keep the community and our traditions honored and preserved. By painting precious scenes from our lives, I'll preserve all that in a new way, and I'm sure it will send more tourists here."

She stood. Her chair scraped back much too loud. "I regret I will not be here to help with *Grossmamm,*" she added, "especially now that Martha will have to take the half-moon pies into the Dutch Farm Table. Martha, I'm leaving you my buggy and Sally, and I know you'll take good care of both."

"I'll help more with *Grossmamm,*" *Mamm* said, sniffling. "I didn't realize how much you two did there, and I'm grateful." Sarah wasn't expecting that kindness. She couldn't hold back her tears.

"I am, too," *Grossmamm* piped up. "But I want both of you girls—Gabe, too, when his bean heals—to meet someone you can marry, get a come-calling friend."

Sarah could feel everyone's eyes on her, even as *Grossmamm* went on about "frolics in the good old days."

"I'm not running away to be with Nate," Sarah told them, "although I respect and—and love him. I'll be leaving late this afternoon. I can pack everything by then. I deeply regret that this decision cuts me off from the people I love, those I will paint with great affection, and that all of you will suffer as I will by our separation. But I have to do this. It's not the accepted thing but it's the right thing."

She turned and ran, thudding up the stairs. Later, as she packed her things in large shopping bags, including the new sketchbook she had almost filled, Martha came in to help and Gabe poked his head in the door, as if to flaunt his twenty scalp stitches as he had in the hospital.

"I think Nate's a great guy," he whispered. "He likes the Amish—maybe he could come live here instead."

"It wouldn't work that way," she told him, hurrying to the door to hug him before he got away. "It has to be like this."

He hugged her back hard and fled.

She left her home and family and people at one-thirty that afternoon, trying not to look back at the Home Valley as her hired car sped away and turned south on the highway. Everyone had embraced her in the kitchen, but no one had helped to carry her things to the car.

"I hope you will feel at home, but I'm sure it will take a while," M.E. said as she and Sarah sat over lemonade and gingersnap cookies later that day in the sunroom where Sarah would paint when she purchased her supplies. An easel Nate had bought for her stood waiting to be used. She and M.E. were both watching the clock. Nate was on assignment in Southern Ohio with VERA but he said he'd be here about 6:00 p.m. For once, M.E. had refused to meet him somewhere so he could avoid coming down the street past the place where his parents had died.

"You've been wonderful, you and Nate both," Sarah said. She was without her bonnet and prayer cap and wore her hair down her back in a loose braid. She figured she'd cut some of it soon, maybe to shoulder length, because, for the first time in her life, it felt too heavy. She also wanted to get some other clothes, conservative ones, but not Amish. Today, she'd borrowed a long denim skirt and long-sleeved blouse from M.E. She was only Amish inside now, not outside, since she'd taken this big step, she kept telling herself.

"And a phone call from home already!" M.E. said. "So how is our friend Ray-Lynn? She said she had a surprise for you that you'd tell me."

"Her good news is that Peter Clawson is going to have to spend so much money for his legal defense that he agreed to let her buy out his share of the restaurant."

"I thought she didn't have the money."

"She doesn't, but Sheriff Freeman does."

"So he's back in her good graces?"

"I wouldn't count on it, not the way she operates. But I still hope she'll partner with me to get my work sold in the Homestead area. M.E., if you don't mind, I'd like to walk down the street to meet Nate. I know he hates to go by the lot where he lost his family, and I thought maybe I could help him through that."

"I've tried, but not with the same skill set you have, my dear." She walked Sarah to the front door with her arm around her shoulders and gently closed the door behind her.

It was a lovely but humid early July day. Several people had their sprinklers twirling water on the lawns they had cut with loud mowers. Kids played in the end of the court, just like Nate probably did when he was young. No sidewalks here, yet there was too much concrete and noise. Well, she'd get used to all that.

She walked briskly to stand in front of the empty, over-grown lot where Nate's parents had died. She could see a ragged concrete foundation amid the weeds and wildflow-ers. The city owned the land now, but evidently no one had wanted to buy and build here. She was standing about ten feet from the curb in the tall grass when she saw a car turn into the court. It was Nate. No VERA, but he had to give his partner back at night when he was here in Columbus.

She wondered if he'd drive on by, not recognizing her or refusing to stop, but he didn't. Frowning, yet looking relieved to see her, he turned off the engine and got out, slamming the car door. But he didn't budge from the curb.

"Thank God you're here," he said, "but why *here?*"

"So we can put our pasts to rest and go on. Outsiders— we've both been that in a way. We've both lost our families, but—I think—we still have each other."

He nodded but did not advance to where she stood her

ground—the ground, she knew, he had not so much as looked at, let alone walked on, for many years.

"You won't believe what happened today," he said, still not moving. "Stan Comstock is retiring in six months, and the state fire marshal has offered me his northeast Ohio supervisor job. If I take it, I'll be stationed not far from Homestead."

"Oh!" she said. "That's wonderful, and my peop—the Amish—will love you."

"But will you love me? If so, I think that move is something we should decide together."

"Yes, I do and will love you, Nathan MacKenzie, and I'm not even jealous of VERA anymore."

He didn't laugh, though his blue eyes lit up. He strode across the wild-grass space between them, lifted her and held her tight.

"Then, wherever we are together—in Amish country or even here on this sad spot," he said, tears in his eyes, "I'm home."

"*Ya*—yes—me, too!"

★ ★ ★ ★ ★

# Author's Note

EACH TIME I VISIT AMISH COUNTRY NOW, I SEE it with new eyes. To write about something, for me, is to become part of it. Unlike most writers who begin with plot or character, I almost always start with a place that intrigues me.

Special thanks to the Amish of Holmes County at such places as the Berlin Helping Hands Quilt Shop and other venues who answered questions. Ray-Lynn's restaurant is partly based on Grandma's Homestead Restaurant in Charm, Ohio, and partly on the various Ohio-based Dutch Kitchen restaurants. I am especially grateful to the Amish who were kind enough to let me visit their barns and to the Amish barn builder, or timber framer, who sketched various styles of barns for me. And I appreciate the interview I had with Shasta Mast, Executive Director of the Holmes County Chamber of Commerce and Tourism Bureau. Her insights were very helpful.

Quilt square paintings on barns are becoming popular in the Midwest. One place to view these online is www.monroecountyohio.net/tourism/barns. Interesting articles about Amish life are available at an excellent website at www.amishnews.com/amishseries.html. Clinton County in Ohio has an excellent Barn Quilt Trail for tourists to enjoy. For information on that, contact Barn Quilts, 2846 Starbuck Road, Wilmington, OH 43177.

Anyone interested in learning more about the Amish book, the *Martyrs Mirror,* in an English translation, can enter in Google "The Martyrs Mirror" + "English translation." Some of the woodcuts and etchings of that book inspired Sarah's nightmares about people being burned tied to ladders—the tragedy of the Amish past when they were persecuted in Europe for being Anabaptists.

The Amish, like many Americans, have been hit hard by the national and global recession. Melvin Troyer, an Ohio craftsman who makes Amish furniture, has said they've been marking items down to "rock bottom" to keep more members of the Amish community earning a living.

Special thanks to Meredith Bair, LPN and Hyperbaric Technician, for her information on burn victims and their treatment at the Cleveland Clinic.

VERA is very much based on the specialized vehicle of the office of the state fire marshal of Ohio; however, it is called MIRV for Major Incident Response Vehicle. I have, however, fictionalized the state fire marshal's name and staff. Any mistakes in investigating techniques are my error, not theirs.

Of course, one of the joys of visiting Amish country is the delicious, homemade food. This story mentions different, favorite dishes, but the half-moon pies were the main focus. A recipe for these can be found online at such charming sites as www.anniesrecipes.com. These pies—which I also see are called preaching pies sometimes, probably because they are good ones to take for individual people at church—are also similar to the popular Amish fry pies.

The other books in the *Home Valley Amish* Trilogy will focus on new main characters—next time Hannah Esh gets center stage—but Sarah and Nate will also return. Happy reading, quilting and eating—and just appreciating life day by day.

*Karen Harper*

NEW YORK TIMES
AND USA TODAY
BESTSELLING AUTHOR

# KAREN HARPER

Policewoman Kat Lindley is running from the big-city job that nearly got her killed, and from memories of the abused boy she failed to save.

Widower Luke Brand is a leader in the Amish community of Maplecreek. But his people are under attack from unknown assailants, forcing Luke to seek outside help from Kat.

Together Luke and Kat are determined to bring justice to the perpetrators, while struggling to suppress the forbidden feelings growing between them. When the case takes a deadly turn, Kat must race to uncover the menace that threatens the people she has grown to respect—before Luke becomes the next victim.

# DARK HARVEST

*Available wherever books are sold.*

www.MIRABooks.com